Second City

Chelsea Keogh

Copyright © 2023 Chelsea Keogh

All rights reserved

The characters and events portrayed in this book are fictitious. Any similarity to real persons, living or dead, is coincidental and not intended by the author.

No part of this book may be reproduced, or stored in a retrieval system, or transmitted in any form or by any means, electronic, mechanical, photocopying, recording, or otherwise, without express written permission of the publisher.

FOREWORD

This book contains content unsuitable for those under 18. The pages you are about to read contain scenes of a graphic nature including consensual sexual content, violence, murder, and abuse of minors. If this is not for you, do not read it. This book is a work of fiction, and the characters are all adults who can make their own decisions. Some scenes may bother some readers, and some characters may not behave appropriately. It's up to the reader's discretion to make of this what they will.

If these things are acceptable to you, please keep reading to dive into a world that I have fallen in love with. I hope you fall in love with it as well.

Chelsea.

CONTENTS

Copyright
Foreword

Chapter 1	1
Chapter 2	7
Chapter 3	18
Chapter 4	37
Chapter 5	51
Chapter 6	68
Chapter 7	81
Chapter 8	91
Chapter 9	106
Chapter 10	128
Chapter 11	138
Chapter 12	155
Chapter 13	170
Chapter 14	181
Chapter 15	193

chapter 16	203
Chapter 17	216
Chapter 18	234
Chapter 19	256
Chapter 20	269
Chapter 21	278
Chapter 22	289
Chapter 23	300
Chapter 24	315
Chapter 25	327
Chapter 26	336
Chapter 27	350
Chapter 28	365
Acknowledgements	373

For Sarah

You told me to Always Remember.

I swear I will.

CHAPTER 1

In another life, I would refuse to take on a man who was easily three times my size. In that life, I would be sitting comfortably at home in oversized loungewear, drinking cheap wine, and watching truly awful reality TV. I would be lazy and absolutely content. Yet here I am, crouched behind a car while the sticky summer heat sends drips of sweat down my back. There is no other life. There is nothing else for me except this. Catching runaway criminals who look like they could eat me for breakfast.

I haven't even had breakfast yet. How is that fair? My perp for the day stands roughly three feet ahead of me. I'm positive this guy is used to being the predator. Little does he know he's about to become prey. My prey. I smile to myself as a rush of adrenaline surges through my blood and – ah, yes, I remember now. This is why I do it. Why I don't have that other life.

I keep my eyes on my prey while I bask in the glory of being the best.

The sun is glaring comically off his bald head. With the right angle, he could probably cause a car accident. His beefy arms are about the same size as my body, and it's clear to anyone with working eyeballs that he's an absolute behemoth. If American football hadn't died alongside the good old American dream, he'd have made one hell of a linebacker. You know, if they could excuse his murderous tendencies and copious amounts of drug use. He's a pretty bad guy, but a very small fish here on the Island.

Golden Island, my home. Yes, it's a very pretentious name. I know. It wouldn't have been my first choice had I been the person in charge of naming it. I would have chosen something a little less...douchey.

A deliberate cough through my earpiece snaps me out of my thoughts and reminds me I have a job to do. I sneak up behind him, my feet barely making a sound as they carry me across the dry cement of the parking lot. The idiot is so engrossed in whatever is on his phone screen that a five-year-old could sneak up on him with no problem.

"Hey, big guy," I say, my voice laced in the closest thing I can muster to sweetness.

He turns slightly towards me, a leering smile already on his face at the mere sound of a woman's voice. Before he has a chance to register who's standing in front of him, I pull the gun from the waistband of my jeans and slam it into the side of his head as hard as I can. I have to jump a little to reach, so I'm pleased when, supersized or not, he goes down like a sack of bricks and is out for the count.

Giant – 0, Me – 1.

A laugh sounds in my ear, and I turn my head to stare at the man in the passenger seat of my car, owner of the intrusive voice. Chase Cameron, my partner in crime. Well, my partner in catching people who commit crimes. That's us, bounty hunters extraordinaire. I give him the finger, and he laughs again. He gets out of the car and makes his way towards me, pulling out his earpiece as he does.

"Damn, Lara, he looks like he could eat you for breakfast," he says as he reaches us, mimicking my exact thoughts.

Sweat beads on his tanned forehead, causing the hair that hangs over it to curl. I've always been jealous of his brown curls – anything would be better than my boring, poker-straight black mane. He's handsome in that boyish way, with dimples that appear when he smiles, blue eyes, and full, plump lips. Standing well above me at 6'4" he's definitely something to look at. Just not for me. There's no way I'll risk one of the best and only friendships I have for some sex. Even if I have a feeling it would be really, really good sex.

It can't – and won't – happen. No matter how much he thinks it should.

"What are you staring at, killer?" he asks when I still haven't taken my eyes off him.

"Nothing. Shut up. How the hell are we gonna get this bastard into the car?" I ask as Chase stares down at the unconscious man, both hands on his hips.

"Uh, you see a forklift anywhere?" he asks, and I snort a laugh in response.

It's easy with us. Simple. A friendship that's dependable and strong; he'd hide a body for me if I asked, and I would drag one across the floor for him. A relationship between us could work. It could be good, strong…or it could ruin us. It's not worth the risk. I sigh before telling him what to do.

"Bring the car over while I cuff him. We have to get him back to the precinct and get our money. I don't want to have to wrestle him into the car while he's awake."

After cuffing him and shoving him inside the car, we're both sweating. The sweltering midday sun beams down from directly above us, and I want nothing more than a cold shower and my bed. I haven't slept in the twenty-four hours I've been following our guy around, and getting him alone has turned out to be a lot more difficult than I originally intended.

I shove the keys at Chase and tell him to drive, hoping to get some shut-eye in the car on the drive home. But the heat makes me too uncomfortable, so I end up with my head against the cool glass window, staring out at Golden City and its inhabitants. This is the one segment of the Island that isn't truly destroyed. And it's exactly how it sounds. The buildings, the streets, the people – all fucking golden. Not literally, of course, although there are rumours that had been the original plan.

Though it's not built from real gold, the smell of money hangs in the air, and the people here are untouchable. Rich beyond comprehension – rich beyond *my* comprehension, at least. They're the last of America's most wealthy population. All bundled together on an Island they built as an escape, surrounded on all sides by a deep, blue ocean and separated in three segments by a very deliberate ocean river. It could have been great, but they botched it.

"So, who exactly is this guy again?" Chase asks.

"Uh, Rick Alesso, twenty-eight years old, originally from Second. Wanted for drug possession and murder.

Along with some other stuff."

Chase isn't shocked at all. It's the same story for most people who lost their way on the Island. It's how we make so much money.

Eventually, we leave the high rises and fancy restaurants of Golden City behind and cross into Purgatory over the large, abandoned metal bridge that crosses East River. A large barrier is built right into the middle, controlled by soldiers in Golden. We approach slowly, waiting for the barrier to open and allow us access.

Chase sticks his head out the window to ensure the cameras see his face – they're used to us by now. The fact that they decommissioned the bridge always angers me. They don't care if Goldens want to travel to Purgatory to get their fix, but they ensured the bridge would no longer let people from there enter Golden City.

The drastic change in scent and scenery somehow still manages to shock me. Dilapidated buildings all the sort of mottled grey colour only years of neglect can create, and the smell of weed and garbage floats in the car, causing both Chase and I to make sounds of disgust. It's the same every time.

I say a silent prayer that we don't run into any trouble, but you can never be certain. There's always some sort of trouble. Purgatory is where it all began, where it all fell apart. Golden City completely abandoned them, and now Gideon Bennet runs the streets. He's the reason it's so bad. The reason drugs are more sought after than food is.

Women roam the street scantily clad, barely batting an

eye at the homeless people they walk past, needles still hanging from some of their arms. As we drive, I see men with their shirts off, scars and wounds marking their skin like badges of honour.

If Golden City is a place for the rich, Purgatory is home to the poor. To the lost. They're not dead yet, but the people aren't really alive either. That's why we call it Purgatory.

I scan the streets, unable to tear my eyes away from the ugliness, the horror. There are no dead bodies today, but it wouldn't be anything I haven't seen before. The rivalry between Gideon and the mysterious newcomer, Roman Black, has never been worse. I get chills even thinking about the sights I've seen thanks to those two men. One of them old and evil, the other...well, the other is a ghost.

There's a groan from behind us – the first sign that our bounty is returning to the land of the living.

I love this part.

CHAPTER 2

"Wakey, wakey sleepy head," I say, turning in my seat to look at Mr. Alesso. His eyes are halfway open, unconsciousness still weighing him down. That is until he sees me smiling at him from the front seat, and he realises that he's gagged and bound in the backseat of my car. He sits up suddenly and fairly smoothly for a guy who's unable to use his hands or feet. His eyes are wide now, and I smile serenely at him as I catch Chase smirking from the driver's seat.

"Now, if I take that tape off your mouth, are you going to be a good little boy and stay quiet, or do I have to leave it on until we get you to the station?" I ask.

The glare he gives me would terrify anyone else, but it's hard to be afraid of him when he's half slumped over and I've already knocked him unconscious once. I take his quiet stare as a yes and lean over as much as I can in a moving vehicle, ripping the tape from his face and immensely enjoying his wince that follows.

"Who the fuck are you?" Alesso says with murder in his eyes. I imagine if this man ever caught me alone, I wouldn't get the upper hand again. He'd squish me like a bug and laugh about it too.

"My name is Lara Miller. Nice to meet you." I extend a hand and can't help but laugh as he looks pointedly at the bound hands he's unable to use. I don't miss the way his eyes flare in recognition when I say my name. Oh, I do love it when they know who I am. It makes my insides go all mushy.

"Ah...so you've heard of me," I say. "All good things, I hope?"

He snorts. "Good things, my fucking ass. You're a rat. A snitch. Daddy's little fucking princess, plucking us off the street and handing us off to the cops when all we're trying to do is make a fucking living. You make me sick. I fucking hate people like you – hypocrites who think they're so much better than us."

He spits his words at me, and I almost flinch at the venom in his voice, except I've heard this little soliloquy a million times and from guys much scarier than him. I am rather impressed by his outburst, though.

Chase and I glance at each other with raised eyebrows and small smiles. "You're a murderer, Mr. Alesso. I choose my bounties very carefully. If you were one of the little guys trying to feed his family, I wouldn't give you a second look. But you've got a rap sheet the length of my life, and I bet the families of the people you've killed would appreciate you paying for your crimes."

I'm unsure why I'm explaining myself. I've never felt the need to before. Sure, my job means I send people to prison, but the way I see it, they put themselves there. A girl's got to make a living, too, and if it weren't me doing it, somebody else would. So, yeah, if I didn't do this, I wouldn't be a rat or a snitch, but I'd also be poor and probably one step closer to living in Purgatory and fucking guys for money just to eat every day.

"Besides, man, you got yourself into this mess. You

deserve to rot for the shit you've done. For the shit you've put out onto the street. Cry me a fucking river, alright? We've all got a sob story." I've somehow managed to piss myself off, or at least Alesso has. I try my best not to let bounties get to me, and usually, I succeed, but something about this guy rubs me the wrong way. His victim complex does him no favours. All it's going to do is make me want to put him behind bars faster.

"Fucking Second City whore," Alesso mutters under his breath, and before I even have a chance to react, the car is pulling over to the side of the road between the rows of houses and bars.

Chase swivels in his seat, and in the space of three seconds, he's got his gun pointed in Alesso's face. I barely contain my sigh. *Men.*

I can't exactly fault him, though. Chase's mom was stuck in Purgatory; a junkie and a prostitute, every day was a struggle for Chase and his sister. He managed to get through it somehow, getting himself into the pitiful police academy before it was dismantled. Before realising that while he wanted to do something about the bad guys and the drug problem, he had an issue keeping within the law.

He was a bit too heavy-handed with suspects, and he enjoyed hunting them down a bit more than he was supposed to. Once Chase realised he couldn't get what he wanted from that job, he showed up at our office. It's easy to see what my father saw in him. To see the determination behind the hard set of his eyes. To feel the warmth beneath his tough exterior. Chase will always get the job done, and he'll always enjoy it a little.

"Say it again, you prick, I dare you!" Chase says, and *his* glare is one I would definitely be afraid of.

His eyes are darkened to a steel grey, and his mouth is set in a firm line. I can see his finger twitch on the trigger, and I know he's dying to pull it. To shut this guy up forever. It wouldn't be the first time he's ended a life, and I can't imagine it will be the last.

"Wow, you've got your little lap dog trained well, *Princess*. Does he scratch at the door to let you know when he needs to go for a piss?" Alesso asks, and I roll my eyes.

"I'm either a princess or a whore, Alesso. Sadly, I can't be both."

I glance back at Chase and can tell by his face that he's struggling with barely-controlled rage. I bet when he looks at Alesso, all he can see is the men who ruined his mother, the men who fucked his sister up so badly she killed herself.

"I'm going to give you four seconds to apologise. If you don't apologise, I'll find out what your brain looks like splattered all over this fucking upholstery."

Chase's voice is flat but dangerous. I don't know what Alesso sees in his eyes, but he doesn't even have to count to one before the man's muttered apology graces my ears. Then, Chase pulls the trigger.

Only instead of a gunshot, there's just the quiet click of an empty chamber. I knew this was coming, of course – it's not the first time Chase has played this little game – but Alesso didn't know. It's fun to see the utter fear wash over his face as his miserable life flashes before his eyes.

"What the fuck, dude!" he shouts, and Chase winks at me before turning in his seat and continuing down the road.

We drive for a few minutes in silence, with Alesso grumbling and whining in the back. Once again, I find myself gazing out at the area around me. There are more bars and clubs and drug dens around here than restaurants. Most of them look terrible enough that I'm not sure people leave without contracting some sort of disease. It's the Purgatory way.

A shiver runs through my body as my eyes meet those of a girl about to slide into the backseat of someone's car. She can't be older than thirteen, skinny and frail and absolutely terrified. Our eyes only meet for a brief second as we drive past, but I can't look away. I turn and watch the car she's getting into, the middle-aged, balding man who's driving, and the tired woman in the passenger seat.

It's clear as day neither woman wants to be in that car. It serves as a reminder. A sickening, stark reminder that this side of the river has no rules. It's a lawless, stinking cesspool full of people who don't give a shit. It's a reminder of why I do the things I do. Why I get as many of these assholes off the streets as I can.

We get to the police station, and that is a very generous definition. The building is an old abandoned house some people used as their station when Golden pulled the real police force. Thick iron bars cover the windows, but whether it's to stop people getting in or stop people getting out is the real question.

I believe someone painted the house yellow once, maybe before it became the police station, but now it's a disgusting grey. Flakes of dirty, yellow paint still stick in some places, and moss hangs from the wet, damp cement. I don't know who turned this place into the station, but they did the best they could. The ground outside is wet and filthy, littered with God knows what. Two officers walk out, and I nod to them before turning back to Alesso.

"Hey, one question before I pass you off to your handlers." There is no way he had the money to pay his own bail and no way he'd skip out on that amount of money. They purposely make the bail too high for the average person to be able to afford.

"Who the hell paid your bail? Who have you got looking out for you that didn't care when you cost them over $20,000?"

The words are barely out of my mouth when Dan, one of the police officers, pulls open the back door. Alesso smirks as he's helped out of the car, ducking his head so he doesn't smash it off the frame of the door. I roll down my window so I can see him as he walks. Right as I'm about to call out and ask him to answer my question, he stops and turns towards me, causing Dan to stop, too, one hand going to his gun.

"There's someone who wanted me free, Princess, and he definitely didn't want me caught by someone like you."

He lets out a sudden bark of laughter that has me raising my eyebrows at him. "Don't worry your pretty little head about it, Princess. I'm sure he'll introduce himself soon enough."

Alesso walks towards the station, and I can't help the sudden fear that seeps into my bones. It isn't the threat; I've been threatened more times than I can count. It's the promise in it. He wasn't threatening me – he was warning me. And I have a feeling there's going to be repercussions to this bounty. Repercussions I'm really not going to like. After all, there are only two people on this Island that men like him work for.

△△△

"You want to go get a drink?" Chase asks as we pull into the parking lot in front of our apartment building.

It's only three stories high since all the real high-rises were built in Golden City, but it's long and wide. Each apartment has a small balcony, and the outside walls are a weird red-orange colour. Not entirely sure what they were going for when they built them, but I don't care; the inside is nice and clean, and it's my own space. Chase managed to get an apartment a floor up from me two years ago, which made my father very happy.

I step out of the car and glance over the road – between a hair salon and a seedy bar is our office. The name painted in gold across the black wooden door is the only way of knowing what's inside. We had the windows blacked out a couple of years ago after an angry relative put a brick through one of them because we arrested his brother. My dad is kind of paranoid, convinced more people would come knocking, and that danger lurks around every corner. He's not wrong, I suppose, but that doesn't mean he's not paranoid too. The security system and a thousand different locks on the door make that building the safest in all of Second City.

At least, it feels that way to me. When I was younger, there was nowhere I'd rather be than there. I'd curl up on the couch while my dad worked and watch his every move, and when I wasn't there, I was in the back room, being taught how to kick ass. That place was more home to me than anywhere else had ever been, and nowhere ever felt as safe. That's probably why my dad was so pissed when I told him I was moving out of the apartment we lived in above it.

Looking at the office, the only light I see is the one on top, the dull orange glow as familiar to me as the back of my own hand. It flickers twice – my dad's sign that he saw me pull in, locked up the shop, and headed on upstairs. I smile at the routineness of it and look back to Chase, who's leaning a shoulder against the car and staring at the shop, too, a small smile on his face. He looks at me and raises an eyebrow, obviously waiting for an answer to his question.

"Nah. I'm so drained I'm not even entirely sure I'll make it to bed. I may just lie on the floor and call it a day," I say. I don't know how he isn't ready to pass out because he's been awake as long as I have. So I ask him as much as he throws the keys to me over the roof of the car. As I walk around towards the front door of my building, I sense him walking behind me.

"No rest for the wicked. You know that killer," he says, reaching around me to open the door. When I'm through, I turn towards him. "I wasn't asking you on a date, you know. Just out for a drink. I've learned my lesson. You don't want me, and I have accepted that and moved on."

The sad smile on his face hurts my heart, and the way my stomach twists at the mention of him moving on confuses me. I shouldn't care; it's not my place to care. I've been telling him to move on since the first time he showed romantic interest in me. I don't want to be the kind of girl that tells him she doesn't want him but doesn't want anyone else to have him. And yet…

"Moved on, huh? Do I know her?" The words are out of my mouth before I can stop them, and even I don't miss the hint of jealousy in my tone. His eyes widen a fraction, and he stands straighter.

"I didn't mean…there's not…I meant…" he fumbles over his words, and I can't help the small smile at seeing him flustered.

I don't think I've ever seen him stutter before.

"I don't think anyone's ever *made* me stutter before," he says, and I realise I must be really tired if I accidentally said that aloud.

We're both silent for a few seconds, and I notice how close we're standing. There's little space between us, and I must be very, *very* sleep deprived because there's definitely no way I'm leaning towards him. And he is absolutely not leaning towards me.

His hand lands on my hip and a small gasp escapes my mouth when he pulls me close to him. Then his face is coming closer, so close. Chase's eyes are boring into mine, and when he stops moving, his warm breath blowing softly against my lips, I realise he's leaving it up to me to close the distance between us. He's giving me the choice, and I know it should be obvious. I should definitely pull away. I should absolutely remove his hand from where it's burning a hole into my hip. I should definitely not be moving closer to—

The shrill ringing of my cell phone breaks the silence in the lobby, the sound echoing off the walls and causing us both to jump apart. I leave it ringing as I stare at him, eyes wide and breathing laboured.

"I-I don't…I really shouldn't have—"

He cuts me off. "Shouldn't have done that. Yeah, yeah, I know. But you wanted to. That's enough for now."

Chase smirks before walking backwards and leaving the door to close behind him, throwing a hand up in goodbye as he turns and walks away. I'm left standing there, confused, listening to the sound of my phone blaring in my pocket, wondering what the hell just happened.

In my apartment I check my phone and groan before I call my dad back.

"How was it?" he asks, and I put the phone on speaker as I potter around my bedroom, getting ready for bed.

"Same as usual. Nothing spectacular. Found bad guy, smacked him across the head, smuggled him unconscious into Purgatory, and then handed him off to the guys. Money will be in our account by tomorrow," I say with a yawn as I finish moisturising. I flop onto the bed, then take my phone off speaker and hold it to my ear.

"Alright, kid, just checking. You done good today."

I smile at the praise and thank him before saying goodnight.

My dad's a good guy. The greatest. He raised me all by himself, and even though he pushed me towards taking after him, he never forced me. Never had to. I naturally gravitated towards the job. I wanted to be exactly like him, and I still do.

I get myself into bed and stare at Chase's name on my phone. I debate texting him a million times, locking and unlocking my phone twelve times before it beeps, and I almost fling it across the room. I glance down at the message waiting for me and don't know whether to laugh or cry.

You can tell me it meant nothing and ask me to forget it if you want. I'll even agree with you and tell you I will. But I know it meant something, and I promise you...I will not be able to forget it. -Chase

I throw my phone onto the bedside table and groan. We didn't even kiss. Nothing happened...nothing *can* happen. I fall asleep with guilt swirling in my stomach. I don't want to lead him on, but I don't want to write us off yet, either. Maybe I do want to be with him. Or maybe I just really need to sleep.

CHAPTER 3

When the Island was first built, the people funding it – the people who would eventually inhabit it – realised they couldn't survive without normal, hard-working, middle-class folk. Who would make their coffee? Do their hair? Who would work in the retail sector and fix their fancy cars? Who would patrol their streets? This was the beginning of what I've heard people call *The Selection*.

They knew they needed people to work jobs they wouldn't, but they didn't want anybody. They wanted the best of the best. People who wouldn't sully their fancy little island. Of course, they chose as many family members as they could, people they already knew, and those they trusted, but they needed more, and so the search began.

Forty years ago, my father was a police officer in New York City, and he was a damn good one. Young, yes, but he'd already proved his talent. When my father was approached by someone claiming to have the means to offer him more money and a house of his own for doing the job he loved on a brand-new island, he didn't believe it for a second. My father was, and still is, a pessimist. A glass-half-empty kind of guy, always looking for what could go wrong, usually going out of his way to make it happen, and then claiming he knew it all along.

By the time the offer came around again, there had been a lot of talk in the news and around the streets about this new island being built off the coast of New York. One full of rich people with money flowing and low crime rates and beautiful empty houses waiting to be filled. My father, unwilling to believe anything unless he saw it with his own two eyes, obviously took the job. He came over on a boat with other young men and women, all of them bristling with excitement over the prospect of this crazy experimental Island.

Bear in mind, that was 2020. There was a global pandemic wreaking havoc, the whole fucking world was either on fire or flooding, and ice caps were melting. The world was on the brink of another world war. It was the year it all came crumbling down, and so the young people on the boat to this magical island could see nothing ahead of them but good things. My father even told me he didn't see things going as horrifically as they did.

He was in the police force here for the eight years that peace lasted. That's how long it took for the gluttons to ruin the place. When Purgatory fell, Golden City pulled their police force from the area and never sent them back. There were riots and violence, and the moment Golden City decided it wasn't worth fighting back was the moment it was all over. Everything that they had worked for and built – gone.

My father never felt right about having to abandon Purgatory like he did. So four years, later when I was two, he left and started the bounty company. It was his way of doing something good for Purgatory – his penance, I suppose, for abandoning the place when it most needed help. He threw himself into the business, built it from the ground up, and gave it his all. He was in this place more than he was home, and I've never begrudged him that for a second.

Throughout my life, whenever I needed him, I could find him behind the desk in his office. And now it's *my* office. It was something I loved when I was young – I always knew he'd be there if I looked, and if he wasn't, he'd be back soon. Now, as a twenty-five-year-old woman, I find there's nothing I hate more than walking into the room and seeing his big frame sitting behind *my* desk.

His chestnut-brown hair is greying around his ears, his handsome face half-covered with a thick beard that he'd recently decided didn't need shaving. That's greying now too. My father is a large man, and he is intimidating. Maybe not to everyone anymore – he's fifty-seven and probably doesn't seem all that imposing to anyone else. But to me, he's the man I have to impress. The guy who handed me the keys to his kingdom and said nothing but, "Don't fuck it up, kid," and I have spent the last four years trying to do just that.

So, when I get to my office first thing in the morning and find my father sitting in my chair with that look that lets me know I'm about to get in trouble for *something*, it derails my entire day in an instant.

"Hello, Father. You're in my seat," I say, even as I drop into the chair on the other side of the desk. The *guest* side of the desk.

"This was my seat long before you even learned how to spell your own name, kid. Don't push me," he replies as he leans forward in the chair to rest his elbows on the desk and temple his hands under his chin. "You never told me your bounty threatened you."

That's what this is about? My dad only comes down here when I'm out for extended periods of time or when I've done something he didn't approve of. What does Rick Alesso being a little bitch have to do with anything?

"I wouldn't exactly say he threatened me. He merely suggested that an important and probably dodgy friend of his may stop in to introduce himself. Where's the threat there?"

I try to cover up my annoyance with sarcasm, something my father doesn't appreciate. He tsks at me before running his eyes over the mess that is my desk. There are files everywhere; expense reports and tax forms and God knows what else. He tsks again in disgust, and it takes everything in me to remain calm. I am absolutely going to kill Chase when I get my hands on his stupid little rat—

"Ah, Chase, come on in. This is important," my dad calls, interrupting my thoughts.

Chase steps into the office, and the glare I shoot him should put him in an early grave. He grimaces and gives me a pleading look before sitting down in the seat next to me. Chase opens his mouth to speak, but my dad continues before he can even take a breath. "Rick Alesso was working for Gideon Bennet."

The silence in the room is audible as Chase and I absorb the information. The name alone causes a shiver to run down my spine. Gideon Bennet is the biggest fucking crook on this entire island; he is evil incarnate.

He and his brother Benny control Purgatory. They took an opportunity when shit hit the fan, and it worked out extremely well for them. The people in Purgatory can't take a shit without asking Gideon or Benny for permission. If he's the friend Alesso was talking about, if I've somehow gotten on the wrong side of Gideon Bennet…I was fucked.

"Fuck." I reiterate my thoughts aloud.

"Double fuck," Chase agrees, and I shoot him another glare.

Double fuck is an inside joke, something we had gotten into the habit of saying over the years. He doesn't get to use it now while he's on the shit list.

"It could be nothing. Alesso was probably just talking big. I doubt Bennet would waste his time on a small fish like him. It doesn't make sense. But, Murphy's Law, and knowing you, Lara, this has put you on Gideon's radar. This is big. As of right now, you're on lockdown. You stay around one of the guys at all times. You're either here or in your apartment, but you're nowhere else, do you understand me? This is serious, Lara. Until we know more, you *lay low*."

My father's words spark a hateful, murderous rage beneath my skin. Being the only woman in this business has put me in plenty of positions where sexism nearly has me pulling my hair out. The constant need to protect me as if I don't possess the ability to protect myself is ridiculous, and right now, it's completely unwarranted.

"You're kidding, right? You're *grounding* me?" I shout, and as I expected, I get the usual sigh from my father.

You know the kind. The "oh, the little woman is being dramatic" sigh? I fucking hate that sigh.

"This is for your safety, Lara. You may be a grown woman, but it's still my job as your father to protect you."

"I don't need you to protect me! You've been teaching me to protect myself since I was old enough to walk. What was the point of it all if when push comes to shove, you're going to be the one pushing and shoving me behind you so you can *protect* me."

"Lara, Gideon Bennet is a monster. He is untouchable, and if the rumours are true that he really survived being shot eleven fucking times, then he might be immortal. I want you to be safe and not wander around the streets where he could have you shot by snapping his fingers. For once in your life, do what I'm telling you and stay inside!"

It's rare for my dad to shout. He is such a respected and authoritative figure that everyone usually listens to him without a second thought. As his daughter, it's my job not to listen to him. It's my job to push his buttons and annoy the life out of him, and so when he does shout, it's usually directed at me. He also taught me how to shout back.

"Fine! But I don't need a bodyguard. I can protect myself better than any of these assholes."

I give it right back to him, but my father has already gotten what he wanted. He's back to his usual calm self as he folds himself out of the chair and stands.

"Fine, no bodyguards. But you let someone know where

you are at all times. I have to talk to a few people and see what I can find out. I'll see you both later. I love you, sweetie."

Then he is out the door, and my anger only has one place left to go.

"You ratted me out to my dad?" I scream, and Chase flinches, obvious regret flashing across his blue eyes. "What the hell is wrong with you? We're supposed to be a team! You and me, not you and my fucking dad."

Chase flinches again and holds up his hands in surrender. "I didn't mean to rat you out. It isn't like I called him to tell him! We were talking, and I mentioned it. How was I supposed to know it would be this big deal? Besides, if I hadn't told him, you sure as shit wouldn't have, and then we wouldn't know that you've pissed off Gideon Bennet!" Halfway into his sentence, his guilt clearly evaporates as admonishment and clear vindication seep into his words.

"The ends don't always justify the means, Chase!"

I'm still furious, and with no other outlet, I can't seem to control my outburst. The words begin flowing from my mouth like word vomit, and I can't stop them.

"Jesus! This isn't the first time you've undermined me. What the hell was that in the car with Alesso anyway? Pulling a gun on him because he called me a whore? I'm not weak, Chase. I don't need anyone to fight my battles for me – especially not you!"

It's his turn to look offended as his eyebrows rise and his eyes widen. "Especially me? What the fuck is that supposed to mean?"

"You know exactly what I mean," I say, still not in control of my anger. "You wouldn't have reacted that way with one of the guys. That was about me and you and whatever unrequited feelings you have for me. I don't need you following me around with your puppy dog eyes defending my fucking honour like my knight in shining armour. I'm my own goddamn knight!"

"Unrequited...you're kidding me, right? Not everything is about you, Lara! Jesus, if you'd take your fucking head out of your ass for five seconds, you'd know damn well that it wasn't because of you. It was because of what he said, and you, more than anyone, should know how that word gets to me!"

He's furious now, and as his anger begins to build further, mine is dissipating, realisation setting in that I was, in fact, in the wrong and probably took it too far. Chase glares at me, and I really don't blame him. But I'm in too deep now. I started this, and my pride refuses to let me back down.

"You want to talk about unrequited feelings?" he continues. "What the hell was last night? Oh wait, let me guess. You want to sweep it under the rug and pretend it never fucking happened. Shocker!"

He throws his hands up in the air, turning around to face the wall as I stand behind him, struggling to find something to say. I don't want to make this worse. While my anger is justified – at least in my humble opinion – the way I spoke to him wasn't.

"I don't want to...I didn't mean...forget I said that, alright? Look, that's not what's important! What's important is that I'm in charge. I'm the boss. You work for me, and you can't undermine me. It makes me look fucking weak, and I am not weak."

There's no conviction in my voice now. All the fight has fled, and the sight of him with his strong back to me, his forearms braced against the wall, makes me feel like a piece of shit. Only the sound of his heavy breathing fills the silence in the air, inhaling through his nose to calm himself down. I reach for something else to say. Something to breach the gap between us.

"If this is too hard – if we can't work together – because of…everything, tell me now. I'll put you with one of the guys. I need to know that you can be professional."

My words are meant to be a peace offering, the only type of apology I'm capable of giving. His loud bark of laughter shocks me, and as he turns to face me, I see nothing but anger in his eyes and indignation on his face.

"I know you think the world of yourself, *Princess*, but I am more than fucking capable of working with you. Despite what you might think, the world does not revolve around you. You want me to be professional? You got it. In fact, I'll start right now." He moves towards the door, yanking it open and pausing right on the threshold. "I've got some work to do, *boss*," he says, and without looking back, he slams the office door behind him.

I wait until his loud footsteps begin to fade, and then after the slam of the front door, I plop myself into my chair and lean forward, groaning a little as I beat my head softly against the hard mahogany.

△△△

Hours later, when my ass is dead, and my fingers are aching from copious amounts of paperwork, I finally leave my desk. The smell of coffee entices me towards the small kitchen we use for lunch. The office is empty as I walk through, and my eyes automatically go to Chase's desk. He never came back after storming out earlier. On the one hand, yes, I could be annoyed at him for it, but I know Chase too well. He works harder than all of us. He puts in the time and the effort, and I know without having to check up on him that he's out doing something important. I hurt his pride, and he's off licking his wounds, so the least I can do is leave him to do it in private.

I sigh as I drag my eyes away from his desk, pushing open the kitchen door and almost colliding with the solid chest of Luke. "Jesus. How is it possible that you've gotten bigger?" I ask, and he waggles his dark eyebrows at me as he steps aside.

"Ain't no stopping me, baby. I'm a growing boy," he replies, and I roll my eyes.

Luke was the first person my dad ever hired when he started the company. At thirty-eight, he's still the fittest guy I've ever met. He's huge, and I thought for sure that all that weight would make it difficult for him to chase or track bounties, but he's fast as shit. It defies all logic, but he's also pretty small.

I say small, but I mean compared to the rest of our guys. He's a very respectable five-foot-seven, and with his bald head, almost black eyes and massive tattooed body, he terrifies his bounties with a simple look. Besides all of that, he's one of the nicest men I've ever met, and I wouldn't dare complain about having him on my team.

"Where is everybody?" I ask as I pour myself a gigantic cup of coffee.

There are only five of us that work here. Chase is with me, Luke is with Carey – our resident comedian – and then there's Eric.

"Carey had to go check on his mom. She's not doing so good. I said I'd stick around here and get some paperwork done for him. We don't have any bounties. Just a PI case we've almost got wrapped up."

Carey is Luke's partner, both at the office and in the biblical sense. I grimace at the reminder of his mom. Linda is an alcoholic and drug addict, living in a shitty apartment in purgatory. When Carey got out of there, she refused to go with him. He goes back and forth, trying to convince her to leave, but all he ends up doing is funding her addiction while getting guilt-tripped for 'abandoning' her. How he manages to keep us all laughing with the shit he has to deal with, I'll never know.

"I don't know where the Kid is, though. Probably in space," he says.

I thank Luke and slap him on the arm as I go past, already wandering towards the small storage closet the guys dubbed *space*. Eric is our most recent employee and a computer genius. I mean an absolute wizard. There's nothing the Kid can't do, and he isn't afraid to break a million laws to get us any information we need. He's a nice boy – a little strange, but in the best way. We call him The Kid because he's only nineteen.

My dad dated his mom for a while a few years ago, and even then, he was constantly on his computer. The countless monitors and consoles and I don't even know what else always glowing around him like the inside of a spaceship. When our parents dated, he didn't speak much to either of us, but last year, when we needed help on a case, I had the idea to reach out and see if he could help. He did. He somehow managed to hack into every single security camera in Golden City, and with some – in his words – "simple facial recognition software," he found the guy we were looking for.

Two days later, he showed up at the office, dragging a huge box behind him that probably weighed more than he did. "Where do you want me?" he asked, and I stood there speechless for a few seconds before realising he thought that he was going to be working for us regularly.

After explaining to him that we hadn't actually hired him and didn't even have space for him, he looked around the room, pulled open the flimsy wooden door to the mostly-empty storage room and said, "This should work."

For the rest of the day, he set himself up in his tiny little office, and I was so impressed – not only by the work he had already done for us but by his gutsy attitude – that I decided to let him stay. I told him I couldn't pay him very well, and he shrugged and carried on setting himself up. He's been here ever since.

I pull open the door and am immediately ambushed by random flashing lights and the odd beep. The room is in complete darkness, having never had a light fixture in the first place, so the only light is coming from the glow of many, many monitors. The entire room is filled with screens and...whatever the other stuff is, and there's only space for a single seat, which Eric occupies for most of the day.

His tall, skinny frame is folded awkwardly into the tiny space, and I can't help but chuckle every time I open this door. "How long you been in there, Kid?" I ask, and he doesn't even turn around to glance at me.

"I don't know. What time is it?" he asks, and I twist my neck to look around at the clock on the wall.

"It's 3:30," I say, and he mumbles something as his fingers fly over the keys. There's something different on every single one of his five screens, and I have no idea how the hell he keeps track of what he's doing. "Earth to Eric. How long's it been? You know the rules."

He tends to lose himself in this room if you don't keep track of him. The third day he was here, we all forgot about him. It wasn't until 8 o'clock that night when I was sitting in my apartment and my dad called to say that Eric's mom had called looking for him that we realised. The poor kid hadn't even noticed that we'd locked him in the office. He had survived all day with nothing but a bottle of water and a packet of chips that he had brought with him.

When my dad went to pull him out of the closet, apologising profusely, Eric had shrugged and said it didn't bother him. After that, we made sure that we checked on him every couple of hours. We send him outside for some sunlight and fresh air – he even eats some food if we're lucky.

He mumbles something else before he rolls himself out the door on his chair, stands, and shoves the chair back into his room. I watch him with an amused smile on my face.

"You know we got you a real desk? And we pay you a real wage? You don't have to sit in that closet all day every day," I joke with him as I swipe a bottle of water from the mini-fridge on the floor and hand it to him. He takes it with a shrug and allows me to direct him to the front door.

Eric pulls open the door and steps aside to let me go first, but before I can take a step, he's back in front of me, his wide eyes locked onto mine.

"What?" I ask, confused by his sudden nervousness.

"Your dad said you shouldn't be outside. That you've got that Gideon guy gunning for you," he says, still standing in my way. He's looking at me with a question in his eyes, and I know he wants me to tell him that I've got it under control.

Over the last year, he's shown more faith in me than almost anyone else. He trusts me implicitly, and the fact that I'm his boss or that I'm a woman doesn't seem to factor into any of it for him. I've always gotten the vibe that it's me as a person who he really trusts. That as the girl who gave him a chance, his loyalty lies with me and me alone.

"It's cool. We're not going far," I say, and he only hesitates for a second before he nods once.

This time, he walks out ahead of me, looking up, down,

left, and right before stepping out of the way. I can't help the smile that comes to my face as I watch him, undisturbed by the fact that he wants to protect me. His reasoning is simply more understandable and far less annoying than the others.

We both lean casually against the blacked-out office window and arch our faces up towards the sun, enjoying the heat. Somehow, even over the noise of everyday life, I can hear the noise of the ocean. Maybe it's the blood rushing through my body, and I'm pretending it's the water, but it's never been a calming presence for me. I've often wondered if anyone else on this island feels claustrophobic. Or deserted.

The Island is huge – so big that I'm not entirely sure how the mechanics of it all worked when it was being built. I don't know if it's because it isn't natural, or if it's the way life is here, but being surrounded on all sides by water, being…enclosed almost, somehow makes me feel stuck. Like I have nowhere to go. No way to escape.

"Do you like it here?" I ask Eric, glancing over at him as he guzzles from his bottle of water. His pale skin is already reddening from the heat, sweat dampening the brown locks of hair that fall haphazardly over his forehead.

"Do you mean that literally or metaphorically?" he asks, and I roll my eyes.

"Literally. As in, on this island? This place they created for us."

He looks around at the buildings on the street, the people milling around, and frowns.

"I guess I've never thought about it before. I like it as much as I'm sure I'd like living anywhere else. I have always wanted to see Chicago."

His reply doesn't surprise me. Eric strikes me as the kind of person who would be content anywhere as long as he had his machines and some people he liked to keep him company.

"Where's Chicago?"

"A place on the mainland. The guy who came up with the idea for the Island called this segment Second City. That's what some people called Chicago. I guess I'd just like to see the place that a man loved so much he wanted to redesign it."

Every day is a school day when you have a friend like Eric.

"I never knew that. Now I kind of want to see Chicago too." I smile at him, but it morphs slowly into a grimace and a sigh. "I don't know. I know the entire world has gone to shit, but sometimes my body aches to leave this place. To go and actually see the rest of the world for myself. This island...there's nothing left here for me to see."

Even though I know life on the mainland is probably worse off than it is here, I want to know for myself. Put truth to what I've heard. Riots ruining cities, governments collapsing. We've been told that the mainland is a raging hot mess, but why should I believe them? What if it's still beautiful? What if it's not as destroyed as it seems in the little glimpses we see of it? Why have I never tried to look before?

A feeling of unrest comes over me, and not for the first time, either. There's nothing new here. I've seen everything this island has to offer, and I'm unimpressed. Even the spotless streets and shiny buildings in Golden City have this fake, unrealistic look about them. Maybe the mainland has fallen to pieces, but maybe it hasn't. Maybe, someday, I should look into a way to find out for myself.

"I think the idea of Golden Island was a good one. What they could have built here? Could have really been something, you know? Maybe the only reason you want to be somewhere else is that you don't have a choice. Also, anything you want to see, I can show you on a computer screen. It might not be the same, but something is better than nothing, right?"

His cheeks go red when I beam at him, and I want nothing more than to pinch them, but that would be entirely too condescending. Also, I'm his boss.

"You're the best guy I know, Eric."

He tries to hide his smile as his cheeks heat further. I laugh at him as he pushes off the window and pulls the front door open for me. As I pass him, he leans in close and whispers, "There're two guys in that car over there, and they've been watching us since we came out."

I glance back over my shoulder, and sure enough, a black jeep sits just down the street. The windows are tinted, so I can barely make out the shape of two people sitting in the front seats. Shit…how did Eric notice that and not me?

His hand comes down on my arm to halt me, and I realise I have taken a step towards the car. Just then, the jeep starts and drives towards us. The window rolls down as the car drives slowly by, and as I make eye contact with the man in the passenger seat, a shiver runs down my back.

His bald head is shiny, and his black eyes bore into mine. One side of his lips turns up into a terrifying smirk as the car passes before he shoves a hand out the window, his thumb and forefinger imitating a gun that he points at me and mouths the word *bang*. I do nothing but stare into his black eyes before Eric yanks me through the door, almost pulling my arm out of my socket in the process.

"Jesus," he says, eyes wide with fear, "was that fucking Sam Bennet?"

I nod, already pulling my phone out of the back pocket of my jeans, my heart racing so fast and so hard it's probably visible through my shirt. "Also known as Benny the Bullet? Also known as Gideon's right handman and brother? Yep. One and the same."

A part of me knows I should tell my dad about this, or at the very least tell Chase – which is basically the same thing – but I stop myself. If they know about this, I'm screwed. They'll try to lock me up and only let me out in a bulletproof vest with four bodyguards flanking me. I'll tell them...just not yet. If anything else happens, I'll tell them then. But for now...

"That never happened. You do not breathe a word of it to anyone, do you understand?" My words are tight, sharp. They leave truly little room for disobedience.

Eric opens his mouth – to tell me that's a terrible idea, I'm sure – but I shoot him a look that I hope says,

"You speak, you die." It must work because he just nods his head, annoyance flashing briefly on his face before slinking off back to his closet.

I've got this completely under control. I'm not scared.

Still, I do spend the rest of the day with uncomfortable anxiety and the feeling of someone watching me.

I get a lot of work done and get paid a fat lot of cash after sending off one of my investigations to a client. Complete with pictures, video, and notes compiled after weeks of following them around, I had compiled evidence that proved without any doubt that this woman's husband was sleeping with his business partner's daughter. Seventeen-year-old daughter.

I'm pretty bummed for her – that's got to suck – but I just saved her in the long run. She's got proof of infidelity for the divorce lawyer, and she's going to get a lot of fucking money in the divorce. The private investigation side of the business has only been running a couple of years, and while I hate anything to do with Golden City, I'm not going to turn away their money.

CHAPTER 4

Leaving work on Friday, I had big plans to go inside, get a bath, and sleep for as many hours as possible. It was weird. I rarely sat around the office. I work outside as much as I can, being active and chasing leads. This week, I had stayed glued to my desk, my head buried in piles of paperwork, and yet I was exhausted. My hand felt like it was stuck in a pen-holding position, and if I hadn't developed arthritis, I would be shocked. The bags under my eyes were deep and prominent, and no amount of makeup in the world seemed to cover them.

As I walk through the gates to my building, I get the feeling someone is watching me again. Fighting the urge to stop and look around, I quicken my pace, racing for the front doors that can only be opened with a fob each resident carries around. After I close the door behind me, a relieved exhale falls from my lips as I make my way towards my apartment. I come to a complete stop three feet from my door, my eyes lingering on a package sitting on the welcome mat outside.

It's a small box wrapped in brown paper. Thankfully, the box isn't large enough to fit a head, so I know I don't have to worry about that. But the hairs rising all over my body make me uneasy. Never one to not follow my gut, I remain where I am as I eye the unidentified package. Call me paranoid, but I swear there's a persistent ticking coming from my welcome mat. A head wouldn't fit into the box; bombs, however, can fit into something as small as a cell phone, so instead of picking it up like an idiot, I call Chase.

He answers on the second ring, and I don't give him a chance to say hello before I tell him I think there's a bomb on my doorstep.

"I'm sorry, a what now?" he asks, sounding more confused than concerned.

"There's a small brown box sitting on the floor in front of my door, and I swear it's…ticking at me. I think someone was watching me on my way over from the office too."

There's silence on the other end of the line until I hear a door open and close, and I know he's on his way to me. Barely a second later, he bursts through the door of the stairwell, and it only takes him four long strides before he's in front of me.

"That's it?" he asks, walking towards the box, not sparing me a second glance. I wonder for a second if maybe telling him was a mistake, but then sense slithers into my head. Better to let the ex-police officer take a look at a possible bomb than me open the box and blow the whole building to smithereens. I know he doesn't actually expect an answer, so I keep quiet and take a tentative step forward until he holds a palm up, silently telling me to halt. I bristle at the gesture but keep my mouth shut. Now is not exactly the time for my pride.

He crouches in front of the door, and it's then that I notice the small device in his hand. He raises it over the box and holds it there for a few seconds before a loud beep sounds. He sighs and looks over at me.

"It's not a bomb," he says, and I release a breath of my own, suddenly feeling foolish for even considering it. Clearly, I'm on edge about everything that's going on. It's the only explanation for my obviously psychotic and paranoid thinking.

"God, I'm sorry. I'm just...paranoid, I guess. The whole Gideon thing. I feel pretty dumb now." I say and then, "Hey!" as he rips the paper off the package and pulls the lid from a small white box.

His eyes widen as he sees what's inside, and my anxiety skyrockets at the sharp inhale that follows. Chase slams the lid back on and holds the box at arm's length as if it's contaminated.

"What? What is it?" I ask. I rush towards him and try to take it from his hands, but he holds it above his head where I can't get it. "Oh, real mature!" I snap.

"Just open your door. Quick."

I hold in my objections since I'm already shoving my keys towards the door to open it.

We walk inside, and relief washes over me to be back in my own space. The few lamps scattered around are on a timer, so the room is awash in a soft orange glow; the sparsely decorated room looks almost pretty in this light. As if the minimal design was a purposeful decision, even if it makes the space seem unlived-in. The few green plants dotted around are the only real signs of life, and it's a small miracle I've managed to keep them alive.

I turn to Chase as he follows me in, holding out my hand expectantly, raising my eyebrows as he sighs and hands over the box. He leans back against the door, an immovable barrier between me and the outside world. His face is twisted with apprehension and worry. I finally understand when I pull open the box and find a watch sitting atop a picture of me, half-naked, clearly taken through my window.

"What the fuck?" I whisper softly, pulling out the rest of the photographs, barely reacting until I get to the last one. The rest of the pictures scatter to the floor. "Oh my god." The words are barely audible, shaky and full of fear as they fall from my mouth.

The picture is of me, asleep, lying face down in my bed, my head turned to the side. My black t-shirt is riding up, showing the expanse of bare skin above my ass. One leg is out straight while the other is bent up, and my black lace underwear barely covers my ass. It's grainy, clearly taken in the dark without a flash, only the light from outside illuminating my skin. The picture would almost be lovely, erotic even – if it hadn't been taken without my permission. Without my knowledge. It would be a little nicer if the tip of a black gun wasn't obviously pointed toward my sleeping figure.

My heart beats thunderously against my chest, and my whole body heats up, sweat beading on my forehead, dripping down my back. "Chase," I say and hold the picture out to him.

He doesn't take his eyes from mine as he reaches out tentatively, then takes a deep breath before looking down. I watch as an array of emotions play across his face – surprise, confusion, anger, realisation, and then, of course, fury. His face turns a dangerous shade of red as he scrunches the picture in his fist. Chase stomps across the room, leaving me to drop into a seat around the old wooden table. He rips the curtains closed, and the noise of the metal hooks against the metal bar jostles me as I wait for him to do the same with the curtains in my bedroom. He walks back into the room and slams the destroyed photograph down on the table.

I can't get my thoughts in order; I'm trying to figure out when the hell I last wore that t-shirt to bed. Trying to remember a single night I'd forgotten to lock my doors. My memory fails me as I look around the room, trying to see if anything is amiss. I feel violated. Unclean. The space I loved so much now feels contaminated.

I'm surprised by the sudden tears in my eyes, and I try to blink them away, furiously wiping at my cheeks. The only emotion I need right now is anger. Those fucking assholes broke into my apartment. Watched me while I fucking slept. God knows what the fuck else they did.

"Benny drove past me on Monday. I was outside the office with Eric. He rolled down the window and faked shooting at me with his hand."

Regret for not telling anyone sooner surges through me, and I hate it. I brace myself as I wait for the onslaught of trouble Chase is about to lay on me. Instead, he turns and slams his fist into my wall. I say nothing. There's nothing I can say, really.

"Okay," He breathes heavily through his nose. "Okay. Get your stuff. You're staying with me."

I'm about to protest, but the thought that someone, that a man, stood so close to me while I slept, and I was unaware, stops me. "Okay," I whisper, already standing and walking towards my bedroom.

I throw whatever I need into a bag, barely paying attention, only aware of the fact that I really want to get out of this room. I take one last glance at my bed, and revulsion turns my stomach. It forces me to walk straight past Chase and out the front door, not stopping as I hear his footfalls behind me. He's already on the phone to someone, asking for camera footage and barking orders.

Tomorrow, I will rage. I will fume over the grossness of this entire situation, but tonight, I'm too exhausted to feel anything more than… numb. I stop outside of Chase's door, waiting for him to unlock it and let me in, which he does, slipping the strap of my bag over my shoulder and taking it from me. I throw myself onto his sofa, resting my elbows on my knees so I can put my head in my hands.

"We have to tell your dad," he says softly.

I'm not stupid. I can hear the anger beneath, feel the rage pulsating from him in waves, but I'm thankful he's reigning it in for now. I glance over at him and almost laugh at the way he's looking at me. I know he's waiting for me to object, to kick up a fuss. In another situation, that's exactly what I would do, but when your apartment gets invaded, and a gun is held to your head while you're photographed in your sleep, you don't keep quiet and hope it doesn't happen again.

"Tomorrow," I say. "Not tonight. I just…want to sleep. I need to…process or something."

My eyes roam over Chase's charcoal walls, adorned

with flashes of black and silver artwork to match the black furniture and silver finishing. It smells good, like fresh linen and men's aftershave, and I inhale deeply, allowing the familiar scent to calm me. Everything about his apartment screams bachelor, not excluding the ginormous television mounted on the wall, a war movie of some sort playing, and the mute sign flashing in the right-hand corner. It's bachelor, but sophisticated and clean.

It's much nicer than my own place, but I'll never admit that to him. I like it. It's warm and cosy, and despite the dark, gloomy colours, it's comforting. Having everything so perfectly neat and organised makes me feel calm. Safe.

"Can I get you anything?" he asks as his body falls into the space beside me. His eyebrows are drawn close as he studies my face, and it actually warms me instead of pissing me off.

"No. No, I just need to sit here for a minute."

Chase nods and leans back, pulling my feet up into his lap, which forces me to twist so my back is against the armrest. He yanks on my feet, and I slide down, my neck now resting on the arm of the chair.

I fall asleep to his calloused fingertips trailing over my calves, offering nothing but friendly, familiar comfort, and, for once, I accept.

△△△

The following day is an exercise in patience. I wake up disoriented in Chase's bed and almost leap out of my skin when I spot him. Perched gently on the side of his own bed, he looks awful, dark shadows filling the space under his eyes. The image of him sitting there, watching me sleep, reminds me just why I'm here.

He must realise at the same time because he apologises and stands, hovering in the doorway. His mouth continues to open and close as he fights the urge to say whatever's on his mind.

"Did you call my dad already?" I ask if only to put him out of his misery. The quick shake of his head allows a sigh of relief to slip from my mouth.

"I thought I'd let you eat some breakfast first. But we need to be quick. He's going to be pissed that we didn't call him sooner."

I drag myself from the bed with great difficulty after burrowing my head under his pillow for what felt like three minutes but, according to Chase, was more like twenty.

He calls my dad as I sit at his kitchen table and shovel food in my mouth. For whatever reason, the panic and horror of last night have faded into mild annoyance, and more than anything else, I find myself dreading the severe over-protectiveness I know is about to ensue. The longer I sit here and pretend to enjoy my breakfast, the more antsy I get. What possible outcome can there be?

In all the years Gideon has been around, no one has ever dealt with him. What hope do we have of getting him off my back when a whole government of rich people lost their island to him? The police here won't be much help. If there was anything they could do, then Gideon wouldn't be an issue in the first place. I allow myself a single moment of panic, wondering if my father would go as far as to try and force me off the island.

Gideon's reach travels far – you don't make that much money and deal in drugs and weapons without off-island help, but being on the mainland would leave me much more space to hide. I refuse for a single second to consider leaving Second City. There's not a chance in hell that I'm going to let some asshole gangsters run me from my home, but even as I think it, I glance around Chase's apartment and realise I've kind of already done that.

The thought alone snaps me from my panic and forces me to stand abruptly from my chair. Breakfast forgotten in the face of sheer stubbornness, I announce as casually as I can that I'm going home while already halfway to the door.

Chase scrambles after me, muttering to my father as he goes, "Jesus, at least let me go check the place out first." He tries to cut in front of me, but I'm already a few steps down from him in the stairwell.

"I'm just as capable of checking out my apartment as you, thank you very much."

But still, I find myself pausing on the threshold of my home. Chase, panting and murmuring to himself, comes to an abrupt halt behind me. He wisely remains quiet as I stand staring at my door, willing myself to go inside. I square my shoulders, but before entering, I realise I have no weapon. "Have you got—" he holds up a gun before I can finish my sentence, and I pluck it from his hand.

I can tell he's trying extremely hard to let me do this my way, even if it goes against every instinct he has. I open the door, shoving the keys back into my pocket, and step slowly and quietly into my apartment.

It's silent, still, and maybe it's just my imagination, but now that I know someone was in here, I can almost feel their lingering presence. As if their ghosts remain behind. Nothing is out of place as I move around the rooms, checking behind doors and in corners, gun held out in front of me.

Chase's breath tickles the back of my neck as he follows closely, not allowing me out of arm's reach. When I'm confident the apartment is empty and there's no imminent danger, I hand Chase his gun and walk into the kitchen. We stand in silence for a moment, looking around the room with fresh eyes, almost as if we'll see the impression the intruder left as he snuck around.

The door bursts open with a loud crash, slamming against the back wall hard enough to leave a dent. Chase immediately stands in front of me, aiming the gun at the newcomer, and I almost laugh when I see my father, eyes wide as he takes in the scene before him and the gun levelled in his direction.

"At ease, soldier," my father says, coming into the room, and Chase lowers the gun before tucking it into the back of his jeans. "Show me the pictures."

He walks towards the table where we left them scattered last night. I jump, running to stand in front of him. No way I want my father to look at them – I'm half naked in most, for shit's sake. I tell him such, and he just rolls his eyes and moves around me. He's so large compared to me that I don't even try to stop him. I only sigh and, once again, find myself dropping into a seat, my cheeks burning in embarrassment.

He looks at them quickly, face darkening in anger before he places them in a brown envelope he's pulled from his pocket. "Now do you see why I was worried?" he asks, condescension dripping from his tone.

"I don't think this is the appropriate situation for an *I told you so,* Dad. If you can't tell, I'm being stalked."

He grunts his agreement, pulls out a chair, and sits, adjusting until he's comfortable and leaving us waiting in tense silence until he levels both me and Chase with a seething look. I settle myself in and resign myself to the fact that this is going to be a *very* long day.

△△△

Hours of arguing, haggling, pleading, and shouting finds us in a terse agreement. The last few hours have been a battle of wills. Compromises are hard to come by when dealing with my dad, and I count myself lucky that I manage to get him to begrudgingly agree to at least some of my terms. The trick is to shoot high and let him come down to where I really want him.

"Alright, you can still come to work. You can work on low-profile cases, nothing that will get you noticed any more than you already are. But only on the condition that you agree you will not leave the house or the office alone. One of the guys is to be with you at all times. You don't have to stay with Chase, but he will check up on you often, as will I. Don't open any packages, don't answer any unknown calls. You will allow me to have extra locks and security cameras fitted to your door and in the hall outside. Does that work for you?"

He's not happy about it, but I argued my way around all the other options he'd thrown at me. Moving back in with him? Not a chance. Moving in with Chase? Absolutely not. Full house arrest? Never going to happen.

"Works for me, Pops." My voice is as sweet as I can make it, and it's only when he leaves, stomping through my apartment like a man on a mission, that I deflate.

I blow out a long breath as my head meets the back of the chair, and my eyes slip closed, losing their battle with exhaustion. My head is pounding, and even after sleeping for nine hours last night, the need to sleep is almost overwhelming.

"He could have been worse, I think," Chase says, startling me. He'd been unusually quiet for the last three hours – so quiet, in fact, I'd just about forgotten he was there.

I look over at him, noticing again how out of sorts he looks. "Yeah. I got off pretty lightly under the circumstances. You should go get some sleep."

He nods but doesn't move. Just continues sitting there, staring at me with those gentle, blue eyes. "I'm sorry, Lara." His voice is soft, and I can't help but frown at him.

"Sorry for what?"

"I was right upstairs. Anything could have happened to you. Anything. I was above right you, and I wouldn't have known until it was too late." He sounds defeated, each word sounding like a sigh.

"How were you to know, Chase? It's not your fault. Seriously, don't beat yourself up about it." I walk over to him and grab one of his hands, squeezing it reassuringly.

When our eyes meet, I'm struck by the level of emotion I see and the depth of emotion I feel in myself. I pull my hand from his, and he reluctantly lets go, a small sigh slipping from his lips.

"I, uh, I'm going to go shower, okay?" I say, but it sounds like a question.

He nods and stands, looking around the room cautiously and a little awkwardly. "I'll just hang out until you're done. Your dad would kill me if I left so soon."

I mutter my agreement, then tell him to help himself to whatever he wants.

I turn the heat of the water up as hot as I can get it, letting it scald my skin in the hopes that I'll be able to wash the violated feeling of being watched from myself. After I'm done, my hair washed and skin pink from the water, I walk out of the bathroom in my robe. I peek into the living room and see Chase sitting upright on the sofa – a position that cannot be comfortable – asleep.

His hands rest behind his head, his gun discarded beside his left thigh. I walk over quietly and pull the blanket from the back of the sofa, placing it over him best I can, before going to check the door. A small laugh slips from my lips when I notice the small bookshelf has been pulled from the wall and placed in front of the door, the lock turned into the correct position. Of course, Chase wouldn't risk falling asleep without a self-made alarm system in place to let him know if someone tried to get in.

I walk back to my room quietly. The shower seems to have removed all my remaining energy, so without putting on clothes or even drying my hair, I fall face-first into bed. I spend a few anxiety-filled moments pouring over the events of the last two days before shoving them out of my head and drifting into a dead, dreamless sleep.

CHAPTER 5

I manage to survive the next two weeks doing the bare minimum. If I'm not in the office, I'm working from home. It's been awful, but I haven't been able to overcome the odd feeling of someone watching me everywhere I go, so I understand why it's necessary. Someone is with me at all times, and if they're not physically with me, everyone is connected to a live viewing of the hallway outside of my apartment door. Eric has it playing in his little closet 24/7 after what happened.

Despite being extremely bored and pissed off about the route my life has taken, time has actually flown by. It's been two weeks since the incident, and nothing else has happened. Well, nothing major, at least. There's been a black car driving around and parking near my building sporadically ever since. It somehow manages to avoid everyone else's notice except for mine, and it almost makes me think I'm insane because no one else has seen it in person.

Sleeping doesn't come as easily as it used to. Instead of nodding off as soon as my head hits the pillow, I find myself lying awake. I listen to every noise, every creak, constantly on edge. It hasn't done much for my appearance; I look dull and haggard most of the time.

My father has been reaching out to everyone he knows,

trying his hardest to find out anything about Gideon and Benny and what they might want from me, besides scaring the shit out of me, but he keeps coming up short. He promises he'll figure out a way to get him off my back, but after two weeks, I wonder what he's actually come up with. How long can this go on? How long am I supposed to leave my life on pause?

I stare out the window, willing some miracle to happen to allow me to live my fucking life again, but when nothing happens, I sigh and sit on the sofa. I've watched more TV in the last two weeks than I have in my entire life.

After a while, I decide to call Chase. The very least he can do is come over and keep me company, save me from going absolutely out of my mind with boredom. The phone rings out, and I frown. It's unlike Chase not to answer the phone. He's with my father, meeting some of our informants and trying to gather intel, but he always answers. I try my dad's phone, and that rings out too. Three times.

My father not answering his phone wouldn't be that unusual if not for the circumstances we've found ourselves in. With Gideon and his henchmen still stalking me, and me technically being on house arrest for my safety, it was usually *me* dodging calls from *him*. I told myself not to be worried after the first two went unanswered. I told myself to maybe not worry too much after the next two were sent to voicemail after barely ringing at all. But I find myself in full-on panic mode when I call Chase again and his phone rings out twice more too.

Antsy, I begin staring out the window and across the

street, squinting to try to see any movement from my father's place. I feel helpless. Useless. I've never been either of those things before, and I don't plan on acting that way now. I try both numbers again, leaving the phone on speaker as I throw on some black jeans and an oversized t-shirt, my usual battle armour. I growl in frustration when neither answers. Throwing my hair into a ponytail and foregoing any efforts whatsoever to make myself look less like death, I call the one person on this island who can find anyone, anywhere.

"Eric, thank God," I breathe into the phone in relief. I had been pacing up and down the living room so aggressively that it was surprising I hadn't worn my footprints into the hardwood.

"Um, hey?" Eric says back, although his greeting sounds like a question, concern filling his voice at the sound of the panic clearly evident in mine.

"I can't find my dad. He and Chase have fucking vanished, and they aren't picking up. You need to find them." I look out the window again, eyes roaming up and down the street, searching for any signs of...well, anything.

"Right, um, give me ten minutes," Eric replies, and I barely register how eerily similar I sound to my father when I say, *"You've got five."*

Six minutes later, I'm glaring at my cell phone. The only thing stopping me from walking out my front door is the fact that if this is some kind of trap, then I'm of no use to them if I get myself captured. While I know that if someone wanted me, they could just as easily break down my door, industrial-sized locks and all, it doesn't take away from the fact that this situation *feels* like some sort of setup.

I'm about to pick up the phone and tear Eric a new one when it rings. I snatch it up and answer, relieved when Eric tells me he found them. "Where are they, and why the hell aren't they answering?" I ask, and he pauses for a moment.

Dread fills my stomach at his heavy silence, and I know I won't like what he's going to say next. "They're...Lara, they're in Purgatory. I...it looks like they're right at the waterfront, up where the warehouses are by East River. I could be wrong but isn't that..." He trails off without finishing, but he doesn't need to.

The warehouses at East River belong to Gideon. That's the only known place he's connected to.

"*Shit*. Shit, shit, shit!" I kick a chair from the kitchen table and send it flying across the room. "Fuck!"

"What do you need me to do?" Eric asks. His voice is calm, but I hear the panic he's trying to hide.

"Where's everyone else?" I ask, but before he can answer, my phone beeps. I glance at the screen to see an incoming call from my father. My blood turns to ice in my veins, and, for a moment, I just stare at the screen. "Eric, my dad's calling. Stay there."

I press the *hold and switch* button on my phone, then hold it to my ear, hoping that it's my dad on the other side, but the cold silence tells me another story. I say nothing, refusing to be the one who speaks first. The feeling in my gut twists and turns until I feel like I might puke. The quiet stretches until I'm about to break, about to ask who the hell is on the phone, when finally, a cool, male voice comes through, sending shivers down my spine.

"Okay, little bounty hunter. I'll go first. I must say, I was hoping you'd be a little bit more desperate to speak to your father after you've been calling and calling," the voice says. I've never heard his voice before, but it's obvious that Gideon Bennet is on the other end of the line.

"I don't do desperate." I force my voice to remain steady, although I feel anything but. My pulse is racing in my ears while I fight to stop my hands from shaking.

"Well, fair enough. You don't want your father back then? Or your lover?" His voice is deep, husky, as if he's been smoking his whole life. I cringe.

"Obviously, I would like them both back, Mr. Bennet." I don't bother to correct him about Chase. "I just don't bend very easily to the whims of men like you. I also don't have time for games. How about you tell me what you want, and I'll tell you if I'm willing to concede to it."

"Oh, I do love a woman who knows what she wants. I do indeed." I can almost hear the smile in his voice, how he uses this odd flirtation to hide the rage simmering underneath.

He's probably never been spoken to like that in his life, and I have to be careful not to push him to the point where he takes it out on either of them more than he already has.

I say nothing, waiting. Finally, after a moment, he sighs.

"I thought you'd be more fun, little hunter. I've heard

some tales about you and your pursuits. Been warned you were a feisty little thing. Perhaps they were wrong."

I grit my teeth, biting my tongue to refrain from biting his head off. To stop myself from begging, showing how desperate I really am to get them both back safely. "I'm waiting for your demands, Mr. Bennet." I finally get out, although what I want to say is, *"I will break your fucking neck and feed you to the sharks if you don't give me back my family."*

"My apologies, dear. All work and no play, and all that. Here's what I need – it's really quite simple. Walk outside your front door and out onto the street. Get into the car that pulls up and behave. When I have you here, with me, I will let your men go. That's all. You see? Very doable, chivalrous even, sending you a car. I could have made you come on your own," Gideon says, and he must be absolutely psychotic because he actually sounds like he believes himself.

This is just business as usual for him, and I'm struck all at once by how few options I really have. I can't get anyone else involved, and the fact that Bennet hasn't already is a small miracle. The thought of poor little Eric being at his mercy makes me feel sick. It's clear to see this is a trap. He won't let them go; there's not a doubt in my mind. My fear is not what he'll do if I do show up – it's what he'll do if I don't.

"So, I just get in your fancy car and come to you, and you'll let them both go. Unharmed and alive?"

"Yes. Well, relatively unharmed. They put up a bit of a fight, you see. They're alive and well, if not bloodied and bruised. If it makes you feel any better, your lover –

Chase, I believe – took out three of my best men. Shame I have to let him go. He would be a good asset to my team." He sounds contemplative towards the end as if keeping Chase is a valid option.

What is it with villains and their long soliloquies? Can't the man just answer my questions instead of running away with himself?

"So, just to reiterate. I come to you of my own free will, and you immediately let Chase and my father free, with no more harm done to them than has already been done?"

He sighs again. "Yes, yes, that is exactly what I've already said."

"I don't believe you," I say, the truth slipping from my mouth before I can stop it.

"Perhaps you have trust issues. You have ten minutes to be downstairs and in that car." He hangs up.

The line beeps, and all the air whooshes out of me in one long breath. My father will never forgive me for this. Chase will never forgive himself. Every self-preservation instinct inside of me is screaming at me not to go. To run and hide, to—

"Lara? What's happening?" Eric's voice startles me out of my thoughts. I had forgotten I'd asked him to wait on the other line.

"Eric, I need you to lock the doors. There's a set of keys in my office. Let yourself into my dad's place and lock those doors too. Set all the alarms and don't fucking move until someone tells you to, okay?" I walk to my room and grab my gun from its place in my wardrobe. I know they'll take it from me, but it feels foolish not to even attempt to bring it.

"Alright, got it, but what's going on? What did your dad say?"

I sigh, leaning my forehead against the front door to my apartment. "Gideon has got him and Chase. I have to... Gideon called me from my dad's phone. I have to get them."

He interrupts with a series of *"No, no nos"* and *"You can't go there – he'll fucking kill you,"* but I speak over him.

"Look, Eric, I got this. I'll be fine. You just do as I said, okay? Call the guys, too, and tell them to get somewhere safe and stay put. I don't want any of you involved in this. I have to go. Do as I say and don't do anything stupid," I pause. "You're a great guy Eric."

There's a lump in my throat; the fact that I might not survive this is suddenly overwhelming. The idea that Eric may have to grieve for me shatters my heart.

"*Please* don't do this, Lara..." he whispers desperately, and it would almost be enough to make me think twice if it wasn't Chase. If it wasn't *my dad*.

"I gotta go. I'll see you soon, kid."

"*Lara—*"

I hang up before I can hear another word.

Then, I pull open my door and go down the stairs and out the front door, my body working on autopilot and fuelled by adrenaline. I glance over at the office, hoping Eric has done what I told him. I see a shape in the upstairs window. A pale, featureless face, a lone hand pressed against the glass. I lift my hand in a wave when I get to the side of the road, still unable to see him clearly but knowing it's Eric all the same.

All of a sudden, the lone hand placed against the window becomes two fists, and I can see the dark circle of Eric's gaping mouth as the fists begin to pound against the glass. The *thump, thump, thump* matches the sound of my heart beating in panic.

My confusion distracts me from the footsteps approaching behind me, and maybe it's only in my head, but I swear I can hear Eric's hoarse voice screaming *no* right before something slams into the side of my head, and everything goes utterly black.

△△△

When consciousness slowly comes back to me, I become aware of two things very quickly. First, my hands are tied behind my back, attached to whatever chair I'm sitting on. Second, either I've been completely blinded by my kidnappers, or the room I'm sitting in is in absolute darkness. I try my hardest to keep my breathing steady, not wanting to alert them that I'm awake.

My fingers are freezing, and I wriggle my wrists as much as possible, trying to get blood back into them, lest I end up with permanently damaged fingers. Without moving my head, I look around the room as much as I can, but in the absolute darkness, I see nothing. My eyes show no signs of adjusting to the lack of light, and there's not a sound to be heard. It's frustrating as hell, and right before I'm about to say fuck it all and start screaming for them to show their faces, I hear a soft click before I see a small amber flash from the corner of my eye. The click sounds again, and the light vanishes.

This happens several times before the sounds registers in my brain, and I realise it's the sound of someone flicking open a lighter and snapping it shut, igniting and extinguishing the flame over and over. I can't help the fear that overcomes me as I try to smell for gasoline, praying whoever has been watching me isn't about to light this place on fire with me inside.

"I know you're awake, little hunter." The words startle me, sending a shiver down my spine as I give up my half-assed ruse and look in the direction of the voice. I hear the *click* again, and for a second, a face is illuminated in the amber glow of the flame before it's once again snapped shut, and only darkness remains. There's a soft creak of what I assume is a chair as the person rises, and I can feel them as they move passed me, the clack of fancy shoes echoing around the room with each step.

Seconds later, the light goes on, flickering a few times before the bright fluorescent light beams, forcing me to squeeze my eyes shut from the assault. He says nothing more as I blink a few times, the silence as loud as I've ever heard it except for the faint buzzing of the overhead light, both of which are agony for my throbbing head.

"There she is," he says, and finally, unable to ignore the need any longer, I look over at the man who has managed to kidnap not only myself but my father and my friend too.

His hair is completely grey, although he looks to be no more than in his late forties. His eyes are a dark brown, set deep in his face, casting shadows around his eye sockets that make him look less human. There's a small smirk on his face, and I imagine he carries that smirk everywhere he goes.

The arrogance, confidence and general sense of power that radiates off of him are hard to ignore, and I find myself wanting to lean as far away from him as possible. There doesn't seem to be anything kind in those dark eyes. Something about him seems unnatural, and I know with absolute certainty that if Gideon Bennet wanted me dead, I would already be buried in an unmarked grave.

"Gideon, I presume?" I say, hating the way my voice cracks. My mouth is so dry I actually feel like I could die of thirst.

One side of his lips tilts up in that villainous smirk I'm always reading about, and I find myself thinking that this man is a walking cliché. It doesn't ease my discomfort, though, because cliché or not, this is a dangerous person. It does give me an odd feeling that I have one-upped him.

"Ah, I see my reputation precedes me. Water?" Gideon asks so politely while holding a bottle of water out towards me that it irks me.

I look at it suspiciously and raise an eyebrow. He understands immediately, murmuring something about me being untrusting before unscrewing the lid and taking a large sip himself. Gideon hands it out to me again, and even though the thought of putting my mouth somewhere his mouth has been makes me feel violently ill, I tilt my head up, allowing him to come closer and pour the water into my mouth.

It's humiliating and dehumanizing, but my thirst wins out over my pride, and it feels like the first sip after years of dehydration. I willingly gulp down as much as I can before rearing back. He continues to pour just a second too long, and the water soaks the front of me, earning an amused *oops* from my captor. The glare I shoot him only makes him grin wider.

"You said if I came willingly, you'd let them go. I had every intention of coming willingly, and yet, I still found myself bashed over the head and tied to a chair. You call me untrusting, yet you have done everything possible to not earn my trust. What is it you want from me?" It's hard to keep the venom from my words, but I remain calm. I cannot get angry. I cannot do anything that might piss Gideon off, considering what he holds over my head.

He places the bottle down on the ground before me, his eyes never leaving mine for a second as he walks backwards towards the metal folding chair he was sitting in while I was unconscious. His black suit is tailored perfectly to his body, and I wonder how much that suit cost him while the people in Purgatory – the section of the island that he is the self-proclaimed master of – starve.

Gideon drags the chair over to where I sit and plants himself in it backwards, resting his forearms on the back. "I took the necessary precautions. From what I heard, you're a feisty little thing. I could hardly give you free rein to cause trouble, now could I?"

His voice is so low and gravelly, yet somehow had that nails on a chalkboard effect on me. The hair all over my body stands on end. This close, I can smell his cologne, and it smells expensive, masculine. It instantly turns my stomach, and if I make it out of here alive, I swear I will find that scent and burn the factory that makes it to the ground.

"Where are Chase and my dad?" I ask.

"They're perfectly safe." His small, secretive smile tells me that I was supposed to hear the silent *for now* at the end of that. "Let's discuss more important matters first."

"Alright, I'll bite. What exactly is it that you want from me?" I only pray he doesn't hear the nerves in my voice.

"You recently handed someone over to Purgatory's sad excuse for a police force, yes?" He doesn't give me a chance to agree or disagree, but Rick Alesso's warning plays loud and clear in my mind. "Mr. Alesso was an... *employee* of mine. He was doing something especially important, something monumental. Now Rick is rotting in the dumpster. I expedited the process because he was stupid enough to get caught, and the work he was meant to be doing remains un-fucking-done."

His anger has risen with every word. With every octave his voice rises, my heart smacks harder against my chest. The instant change in his mood sets off alarm bells in my mind, reminding me that he has the upper hand. I have no other choice but to play along.

"I had no idea he was working for you. I was just doing

my job." My excuse is weak, but after he takes a breath, he seems to melt back into his pleasantly polite persona. The shift is quick and terrifying, and if nothing else, it proves that this man is unhinged.

"Ah, yes. Yes, how were you to know, little hunter?" He raises a hand, brushing stray hairs out of my face, and I rear back as much as I can, desperately trying to avoid his fingers anywhere near my skin. "Alas, what is done is done. You got your money, but I was screwed. Fear not, though, little one. I do believe I have produced a solution that may well work for us both."

His smile is ugly, calculated – he knows he has me. He knows that him having my father, him having Chase, means I have to do whatever the fuck he says. Otherwise, I'll probably never see them again.

"I'm listening." I let a touch of feigned boredom slip into my voice, though bored is the last thing I am. He seems to enjoy my brand of sass, and it's not a hardship to give it to him.

"Rick Alesso had wormed his way into the inner crew of a rival...business. He was my in. Now you, my fierce little hunter, will take his place."

I almost laugh. I mean, he has to be joking, right? There was no conceivable way he could think for even a second that I would somehow be able to get myself into the inner circle of some gang. I don't even know which gang he's talking about. In fact...

"What...*business* might that be?"

"I want you to find your way into Roman Black's inner circle. Then I want you to help me burn his entire organisation to the fucking ground."

This time I can't help it. I do laugh. And laugh and laugh and laugh. This is not the time or the place for a fit of the giggles, but I absolutely could not stop if I tried. Gideon's face is one of obvious disapproval, his eyebrows low and lips pulled into a tight line. It isn't until he clears his throat menacingly, obviously indicating for me to stop, that I manage to rein it in.

"Roman Black? As in the boogeyman? The fictional character parents tell their children about at bedtime to scare them into never being bold again. That Roman Black?"

I'm kind of exaggerating in my description. I've heard about the man, of course – everyone on the Island has. The name is infamous in our office, his file coming up so many times that I could recite it verbatim. Not that there's much in it besides a detailed list of all the crimes he's supposedly committed. Nothing ever about *him*.

To my knowledge, no one has seen him. No one knows what he looks like, where on the Island he hides himself, or any has idea where he came from. His name is one of legend, myth. A man so evil, so violent and volatile, that he makes Gideon look like a fucking saint. Maybe I'm being slightly dramatic, but in my current situation I think that's allowed.

Gideon looks disgusted by my outburst, anger radiating from him in waves, and I wisely decide to keep my mouth shut and stop making Roman look like the big bad wolf to Gideon's sheep.

"I can assure you, Miss. Miller, Roman Black is real. The stories about him are gravely exaggerated – that I can attest to. He is nothing more than a thorn in my side, a pest I have waited too long to exterminate. A few years ago, he was nothing more than an annoyance. I ignored him, assuming he would crash and burn like many others who tried to rise up against me. Like a cockroach, Mr. Black keeps slipping through the cracks, his organisation tripling in size to the point that something needs to be done. There can only be one king, Ms. Miller, and I have no plans to give up my throne."

He extricates himself from the chair, kicking it off to the side where it crashes against the wall. "I don't care how you do it. I don't care if you have to sweet talk him or fuck him so fucking good you can read his mind, but you will find yourself at his side, and you will report every fucking move he makes to me."

"But how am I—"

He cuts me off, his tether snapping, anger taking over every inch of his body. His hand snaps out, gripping the bottom of my face in one large hand.

"I tire of this. You know what I want. I don't care how the fuck you do it. Just get it done."

He tilts my head to one side, then to the other, his eyes completely black, fury shining in them unlike anything I have ever seen before. Gideon leans his face in so close to mine that I can feel drops of spit landing on my cheeks, the burning smell of bourbon wafting from his mouth. My eyes water as he squeezes my face with more force than necessary.

"Perhaps you can beguile him as you have your lover. He fought so hard to protect your father. Oh, the threats he made if I were to harm a hair on your head were violent enough to make even me shiver." He pushes my head back suddenly, and the chair rocks back on two legs before dropping back. He returns to his full height and glares down at me.

"Your father is staying with me until you do what needs to be done," he speaks over me as I try to protest. "As a gesture of good faith, however, I will give you the location of your lover. You may go retrieve him. Perhaps he can help you."

"You can't keep my father. I'll do it. I'll do what you ask, I'll help you take Roman down – whatever it takes – but you let my father go. You gave me your word." I'm fuming now, pulling at the ropes restraining me, my heart racing and mind spinning at the thought of leaving my father in the hands of this…monster. Knowing this could happen and actually having it confirmed… at least I'll have Chase. Relief pours through me at that realisation, even if I still want to vomit.

"My mind is made up. You won't change it. All you're going to accomplish here is pissing me off." He gestures to my arms, still struggling against my restraints, "And perhaps dislocate your shoulder."

With that, he walks from the room, the heavy metal door slamming behind him, and I can hear him calling for Benny as I continue to shout and scream and struggle. I cannot leave my father here. I cannot fucking leave my father here.

CHAPTER 6

I left my father there. My head throbs as I walk through the warehouse district of Purgatory. I'm right by East River, on the very coast of the Island, the sounds of the ocean so loud I can barely think. After Gideon left, I screamed my head off for what felt like hours, struggling with my ropes until my skin burned and bled. It didn't work. I was left there, alone, until Benny showed up. Without saying a word, he held up his phone, and my heart almost beat out of my chest.

"Daddy!" I had cried, tears escaping even when I willed them not to. The video on the screen showed my father standing behind the bars of some kind of cell, his face bruised and beaten. He shouted, cursed, and threatened everyone and anyone near him before finally calming down enough to have a coherent conversation.

I told him what was expected of me, and he begged me not to do it. Told me to leave him there, to get Chase and forget about all of it. As if that were even a possibility. I told him I'd get him out, that I loved him, and then hung up the phone in the middle of another of his tirades. There wasn't a chance I couldn't go through with this. Even if I wanted to, Gideon would kill me for disobeying him. I had no choice. No options.

Afterwards, Benny cut the ropes from my wrist, and I almost cried in agony and relief at the sensation of blood flowing through my fingers again. He handed me my gun, sans bullets, my phone, and two pieces of paper.

One piece had the address of the storage facility where they had left Chase. The other was the address for Roman Black's warehouse. I almost couldn't believe it. In fact, when I asked Benny if it was a joke, he merely scowled at me before shoving me out the door.

Roman Black was in Second City all this time, right under my goddamn nose.

This section of Purgatory is made up entirely of warehouses, storage facilities, and factories. It's huge, right on the waterfront, and an absolute maze to try to navigate. I got lost four times, had to stop twice when the throbbing in my head made me dizzy, and even screamed aloud when I discovered I'd been walking in circles for an hour. Turns out that screaming, "Oh fuck you right to hell!" is the best possible thing to do because right after, I hear Chase screaming my name from the small storage building to my left.

I run at full speed towards the ugly grey building, slamming my fists against the faded, red metal door. "Chase? Chase, are you in there?" I shout.

There's a groan, followed by shuffling noises. I let out a breath when I hear him.

"I'm here. Open this fucking door," he says.

I look around, trying to figure out how the hell I'm supposed to do that, when I spot the padlock keeping the grate closed. I see rocks all over the ground, pick up the biggest one I can find, and smash the absolute shit out of the lock. My arm is getting weak, and sweat is dripping off me in ridiculous amounts. I'm convinced it's not going to work when I swing one final time, letting every ounce of frustration pour out of me, along with a very effeminate grunt, and I'm pleasantly surprised to see the newly deformed lock pop open. Without wasting a second, I pull the shutter door up and push it as far as it will go. It's pitch-black inside, and a gasp escapes me when I finally let enough light in to make Chase's form visible.

He's on the floor, his face nothing more than a mass of bruises, one arm cradled to his chest – I assume it's broken. "Oh, Chase."

The words fall from my mouth in a whisper, but he hears them. With visible effort, he lifts his face to look at me, and I'm not even ashamed to let out a whimper at the sight of him. The relief, the pure relief at seeing him here, in front of me, alive, almost brings me to my knees. I walk to him on shaky legs and drop down beside him, gently resting my head on his uninjured shoulder.

"They've still got your dad," he says, and it's not a question. I say nothing in response and merely wrap my hand around his bicep. "What happened?"

He coughs at the effort it takes him to speak. I sigh heavily, searching for any possible words I can use to make the situation sound better than it is. I open my mouth, intent on reassuring him, and instead, the only thing that falls out is, "We're so fucked."

△△△

As we walk into the office after calling Luke to come pick us up, the relief of being in the familiar building with its chipped paint and homey smell is astounding. The sun is setting, casting an orange glow around the small room. It's only been hours since I was taken – not even an entire day – yet it feels as though I'm coming home after months, years.

Eric and Carey are sitting on the worn leather sofa that's pushed up against the wall, but they both jump to their feet when we stumble in, Luke and I dragging Chase between us with considerable effort. The fear on their faces morphs into relief, and Eric rushes forward, wrapping his long gangly arms around me in a crushing hug. It's awkward with one of my arms around Chase, but my other arm comes around him for a quick squeeze.

"I thought you were dead," he says. "I saw Benny smash something into the side of your head, and I thought for sure I'd never see you again." He pulls away, and his cheeks are flushed, his eyes brimming with tears that he quickly tries to blink away.

"Hey, come on. It would take more than that to keep me down." I give him my most reassuring smile, and then we move to lay Chase down on the couch. "Someone call Sophie. Get her here now."

Carey winks as he wiggles the phone he already has pressed to his ear.

Sophie is our doctor. The daughter of two other doctors who came over here when the Island was first built. They brought her up in Golden City and made sure she followed in their footsteps. Soph is a ray of sunshine. You wouldn't think she was an absolute genius just by talking to her, her bubbly personality is almost overwhelming, nearly eclipsing that giant brain of hers. I met her in hospital after an arrest left me needing stitches a few years ago. She gave me her number after I told her my line of work.

From then on, she was my reminder that perhaps not everyone in Golden City should be painted with the same brush. She's a genius and an honest-to-God great person, but she's also pretty badass. She patches us up on the road, in the back of cars, in alleyways. Sophie's our friend, and if she weren't so dedicated to her patients at the hospital, I would have her working here full-time. She's a force to be reckoned with; even my father follows her orders like a sick child.

Once, after a bounty gone wrong, my father wound up getting a knife to the abdomen. I called Sophie against his wishes, and when he refused to be treated, claiming he was absolutely fine, she stared him down until he relented and lay down on the same sofa Chase is on now.

I sigh, a weight as heavy as an elephant pushing my shoulders down, and Eric shoves me into a chair before I collapse on the floor.

Everyone is silent for a moment, but I can see the questions in all of their eyes. *"Where is your father,"* they ask, without making a sound. My heart cracks at the reminder, and it's all I can do not to cry. Luke tried to drag information out of me on the ride home, but I dodged his questions. I want to tell this story once and once only. Repeating it would wreak havoc on my already fragile nervous system.

"Look, I know you all want to know what's going on, and I swear I will tell you everything. But right now, I just want to shower and change and make sure Chase is alright," I say, and even I don't miss the exhausted, defeated sound of my voice. "I'm heading upstairs. Call me when Soph gets here."

Luke gives my shoulder a quick squeeze as I pass.

My feet drag on every step to my father's apartment, and I thank God when I reach the top of the stairs that they left the door unlocked because I may not have made it back down there to retrieve the keys. I shut the door quietly behind me, resisting the temptation to lean back against it and slide down until my ass hits the floor. My brain is in overdrive with worries about my father, Chase, and what I have to do.

Roman Black. A chill washes over me at the mere thought of his name. As I reach into the shower to turn it on, I catch a glimpse of myself in the mirror. The left side of my head looks swollen, with dried blood still stuck to my temple, and a dark bruise blooms at my hairline. It's not pretty – not that I care too much about vanity, but still. I can't help but wince as I peel off my clothes; my skin feels grubby and gross, and I can't wait for the scalding hot water to wash the grime from my body. Everything is better after a shower, almost as if the stream of water can wash away not only the dirt but also today's events.

The water stings, and my skin pinks up almost at once, but I welcome it. I welcome the burning heat of the water, and with no one around to be strong for, I cry. Great big sobs explode from my chest, and tears mingle with the scalding water, circling the drain and then disappearing right before my eyes. My tears are of sadness, frustration, desperation. Guilt. If I had paid more attention to my bounties, if I had done more research into Rick Alesso, I might have seen that he worked for Gideon and dodged a bullet. The realisation smacks me over the head with the same force as the gun earlier, and I lean my head against the wall and allow the tears to continue falling.

I'm not someone who believes crying is a weakness. Crying is necessary. Feelings demand to be felt, regardless of how strong you are. There may be a time and a place, but every now and then, it's necessary to let your guard down and release everything you've been hiding away. I give my sorrow three more minutes, then pull myself together.

My tears have reinvigorated me, and just like I hoped, I exit the shower with freshly washed hair, pink skin, and a whole new mindset. I can do this. I *will* do this. Roman Black won't know what hit him; he is a monster, just like Gideon, and if taking down a monster is all it takes to get my father back, then I suppose that's no price to pay at all. Perhaps it's a privilege.

Sophie is finishing with Chase as I make my way downstairs, her long braids twisted into a bun behind her head. He's been cleaned, disinfected, wrapped, and thoroughly drugged up for pain relief. I run a hand through his hair once and then turn, the solemn faces of my team staring back at me. I pull up a chair, take a deep breath, and tell them everything.

Their reactions range from fear to anger, then from rage to shock and denial as I fill them in, and at the mention of Roman, every one of their faces drops. When I'm finished, there's a cacophony of voices as they all bark over each other. Even Sophie raises her voice to ask her questions.

"Alright, alright. Jesus, one a time," I say and point to Luke, whose face has never been so animated.

"You're aware that this is a terrible idea, yes? If you get caught, Roman won't feed you to the fishes. He'll probably eat you himself."

There are murmurs of agreement, and even Carey, who likes to live life on the wild side, is wide-eyed and sweating. I let them all have their moment before standing up.

"Look. I understand the risks, and I get why you're worried – hell, I'm worried too. There's a lot riding on this, on me not fucking this up or getting caught. On me actually getting in in the first place. I understand, but I don't have a choice. I will not leave my father there willingly. Even if I wanted to say fuck it and not do it, do you think Gideon wouldn't have me killed regardless? My father killed? Hell, even you guys."

They aren't happy, but they're quiet, listening. All of them focused on me, giving me their undivided attention, makes my heart feel full. This could potentially be the death of me, but I have no problem dying for the people I love most in the world.

"This is how it's going to go. Eric, I need you to find everything you can about Roman Black. Everything. Go deep. I need an in, and you're going to get it for me. While you're at it, find what you can on Gideon. Find his safe houses. I want to at least know where they're keeping my dad. If there's another way to get him out,

I'll take it.

"Carey and Luke – sorry, guys, but you're going to have to take over the cases here. All of them. You have to keep this place going. I'll help where I can, but my focus has to be here," I pause, and they nod at me, more than willing to do whatever they can to help, even if Carey looks mildly disappointed that he won't be working with me.

"And, Chase . . ." I say, turning to look at his sleeping form on the couch. He's going to be pissed that he missed all this. "Chase is with me. I'm going to need him close. If it all goes tits up, I may need him to pull me out. I may need all of you. Look, this is dangerous. We're not just messing with petty criminals anymore, and if you guys want to walk, I understand."

I say the words honestly, but inside, I'm praying none of my friends leave me. I need them. They've been like my family for so long that I'm not entirely sure what I would do without them.

They all look at me in disgust, their chorus of, "*Where the hell else would we go?*" echoing in my ears and filling my heart with warmth.

"Meh, we're all going to die one day anyway," Carey says, eyes shining mischievously. "Why not make it *exciting?*"

△△△

When Chase finally wakes, it's hours later. He tries to hold his groan of pain as he sits up, but two of his ribs are broken, so I assume he's in agony. He didn't even flinch when I had the guys push the sofa into my office, and I've barely taken my eyes off his sleeping form since. I already know that because he's clearer-headed now, his guilt will be overwhelming. I intend to squish that before it even begins.

He finally rights himself in the chair, wincing and holding his uninjured hand against his ribs. His eyes meet mine, and I jolt at that spark of electricity between us. I clear my throat – now isn't the time or place to touch on that – and glance pointedly down at his injuries.

"So, what's the damage?" he asks, and I sigh for what feels like the millionth time today.

"Not as bad as we thought. Two broken ribs, probable concussion. Your wrist is sprained, not broken, your shoulder was dislocated, but Soph popped it right back in. I missed the show." *Thank God.* "More bruises and cuts than we can count, and then there's the most obvious injury..." I say gravely, leaving him hanging as his face morphs into confusion. He glances down at his body as if scanning for hidden injuries and a small laugh escapes me. "Your wounded ego," I tell him, and that earns me the first smile I've gotten from him all day.

I lean back in my chair, my back and limbs aching, exhaustion seeping into my bones. I've spent the last few hours on the phone with contacts, trying to find out everything I can, which has turned out to be a fat load of nothing. Nobody knows anything, or if they do, they're not talking. It's just like when my father was trying. It's irritating, but to be expected. Even Soph has plans to talk to some higher-ups in Golden City to see if any of the big dogs know anything about the elusive Roman Black.

"Everybody gone?" Chase asks, and I nod, pointing at the clock on the wall that reads 2:34 A.M.

He frowns, informing me I should have woken him up. I tried. He was sleeping like the dead, hence the reason I'd been watching him so closely.

"You're really going through with this?" he asks, and I shrug. He already knows the answer.

"I don't have any other choice," I say softly.

Chase is not happy with my response. He's rigid, and not just from the pain – he's furious that I'm in this position. That he wasn't able to prevent it.

"I can get you off the Island," he says suddenly. "Say the word, and I'll get you off the Island. I can worm my way in with Roman. Let me take you somewhere safe, and then I'll get your dad back."

His idea is a desperate plea; the only way he thinks he can keep me safe. I love him for it, truly, but it's not an option, though tempting. Even if getting off the Island and forgetting all about the assholes that run our streets is all I want, I could never do it. I couldn't let anyone, let alone him, risk his life for me. I'd never be able to live with myself if anything happened to him.

"Chase…"

"Yeah, I know. Not gonna happen. I had to try." His sad smile breaks my heart.

We talk for a few minutes, going over what happened, what we know. What we've found so far does nothing for us, and when Chase sees me rubbing my temples, the first signs of me preparing for a meltdown, he gets up and holds out a hand. I smile gratefully at him as we walk out of the office, him turning off the lights behind me. The place is already locked up – it was the first thing I did as soon as the guys left – but Chase hobbles over to double-check before following me up the stairs.

He locks the door behind us when we enter my dad's apartment, and as we walk through the small living area and down the hall, we both pause outside my father's door. Neither one of saying anything, just pausing at the reminder of what we're doing all this for. I place my hand against the door quickly and then continue on to the small bedroom in the back. The room is mostly bare; I took most of my stuff with me when I left. A few of my childhood belongings are still peppered around.

My clothes and towel from earlier are in a pile on the floor, and I vow to myself that I will pick them up tomorrow. I climb onto the double bed, pulling back the duvet to slip inside, frowning when I see Chase still standing at the foot of the bed. I look at him pointedly.

"I can sleep on the—" he starts, but I cut him off.

"Get into the bed, Chase. It's been a long day."

He sighs and pulls off his t-shirt with only half the struggle it would have taken me if I had all his injuries. Chase looks around the room, spotting my pile of laundry on the floor and throws his shirt on top of the heap before climbing into bed beside me. The bed is small, but he manages to leave a healthy distance between us. I appreciate it, and I hate it.

The room is silent for a moment, only the distant sounds of the outside world bursting our quiet bubble.

"Chase," I whisper, and my breath catches.

I pray he doesn't hear it, but of course he does. He hears everything, even the things I don't say. He says nothing and holds out his arm towards me. I don't hesitate before rolling to him, careful to be gentle with his ribs. Chase grunts and shifts a little, getting comfortable before wrapping his arms around me. His warmth and smell engulf me, and the panic that had risen just a second ago begins to ebb away in the safety of his arms.

We're quiet again when he presses a soft kiss to the top of my head, and I return the favour, pressing my lips gently and chastely against his chest. We say nothing, do nothing but hold each other in the aftermath of a horrific day. And before long, I'm drifting off to sleep with his arm around my shoulders and the sound of his steady heartbeat thrumming in my ear.

CHAPTER 7

It's two days before we get anything we can use. We've all been running around like headless chickens, trying our hardest to think of ways that I can get Roman to let me into his network. Eric has been working relentlessly, sleeping on the sofa in the office and barely leaving his little spaceship. He even brought over a friend – a small brunette named Andi, who is almost as good on a computer as he is. They suit each other too. Both slim, both adorably dorky and both so pale they look as though they have never seen the sun.

He's brought her around before on cases where he needed the extra help. She's a great girl. I always kind of wanted to hire her for real, just for some extra oestrogen. I don't know how they both manage to squish inside Eric's tiny room, but they do, barely coming out to eat. Andi has turned out to be a godsend, bringing food for everybody from her father's restaurant and just being an absolute delight to have around. The fact that she doesn't know my dad means she's able to remain positive and bubbly when the rest of us are collectively losing our shit. It's nice to have someone who isn't in panic mode.

When we finally do get our in, it's almost accidental. We're all sitting around eating lunch, a sombre silence and tension surrounding us, when Eric bursts from his closet, muttering to himself, flipping through pages and folders that we've all compiled onto Carey's desk.

"I know it's here. I've seen something. It's…I know… where did…" he stammers to himself. We all watch in confusion as he continues searching, his incoherent sentences bringing a smile to our faces.

"Hey, Kid, you want to tell us what you're doing?" Chase asks, leaning back in his seat with unbelievable ease as if he isn't just a giant walking bruise.

I look him over, my gaze roaming over his handsome yet battered face, then quickly look away when he catches me staring, a knowing smirk on his face.

"I had a thought, but it's…and I can't…" he trails off again, his eyes going wide as he finds what I assume he was looking for. "Yes!" he exclaims excitedly, pushing his glasses up on his face and turning to us with the seemingly important document in hand.

"So, I've been looking into Roman," he begins, and I settle in for his explanation. "There's not much about him. I mean, the guy's basically a ghost. I looked into his family, and they're all dead except his sister. I looked into her a little bit, but I guess I got distracted or something, because I forgot all about it." Eric begins to pace, and the rest of us look at each other in confusion.

"What does his sister have to do with anything?" Carey asks, voicing my own thoughts.

"Well, nothing. Or so I thought. But then I looked into her again, and this is where it gets interesting." A look of guilt flashes across his face. "Interesting is the wrong choice of words. I found some stuff, some pretty bad shit. Turns out, little Alisha Black got hooked on heroin when she was sixteen. At first, I thought, man, Roman must be a cold-ass guy to get his sister hooked on drugs, but then I remembered that heroin is *not* his area. He sells cocaine. Everything I have on him is connected to cocaine, marijuana, and guns, but never heroin. I thought…well, heroin is Gideon's turf, and if Gideon was the one supplying Roman's sister with drugs, surely there'd be…

"I don't know what I was thinking, but it seemed worth looking into. This is where it gets weird. Three years ago, Alisha vanished. There's nothing about her – no arrest warrants, no hospital visits, nothing. Facial recognition would have picked her up somewhere. So, I thought, ok, Roman got her off the island…but then something twigged with me."

He slams the piece of paper down on the desk in front of us, and we all lean over in tandem to see what's written on it. The writing on the page is Carey's. It's the notes he took when he visited his mother to see if she'd heard any rumours around Purgatory. The writing is terrible, so I can't make out what she says. Carey and Luke do, though, and they whisper, "*Holy shit,*" as whatever it is becomes clear to them.

"Someone explain. I'm lost," I say, annoyed at being in the dark.

"When I went to speak with my mom, she wouldn't say shit. Just gave me all these rumours and stuff I already knew. She was high, obviously.

"Then, out of nowhere, she says, 'God, what Gideon did to poor Alisha…I'm surprised Roman hasn't burned him alive yet.' I didn't know what she was talking about. Didn't think it was important 'cause, as I said, the woman was high as a kite. But I didn't know that this Alisha was Roman's sister," Carey explains, and my eyebrows rise as I sit back and contemplate what this means.

So, Gideon did something awful to Roman's sister. How does that help us? I'm sure it does – it's too convenient not to have a use – but I'm just not sure how I can play it to our advantage. My head begins to throb. Wondering how I can use the possible death of a young girl to my advantage makes me feel sick to my stomach, but apparently, that's where I'm at right now.

"I don't know how this helps us," Chase announces, with Carey and Luke muttering agreements. I go to voice my own agreement when a thought comes to me.

Gideon, whether he killed Alisha or just got her hooked on the drugs that probably killed her, took something from Roman. Gideon also took something from me.

"It's my in. I'm going to tell Roman the truth. Well, half-truth." Everyone looks at me like I'm speaking another language. I take a moment to gather my thoughts while everyone waits.

"I'm going to tell him that Gideon killed my father. I'm going to convince Roman to help me take him down," I say, and all eyes bulge at the idea. I don't look at any of them – there are too many plans, too many problems spinning around in my head, and I can't for the life of me settle the thoughts that are going a mile a minute.

"I don't understand." Luke says, "Are you telling me you're going to double-cross them both?"

I smirk as if Luke's words finally put a voice to what I was thinking. I let my eyes roam over each and every one of them.

"That is exactly what I'm telling you. And, if I do it right, the two of them might just fucking take each other down for me."

My eyes land on Chase, and we stare each other down. I see the worry in his eyes, but beneath it, I see pride. He may care about me, he may want to keep me safe, but I know him. I know what he hides under those boy-next-door looks. Chase thrives in chaos, and pitting these two monsters against each other, watching them be their own downfall, is exactly the kind of revenge he's spent his life searching for.

I smile at him, and slowly he smiles back, one side of his mouth tipping up higher than the other. I look away, ignoring the extra beat my heart makes, and glance at my team as they talk amongst themselves, going over the plan. I wink at Eric, who looks thrilled that he was the one who figured it out, and he smiles back.

Finally, with a plan in place, I've regained some semblance of control over the situation. The guys are discussing the plan – the possible problems, a back story, the best way to approach the situation – when Andi bursts from the closet herself, doing a great impression of Eric only moments ago.

"I've got it. I got into Roman's security system. I can disable the alarms," she announces, and all eyes swing back to me as I lean back onto the old sofa, reaching my arms above my head to stretch and then resting them both on the top of my head.

Carey reaches into the drawer of his desk and pulls out a half-empty bottle of tequila. "This definitely calls for some shots, right?"

I feel Luke's sigh to the bottom of my toes, but it doesn't stop me reaching a hand out for the bottle. Carey grins wickedly as he unscrews the top and hands it over, eyes gleaming mischievously.

"Atta girl," he says as I take a sip and grimace as it burns my throat. "Let's get to fucking work!"

ΔΔΔ

The following night, I'm dressed in my tightest, black leather trousers, black boots, and ripped oversized t-shirt. Chase hates the way the collar of the t-shirt is ripped halfway down the front, stopped from falling open by a string crisscrossing from below my boobs to my neck.

"You don't need to show yourself off to get this…this guy to pay attention to you," Chase had said, and I rolled my eyes at his comment.

"Can't hurt, though," I replied before sauntering toward the door.

Carey, Sophie and Andi think I look great, but Luke, doing his best dad impression, only grumbles quietly, saying, "I don't like this," before glaring at Carey and storming off in a huff.

Eric, in his own world as usual, barely glances at me as I head out the door with Chase.

I'm not usually the type to use my body to get what I

want from men. I have no issue with it, of course – for so many years, women were taught to be ashamed of their bodies, and we're finally coming to terms with the fact that they can be powerful tools when necessary. Men are hot-blooded creatures, and I'm not too prideful to use everything I have in my arsenal. While I'm hoping I can get Roman to trust me with my wits alone, if I have to show some cleavage to make him think I'm just a sad little woman looking to avenge her father, then hey, more power to me.

We get to the address Benny gave me, and Chase drops me off down the street so as not to draw attention to the car. I crouch low as I make my way over to a wall I can hide behind before I get the all-clear to go ahead. About five seconds ago, Andi and Eric disconnected the security cameras inside and outside Roman's building. They tripped the alarms, giving me five minutes to get in the door before anyone is notified about the breach in security. I already know I'm going to get caught. That's my plan.

I'm simply counting on the fact that me breaking in and maybe making it to Roman's office will earn me enough respect to at least get him to hear me out. Chase wasn't happy with the plan, of course. He'd spent all day scoping the place out, and apparently, the men working for Roman didn't look cute and cuddly. His precise words were, "I hope you're faster than them, cause you sure as shit ain't stronger."

That, as I'm sure he intended, filled me with absolute confidence. He begged and pleaded with me to arrange a meeting, something public and "*safer*." But I had a plan, and it was damn well going to work. Men like Roman need to be challenged, impressed. If he doesn't think I might be useful, he won't hesitate to tell me to fuck off. Or murder me.

"Go. Now." Andi's voice comes through my earpiece.

I don't wait for a second and sprint across the parking lot. I see the glass door Chase told me about, so, without stopping to think, I take out the rock I'd put in my pocket and hurl it at the door. I have a moment of panic, thinking that the glass is bulletproof or something, before the sound of glass shattering informs me it was, in fact, not.

Then I'm moving again as fast as I can. Through the broken door and down the dark hallway, repeating the directions in my head over and over again. After Andi hacked into the cameras, she made a point of memorizing the layout and forced me to do the same. I'm thankful because the inside of the warehouse is too dark to see much. I knew what I was walking into, but in the blackness, it's almost impossible to see where I'm going.

I walk forward down the hallway, feeling my way along the wall, stopping when I get to a door on my right. I keep going, knowing I should come upon another door that will lead me to stairs. A few more steps and I'm there, pushing it open and running up the stairs, two at a time. My heart is hammering, even knowing it's my intention to get caught. Breaking and entering allows a certain amount of adrenaline to enter your bloodstream, and I can't help the nervous energy bouncing around inside me as I bound up the stairs.

When I reach the top, I almost fall, thinking there's

another step where there isn't, and a choked yelp falls from my lips as the earpiece clatters to the ground somewhere. I immediately smack my hand over my mouth, even though the attempt at hiding myself is futile. Roman's office is on the first floor of the three-story building, so I turn to my left and feel my way along the wall. There's only a small portion of light creeping in through a minuscule window, and I thank all the gods there are that I'm not afraid of the dark anymore. I place my hand on the handle and push, my heart dropping when it doesn't budge.

"Shit, shit, shit," I mutter to myself. I hadn't accounted for any of the doors on the inside of the building being locked. I shove at the door again and then smack my hands against it for good measure.

"It's pull."

The deep, muffled voice feels like it comes out of nowhere, and God help me, but I can't stop the scream slipping out of my throat as I spin and slam my back against the door, my hand coming to my chest to rest against my racing heart. Roman. My eyes look around in the darkness, and it's then that I spot the small flashing red light in the corner. The cameras are back on. Shit.

My phone buzzes in my pocket, but I ignore it. I let out a calming breath and turn, trying the handle again – this time pulling it towards me – and it swings open with ease.

I make it two steps before the lights flick on, and I find myself standing in Roman Black's office. My gaze roams over the space. It's big, masculine. All dark wood and bare walls, the musky scent of man and aftershave fills my nostrils. I don't have a second longer to take in the room before I hear the tell-tale sign of a bullet slipping into the chamber of a gun as Roman cocks it and holds it to the back of my head. I can't see him, and unless I risk turning my head to look at him, I'm not going to until he lets me.

"I'm going to give you ten seconds to explain who you are and why the fuck you broke into my building."

CHAPTER 8

There's that voice again. It's deep. Rich. It flows from his mouth with a confidence only a man with real power has. Goosebumps raise the hair on my arms, and for all my bullshit and bravado earlier today, I can't help but stammer over my words.

"I…I just want to talk…I have…there're things…"

"Five seconds. Speak," he says, pressing the gun harder against my head, and I squeeze my eyes shut tight. Before I can stop myself, I say the only thing that comes to mind.

"A-Alisha. I want to talk about Alisha." The words come out in a rush, and in a matter of seconds, he has me spun around, my back to the cold, empty wall, and a strong, rough hand is wrapped around my throat. His eyes darken in an instant.

This is the first time I see him. The first time anyone who doesn't work for him has seen him. He's… terrifying. All of the stories, everything I've heard, the nightmares and the horror…it's all there, blazing in the depths of his eyes. I blink up at him, and I really do mean up. He's tall, at least as tall as Chase, maybe taller. Of all the things I had heard, every story and rumour, every whisper in dark corners, no one told me he looked like this. He's…beautiful. Temptingly beautiful as dangerous things often are.

His eyes are brown but so light they appear amber. They're framed by dark, black eyebrows, matching the jet-black hair on top of his head, clearly messy from perhaps having run his hands through it countless times throughout the day. His lips are full, wide, and with his face this close to mine, they seem unnaturally soft. My eyes roam over every inch of his face, and I think that even without his hand around my throat, the slight pressure enough to half my air supply, he would take my breath away.

"How do you know that name?" he demands, adding more pressure to the sides of my neck as my hands come up to wrap around his wrists, trying to pry his hands off of me.

I ignore the zing of electricity I feel when my hands touch his skin and instead focus on trying to breathe. Trying to convince him not to snap my fucking neck.

"I know what Gideon did," the words come out as a quiet rasp, my throat burning from the effort, "I-I know h-he killed her. He killed my father too."

His grip loosens a touch, his eyes look between mine, and for a moment, I'm almost distracted by the length of his long black eyelashes.

"What the fuck has that got to do with me?" he asks, but there's less anger in his voice now, more curiosity, and hope flares inside of me at the sound of it.

"I want to t-take him down. I want him gone, and I... you're the only one who can do it. I want – I need to help."

His eyes continue to dart between mine, searching for

something I'm not sure I want him to find. The hand that's not wrapped around my neck moves, and I hear him tuck his gun into his trousers. The same hand lands on my waist, and I gasp in shock, panic at what he could do to me flaring up until I realise he's patting me down. "Behind me. Left side." I say, telling him exactly where my gun is.

He raises an eyebrow and steps closer, reaching his hand around my back to grab it. We're chest to chest, and I can't help but lean farther away from him and into the wall. He might be one of the best-looking men I've ever seen, but I am absolutely terrified of him and the untapped power that radiates from every inch of him. I want to be away from him, not closer. He grabs the gun and holds it at his side before taking one final look at me, frowning as he looks over my face, and then, finally, releases his hold and steps back. My hands instantly go to my sore throat, rubbing at bruises that are sure to appear.

"Sit," he says, turning his back to me without fear I'm going to stab him in it, which, ironically, is exactly what I intend to do. "Let's talk."

With more bravery than I really feel, I do as he says.

We both sit. Him, comfortably behind his dark mahogany desk, and me, uncomfortably in front of it. I'm glad for the space between us. Being close to him is oddly intoxicating. The energy he emanates is insane, and even after only being in his presence for a few short minutes, it's easy to understand how a person could drown in it. I adjust the way I'm sitting, placing one leg over the other, and then force myself to stop fidgeting. I'm supposed to convince him that I'm an asset, not a nervous wreck.

"You have a plan then, I presume?" he asks, jumping right into it. His eyes bore into mine as he waits for an answer I can't seem to get out. The words are there, memorised for this exact moment, but I'm choking. Shit. Get it together.

"Not necessarily," I say, lifting my chin, "I want him gone. Dead or excommunicated or buried alive – I don't really care. I want him off the streets. He's done enough damage." I don't have to fake the emotion in my words. I mean them wholeheartedly.

The man is a monster, and he deserves to go swimming with the fishes indefinitely. The corner of Roman's mouth lifts up, and my heart pounds in my chest. He agrees with me, and even finds my hatred for the other man amusing. This is good; this is what we wanted. I just need to remember that Roman needs to be taken down too. That's the main goal of this operation, but if I can get Gideon off my back while I'm at it, that would be great.

"I agree with that sentiment, Lara," he says, and my blood runs cold.

"How do you know my name?" I ask too quickly. This I had not planned on. I didn't want him to know anything more about me than I would tell him. Him looking into me could seriously fuck things up.

"Did you think you could have my cameras and security system disabled, break into my building, and I wouldn't know who you are? Honestly, I've been waiting for you." He leans back in his chair nonchalantly, spreading his legs wide and resting his forearms on the arms of the chair.

My voice wavers when I answer him, and I have to remind myself to keep it together. Now is not the time for nerves. I can bullshit my way through this. "I was planning on getting caught. I needed to get your attention. I needed you to see I was capable." Not a lie. I had to tell him as much truth as possible, make sure I didn't trip myself up. This was a dangerous game, of which there could only be one winner. I had to make sure the winner was me.

Roman makes a soft *hmm* noise as he looks me over. His stare is penetrating, damning. I feel like he can see through my clothes, see through me. It's unnerving. I usually hold my own with men. I grew up around strong men, and I learned incredibly early on that the only way to stay on equal footing with them was not to let them intimidate you.

"I am curious about how you managed to get into my systems. You're a bounty hunter, no? I wasn't aware that the job description included the word hacker. And a good one at that. It took my best men far too long to trace it back to your building, and by then, you were already waiting outside to break in."

I take pride in his words. Not in myself, but in Eric and Andi. Roman is one of the most dangerous men on the Island, the people he has working for him would be some of the best, too, and yet it was *my friends* who were able to fuck them.

"I can't take credit for any of that, Mr. Black. Some friends of mine did all the hard work. I just stick to the breaking and entering," I say, uncrossing my legs to switch them. His eyes tip down to watch the movement. There's a glint in his eye – there and gone in a second – but it tells me all I need to know. The pants are doing their job.

"Break and enter, you did. I'm sure you were just about to offer to fix my door." He raises an eyebrow, so I raise one back.

"I'm absolutely positive you have the means to get it fixed yourself."

He grunts, and I take it as a yes. I'm not entirely sure where we go from here. The conversation has taken an unexpected turn, and it has me in a bit of a spin. I decide to just go right ahead and ask him.

"So, what do you think of my proposal?" I say, batting my lashes just the tiniest bit as I lean forward and rest an elbow on my knee, holding my hand out to rest my chin in it.

"What makes you think I'll help you? You obviously know who I am. Surely you know that if I wanted someone dead, they would already be dead."

It's not a threat, and he's not bragging; he's simply stating a fact. It's terrifying, actually, how confident he is that he can do whatever he wants, whenever he wants. Roman also doesn't even glance at the view I'm offering him. I sit back up.

"Yes, but actively going against Gideon would basically be an act of war. Going to war on an island of this size would be catastrophic, not just to your own men but to civilians, innocents. Also,"—I'm going out on a limb here, bringing up his sister based on the reaction he had when I mentioned her just a few minutes ago—"this is personal for you. Revenge takes time. It takes planning. Which I'm betting is hard to do when Gideon's army is bigger than yours, more brutal. I bet he keeps a remarkably close eye on you, just waiting for you to make a move so he can paint this island with your blood. That's where I can help. I'm not important enough for him to watch. Sure he knows who I am, but he's too narcissistic to expect me to come for him. I can do things you can't, and as you have seen, my friends are exceptionally good at what they do."

It's the most I've spoken since I've been here, and I can tell by the look on his face, the way his eyebrows are scrunched and how he's biting the inside of his lip that he's intrigued. I just hope it's enough.

Roman doesn't say anything, just stares at me, his eyes holding mine so sturdily that I can't look away. I'm trapped there in his gaze, and there's no way out. Suddenly he says, "I'm sorry about your father."

I don't have to fake my reaction. I flinch, and I can only imagine the sadness that takes over my face. My father may not really be dead, but he could be if I don't pull this off. If I don't make this right. I don't know what to say, and I don't trust myself to say much else, so instead, I settle on, "I'm sorry about your sister."

He doesn't move, doesn't break my gaze for a second, and then all he gives is a firm nod. We are in the same position. Both of us fucked over by a demon wearing a fucking suit. Both of us hurting because of the actions of a mutual enemy, and for a split second, I feel guilty. I'm using his pain, his loss against him. I feel like scum, and I should. It takes me a moment to remind myself that while he doesn't *seem* to be as evil as Gideon, it doesn't mean he's not, and it also doesn't mean he's not still a bad man. This is what I do. I find bad men and make sure they pay for their actions.

"Alright, Lara. You have yourself a deal. We'll take down Gideon. We'll bring him and his whole fucking organisation to their knees. But, from now until then, you'll work for me. If I'm going to put everything on the line for this, I want your services in return," Roman says, any hint of emotion gone from his face. He's business Roman now – all work and no play.

Work for him how? Why? This wasn't in the plan. I had anticipated some pushback, but it's obvious Roman was going to go after Gideon eventually. So why does he want me to work for him, and what the fuck is he going to make me do?

"Work for you how? Why?" I ask cautiously.

"You get nothing in this world for free. You want my help? I'll give it to you, but I want yours in return. You think nobody knows who you are? You couldn't be more wrong. Even before tonight, I had heard of you. Whisperings and rumours here and there. Every time I went out in public, I wondered if that would be the day the infamous bounty hunter came to collect me. It was...unexpected. *You* are unexpected."

I'm shocked into silence. I had known I wasn't exactly a nobody. I had worked for some particularly important people in Golden City and probably put some of his own guys behind bars. But the fact that Roman Black, and even Gideon, had my name cross their paths is...wild. I don't want to, but I have no other choice.

"Alright then. Okay, I'll work for you. But…I can't…I don't want to hurt anybody."

His eyebrows shoot up to the top of his head, and an unexpected laugh barks out of his mouth. He looks just as shocked by it as I am, even though it was quite a… lovely sound. "Relax, Miss Miller. I'm not hiring you as a hit woman, tempting as it might be. But you're in the business of hunting people, and I have some names on my list. Some people I have allowed to hide from me for far too long. I've been busy, but with your help, I can check them off my list without spending my own or my men's time."

He stands, buttons his suit jacket, walks over to the large window, and looks out at the nearly full moon that's surrounded by thousands of twinkling stars. In the glow of the moonlight, he's even more handsome, and I have to force myself to look away, to fix my gaze to the desk in front of me. "I want to meet your friends. I must see the men who cracked my security."

"It was a girl, actually. A woman," I say, and the pride is evident in my voice as I think of Andi. I look at him and smirk at the shock on his face.

"I apologise. Rude of me to assume a woman wouldn't be capable of such a thing – especially one who is friends with you."

He turns his back to the window to fully face me, looking pointedly in my direction. I'm unsure what he meant by that, but choose to ignore it and focus on his apology.

"No offense taken. Men never expect to be bested by a woman." I hope he falls into that category. If all goes according to plan, he will be well and truly bested by me as soon as possible.

He makes a noise, which sounds like an agreement and walks over to his desk again.

Roman takes out his phone, tapping away at the screen while I sit there and wait for... something. I can sense this meeting is coming to an end. I have no idea how long I've been here, but I'm ready to be home. Scheming is exhausting.

"You'll work from here. I want to keep an eye on you until I know I can trust you. I want you here where I can be sure you won't fuck anything up," he says, and I'm suddenly offended. Pissed off. Fuck this guy. Work from here? In this office with him? Was he out of his fucking mind?

"What reason have I given you to think I'm the type of person to fuck things up?" I ask, and then referring back to our last point of conversation, add, "Because I'm a woman?"

He looks up from his phone slowly, and his eyes trail over me from the tip of my head, down my face and neck, stopping for the briefest moment on my chest and continuing all the way down to the top of my black boots. It's impossible, but I swear I can feel his gaze on me, his blatant perusal. I can feel it like it's a physical touch, and I will deny it until the day that I die, but a thrill races through me at being the object of such a powerful man's attention.

His gaze sweeps back up, stopping on my eyes again, and I feel my cheeks redden just slightly. "The fact that you are a woman barely even crossed my mind," he says, and it's like having a bucket of ice water thrown over me.

I had forgotten myself for a moment. Forgotten what the fuck I was doing. This was not a man I wanted attention from—he's a killer, a gangster. There was nothing I wanted from him except his swift demise so my father could come home. I hated him. Roman Black was just a means to a fucking end.

"Yeah, if you say so," I mutter as I stand, keeping the reigns on my temper and refusing to be embarrassed by his obvious dismissal.

"I'll be in contact about when I expect to see you here. And I was serious. I want to meet these friends, Lara." He's basically throwing me out, which is rude, but fine by me. I don't want to be here a second longer anyway.

"Pleasure doing business with you, Mr Black," I say, holding my hand out across the desk to him.

He looks at it like he's never shaken a hand before, and I swear if he refuses to shake, I'll have to throw myself out the window. Slowly, Roman raises his to meet mine. He clasps my hand in his, and the sheer size of it makes my own look like a child's. His fingers reach just above my wrist, and I'm worried for a moment he'll be able to feel my racing pulse. I notice how calloused his hands are, how prominent the veins poking out from beneath his skin, and I have to look away.

I grip his hand tightly, and he matches it. We don't so much shake hands as we just...hold them there. Our eyes meet, and my heart leaps. I need to get out of here. I need air and space and a moment to breathe or think or throw up or something. I go to pull away, and as I do, his index finger caresses the inside of my wrist, grazing the point where my blood pulses. I yank my hand back and look away, quickly turning towards the door.

"Forgetting something?" he asks just as I get to it, and I turn to see him holding my gun out to me, flat in his palm.

Even the gun looks dwarfed by the size of his hand. I walk back and gently take the gun, careful not to let my fingers touch his, and the smirk on his face lets me know that he knows. He knows I'm affected by him, and I want to stomp my foot and yell. I can't be blamed for hormones – any straight woman with working eyeballs would be affected.

I nod and turn to leave, but just as I get to the door again, he speaks. "Lara?"

"Yes?" I say, not looking back at him, keeping my gaze on the door I desperately want to walk through.

"You really do not want to fuck with me." His voice is cold. Serious. Terrifying.

I roll my shoulders, wipe my face clean of any emotion, and turn to look him dead in the eye.

"Wouldn't dream of it," I say.

And then I walk out the door, moving quickly through the building and not stopping until I exit the shattered glass door. I take the biggest breath I can manage once I'm in the fresh air. I continue to walk in the direction I told Chase to be waiting, and the whole time, I can feel his eyes on me, burning a hole into my back. I don't turn around. I keep my head high, my shoulders squared, and say a silent prayer that I manage to fuck him over before he does the same to me.

Chase steps out of the car the minute he sees me, worry etched on his face as he walks around to the passenger side. "Is it on?" he asks, and a small smile graces my face.

"It's on. He's in."

His smile lights up his whole face, and I'm glad he's more supportive of the plan now than he was in the beginning. "I knew you could do it, you know," he says, pulling open the passenger door and waiting for me to get in before shutting it behind me again.

I let out a breath while I wait for him to get back into the car, trying to calm my nerves. I'm not entirely sure where my reaction is coming from, why my heart is still racing while my stomach does summersaults, but I'm willing to say it's simply because I survived an encounter with Roman when few people do. When Chase slips back into the car, he watches me quietly, and I know he's dying to ask. I let myself laugh for a second and then say he can ask if he wants to.

"What was he like? Did he do anything?" I know Chase wants to know how dangerous Roman really is, how dangerous this situation is. I could be honest – I could tell him Roman scares the shit out of me, that he's huge, that he wrapped his hand around my throat after holding a gun to my head, but for some reason, I don't want to.

"He's…not so bad. Arrogant. Rude. Very…confident in his abilities…" I trail off, choosing not to add that I think I might hate him.

"He didn't hurt you, though? When you got there?"

Chase asks, but I wave him off with a flick of my hand.

"Pulled a gun on me, as expected, but other than that, he was actually kind of...polite. He hates Gideon just as much as we do. It didn't take much to convince him anyway, and once I agreed to work for him, things went pretty smoothly."

Chase is staring out towards the way I came, distractedly, and so he just *hmms* in response while I stare at him and wait for the words to register. A second later, his eyebrows slam down, his head swinging towards me so fast I'm surprised he doesn't give himself whiplash.

"Wait. I'm sorry, you said you would do what now?"

I can't help but laugh at the look of confusion on his face, and once I start laughing, I find that I can't stop.

Maybe it's the lack of sleep or that my nerves are constantly on edge worrying about my father, but before long, tears roll down my face and my stomach aches from laughing so much. Chase looks puzzled, glancing left and right as if checking to see if there's anyone else around to witness my clear mental breakdown.

It's a relief to laugh, like a weight lifting off my chest, so I don't try to stop myself. I just continue laughing as Chase watches with a lovely little smile on his face. Eventually, my guffaws become giggles, and then even they quieten too, and I'm left wiping the tears from under my eyes.

"You're beautiful," Chase says, his face very serious, as if he was delivering important news.

I blink, speechless. My cheeks redden slightly, and I open my mouth to say something, but nothing comes out.

His face clears as he shakes his head. "Don't worry. Maybe when all this shit is done, we can finally have *that* talk."

I'm grateful he gave me an out. I'm not ready to go there with him. Maybe I never will be. I love him, that's obvious, but loving is different to being in love with someone, and I'm not sure I could ruin our friendship on a *maybe*. I say nothing, and he starts the car, checking his mirrors before pulling from the side of the street into the empty road.

"He's got a list of people he wants me to find. Says they've been hidden too long or some shit. He knew who I was. Guess he figured he could kill two birds with one stone." It's the only thing I can say to break the semi-awkward silence.

"Well then, I suppose it's time for you to do what you do best. It's time to go hunting, killer."

We drive the rest of the way home in silence, but inside my head is the loudest it's ever been.

CHAPTER 9

I've never been a big fan of lying, and I absolutely hate secrets. They build, and they fester and, eventually, they explode. Secrets are ticking time bombs, and lies are gunshots to the chest. They might not always kill you, but they'll definitely leave some damage. I was never one to lie, preferring blunt honesty when it's needed and soft truths to lessen the blow when not. I can lie to my father, which doesn't bother me so much – little white lies here and there to get away with things I shouldn't be doing. It's every child's rite of passage to lie to their parents. Other lies, though? I hate them.

I suppose the first big one is the lie I tell myself about Chase every day. The secret I cannot admit to myself, let alone him. That lie has been going on so long I'm not entirely sure where it begins and I end. The next big lie was not telling my father about Rick Alesso the moment I had the chance – we may have avoided this whole mess to begin with. Then there are the lies I fed to Roman. Pretending my father is dead is a whole new low I never thought I would sink to.

The fact that it wasn't really my choice, that someone like Gideon has put me in a position where I have to bend my morals, really pisses me off. That's not the last of the lies, though, because now I also have to lie to Gideon. Pretend I'm working with him to bring Roman down, when in reality, I suppose I'm just working with myself to bring them both down. It's a slippery slope, and I have to be sure I'm not going to trip myself up.

On top of all of this, I have to lie to my friends because the questions they have about Roman are not easy for me to answer. It would be easy to say that he's just like Gideon. To say that, yes, he is the monster we've all been taught to see him as. The thing is, though, I find myself not wanting to put him in the same bracket as that bastard. Roman seemed like an asshole. Like someone who knows exactly how to push people's buttons and I hate that. But Gideon is... insane. Unpredictable.

I have no doubt that Roman is not a good man. The threat he made as I walked out of his office is fresh in my mind, and I also don't doubt for a single second that crossing him will be the worst mistake I'll ever make. While it would be easy for me to say that he and Gideon are two sides of the same coin...it doesn't feel true. One of them may just be a lesser evil. I'll take that.

After being in Roman's presence, I didn't get the sense that he was bad just for the sake of being bad. I didn't walk out of that meeting feeling like I needed a hundred showers to scrub off the grime he left the same way I did with Gideon. They're the same on paper – both their crimes are just as bad as the other one's – but there's something about Roman that doesn't seem entirely evil.

Of course, I can say none of this to my friends because I would sound like a crazy person. They wouldn't understand, and I wouldn't expect them to because I certainly don't. That's how I find myself telling more lies, further lowering my morals just to make sure everything stays on track.

"Look, what I really want to know is…is he hot? He totally seems like he'd be hot." Andi says.

"Yes! That is absolutely the vibe I get. Is he all dark, sexy, and dangerous?" This is from Sophie, who's currently doing sutures on the side of Carey's face after he got into it with a bounty.

He winces as he adds in his agreement, and I place both my hands over my face and groan. My mind is reeling after telling them all about the events of the meeting last night, and the sudden shift in direction is giving me whiplash. I say nothing, hiding my face so they don't see just how attractive I actually found him.

"Well?" Andi asks, and I peek at her through the cracks in my fingers.

"Well, what?" I ask, my words muffled through my hands. I can feel Chase's gaze on me from where he sits behind his desk.

"Oh Jesus, he is, isn't he? He's a God. You can't even look me in the eye!" Andi squeals, and she's not wrong,

I've abandoned my hiding place behind my hands and begun counting how many tiles are on the ceiling as I contemplate ways to disappear into the cracks of the couch. Andi scoots her chair over to me and grabs my face in her hands, forcing me to look directly at her, raising both eyebrows and cocking her head a little, very clearly telling me she's not going to let this go. *Sigh.*

"He's…attractive, I guess. If you're into that sort of thing." I pull my face out of her hands as I answer her and have to cover my ears as she and Sophie squeal again.

Having not had many girlfriends growing up, I'm never quite sure how to communicate with them. I try my best to get excited about things that excite them, and I make sure to include them in things that excite me, but I always get the feeling that I'm an odd one out. The one who has to walk behind on the sidewalk because there's only space enough for two. It's been this way my whole life, and now with Andi and Sophie, I have to force myself to work harder to ensure our friendship is a lasting one, an equal one.

I draw the line here, though. There is no way in hell I'm going to squeal and giggle because Roman is as hot as the surface of the sun. I can't pull it off. Andi and Sophie are two of the biggest badasses I know, and somehow, they manage to do it while still maintaining femininity and grace. The best I can produce is a wobbly smile at their dramatic display.

"Are you into that sort of thing?" Chase asks.

The smile slips from my face and melts into a grimace. "What, murder and arms dealing? No. I don't find that I am."

He eyes me, and I hold his gaze, unflinching. He's trying to read me, and there's nothing to be read. Chase breaks first, looking quickly down to the files spread across his desk.

Sophie continues her sutures as Carey drinks from the bottle of liquor clutched in his fist. Andi makes her way back into her shared closet space, and I get the briefest glance of the back of Eric's head. Everyone has gone back to their business, and I'm left feeling bereft.

There's not much for me to do around here anymore

but wait. Wait for Roman to call, or whatever it is he intends to do to contact me. Wait for Gideon to call and give me some proof that my father is still alive. Wait for information on the men Roman wants me to find. Wait to find information on Roman that I can give to Gideon. *Wait, wait, wait.*

I've never had a lot of patience, and I've always kept myself busy – idle hands and all that. But with the severe lack of sleep, I've caught up on all the office paperwork. All my cases have been spread between Carey and Luke, and even Eric has taken on some of the more difficult PI cases, with Andi acting as his sidekick. Chase still has his cases. I didn't see a need to pull him off them to focus on this with me, especially now when we don't exactly have anything we can do but fucking *wait.*

I'm cursing the Gods and whoever else I can when the phone rings, startling me onto my feet. All eyes swing my way because we all know the only people who call me are the ones in this room and my father. I search for my phone, shoving my hands down into my pockets until I grab hold of it. It's my father's number, and immediately my stomach flips. I show the screen to Chase, and he stands, walking towards me as I answer the call.

"Hello?" I say, my voice wavering just the tiniest bit.

"Hi, sweetheart." At the sound of my father's voice, deep, strong, and warm, I sigh in relief, and my ass hits the sofa behind me.

"Hey, Daddy." It feels so good to say the words. To know he's alive, capable of speaking.

"Gideon thought you'd like to know I'm alive and well. I am. He's been a very..." he pauses in search of a word, and I can already hear the sarcasm dripping from his words, "hospitable host. I've been moved. No more prison cell, I now have a room with a door and the toilet flushes."

I almost cry when I hear he's not in that tiny cell anymore. The fact that Gideon has actually put him somewhere comfortable is reassuring that he's not just going to kill my father, regardless of what I manage to get from Roman. I don't have complete faith that he's not going to do just that anyway, but hearing he's treating my father even a little bit well is music to my ears.

"Well, you know, a toilet that flushes is pretty great. Not everyone has that."

My voice doesn't really sound like my own, and I'm struggling for what to say. There's too much, too many questions, too many I love yous, too many I miss yous. I want to say it all, but before I have a chance, there's a shuffle on the other side of the phone, and then my blood runs cold at the sound of Gideon's voice. It's so different from my father's. Gideon's words are cold and dead and all around unpleasant.

"Hello, little bounty hunter. It's been a while," he says into my ear, and I see Chase's fists clench beside me.

I reach down and place my hand over his. He immediately loosens his grip and flips his hand up to let his fingers intertwine with mine. It's not exactly what I had in mind, but even I can appreciate the comfort.

"Not long enough." The words are out before I can stop

them, and I'm thankful when Gideon chuckles instead of getting angry. He's amused by me, and right now, that's very useful. It means he might like me just enough not to kill me.

"I've got my in. I had a meeting with Roman. He wants me to work for him, and I agreed. Now, I'm just waiting for him to get in contact."

Gideon makes a pleased *aha* sound, and I grimace. Happiness doesn't sound right coming from him – it seems unnatural, fake.

"I knew you'd do it. See, that wasn't so bad. Looks like we're all on our way to getting exactly what we want. Even your father is in perfect condition – three square meals a day, and he's catching up on his beauty sleep. How wonderful this little partnership is turning out to be."

Chase and I give each other a look as Gideon rambles on. It's possible that Gideon is certifiably insane. There's something unhinged about the way he talks, the way his words sound, and his moods change. It's like he is constantly on the verge of losing it, and I'm constantly unable to tell just what his tone entails.

"Yeah, it's working out very well. I'll let you know when he calls. Or I suppose I'll wait for you to call and tell you then." I say.

"Very good. I'll call you. I'm very busy, you see. Very busy indeed."

"Um, sure. So, is that...all?" I ask, dying to get the noise of him out of my head.

"That is all. Thank you for the update. I'll give your

father your best."

"Thanks."

"Oh, little hunter?" he sings, just as I'm pulling the phone from my face.

"Mhh?"

"Don't fuck this up," he says, then hangs up.

It takes me a moment to pull the phone away from my ear this time. I let out a long breath that's part relief at the phone call being over and part steadying myself. Somehow, his less threatening version of what Roman said as I left his office sounded far worse. Not because Roman isn't as terrifying as Gideon is, but because there's just something missing inside of Gideon. I look around at the faces of my friends, their expressions varying between anger and fear, and I give them the best smile I can muster.

"Looks like we're in business, folks."

Carey wobbles as he stands, sutures now finished, bows dramatically, and then face-plants on the floor. No one moves a muscle to help him as all our faces drop to his unconscious form. Luke emits his famous sigh as he looks at his boyfriend lying on the floor.

"Yeah, business as usual."

As one, we move to pick him up, smiling despite ourselves.

△△△

It takes two days to hear from Roman again. I kept myself busy doing as much work as possible, but I'd be lying if I said I didn't spend most of my time pouring over the information we collected on him. We hadn't really found anything new; the man is practically a ghost.

The file we have on him is barely an inch thick, and most of it is just stories we heard from other people. It's as if he doesn't exist at all – no bank accounts in his name, no family that we could find besides his sister, no shady business deals with his name on them, and no arrests where his name was mentioned, even by affiliation. Roman was a hard man to track and an even harder man to know. It makes sense that I wouldn't have known he was living so close in Second City.

I spent the rest of my time gathering everything I could on Gideon. The best news we have is that Eric and Andi managed to find all his known locations. One of them, a shitty house in Purgatory, seems to be more heavily protected than the rest. I can't go myself because I'd be dead if he saw me, but Luke and Carey have been staking it out. We have no definitive proof, but going by the added security, we think it's where my dad is being held. The two of them have been going over there as well as to his other houses and warehouses to see if there's a chance we could break my dad out.

It would be messy and dangerous, probably a suicide mission. But it's an option. The only problem is none of them are ever left unguarded, and we don't have the manpower to take on that kind of thing. That doesn't mean they're going to stop keeping an eye out. It eases my mind a little that we probably know where my dad is. To know that the people I trust the most are watching him as best they can.

The rest of the stuff we have on Gideon is insane. His file is so thick it's currently being held together with rubber bands, not to mention the box full of stuff I haven't even made it through yet. Gideon isn't as careful with hiding his identity – he's so untouchable that he never had to bother before. I've gone over it and over it, and it seems absolutely impossible that he hasn't been arrested yet.

To think of the people he must have in his pocket, the piles and piles of money he must have lying around blows my mind. I immersed myself in his world while waiting for Roman to reach out and had nightmares every night after reading of the atrocities he's committed.

I'm just taking a break when Roman shows up. If I'm being honest, I'd been expecting a phone call from some unknown number, with Roman on the other end of the line, his voice obscured by some sort of device so he could remain anonymous. What I hadn't been expecting was for him to show up at my office. So, when he finally does, it's at the worst possible time.

I'm sitting on top of Chase's shoulders, trying to change a light bulb. Yes, I could have made Chase change it for me. Yes, I could have gone upstairs to my father's apartment and retrieved the step ladder, and, yes, I probably could have stood on a desk to reach the offensive flickering bulb, but I didn't. I have been changing lightbulbs from Chase's shoulders for so long it's almost ritualistic.

As usual, everyone has gathered around, laughing as Chase wobbles and sways, pretending to lose his balance and drop me. I'm reaching up, one hand braced on the ceiling to hold myself steady, the other gripping the broken bulb.

"Chase, I swear to God I will end your life if you don't stay still," I say, deadly serious, despite the smile on my face.

The door shuts, and every one of us says, "We're closed," in unison. We hadn't been allowing anyone but ourselves into the office – it wouldn't be good for business if a customer was inside and Gideon decided to stop by. Who the fuck forgot to lock the door?

"This is a...unique way to conduct a business, the voice says, and I recognise it immediately.

In my shock, the lightbulb I'd just managed to remove slips from my fingers and shatters on the floor. "Way to go, Lara."

Chase laughs, clearly not recognising the man standing at the door, just out of sight.

"Roman," I whisper, twisting to see him.

Chase spins so fast I have to tug on his hair to keep from falling, and his hands slide higher up my thighs, gripping the very top of them to hold me steady. Silence falls over our office as everyone turns to take in the man on our doorstep. I take a moment to look him over as his gaze looks around the shop and the people huddled within it.

He's in a navy suit; the crisp white shirt is almost blinding against the sun-kissed tan of his skin. Roman looks ridiculous standing there. In this shabby office. Everything about him screams money, from his artfully messy black hair right down to the tips of his brown leather dress shoes.

I pull my gaze from him and look over at my friends, whose eyes are all locked on him. I almost die when I notice Andi, her phone tilted up towards him. Before I can say anything, the flash goes off, and Roman's eyes zero in on her. He narrows his eyes as hers widen, and she mumbles something incoherent. Eric moves slightly, angling his body in front of hers.

"I'd appreciate it if you would delete that," Roman says, his voice like gravel. "Please."

Andi squeaks in response as she lowers her phone back into her lap.

Roman's eyes finally come back to me, roaming half of my body until they come to rest on Chase. Of all the fucking compromising, embarrassing, awful positions Roman could have caught me in, this hardly seems the worst, and yet when he sees Chase's hands still gripping my thighs, his eyes flick back up to mine, and he cocks an eyebrow.

"Chase, uh, put me down," I say, patting him on the head.

To his credit, he does it immediately, albeit slightly... possessively. He swings me around, and his face is basically in my...area... Then lifts me slightly so my legs come off his shoulders before lowering me down, our bodies touching every step of the way. Unnecessary.

I turn and face Roman, already feeling better now that

my feet are actually touching the ground.

"What are you doing here?" I ask, glaring at him.

"I said I would be in touch. I also said I wanted to meet your hacker friends."

"Oh...that's me!" Andi, for reasons I cannot fathom, doesn't appear afraid or threatened by the actual murderer standing in our office. Instead, she bounces over, hand outstretched for him to take. "Andi Devlin."

Her smile, apparently, is contagious, even for the likes of Roman. It's difficult to hide my shock when a genuine smile lights up his face as he takes her hand.

"Andi. Roman," he says, introducing himself. "Very nice work. You should come work for me. You could teach my men a thing or two."

Andi beams at him, turning to Eric with wide, proud eyes.

"Thanks, but no thanks. I don't really work for anybody. Except Lara, of course, when Eric decides to let me play with his machines." She glares at Eric, and he glares back.

Roman nods his head towards Eric then, who nods it back in that weird male greeting. He pulls his hand from Andi's. She seems reluctant to let him go, and I can almost see the hearts in her eyes as she stares at him.

"We can talk in my office," I say, suddenly wanting to get away from the observing eyes of my friends. I don't want them any more involved than they have to be. I need to get whatever he came for out of the way so I can shove him out the door and tell him not to come back here.

I begin to walk towards my office door, only stopping when I don't feel his presence behind me.

Then I hear, "Chase."

When I turn, he and Roman are shaking hands. Even from here, I can see their veins bulging.

Ah, a pissing contest. How fun.

They look at each other, sly little smirks on their faces. It's a disgusting display of masculinity, and I can't wait for it to be over.

"Alright, when you two are done eye-fucking each other, I believe we have shit to talk about." I say it loudly enough that they both drop their hands immediately.

Roman strides towards me, glowering, and I feel more at ease with that glower on his face than I did when he smiled. Strange.

We enter my office, and I close the door behind me after giving Chace a *"what the fuck"* glance and grimacing when Carey and Andi make crude gestures at Roman's back.

When we're inside, I turn to look at the room, trying to see it as Roman is for the first time. It's nothing like his office. Mine is cluttered with paperwork, random knick-knacks are scattered across the desk, photos adorn the walls, and the mismatched furniture that I once thought added character now feels entirely too out of place. I walk over to my desk, feeling like the room has shrunk since the last time I was in it.

Roman continues to stand, eying the pictures on the walls. There are photos of all of us. Me, Chase, my dad, Eric, Carey, and Luke. Even more recent ones with

Sophie and Andi from nights out or from cases we all decided to work on together. He makes a noise as he looks them over, and I have to fight the urge to tell him to hurry up. I don't want to be rude, but he needs to get the fuck out.

"So...you're here," I say, and very much want to slap myself. *Well done, Captain Obvious. Of course, he's fucking here.*

"I am," is all he says, still taking in the room. My patience snaps.

"God, would you sit down? You're making the place look untidy."

He eyes the mess that is my desk. "It's Roman, and I think you've done a good job of that all on your own."

I ignore his terrible attempt at a joke. He sits, his ginormous frame barely fitting in the cheap chair. The only reason I'm not worried it's going to break is because Chase has sat there, and we haven't had any accidents just yet.

"This is a nice little place you've got here. It's...homey," he says, and I bristle. Homey is a nice word, but from him, it feels like a back-handed compliment. Stupid, rich, law-breaking asshole.

"Thank you," I say, folding my hands together on the desk to ensure I don't fidget. One would think I'd be more comfortable now that I'm in my own space, but having him here seems so wrong on so many levels that it has me on edge. Not to mention that chances are he's here to discuss what he wants me to do for him, and that's not bound to be a fun conversation.

"So, what are you here to—"

"Is he your boyfriend?"

He interrupts so suddenly that I know for sure if I'd been drinking something, I would have spit it out all over him and his fancy suit. I almost want to take a sip of something just so I can do exactly that.

"Who, Chase? No. I mean, I don't—" I don't want to deny it vehemently because that seems unfair to Chase, but he saves me the worry.

"He wants to be."

"Well, that's none of your—"

He cuts me off again. "You don't want him to be."

"It's really none of your—"

"Oh, I was wrong. You don't actually know what you want."

"Seriously, what has this got to do with—"

"You two seem very…intimate, is all."

My blood reaches boiling point. I'm at a complete loss as to why this is relevant, why he even cares. His replies are so nonchalant as if he discusses people's love lives with them on a daily basis, and it is really inappropriate and terribly annoying.

"I swear to God, if you cut me off one more time, I will shoot you in the foot." I finally make it through a sentence and take great pleasure as he raises his eyebrows in shock at my outburst.

"Well, I do apologise."

"Apology accepted. You're very nosy," I say, "and…

perceptive."

"It's my job to be both. It's important to me to know about the lives of the people who work for me. That, now, is you. I need to know if your boyfriend, or whatever it is you're calling it, is going to try to murder me in a jealous rage if you get home late from work." His voice is cool, calm, and collected, while my mind is still stuck on, *"Is he your boyfriend?"*

"He won't. Or, rather, wouldn't. If he was." I fail to use words. "Was my boyfriend, that is, not jealous. Which he isn't."

Dear God, compose yourself, woman.

"My boyfriend. Or jealous. He's neither. It's…well…it's irrelevant in any case." I finally manage to shut my mouth and silently make a vow to myself to never open it ever again.

Roman looks amused, and I find myself revisiting that idea I had to shoot him in the foot.

"Yeah, I understand… Somehow. Tomorrow, I'd like you to come to my office. I have the files on the men I want you to find."

Resisting the urge to scream, I nod silently. Still unsure if opening my mouth is worth the absolute word vomit that is still threatening to erupt from it.

"Great," he says, "I'll be there early – shall we say nine?"

I nod again, and he frowns at me.

"I'm very private, as I'm sure you've realised in your thorough background search. I'd prefer you to work from my office and not take anything home. At least until I know I can trust you. If you need help from your…friends, I suggest you bring them with you."

Never going to happen, I think to myself when he's finished speaking. It'll be a cold day in hell when I voluntarily bring one of these guys into the devil's lair. A cold day in hell indeed.

"Look," I say. "You don't trust me, and that's fine. I don't trust you either. Maybe that will change, and maybe it won't. Either way is fine by me as long as we both agree that the end goal is Gideon no longer breathing. That's all I really need from you, and as long as you can give that to me, I don't think we'll have a problem."

Roman looks thoughtful at my words. I remain still as he eyes me, clearly evaluating what I've said. I can't try too hard to make him trust me, or he'll suspect something. Any information I'm going to get out of him, he's going to have to offer to me himself. Other than that, it's up to me.

Honestly, the fact that he wants me to work in his building makes it much easier. Sneaking around and looking through his things will be a lot less difficult if I don't have to worry about breaking and entering to do so. If I can just get a peek at his computer, or even better, his phone, I'm sure I'll find plenty. The rest…I'm going to have to rely on eavesdropping. As long as he doesn't speak in riddles when he's talking to his men, I should be able to learn. Also, being so close to him will make it easier to memorise his movements.

So far, Roman hasn't been awful, which means even though I don't particularly like him, it won't be too much of a chore to be in his presence. I just need to keep my head in the game, my eyes on the goal, and hopefully everything will work out in my favour. Roman and Gideon can kill each other, my dad can come home, and life can continue the way it has been.

The thought of Roman being killed inadvertently by my hand leaves a sick feeling in my stomach, but before I have time to ruminate on it, I realise I've just been staring at him for the last few seconds.

"Sorry, got lost in my thoughts for a second there. Did you say something?" I ask after he clears his throat to get my attention. He considers me for a moment before speaking.

"No. Nothing important. I think we'll get along just fine. You find the men, and I'll work on Gideon. How much involvement would you like in the actual murdering of him?"

I'm a little bit taken aback by his question. He doesn't strike me as the type to consider what other people want. Also, I don't know how to answer that. I've never actually killed anybody, and I don't necessarily want to start now, even if it is only Gideon. He takes in my pause.

"I only ask because we're partners in this. We made a deal, and I will hold up my end. You can be involved as much or as little as you'd like. I just assumed after what he did to your father, you'd like to get your hands dirty." His eyes are questioning, and I mentally slap myself.

Roman thinks Gideon killed my father, so of course, he'd expect me to want to be there when the head is chopped off the beast. I'm also going to need to be in the loop on everything. If he does something without my knowing and it goes wrong, it could all come crashing down on my dad.

"I want to be involved in it all. I want to know everything. Don't leave me out," I say, and I mean it. I just hope I don't fuck it all up.

"Fine," he says.

His face has returned to the dark, stony mask I witnessed the first time we met, and I'm glad for it. It's easy to remember I hate him when he doesn't seem entirely human.

"Alright. Well, if that's everything…" I say, trailing off so I don't seem rude, but he knows what I mean.

He stands and buttons his suit jacket before adjusting the watch on his wrist; he seems purely professional now, and I feel a little bit out of my depth. I put my own business face on, and I know that, on the outside, I appear nothing but calm, cool, and collected. Roman sticks out his hand, and I get déjà vu remembering the last time we shook hands.

I reach over and place my hand in his, except this time, I manage to retain my composure. Our eyes meet, and he nods just slightly. "I look forward to working with you," he says, and I return the sentiment. His eyes slip down my neck, and I realise the moment he notices the bruises he left on my neck.

Our hands stay connected for a beat too long, so I slip mine out and make my way towards the office door to open it for him.

"I'll see you Monday?"

"Monday," he replies but he's still gazing at my neck.

He comes towards me, stopping only when we're toe to toe. His finger tip skims my throat light as a feather. He inhales, opens his mouth and I expect and apology, but instead he shuts his mouth with a click of his teeth and then he's leaving, striding through the office, offering a brief nod to everyone in the room.

Andi calls out goodbye, and he returns it, but there's no smile on his face this time. He pulls the door open, sliding his phone out of his pocket as he does so, and then he's gone.

I let out my breath, feeling like it's the first time I've breathed since he walked in. I do it again for good measure.

The office returns to normal size now that he's no longer here, taking up all of the space and stealing all of the air.

"That was bizarre," Carey says, and then everyone is speaking over each other, commenting on his visit and how strange it is to see the devil made flesh. I remain standing at the office door, still staring at the one he just walked out of, my own fingertips touching the spot he just traced.

"Hey, you ok? What happened?" Luke asks, coming from the kitchen with a hot cup of coffee in his hands, snapping me out of my trance. Thank God.

He passes it to me, and I take it, glad to have him here. Sometimes he's the only normal, level-headed person in my entire life.

"Nothing. He wants me to come in on Monday."

"That's it? You were in there a while," Chase remarks.

"Yeah, pretty much. He just wanted to let me know he's a private person. I'm guessing he also wanted to remind me he knows where I work, where I live. He's...well, you saw how he is." I smile at everyone and walk back into the office, shutting the door behind me to lean against it.

Sometimes it shocks me how drastically things have changed. A few weeks ago, I was just a girl. Just a bounty hunter. Now, I'm some sort of double-crossing spy trying to save her father by taking down the two biggest crime bosses in the city.

I suppose, in a way, it's good it happened to me. I'm trained for this. Not this *exactly*, of course, but this line of work. I've got the skills to make this happen – I can protect myself and the people I love. Even though I know I can do it, I have no room to think otherwise because my nerves are shot. Fried. I've never felt this stressed in my entire life, and all I want is for it to be over.

Having someone's life resting on your shoulders is a *lot* of pressure. Having my own *father's* life on my shoulders? Yeah, that's about as heavy as it gets.

CHAPTER 10

It feels like so long ago since the day Chase and I almost kissed. The moment remains where I left it, trapped somewhere in the back of my mind. Locked away for safekeeping until I have the time to evaluate it, to determine what it meant, and what I even wanted it to mean. It would have been a good kiss, and I haven't forgotten how it felt to have it within my reach.

It's just that kisses like that, important ones, need the proper time allocated to them in order to really consider them. I'm not usually the type of person who evaluates kisses, not that there's been a lot of them or a lot of guys for that matter. But Chase's almost-kiss is an important one, and I have to decide whether or not it's something I want to happen for real. And I will...just not right now. Right now, I want to not think about anything. I just need a moment of peace, of silence. So, I'll think about anything else instead.

Second City is dark as I drive through the near-empty streets. Most of the streetlights are broken, and nobody has bothered to fix them. They probably never will either, because unless you're in Golden City, you don't get anything done unless you fight for it. This is what I'm thinking about as I drive past the small school I went to as a child. The lights are all off, obviously, considering it's nine at night, but I can still catch glimpses of multi-coloured paintings stuck to the windows. The memory of little red chairs and small blue-legged tables is still fresh in my mind.

There are only two schools on the Island. As you can imagine, neither of them is situated in Purgatory. Golden City is host to a huge private school that houses children all the way up until high school. The college, while it may be the only one on the actual Island, is a good one. Due to the fact that it's the only one, it caters to all types of education. Whatever it is you want to study, you can do it right there on the Golden campus.

The problem, however, is that the only way you're getting in is if you're rich. There are no scholarships offered here, and as long as the rich intend to stay rich and keep the rest of us away from their part of the Island, there never will be. My anger ignites as I think about it. As I think about the unfairness of the whole thing. It's very rare that kids from Purgatory ever even make it to school – their parents either don't care or, if they do, they can't afford it. It's shocking, really, how little Golden City cares about the cycle of poverty. If they just tried to help those less fortunate, then there'd be a chance this Island could be something great.

As it stands, the only way poor people get an education is through the generosity of others. People offering tutoring in their own homes, makeshift day cares and pretend schools set up in backyards just to give some sort of education to children. It's a joke, and it won't change. We all spend our lives fighting over scraps when just over the river, the very people who built the Island live in luxury.

When they built this place, and over the years that followed, only one thing remained the same. The only thing they ever did right. They vetted the people they brought over so thoroughly that discrimination – like homophobia, racism, or even sexism – was pretty much the least of anyone's problems. There's such a mix of races and religions that the people born here, like me, wouldn't even understand bigotry if we weren't taught about it. Everyone is equal except the poor.

The struggles on the mainland weren't welcome here, and that's probably the only thing the island managed to maintain. It's not perfect, of course. Sometimes people are just assholes. Sadly, assholes can't be completely eradicated. But still, the issue we have, the biggest issue, is the class structure. If you could even call it that.

There's the Goldens and all of their millions, and then there's everybody else. Second City might be more privileged than Purgatory, but to the Goldens, we're all the same. We are the scum beneath them, and the only reason they haven't found a way to get us off the Island is that there's more of us than them. It would be too much trouble, too much work.

Instead, they make things easier for themselves and more difficult for us. So difficult that the price to even get off the Island, to risk seeing if there's a better life for yourself on the mainland, is nearly impossible. Leaving the Island is extremely discouraged. I'm not even sure I know anyone who's managed it. It makes little sense. Why make leaving hard when it would solve all their problems? Why force people to stay where they aren't wanted?

My anger simmers just beneath the surface of my skin as I finally get past the school. Without even noticing,

I've made my way towards the bridge that will take me into Purgatory. The scenery changes dramatically, and almost instantly, I wish I'd driven the other way.

The street lights in Second might be broken, but while we've got a few left, there's not a single one around Purgatory that hasn't been smashed to pieces. That doesn't matter much, though, because light floods into the dirty streets by way of neon lights from seedy bars and strip clubs. In the near distance, you can see the bright lights from the mass of casinos. Flashing signs from what were once fancy hotels that became homes for crack addicts and anyone else who finds a place there to rest their head light the way to the Gambling Quarter, the name given to the cluster of casinos on the edge of Purgatory.

Without a conscious thought, I realise I've driven towards the address we think my father is being held at. I slow to a stop down the road, close enough that I can just about make out the house but far enough that, hopefully, they won't spot me. I shouldn't be here. If Gideon saw me, who knows what he would do to me. To my father. I shouldn't be here, and yet I can't force myself to leave. I have to squint to make out the house in the darkness. It's small and dirty, run down and unkempt. Three men stand outside, arms folded across their chests as they speak to each other. I hate them. I hate this.

As I watch, a light flicks on in the upstairs window. I can barely see through it because of how far away I am and how dirty the glass is. My heart aches as a shadow passes the window. Is that my dad? Is he this close to me? I want to get out of the car, to fight my way in there and not walk out without my father beside me. I want to so badly, but I can't. There's nothing I can do from here. Not alone, and not with those men and whoever else might be inside. Plus, for all I know, this isn't even the house he's being held in.

Frustration heats my blood, and I have to start the car and drive before I do something stupid. If anyone knew I was here – Luke, Chase, or any of my friends – they'd kill me. I throw one last glance at the house, chest aching, before I turn the car around and leave. I can't help but feel like I'm abandoning my father all over again.

I drive through the streets, allowing my eyes to take everything in, letting the sights take my mind away from the dark road it's been going down. I focus all my attention on the world around me, on the streets lined with people who were never really given a fighting chance. It's not pretty, but these people deserve to be seen. I may not want to, but the least I can do is look at the mess they're living in.

I'm aware people make their own choices, but sometimes you don't have a choice. Most of these people didn't. My eyes linger on a group of women – or girls. It's hard to tell with the heavy makeup and the sky-high heels. They stand together, smoking and laughing, waiting for a customer to pick them up and pay them for their company.

Is that really a choice? When it's your only option, the only way you're going to get food on the table, is it really a choice? People do what they have to do to survive, and I can't fault them for that. Not everyone is Rick Alesso, and with Gideon being the one in control of these streets, supplying the drugs and keeping the casinos running without doing a damn thing to actually help, do they stand a chance?

My headlights illuminate a girl sitting on a bench outside of a liquor store, and quickly I recognise her as the young girl I saw the day we arrested Rick. Her knees are huddled up into her chest. It's not cold out, but she looks like she's freezing. Starving. Before I really have a chance to decide anything for myself, my car is pulling over beside her, and she peeks up over her knees. The look of dread and fear in her eyes shatters me, and the relief in her eyes as I roll down the window and she notices I'm a woman almost kills me dead.

"Hey," I say gently, leaning over to see her out the window.

"Hi." Her voice is so tiny, so soft and broken. The rage inside me simmers, boiling my blood.

"You okay?" Of course, she's not, but I don't know what else to say.

"Fine." She's wary, eyebrows drawn together. I don't blame her. I doubt anyone has asked her if she's okay in a very long time.

"What's your name?" I ask, and she unfurls her legs slowly.

They're so skinny, peppered with bruises and small cuts. It's devastating. I have no idea what I'm doing here. I can't help this kid, bar giving her some money, but I'm already here.

She steps closer to the car, looking through the window into the back, probably trying to ensure there's no one else in the car with me. I admire her for being cautious – little good it's done her before, I'm sure.

"It's alright. It's just me. I don't want to hurt you. I'm just…" I trail off because I don't actually know what I'm doing or why.

I shouldn't even be here. Tomorrow is Monday, and I'm going to have to face Roman. Driving around Purgatory and talking to random kids is not how I should be preparing for that.

"What do you want?" she asks, and she looks braver now that she knows it's just me. Her head is high, and she's taller than she looked when she was huddled on the bench.

"I just wanted to see if you were okay. Shouldn't you be at home?"

"I can't. My mom's got a…visitor. She doesn't like it when I'm there while she works." At least her mother cares enough not to want her near male clients, but sending her out into these streets at night isn't really much better.

"Oh." I stop and look around as if I'd see her mother waiting for her. "You got any friends you can go stay with?"

She shakes her head no, and I find myself at a loss. I can't take her with me. Things are too dangerous around me right now, and besides, that's kidnapping. I reach down towards my bag on the floor of the passenger seat and pull out my purse. She eyes me warily as I do, taking a small step back. I try to give her a reassuring smile, but I'm not entirely sure she would even know one if she saw it.

I pull out some money – I've only got about sixty on me – but to her, that would be enough. Plenty, in fact. I go to shove my purse back into my bag before I open it again and pull out my business card. I look around to see if anyone is watching, and when I'm sure there isn't, I hand her the money and the card.

"Here. Take it. That's my number. I don't know if you… Well…look, if you ever need help or if you're ever in trouble, call. I can help."

She looks at me like I'm crazy, but then her hand jerks out so fast that the money and card are gone in an instant. She doesn't say thank you, just continues staring at me while shoving both the money and card deep into the front pocket of her shorts.

I hesitate a moment, sure what I'm about to do is a terrible idea, but the thought of this kid being defenceless and getting hurt will keep me awake at night. I reach into the glove compartment and find my small switchblade. My dad gave it to me when I started working with him, and I've never actually had to use it. I pray this kid never has to either. I shove the blade out the window, and she just eyes it wearily.

"What's that?"

"It's…a knife. It's mine. It's dangerous around here. You need to protect yourself."

"I don't know how to use that," she says, staring at the knife with a mix of curiosity and fear.

"That's okay. I hope you won't ever have to, but…if you keep it on you all the time and you ever do need to, well, you'll know what to do. Only if you need to. To protect yourself. Maybe now you don't have to be scared of your mom's…friends."

Her hand reaches out tentatively, and she takes the knife, flicking it open quickly and then shutting it, her eyes wide as she realises how sharp it is. The knife goes in the front pocket with the rest of the stuff I gave her.

"It's Adeline," she says finally, and I smile as I hold my empty hand out the window.

"Hello, Adeline, I'm Lara."

She smiles softly, and you can see she's a beautiful girl. Two small dimples mark her cheeks, and I immediately want to hug her.

"You'll call if you need anything?"

"I'll try," she says, and then there's a woman calling her name. Her smile slips from her face, her round eyes turning in search of the voice I assume is her mom's.

"Go on. Go home. Be careful, okay? And keep that money for yourself, alright?" I say, worried she'll give it to her mother, who might spend it on drugs.

She nods at me and then turns and jogs towards what I assume is home. My shoulders slump as I watch her go, feeling shitty in my warm car, about to go home to my warm house and my nice friends.

My drive home is much different. Instead of being angry at the Goldens alone, I'm angry at the whole goddamn island. Instead of bitching about how nothing is going to change, I think about how good it will feel when Gideon is dead. That's what I can do to help that girl and all the others like her.

I'm going to cut the head off the beast and then swoop in before another can grow. I want them all to pay – everyone who has the money to really help but doesn't. Everyone putting guns and drugs and God knows what else onto the streets. They're all going fucking down, and I will bask in being the one to do it.

CHAPTER 11

Chase and I sit in the car, parked on the side of the road just like the last time we were outside of Roman's warehouse. He shuts off the car, and for a moment, we sit in silence. I don't feel nervous like I thought I would. This time, when I walk into the lion's den, I'm doing so with an invitation, and my mind is focused solely on my goal.

After my run-in with Adeline last night, there's no room left inside me for indecisiveness. Gideon needs to go. I've known it all along, but now it feels more important. I'm willing to play my part to get things on this Island to a better place.

"You ready?" Chase asks, turning to face me.

"As I'll ever be," I reply, fiddling with the hem of my black denim shorts. The white shirt I'm wearing belongs to Chase, and I haven't missed the small smiles he's been hiding the few times he's glanced at it.

"I have to go." It's five minutes to nine. I didn't want to be early, but I also knew Roman would have something to say if I showed up late. "Wish me luck."

I step out of the car, but just before I shut the door behind me, Chase calls my name.

"Yeah?" I bend down to look through the open door at him. He doesn't say anything for a moment, just smiles.

"You don't need it," he says, finally.

"What?"

"Luck. You don't need it. If anyone can pull off this whole thing, it's you."

His comment warms my heart, and I scrunch up my nose to hide my smile before closing the door and making my way across the parking lot.

The gravel crunches satisfyingly under my feet as I walk, and I resist the urge to look back as I hear Chase pull away. My back is straight, and my head is high when I approach the door. The glass has been repaired since my last visit, and part of me wants to break it again, just because, but I don't. I avoid giving myself a pep talk. I don't need one today. Instead, I take a deep breath and let it out slowly before pulling the door open and making my way through the building.

The whole thing looks different in the daylight, of course. It really is just a warehouse – you can see where work has been done to separate this hallway from where they store whatever it is that they store here. Actually, that's something I should figure out. I pass the door I felt on my way in last time and have to fight with myself not to open it and have a peek. It's too early to start snooping; I need Roman to trust me at least a little bit.

I don't stop when I hear voices on the other side of the wall. Clearly, Roman's men are in there working. I make my way up the stairs and stop at the door to his office. I know now that it's pull, but I doubt barging in like I did last time is the right way to play this, so I raise my fist and knock twice.

"Come in," Roman calls from the other side, and I steel myself as I enter. "Lara. You're here," he says, mimicking my words from when he showed up at my office.

"I'm here," I reply, slowly taking him in.

Again, he's in a perfectly tailored suit, although I can only see the top half of him sitting behind his desk, laptop open, and manila folders spread out in front of him. He doesn't stand to greet me, and I'm thankful. He's a lot less intimidating when he's not at his full height.

"Where do you want me?" I ask, but just then, I notice the small desk situated right next to his own.

His desk has been moved over a few inches to make space, and while this new desk is small, it looks in no way less expensive. It's the same shade as his own, and the high-backed chair behind it looks to be the same as the one he's sitting in.

Roman nods his head in the direction of the desk, and a sigh slips from my lips as I realise that when he said he wanted me close to keep an eye on me, he really meant close. This is good and bad. Good because I can keep an eye on what he's doing, and I'm close enough that I won't be far from my own seat if I get a chance to snoop. Bad because just as I'll be able to watch his every move, Roman will be able to watch mine.

I make my way over, pausing to look out the window. There's not much of a view – just the parking lot and other warehouses. In the distance, you can just about see South River and the tops of the casinos and high-rises in Purgatory.

I look down at my desk, and my eyebrows shoot up at the brand-new high tec laptop sitting on top, along with three manila folders, each with a name written neatly in the top right corner. He watches as I make my way around the desk, and I have to force myself not to look at him. Looking at him is dangerous – it's very easy to forget he's a villain when his face looks the way it does. Stupid, beautiful man. I finally get myself into the seat, and he swivels in his own chair to face me.

"Everything to your liking?" he asks, and I look over at him.

He has one ankle across the opposite knee, his elbow resting on it as he rubs the nail of his thumb over his bottom lip, eyebrows raised in question.

"Uh, sure. I mean, it's unnecessary. I have a laptop already so…"

I let my words trail off, uncaring of how ungrateful they sound. He didn't do any of this for my benefit, and I won't give him an ounce of gratitude for wasting money on things when there are people that are starving.

"Unnecessary? You needed a place to work, and I had a spare laptop."

A laugh falls from my lips as I adjust the seat to the right height, avoiding his eyes as I feel them boring holes into the side of my face.

"People are starving in Purgatory, and you just had a spare laptop lying around? Imported from the mainland, no less, which I'm sure costs a lot of money."

I don't want to open the files just yet, and I don't want to continue fidgeting, so I turn my chair until we're facing each other.

He looks annoyed, although that's how he usually looks, so I'm not entirely sure my assumption is correct.

"I'm not responsible for the people in Purgatory," he says flatly.

"Aren't you, though? I mean, Golden City pulled everyone in power out, and from what I heard, the place runs on Gideon's word and somebody else's. Are you saying that's not you? That the wars on the streets had nothing to do with you?" I ask, baiting him.

I know of few other small-time dealers, none of which would dare go against Gideon so publicly, which only leaves Roman. The only other name that instils fear in people.

"I never said that. I said those people aren't my responsibility." His voice is calm and flat, but there is anger in the frown lines on his forehead, and I feel like I've somehow hit a nerve.

"Seems awfully convenient to me. You sell them your drugs, but you don't care about them once the money's been exchanged."

"I don't sell drugs in Purgatory."

I raise an eyebrow because that can't be true. Almost everyone in Purgatory is on drugs, and there's no way he doesn't sell where his biggest market would be. Although he didn't say he doesn't sell *at all*.

"Believe me or not – that's your own prerogative. Honestly, I don't care to convince you, nor do I wish to explain myself any further," he says, and his phone buzzes on the desk in front of him.

He glances at the screen before pressing the button to hang up. I decide this conversation is not one ready to be had yet, although I'm confused. If Gideon wants him out of the way because Roman is a threat to his business, how is that possible if Roman doesn't deal in Purgatory? Someone's lying, and while I'm willing to bet it's Gideon, I wouldn't wager much on it. I have no idea who Roman really is.

"You're not going to get that?" I ask.

He shakes his head and stands, coming over to my desk and standing over me. "These are the men I need you to find. I won't lie – I haven't looked too hard, and I haven't had anyone look into it besides myself."

I crane my neck up as he opens one of the folders and places it on the desk in front of me.

"Why not?" I ask, but I'm already not listening because I'm looking at the file in front of me.

Ryan Foster, 28, Purgatory-born and raised. His last known address, phone number, and photo stare up at me, and he looks like a mean piece of work. Tattoos cover almost the entirety of his face, neck, and arms, and even in the grainy photograph, it's easy to see how huge he is.

"Well, he looks mean," I say, only getting a grunt in return. I look over my shoulder at him and see he's staring down at the photograph of Ryan with unhidden hatred. "You want me to start with him? I could do them all at once, but I prefer working one case at a time."

He finally pulls his gaze away from the file to look at me. "Yes. Him first."

We go over a few things, mainly him telling me pieces of information on Ryan. It's not entirely necessary – I'll be able to find out anything I need to know for myself – but he seems to want to help, so I let him. After a few moments, he sits back at his desk. Without a word, he begins looking over his own work, so I decide it's time to jump straight to it. I pull my own laptop out of the bag I brought with me and start it up. I can feel Roman's eyes on me, sense his suspicion.

"Eric has put tons of stuff on here. I'll be completely honest and say I have no idea what most of it is or how it works, but it's somehow connected to the database the police use. It gives us access to all their files – the ones they've given us permission to use *and* the ones they haven't" I find myself explaining, even though he didn't ask. If Eric was here or if I sent the names over to him, he could probably find them in minutes, but it's been a while since I've gotten my hands dirty, and I'm actually kind of excited to do some sleuthing.

"I didn't ask."

I glare at him. "I could feel your mistrust from all the way over here. I thought you'd like to know why I was using my own—"

"Work, Lara. I trust that you value your life enough that you wouldn't be so stupid as to fuck me over right under my nose." With that, he turns back to his desk, leaving my heart racing with the reminder that if I'm caught, or if I fail, I'm dead.

I type Ryan's name into the system, trying to only focus on my new task, and he's the first to pop up. It's very easy to keep track of people on the Island. You can trace everyone back to the very first people who came over. Most of it isn't public information, per se, but with the right connections – which I have – it's very easy to see where people come from. Ryan Foster's mother came over with her parents. They both worked in one of the casinos in Purgatory. Reading through each of their files is unnecessary, but I do enjoy being thorough.

It's all fairly basic, the usual story. The parents were good people, but when it all went to shit, they got screwed. His mother turned to drugs, and Ryan has been a piece of shit since the day he was born. Nothing on his file was bad enough to send him to the dumpster, and a lot of criminals get away with paying fines because all Golden City really wants is money. They're fine with these people being on the streets once it's not their streets, and once they're contributing to Golden City's large bank accounts. Such a shame.

Roman and I work in silence for a while, and as much as I hate to admit it, I'm kind of having fun. I've got Ryan's last known address, which is updated to the one Roman had on file. I've also pinpointed where he likes to hang out, judging by reports of places he's been caught dealing. I keep working, my face almost inside my laptop screen until I feel Roman's gaze on me. I've resisted the urge to look at him for the last hour, but the feeling of his eyes on me hasn't gone unnoticed. It's like my presence alone is irritating him. He put me here. I didn't ask for it.

I look over, and, sure enough, he's watching me. It's unnerving and unwanted, but when my eyes meet his, there's an unmistakable tension. Mutual hatred, probably.

"Can I help you?" I ask.

His face gives me nothing; it's blank as usual, and I want to shake him. It's impossible to know what he's thinking, and when you're dealing with your enemy, it's important to know what's going on inside their head. The thought strikes me as I look at him. Is he really my enemy? He said he wasn't dealing in Purgatory, but that doesn't mean he's not dealing in general. Drugs ruin lives whether you're poor or rich. But is *enemy* the right word? I'm not sure. A means to an end is what he is. A casualty of the deal between me and Gideon.

"You really love what you do," he says suddenly. It's a statement, not a question. I hate how easily he seems to read me as if he knows what I'm thinking.

"I do love it. It's what I was raised to do."

Roman regards me quietly, his thumb running over his bottom lip again. He's not doing it to be sexy – it's clearly just a thing he does. I catch my tongue darting out to lick my own bottom lip at the sight of it and immediately force myself to stop paying attention to his lips. And his hands.

"Is there much work in it? There can't be that many bad guys to catch that the police here can't do it themselves." Roman asks so innocently that I laugh, assuming he's joking. He isn't. His dark eyebrows get lost somewhere under his hairline, and I realise he actually wants an answer.

"There are no cops. Not really. Golden City only gives us the leftovers from their little army, and the civilians that join to try and help are barely trained. They do their best, all of them, but things are so bad that they usually end up letting people go when Golden City realises putting them on trial will probably just cost more money. So, Golden City pays the cops to pay me to catch people, but then the majority of the time they just let them go with a warning or a fine. Mostly it's just to make it look like they're doing something. Come on, you have to know this already."

I sigh when I finish my explanation and am quite pleased – albeit shocked – to realised Roman seems to be genuinely considering this.

"Although," I continue, "seeing as you yourself are one of the guys I've been paid to catch, none of this is an issue to you. You'd probably flash your pretty little smile at some woman in Golden, and she'd let you walk out the door." This time he looks mildly amused, thumb still brushing his lip.

"Well the lack of policing is beneficial to me. I don't pay attention to what doesn't concern me and mine."

"That's because it doesn't *affect* you, living up here in your ivory tower. Also, being the big bad Roman Black means nobody's going to fuck with you. It's us little people who have to worry about it."

"Well, that's—" but he doesn't get to finish because his phone rings again.

This time, instead of ignoring it, he brings it to his ear. I turn back to my computer and pretend not to pay attention, but as discretely as I can, I activate the voice recorder on my laptop.

"Speak," he barks into the phone, all the softness from a moment ago banished from his voice, and even I startle a little at the rude command.

I flick through random things on my laptop, actively trying not to listen. I expect him to get up and leave the room, but he doesn't. His ass stays firmly planted in his seat, and as I peek at him out of the corner of my eye, I see him sprawled in the chair, his long, muscular legs spread wide with his feet planted on the floor. He uses his feet to spin his chair from left to right as he talks, and the movement is so…normal that, for a moment, I forget I'm not supposed to be paying attention. Roman looks so boyish and human while barking orders down the phone. He has a face like thunder while he practically *spins* his chair around like a child.

"I want it today." Pause. "That's really no concern of mine. I said today, and I meant it." Longer pause, louder muffled words. "You have until the end of day." Pause. "Not my problem." Pause. "I'm done with this. End of the day. If it's not in front of me by then, you will not like the consequences, I assure you." Much longer pause. My eyes widen as his tone changes. "Wonderful. I'm delighted we could come to an agreement. Thank you, Micah." He hangs up without saying goodbye and throws the phone onto the desk in front of him.

He appears to be zoned out, but that all changes when, against my own wishes, I start to laugh.

"Did you just greet someone with the word 'speak?'" I ask, absolutely bewildered.

"No." He frowns. "Did I?"

"You absolutely did." I'm laughing hard now. "That is so. Fucking. Rude."

I can't stop, and his lips twist up into an almost smile as if he's holding back his own laugh. That's just wishful thinking. I don't think he knows how to really laugh.

I'm still cracking up when my own phone rings. He doesn't even pretend not to listen as I answer, and I catch his eye as I hold it to my ear.

"Speak," I say, and I'm greeted with silence. I look at the phone again, confirming the call is still holding and that it was Sophie's name I saw on the screen. I hold it back to my ear and ask if she's there.

"Did you just answer the phone with 'speak?' What am I a fucking dog?"

I can't help but snort in response. "Yeah. I was just testing something."

"Well, it's not going to work out."

"I see that now, thanks. Can I do something for you?"

"You can start with explaining why you said Roman was just *attractive* when you clearly meant he was a fucking God on Earth."

Oh. Oh no.

"Um, Soph, I'm working right now." *Please don't be looking at me. Please be focused on your work.* He's not looking at me. He's also not focused on his work if the slight quirk of his lips is any indication. I stand, trying to get far enough away so that Roman can't hear her, but I'm flustered and my chair wont roll back enough for me to step out easily and Sophie just keeps on talking. I try to interrupt but she's still going and why is my phone *so loud* anyway. I try the volume down button, but she just seems to be getting louder.

"So? I think extremely hot, murderous bad boys are more important. Are you at the office? I'm on my way there. I need you to describe him to me again. I don't think I heard you right the first time." Sophie screeches when she's excited, and right now her she is basically shouting down the phone at me.

Oh please, God, make her stop.

"No, Sophie, I'm not at the office. I'm working somewhere else. You remember?"

The line finally goes silent before her voice comes through again, filled with understanding. "*Ohhh...*"

"Yep."

"You're with Roman, aren't you?"

"Yes."

"He's right beside you, isn't he."

"That is correct."

"Did he hear everything I just said?"

I twist in my chair to face him, and he's not even pretending anymore. He's staring right at me, and the quirk of his lips is now a cocky smirk.

"That is the obvious conclusion one would come to, yes."

"I see. Okay. Well then...goodbye."

The phone goes silent once again, and I lower it slowly to the desk as Roman runs a hand over his face, clearly trying to wipe the smile from it. It doesn't quite work. I fight the urge to run from the room and spin my chair back to face the desk. I stare intently at the screen but focus on nothing. I could have hung up. Why didn't I just hang up?

"You heard?" I ask, and he clears his throat before answering.

"Yes."

"Wonderful." The word is layered in sarcasm. I hate my entire life. I am an adult woman! How is this happening in real life?

"So, which would you say it is?" he asks, and I can't help but look at him again in confusion. "Am I attractive, or am I a God?"

Death. Quickly, please.

I scoff, once again turning away from his eyes. Ridiculous orange eyes that always look right through me.

"Neither. Obviously." I say.

"But your friend said you said—"

"I," I interrupt, "was simply humouring two girls who wanted some entertainment. I didn't mean a word of it. You are…adequate. No more, no less. Now, let's move on, shall we?"

He rises from his desk, and my gaze snags on his wrist as he adjusts the sleeve of his shirt, twisting his watch slightly to sit correctly on his wrist. I ignore him, focusing again on nothing instead of him.

"Ok, Miss Miller. My lips are sealed." He picks up his phone and informs me that he has to go before telling me I can leave whenever I want.

"Shall I come back tomorrow then?"

"Please."

I'm glad he doesn't want to shake hands this time.

I hold off getting ready to leave, slowly collecting my things so we don't have to walk out together, when I notice he's stopped in the doorway, looking at me. *Looking* at me.

"Yes?" I ask.

"I suppose you are perfectly adequate too," he says, and then he's gone, his footsteps echoing loudly in the stairwell.

A blush rises to my cheeks, and I open and close my mouth in shock like a fish. Fucking asshole. I have no idea if he meant that as an insult or compliment. I'm going to take it as the former because that makes more sense.

What it doesn't do, though, is explain why my heart is beating rapidly inside my chest and why my blood suddenly seems fifteen degrees hotter.

△△△

Chase picks me up again, and the ride home is quiet. He asks me how it went, and I tell him it was fine. I'm unable to muster much enthusiasm, struggling to rip myself out of my turbulent thoughts. I can't help the way I react to Roman. It's not my fault that he looks the way he looks and sounds the way he sounds. Nor can I help the way he smells or how that makes me feel. I'm conflicted, torn.

I hate him as a human. I suppose I'm morally obliged to hate him – he's a bad guy and everything else that goes with that. The thing is, if I had just met him in completely different circumstances, I would absolutely go for it. Moral compass or no, I'm attracted to him on a purely physical level, and denying that is only going to make the attraction stronger.

Admitting it to myself means I can control it, shut it down, and work harder to remember who he is and why I'm even around him. Like countless times throughout today when I'd catch him staring at me, and I didn't want him to stop. Times when he smiled at me so casually, or touched me so briefly, that I had to remind myself about all the reasons I hate him. Remind myself that being interested in a guy like him would be utterly detrimental to my health.

My thoughts remain like this until well after we make it home. I'm lost in my own head as I talk to the team before they all leave for the day, absentmindedly nodding along as they give me progress reports and updates. I don't miss the glances they give me and each other. They know it's getting to me. My friends can tell I'm struggling, but they know I wont talk if they ask me why.

Eventually, everyone leaves, and Chase and I lock up. Then we make our way across the street to our building. I shut down his attempts at conversation, not wanting to even have to look at him. There's too much going on in my life at the moment for me to be thinking about not one but two men, and so, as I settle into bed that night, wrapped tightly in the covers, I vow to let it go.

To do what I came to do and nothing else. I promise to remain focused and not lose sight of the main goal.

I make the promises, then drift off to sleep where my dreams are filled with amber eyes and everything I swore not to let myself think about.

CHAPTER 12

The rest of the week passes in a blur and then rolls into the next. I work with Roman almost every second of the day, except for when he has to leave to do business. I make note of anything that might be useful for Gideon, ensuring I have at least a little something to give him the next time he calls. Roman is his usual polite yet aloof self. There was no more mention of my adequateness or his, but it was getting easier and easier to feel his stare on me. To catch him watching me. I lost track of how many times he told me to stop typing so loud. Stop fidgeting. Sometimes I caught myself glaring at him so hard he's actually flinch.

Yesterday, I met him in the parking lot as we both walked into the building. He pulled the door open as I walked in, placing his hand on the small of my back, burning the skin there so badly I thought he'd leave a handprint. He asked questions about the business, most of which I answered, and I asked questions about him, most of which he shut down or gave the bare minimum for an answer. It was frustrating not to be getting more out of him, but it had only been two weeks, and this was not really something I could rush without making a mistake and getting caught.

I was busy, though. I had multiple sightings of Ryan, and after sending Chase out to follow him, it's looking like today, Friday, is the best day to pick him up. Chase had arranged it so that he bumped into him accidentally on Thursday. I liked to see how responsive or volatile perps might be before I went after them. If they got aggressive over a 'stranger,' it would be easy to conclude I might need backup. It didn't always work this way, of course – sometimes you just had to go for them.

I wanted to be absolutely certain I could get him with the least amount of stress possible, so when Chase bumped into him yesterday and inquired about buying drugs, they set up a meeting for today. A meeting that I, unbeknownst to Ryan, was going to crash. I didn't want anything to go wrong.

I'm in Roman's office that morning, but he hasn't shown up yet. I contemplate calling him, but since we exchanged numbers, I haven't yet had to use his, and for whatever reason, I'm reluctant to change that. I'm only here to let him know I'm going to get Ryan. Chase let me know the details at my apartment last night, so Roman isn't aware that today is the day. It isn't that I necessarily have to check in with him, but I'm trying to build a trust between us, and it feels like the right thing to do.

I plonk myself down in the chair behind his desk and take a moment to pretend that I'm him. That I'm all powerful and brutally dominating. I rest my hands behind my head, spinning from left to right as I'd watched him do so many times this week. Sitting here makes it easy to understand the power he must feel on a daily basis. The wealth and opportunities at his fingertips, the—

"That chair looks a lot better with you in it." His voice startles me out of my thoughts, and I sit upright, letting my hands fall from my head while struggling to stop the left-to-right motion I had created. His eyes are directly on me, and I clear my throat as I avoid his heated gaze, doing my best to ignore his strange compliment.

"Sorry. I was waiting for you," I say, standing up and fiddling with the end of my oversized t-shirt.

"I had some things to get done."

"That's alright. I'm not staying. I'm going to get Ryan."

He'd begun to hang his suit jacket on a rack, but at the mention of Ryan's name, his head whips towards me. "You're going now?" he asks, anger in his tone.

"Yes. Now. Chase set up a meeting under the pretence of buying coke, so while he does that, I'm going to swoop in and grab him."

"Why didn't you tell me?"

"I just did."

"I'm coming," he says, and then he's swinging his jacket back on and marching towards his desk.

"Uh. No, you're not."

Roman opens the safe concealed in one of his drawers, and I watch, transfixed, as he pulls out his gun. He slides it open to check the magazine and loads it again so quickly I almost can't keep track. After he slams the magazine back in with a resounding snap, my attention turns to his face. He looks angrier than I've ever seen him, his shoulders tight, and he looks about ready to kill someone. Suddenly, I'm not entirely confident Roman didn't want me to find Ryan just so he could kill him.

"Yes, I am. Let's go. I'll drive."

I clench my jaw as he storms past me, but before he can make it out the door, I slam it and stand in front of it. He stops abruptly, and then we're toe to toe.

"What are you doing?" he asks, eyes flicking between mine. They're darker now, more brown than amber, and entirely too dangerous to be legal.

"Listen to me. Very carefully. I understand that you're used to being the boss, the one in control. That's fine by me on your turf, but this? This is my turf. My arena. I'm the one in control here. Do you understand?"

He says nothing, just tips his head slightly in acknowledgement of my words. I look into his eyes directly now, and I'm relieved when I feel nothing but indignation. I'm in control here; his face has no power over me at this moment.

"I'll decide if you get to come," I continue, and his lips open to dish out a response to my questionable words, but I cut him off with a roll of my eyes and continue, "Chase is coming. *I* am driving. You can sit in the back. But first…Ryan. Why him?"

Roman doesn't answer me for a moment, just stands there in my space, chest rising and falling so close it almost touches mine. His brows furrow as he glares at me, his eyes flickering all over my face. It doesn't seem like he's going to answer me, but I make no move to get out of his way. This is one question he's not getting out of answering. Finally, he rolls his eyes and takes a slight step backwards.

"That…man…" He lifts his wrist and begins to adjust his watch. He does that around me a lot, and I have to fight to stop my eyes from looking. "He sold my sister the drugs that she overdosed on. The first time."

Roman's eyes don't meet mine as he begins to adjust the rest of his attire. He loosens the knot on his tie, sliding it down and then pulling it over his head before opening up the top button of his shirt, fingers fiddling with his collar. "He introduced her to Gideon. Then Gideon ruined her."

No wonder he wants to get his hands on this guy. Guilt rises inside of me, and I work to quash it. Guilt has no place here. His sister is dead – I can't change that, and I can't feel bad for using it as a chip to save my father's life. I'm not quite sure what to say, so instead, I step out of the way and pull open the door, motioning with my hand for him to lead the way. He nods, but the movement is stiff. His whole body is stiff. I'm so used to him moving with such grace, sauntering across the room effortlessly.

As I watch him exit, everything about him is tight, wound up. Our eyes catch as he waits outside the door for me, and he nods again. He's vulnerable, and I don't like it. This is a chink in his armour – unquestionable humanity slipping through the cracks of his bulletproof shield. It makes him relatable; it makes him human, and I hate him for it. How dare he make me feel anything? How dare he, of all people, invoke such a ridiculous reaction from me when he's the very type of person I'm trying to rid the island of?

Roman follows me down the stairs, a quiet tension surrounding us.

"You're still sitting in the back. You need to be invisible," I say when we reach the bottom. I look in his direction as he steps to my level, and as usual, have to crane my neck up to see him. I allow my eyes to travel the length of his body. "I don't think you've ever been invisible a day in your life."

He smirks, just barely, so I turn away from him in mock disgust. The stupid giant is going to get us caught.

Chase is leaning against the car as we approach. His smile slips from his face when he notices Roman at my side, and he stands up straight, crossing his arms over his chest.

"Hazel," he says in greeting using an old nickname I haven't heard in a while, so I know it's a question. I've heard the tone enough times to know it means, *"What the fuck is going on?"*

"Hi," I say, walking around to the driver's side. "Roman's coming."

The two of them eye each other, just like the last time they met in the office. It's disturbing.

"Get in the fucking car," I say, and they both snap into action, unaware of how similar their movements are. They both slam their doors in a synchronised fashion. I turn to look at them both with raised eyebrows, getting nothing but a glare from both of them in return.

It's then that I notice how small the space is. There are two six foot four men sitting in my car, both of them taking up far too much room and breathing far too much air and smelling entirely too manly. Each of their aftershaves reach my nose, and I roll down the window, desperately in need of air. The silence is thick in the car, and I can't help but take another look at them.

Chase sits stoically in the front with arms crossed over his chest, a black baseball cap turned backwards on his head, covering the mess of brown waves I've always adored. Those blue eyes are trained on the windshield in front of him. His t-shirt is tight, showing off the defined muscles in his chest and shoulders and the golden-brown tan and dark veins down the length of his forearms and hands. My mouth is suddenly very dry, and I avert my eyes, choosing instead to look at Roman.

His black hair is its usual perfection, short on the sides with some sort of artfully messy situation on top. Roman's eyes are aimed out the window, too, and I take a moment to look over him. His suit is expensive and tight enough to hint at a pretty decent body beneath. There's a slight shadow on his carved jaw like he didn't bother to shave this morning, and then my eyes travel down to where his hands rest in his lap. The edges of his tattoos peeks out, his veins travelling down the back of his hands to his long fingers. The middle one on Roman's left hand is adorned by a silver ring, while the ring finger of his right hand carries a silver ring with a black stone.

It's stifling in the car. The rising morning heat is obviously the only reason I'm sweating. I tear my eyes away from him, realising if I don't move soon, one of them is going to ask what I'm doing. I shake my head slightly.

I'll just have to ignore them and rid myself of any and all thoughts of the two men occupying both my car and my fucking dreams and get on with shit without acting like a dog in heat. Absolutely ridiculous behaviour out of me. Disgusting really. I am utterly ashamed of myself.

My eyes slide back to Chase's forearm, and then my head turns without my permission, eyes zeroing in on Roman's ring and – fuck me, it's hot in this car.

The sound of a throat clearing snaps me out of my stupor, and I mentally slap myself as Roman flashes me a crooked smile, earning a confused glance from Chase. I grumble to myself and start the car as we begin the journey to Purgatory, where, hopefully, we'll nab Ryan.

Chase reaches over to squeeze my knee, mistaking my discomfort for nerves. I give him a small smile, looking in the rear-view mirror to glare at Roman when he lets out a small laugh, clearly having seen the interaction between us. He just raises an eyebrow as I huff.

"Why did he call you Hazel? I thought your name was Lara?" Roman asks after a few moments, breaking the silence.

Immediately, my eyes roll right into the back of my head, and I groan while Chase lets out a bark of smug laughter. I resist the urge to reach over and smack him, even though my hand itches for it.

"You want to tell him, or should I, *Hazel?*" Chase asks, and I want to shove him out of the moving vehicle.

Instead, I tell him to go ahead. He does love telling the story. His grin widens and he goes on to tell the most embarrassing story of all time.

"When I started working for Hazel's - *Lara's* – dad, she was only eighteen. She was going through some sort of rebellious phase. You should have seen her! She cut her hair real short and only ever wore short black skirts and fishnet tights just to piss off her old man," he pauses to laugh a little, and I roll my eyes, but a small smile still takes over my face. Fond memories.

"Anyway, Lara goes out with some friends one night and gets absolutely blind drunk. I mean, she was…just fucked up. Her dad's gone for the night working a case, which is fine because the guys and I were always around to check on her, and she was living above the office still. So, she calls me. She somehow managed to sneak out without Luke, who was asleep downstairs, noticing." He looks over at me and raises an eyebrow in a, *"Are you sure you want me to continue?"* fashion.

As if I have a choice. He'll be telling people this story when he's old and grey. "Get it over with," I say.

"So, I go and get her and put her in the passenger seat of my car. She's laughing and babbling, and then she goes dead silent, and I tell you I about shit myself. I thought she was choking on her own vomit or something, but when I looked over, she's just leaning towards me, staring at me. So, I ask her what's wrong, and she just keeps staring. I pull over to make sure everything's okay and she isn't having a seizure or something.

"I ask her what's wrong again and she's just staring at me with these googly eyes, and she says, 'So pretty. You're so pretty, Hazel.' I was so confused. I was like, *who the fuck is Hazel*? She starts laughing, and she says, 'Your eyes. Pretty hazel eyes. Stupid, pretty hazel eyes.' Then she reaches up, pokes me in the eye hard enough to blind me, and promptly passes out. I swear she repeated 'pretty hazel eyes' about a hundred times while she was asleep. Luke heard it, too, when the two of us put her on the sofa in the office to sleep it off, and we couldn't stop laughing.

"It's so rare for her to say something nice to me or anyone, so I've been calling her Hazel ever since to remind her of it." His eyes burn holes into the side of my face, and I glance over to give him a smile.

He looks so smug at the reminder that I got drunk and was unable to hide how pretty I thought his eyes were. It was so embarrassing waking up the next day without even the benefit of blacking out the night before. I remembered every awkward detail. Luke and Chase were merciless with it, staring at me with their own impression of the face I was making and whispering "pretty hazel eyes" over and over again. It was the worst.

"Alright, alright. I called your eyes pretty and identified their colour, big deal. You ever gonna let it go?" I ask jokingly.

"You personified my eyeballs. You said, 'You're so pretty, Hazel.' It was adorable. Of course, I'll never let it go."

Those were the easy days when I was too young for Chase to pay any attention to whatsoever. In fact, it wasn't until I was twenty-one that Chase stopped treating me like a kid and began treating me like a woman. Those were simpler times. Now I'm twenty-five, and he wants whatever it was he wants, and I'm just as confused now as I was then. Stupid, pretty hazel eyes.

Roman hasn't said anything, and I glance in the rear-view mirror in time to see his eyes bouncing between me and Chase, his face an unreadable slate. He looks at me, then raises his eyebrows and drops them just as quickly.

"Huh," he says, and then nothing. Roman stares out the

window and the rest of the car ride is silent except for me and Chase planning out how this retrieval is going to go down.

Eventually, after what is the longest yet shortest car ride in all of human history, we arrive on a filthy street, both sides lined with homeless people. Just a little further along, the bright lights of Purgatory's casinos shine down as if this was a holiday destination and not a last stop before death.

We stop not far from the bar where Chase is supposed to meet Ryan. The alley beside it is dark and deserted, except for the few homeless men we spotted as we drove past. My heart races with adrenaline; it's been so long since I've done this that it's difficult to hide my excitement. Is it wrong that I hope he puts up a fight? Probably. Do I care at all? No.

"Alright. Chase, you've got fifteen minutes until you're meant to meet with him, so go scope out the alley. If there's a way to get those people out of there, do it. If not…well, we tried." I say, turning in my seat to look at both of them.

Chase nods his head as he pulls open the door. "You got it, boss. Good to have my partner back." He winks, and then he's gone.

I watch his huge menacing frame as he walks towards the alleyway.

"You, slouch down. You're hard to miss, and I don't want Ryan bottling it if he sees you." I give Roman a hard stare when he raises an incredulous eyebrow, and finally, he slouches a little. He's so large he's still entirely visible, and I just hope the lack of street lights makes it difficult to see into the car.

"You really love this, don't you?" he asks again, just like in the office.

I keep my eyes out the window, watching the alley for any signs of Ryan. I don't have to think about his question; the answer, the truth, rolls off my tongue so quickly I couldn't have planned it if I'd tried. "Of course I do. There's nothing better than this. There's no one better *at* this."

I don't look at him, but I can almost hear him contemplating my answer.

"You look..." He drifts off, so I turn to look at him and see he's staring at me, studying me like a puzzle he can't figure out. Like I'm a mystery.

It's disturbing because I'm mostly an open book. At least I used to be. I didn't hide myself from anyone. The people who knew me knew me, and I don't have to worry about anyone else. Roman, though...Roman only knows most of me. I haven't changed myself to be around him. I've just lied to him. In a way, I guess that's meant changing myself. With him, I'm an orphan, a girl with vengeance in her blood but with very little emotion to show for it. I suppose, for him, I'm confusing. Maybe I'm not playing the part as well as I should.

Before I can say anything, movement catches my eye, and I look back out the window. A man walks into the alley, throwing cautionary glances over his shoulders. It's too dark to see for sure, but it has to be Ryan. He's about the same height and build.

"Go time. Stay in the car. Seriously – stay here, keep the doors locked, and don't be seen. Who knows if he has someone watching," I say, shoving open the door.

"*Keep the door locked,*" he mimics my voice. "I am not a fucking child, *Hazel.*"

The sound of the nickname coming out of his mouth pisses me off. "Shut up," I say, in a fine display of immaturity.

Sick burn, Lara. I slam the door behind me and make my way up the street. One hand immediately goes to the gun tucked into my waist, but I don't pull it out until I reach the alley's entrance. I hear Chase's mumbled voice and hesitate a second to make sure I'm approaching at the right moment.

"You know what you're doing with this, right?" Ryan asks.

"Yeah, I'll figure it out." Chase catches my eye over his shoulder. "That a friend of yours?" he asks then, nodding his head towards me, pretending like he doesn't know who I am.

I take a step towards the both of them, and Ryan looks me over. My skin prickles in disgust at his attention, and I'm suddenly glad I'm all covered up.

"Hey, baby. You looking to score?" He slides his hand back into his pocket, obviously in search of drugs to give me.

I leave my dignity behind as I give him my best sultry voice. "I think the real question is, are *you* looking to score?" I wink and sashay my hips a little, cringing internally as he looks me over again, a leer spreading across his face.

"Well, fine little thing like you and I just might be," he glances over his shoulder at Chase, who is looking at me, clearly trying not to laugh at my faux seduction. "You can go now," Ryan says to Chase, who smirks.

"Actually…"

I pull the gun from my waistband so quickly that by the time Ryan turns his head back to look at me, it's already pointed in between his eyes. They widen in fear and confusion before finally realisation – or at least assumption – sets in, and he thinks he's being robbed.

"You fuckers. Do you know who the fuck I am?" he asks.

I laugh, using my previous line. "I think the real question is, do you know who the fuck *I* am?"

Ryan makes to turn the other way, and he either doesn't have a weapon on him or he knows it would be extremely unwise for him to pull it out now. Especially when he turns and gets a good look at the gun Chase is holding in his face. He's surrounded, and he knows it.

"What the fuck is this?" he asks, looking back and forth between us.

"I'm so glad you asked. You want to tell him, Chase?" I ask.

"Nah, I'm good. You go ahead. You're better at the talking part."

"Aw, thank you, you're so sweet."

"Anytime, partner."

"WHAT THE FUCK IS GOING ON?" Ryan roars, clearly

fed up with our little display.

My smile widens at his clear annoyance. I do enjoy fucking with people. "My name is Lara. I'm a bounty hunter, and you, I'm afraid, are going to need to come with me."

His shoulders droop, and I see the recognition on his face. "Fuck," he whispers.

"Let's make this nice and easy. Come with us, and we won't have to shoot you—"

"I never made that promise." The deep, rumbling voice comes from behind us, and I sigh. Didn't I tell him to stay in the fucking car?

CHAPTER 13

I don't take my eyes off of Ryan, so I don't miss the way his eyes widen, and his already pale face loses all trace of colour. His eyes are full of fear as he watches Roman approach us, the sound of his footsteps echoing in the alley. I glance around and notice the alley is empty. Chase must have had no issue getting rid of whoever was in here.

"R-Roman. Look, man, I-I...I'm sorry. I didn't...She wasn't supposed to—" Ryan stutters, and finally, Roman is at my side, his own gun levelled at the man who is now trembling before us.

Chase remains where he is, but the anger is evident. He doesn't like surprises. Neither do I. I take my first look at Roman, and in the dimly lit alleyway, there's nothing but a blank look on his face. I had expected rage, but he seems entirely devoid of emotion.

"Shut the fuck up. On your knees. Now," Roman says.

I want to say something but find myself unable to speak. Chase catches my eye and gives me a questioning look that I return with a shake of my head. I need to stay on Roman's good side, and I want to see where this is going.

Ryan drops to his knees, apologies falling from his lips. The stench of desperation wafting from him is almost enough to make me feel bad for him. Almost.

Roman watches him, his face still blank apart from the predatory look in his eyes.

"Apologise," he says calmly, and the sound of his voice sends chills down my spine.

While his voice has had that effect on me before, it's never quite been to this extent. In this moment, it's very easy to see the Roman that people are terrified of. The name whispered in dark corners and used to scare children into doing what they're told. This is the Roman I'd heard of – the myth finally come to life.

He seems so far removed from the serious, almost business-like guy I'd been working with all week. The man who had slipped into easy, sarcastic banter and asked me personal questions. The one who seemed so sad about the death of his little sister. This wasn't that Roman – this was the other one, and I didn't know which one of them intrigued me more.

I didn't have time to think more about it. I lower my gun, obviously no longer needed, and Chase follows suit, walking around to stand beside me, both of us just an inch behind where Roman stands. He towers over the man who had a hand in the death of his little sister.

"I'm sorry. I said it. I didn't mean for her to die. How was I supposed to know Gideon would fuck her up so bad? It wasn't my fault."

"Don't fucking apologise to me, you piece of shit. Apologise to her. To Alisha." The anger in Roman's voice becomes more obvious with each word, and I find myself taking a step back, Chase's hand coming to rest on my lower back for reassurance. "Beg for fucking mercy."

Ryan looks confused for a moment, only staring up at Roman with pleading eyes. At first, I don't think he'll do it, I think he's dumb enough to ignore Roman's request, but then he begins. Words fall from his lips so quickly that I only catch a few of them. Alisha's name is said over and over, and tears fall from his eyes.

"I loved her, man. I loved her. I didn't want her to fucking die." He finally finishes, and I look to Roman, his blank face now morphed into one of disgust.

"Not enough," he says calmly and then pulls the trigger.

It happens so quickly I can't help the small gasp that slips from my mouth, the slight jump as the noise of the gunshot bounces off the walls. One minute, Ryan is there, kneeling on the ground in front of me, and the next, he's lying awkwardly on the filthy cement, a hole in his face where his eye used to be.

"Not enough," Roman repeats, as he uses the sleeve of his jacket to wipe blood from his face, his crisp white shirt covered with speckles of blood, stark against the white.

Roman stares at the body for only a moment, then as suddenly as he pulled the trigger, he shoves the gun into the back of his pants, turns on his heel, and walks back towards the car. He is unhurried, clearly not afraid of being caught, which isn't surprising. Chase and I glance at each other and then down at the body before turning and walking away.

∆∆∆

When we get back to the car, Roman is already sitting in the back. His jacket is off, shirt sleeves rolled up to his elbow. His right arm is up over his face covering his eyes. He says nothing as we climb into the car, and neither of us speaks. Honestly, I'm not even entirely sure what to say. My emotions are all over the place.

Part of me is angry at him for disobeying simple instructions, although I'm unsure what made me think I could give Roman Black an order in the first place. I'm a little bit shell-shocked, what with just having a man murdered in front of me, but also, I'm worried about my lack of feelings on the situation. Some piece of me knew that Roman didn't just want to catch Ryan for a chat. I just hadn't really admitted to myself that I was sending a man to his death.

But part of me is happy that Ryan is dead. Another piece of scum off the streets, right? My brain is flooded with these thoughts the entire ride back to Roman's warehouse, and I'm not entirely sure how I managed to drive home without crashing the car. I park at the usual spot, but nobody moves. Chase and I glance at each other again, speaking in that silent way that we often do.

"What the fuck happens now?" his look says.

"I have no idea," mine says back.

Eventually, after I clear my throat in an obvious attempt to catch his attention, Roman looks out the window. I watch him in the rear view as he grabs the door handle.

"Come with me," he says, then slams the door behind him.

I shrug at Chase, and then we both get out.

Roman's eyes land on Chase. "Not you," he says coldly, and Chase glares at him.

"I'm not leaving her alone after—"

"Get back in the car, lover boy. I'd never hurt her. Besides, she can fucking take care of herself."

Chase's look is downright hostile, and as he takes a step towards Roman and Roman takes a step towards him, I dive between them, my hand coming to rest on Chase's chest.

"I'm fine, Chase. It's fine. Go. I'll be home later."

Roman scoffs behind me and begins walking towards the door.

"You need your car," Chase tries, but Roman, clearly dying to get rid of him, shuts him down.

"I'm more than capable of driving her home, Jace. Do me a favour and fuck off."

"Shut up, Roman. Jesus Christ," I bark at him and then calmly tell Chase he can go. Ensuring I'll be fine. "I've still got my gun," I remind him, patting the back of my jeans where it rests.

He doesn't like it, and it shows, but he gets back into the car, slamming the door so hard I'm surprised it didn't come off his hinges.

I follow Roman, who's waiting patiently at the door. He pulls it open so I can walk in ahead of him, both of us silent until we get to his office.

"What the fuck was that?" I demand, trying not to watch as he unbuttons his blood-splattered shirt. I catch a glimpse of a defined chest before I avert my eyes, looking anywhere but at him.

"Which part, exactly?" he asks, and I look over to see his muscled back as he pulls open a wardrobe and slips out a t-shirt.

The fact that he has a wardrobe for clean clothes in his office is worrying, but I ignore it, filing it away for later pondering. His back is covered in tattoos, and as much as I would like to see what they are, I look away again. *Must not ogle the murderer's back.* I repeat the words to myself like a mantra.

"I don't even...Jesus. Where do I begin? All of it?" I say, relieved when, finally, the shirt is on, and I can look at him again.

He looks tired, but the anger from before is gone. Clearly, the ride home was enough time for him to go from Roman the Myth to Roman the Man. He rubs a hand down his face after falling into his desk chair, legs spread in his favourite position.

"I apologise for putting you in that situation. I had intended to bring him back here, ask him some questions, but..."

"Well, you didn't, and now Chase and I are accomplices to an alleyway murder, so, you know, thanks for that!" I spit and find that I'm actually angrier than I thought I was. "Jesus. I told you to wait in the car!"

"I don't take orders from you, sweetheart," he says, and

I almost, *almost*, shoot him myself. Fucking *sweetheart*? Who does he think he is?

"Out there, doing *my* job, you fucking do. If you want me to risk my life catching these men for *you*, then do what the fuck I say so that next time, I'm not standing next to you when you blow someone's fucking brains out!"

"And if you want *me* to risk my life taking Gideon down for *you*, then you'll learn to understand that I take orders from no one." He snaps back, standing from his chair and glaring at me from behind his desk.

"Oh, give me a break. You want him gone as much as I do, if not more. You get more out of it than me, anyway. You'll get the man who is partially responsible for the death of your sister, and you get to take over his fucking turf too."

Technically, he won't because Gideon's planning to kill him, but I ignore the little pain in my stomach at the thought. Another thing I can add to the ever-growing list of shit I need to ruminate on at a later date.

"Ryan deserved to fucking die, and now he's dead. That's it. Move on," he says simply, ignoring everything else I've said.

"Move…I don't care that he's fucking dead!" I say and am a little bit shocked at how true that is. "I care that you shot him in front of me and forced me to leave his body in an alley. Have you forgotten that it's my job to catch the people who do shit like that? God! Give a girl a warning next time you want her to be complicit in your crimes!" My chest is heaving after my rant. He stares at me, looking me over with that puzzled expression.

"Fine. Next time I intend to kill someone in your presence, I will alert you beforehand."

"That's not…" I shake my head. This is irrelevant in the grand scheme of things. "Whatever. Fine."

I take a deep breath, only realising that, in all my ranting, I'd walked myself over to the front of his desk. I take another step towards the corner and raise my thigh so that I'm partially sitting on top of it.

"And down there? What the fuck was that with Chase?"

"Chase," he says, disgust in his voice.

"*Jace?*" I mock, and he smirks, clearly proud of himself for his immense maturity.

"Not a fan," he says as if that explains the whole thing.

"Of what?"

Our eyes connect, and I feel that current between us again. My tongue darts out to wet my dry lips, and his eyes follow the motion as his thumbnail runs over that bottom lip in a now familiar gesture, my own eyes following his motion. Roman drops his hand and takes a small step forward, and for a second, I feel my own body lean forward of its own volition.

Abort. Abort. Abort.

I clear my throat and jump off the edge of the desk, ignoring his fucking smirk as I do.

"Of him," he says. "Of him and you. Not a fan."

"What?"

"Nothing."

Again, what? "So that little display of toxic masculinity

was all for...?"

"I felt like pissing him off. He's easy to rile up."

True, but...Christ. What is happening? What is this entire situation? I am far too drained to deal with this. The adrenaline from before is well and truly gone, and my emotions are clearly wreaking havoc on my body. If my staring at Roman's lips and leaning towards his body like a desperate idiot are anything to go by, I really need to figure my shit out.

"Alright. Okay. Whatever. Why did you need me to come back here?" I ask, and he frowns. His mouth opens and closes before he finally seems to remember.

"Actually, my intention was to apologise. For shooting Ryan in front of you."

"Are you serious?" I ask. Why did he argue with me if he had wanted to apologise anyway?

"Yes."

"Well, don't let me stop you."

Roman says nothing. His phone rings, but he lets it continue. Instead of answering, he looks at me – why is he always looking at me?

He walks towards me, his strides long, his steps sure. I tilt my head to look up at him when he's close enough to touch, and my heart races at the proximity. I curse myself; I really need to get a handle on that. His hand comes up, and heat pools low in my stomach at the simple feel of his fingers on my skin.

The whisper of them against my face and then my ear as he pushes an errant strand of hair behind it. His hand rests there for a moment until he slowly trails his fingers down the side of my neck. My pulse jumps as I intake a sharp breath, and I feel the touch all the way down my body.

"I'm sorry," he says, a slight frown marring his face.

His eyebrows are pulled together as his amber eyes bounce between mine. The moment is electric, and just as I'm beginning to wonder how I went from wanting to shoot him to wanting to rip his clothes off and fuck him, his phone rings again, a different sound this time. He curses under his breath and takes the call.

"Speak," he says, casting a slight glance my way, and I fight my smile as he raises an eyebrow. "I'll see you at the dock in an hour. Wait for me." He looks at me again, and the blank face has returned, the moment gone. The remaining sexual tension in the room dissipates, and with a single sentence, I'm back to wanting to shoot him again.

"Let's get you back to your castle, *Princess*."

The ride home is mostly silent, but there's a question that's been bothering me.

"If you hated him so much, if you know what he'd done...why hadn't you just gone after him yourself? I know you could have if you wanted to."

Roman doesn't look at me, just continues his focus on the road.

"I could have. I've been thinking about what I'd do to him for so long," he pauses, looks at me quickly before looking away. "I could have found him. But then it would have been over. Now it is. It's done."

His hands tighten on the steering wheel, eyebrows pulled tight. He says nothing else, but somehow I understand anyway. He was putting it off because once it was over he had no choice but to let it go, to let his sister go. He killed him, and now all his anger... all his rage... he has to find something else to do with it.

I let the silence continue the rest of the drive, he doesn't look like he feels like talking anymore anyway.

I get out of his car at the gate to my apartment, walking inside without a goodbye or a second glance. When I get into my apartment and look out the window, his car is already gone. Before I can talk myself out of it, I type out a text to my father's phone, knowing Gideon will be the one to see it.

Something happening at the dock tonight. He's on his way there now.

A message comes back almost instantly.

Thank you, little hunter. What a clever little spy you are.

I glare at my phone and fling it onto my kitchen table, reminding myself that I'm doing this for my dad. Reminding myself that I owe Roman nothing.

CHAPTER 14

I spend the weekend strategizing with everybody. We meet and discuss and my life has turned into some sort of alternate universe. I go home and I clean and I cook, I read and I watch tv. I check in on Carey and Luke, who are still watching the house my father is in. The two of them are starting to ignore my texts because I contact them every hour to see if they've spotted my dad yet. We haven't seen him once, which means he's either not even allowed outside for some fresh air, or we've been watching the wrong house. I don't know which is worse.

I ignore messages from Andi and Sophie, shoving the friend guilt aside as I do so. It's been a whirlwind few weeks, and this feels like the first time I'm actually able to take some time to myself. I think up a million ways to save my dad, to break in and get him out, and then I throw every single idea into the metaphorical trash because none of them would work without someone I love being hurt or worse. That basically means I'm in a mood the whole weekend.

I lie to myself and say it has nothing to do with the way I felt with Roman on Friday after what happened. I lie to myself in an attempt to avoid admitting that giving Gideon that information made me feel like a horrible person. I lie and I lie and continue to lie because that's what I have become recently. A professional liar. Can't wait to add that to my resume when this is all over. I'd thought it would be easy, but the more my mood worsens over the weekend, the harder I have to fight to shove what I'm feeling deep down inside of me. This was never meant to be my life, my job. Yet I've somehow found myself right in the middle of it all.

My sorrows brighten after a phone call with my dad, who, according to him, is still being treated just fine. I've tried to ask if he knows where he is, but he either doesn't, or he does and just can't tell me because they're listening. He puts on a happy voice, but he's tired. I can hear the falseness in how he speaks. It breaks my heart listening to him beg me to stop whatever it is I'm doing.

Part of me wanted to tell him everything's fine, that he has nothing to worry about, that I'm going to do everything in my power to get him out of there. The other part of me, though, the part that has always had her father there to help her if she needed him, wanted to tell him she hates the situation she's in and the man she's been forced to spend time with.

It's crushing to not be able to tell him things, to not get his input on my plan, but there's no way I can risk telling him anything, not with Gideon probably lurking over his shoulder. I miss him. My dad, obviously, not Gideon. I'm so used to having him there, so used to looking out my window and seeing the light on in his apartment above the office.

△△△

After the weekend, when I'm no more rested than before and not at all rejuvenated, I head back to Roman's office, where he avoids me like the plague for three whole days. I barely see him, and when I do, he doesn't speak to me- just watches me. He hasn't been showing up to his office as often, and so I have found myself there alone, more often than not, giving me opportunities to look through his stuff as discreetly as I can. I snap pictures of random paperwork, numbers he's written down, and names of people who work for him, but there's nothing interesting. He's far too smart to leave anything important around, he doesn't trust me and I know it.

When I'm not doing that, I'm working from my own office, using Eric and Andi to help. Finding Roman's next *victim* is proving to be a lot more difficult, and with Roman only speaking to me in monosyllables, it's like pulling teeth trying to get more information from him. Nobody has seen victim number two in weeks, and even Eric hasn't been able to find a trace of him. So, either he's extremely off-grid, or he's already a corpse. Either way, Roman isn't happy with how I'm progressing. His mood is a clear indicator of that.

He's apparently having issues with the business. Issues that I've caused – or at least Gideon has. Over the last few days, and during the few snippets of conversation I've been able to gather, I've learned that the information I gave to Gideon was useful. He managed to hijack a huge delivery containing more than just the weapons and drugs I had assumed. There were also regular things being brought in for Roman's legitimate businesses.

Roman owns multiple restaurants, bars, and even part of a shopping mall that's located in Golden City. So the delivery containing furniture, food, alcohol, and all sorts of stuff was stolen by Gideon. None of this I would have known without the snooping I've been able to do in his absence, which only partially eased my guilty conscience.

Going through his desk while he was gone was the most nerve-wracking thing I'd ever done. I kept waiting for him to walk in and bust me, but he was so preoccupied and very clearly stressed that he paid me no attention when he *was* in his office, never mind when he wasn't. It was a nice reprieve from looking at him and listening to him and speaking to him.

When Roman wasn't around, it was so much easier to pretend he wasn't a real person. It was easy to see him as the villain, and when he was just a villain, I could hate him without any additional feelings. When I wasn't listening to him speak or watching him do mundane things, I could escape the guilt and the sinking feeling that Roman Black is not the devil he's been made out to be.

I'm surprised to find Roman sitting behind his desk when I arrive one morning. He doesn't look up as I walk in, just continues staring down at whatever he has in front of him. I sneak glances at him as I sit down at my desk beside his, but he doesn't pay me any attention. I'm not really sure why I'm here at all, why him making this space for me was necessary. There's nothing I can do here that I can't do back in my own office. It seems the only person who benefits from being here is me, secretly, but Roman doesn't know that.

"Good morning," he announces abruptly after a few minutes of awkward silence.

I let a dramatic gasp fall from my lips, raising a hand to my chest in mock shock. "He speaks."

His eyes roll so hard I'm surprised they don't pop out of his head. "I've always spoken." He turns his chair to face me the same way I've done, and I marvel at the frown on his face. If I slapped him right now, he'd probably get stuck that way.

"Walked out of the womb with a full vocabulary, did you?" I ask, and to my shock, he barks out a laugh, the sound so foreign and wonderful I almost fall out of my chair.

"That is quite a disturbing image," he finally says after he finishes laughing. Unwanted pride warms my belly at the fact that I actually made him laugh. This... God. Is it awful that I kind of missed this while he was M.I.A?

"You've been a grump the last few days," I tease.

"I'm a grown man. I was not *grumpy*."

"You absolutely were grumpy." His glare brings a smile to my face, and I quickly wipe it away. Bad smile.

"You are the most infuriating woman I have ever met." He does the famous eye roll again, and I don't manage to rid myself of the smile this time.

"Well, it's my pleasure." I pause for dramatic effect, but I already know what I want to ask. "Speaking of..."

"Your pleasure?" he questions with a smirk and a lift of one of those dark eyebrows.

I flush and scoff. I haven't noticed him with anyone important, anyone who might actually mean something to him. I need to know if there's anyone I can give to Gideon to use as leverage. I don't want to, but I know I need to keep the ball rolling.

"No, asshole. Of women. Of *your* pleasure…" I leave the implied question hanging in the air. I'm only asking for snooping reasons, of course. Yes, I've been curious about what or *who* he does in his spare time, but the only reason I'm asking is so I can slip the information on to Gideon. Obviously.

The whole time I've been working with him, which, granted, has only been a few weeks, I haven't seen or heard him mention a woman. A man like him, a man who looks like him, surely has…appetites.

He leans forward in his chair, resting both elbows on his spread knees. It's such a boyish position I can't help but gawk.

"Oh. She's interested in my pleasure." His smirk is full of delight, eyes dancing with obvious mischief. It's such a strange side to him, one I hadn't expected he even had.

"No," I begin, already scolding myself for having even brought it up, "I'm just wondering if there's a special lady in your life. Or man, if that's more your type."

He laughs. "Do I seem like the type who has time for women? Or men, for that matter?"

My eyebrows raise. Is he into men too?

"Which is it then? Or is it both? Either is fine, obviously. I'm just curious…" I realise now how intrusive my line of questioning is and decide to backtrack in case I have made him uncomfortable. If I press too hard, he might get suspicious. "Never mind. Sorry."

He says nothing for a moment, enjoying leaving

me in my self-made awkwardness. "It's women," he says finally, smirking. "*Generally*. But to answer your question, no. There's no one." He doesn't need to tack on the *right now* at the end of his sentence. I can hear it. I say nothing, just nod and spin slowly back to face my desk.

"Why? Are you offering, sweetheart?"

Heat rushes to inappropriate places at the thought, and I mentally chastise my vagina for being such a whore as I laugh out loud. "Absolutely not. I'd much rather die."

"Very defensive, aren't you?"

I turn to face him again and see that he's enjoying this. Watching me squirm. It's my own fault, I suppose, for bringing up this line of questioning.

"Not if you were the last man on the Island," I say as sweetly as possible, looking him dead in the eye so he knows he's not winning this round.

My words are at complete odds with what I'm feeling, and I must really need an orgasm or twelve because my body is ridiculously in tune with the way he sits and how he smells. I swallow as I catch a glimpse of the thick veins on the back of his hands.

Fuck me.

"Hmm. You couldn't handle me anyway."

I rear my head back in shock, a surprised laugh falling from my lips. "Are you trying to goad me into sleeping with you? Because there's got to be laws against that."

"Believe me, love, if I wanted to sleep with you, I wouldn't have to goad you into it. If I wanted to sleep with you, all I'd have to do is make you aware that I want to."

He scoots forward in his chair. In a single graceful move, he uses one long leg to pull himself closer to me. If I had tried it, I would have made it an inch, but as it is, his legs are so long, he manages to stop his chair right in front of me.

"If I wanted to fuck you,"—his face is terribly close to mine, and as much as I want to run out the door, I remain frozen where I am, eyes fixed on his mouth as the words tumble from it—"you would beg for it.

"I've never begged a day in my life," I say, but the words are breathy. His lips are so close I would just have to lean forward to put my own on them.

"There's a first time for everything," he replies.

"It's highly unlikely."

"I notice you didn't say impossible."

"Well, you would, wouldn't you?"

"So, it's not then?" he asks.

The air is filled with static tension, and my skin is on fire. There's a delicious ache in my stomach and below, and I've mostly been staring at his lips instead of paying attention to our conversation.

"What?" I say weakly, my voice barely a whisper.

"It's not impossible to make you beg?" he asks.

Finally, my libido shuts up, my brain takes over, and I realise I can't let this end with him being in control and me being horny. I lower my head, looking up at him through my long black eyelashes.

"If anyone was going to beg in any scenario…" I reach my hand out and lay my palm flat over his knee, pushing upwards with slight pressure as the muscle in his thigh twitches. His lips part and he sucks in a breath that's almost inaudible, but I don't miss it. "…it would definitely be you."

My hand is dangerously close to his dick, and I hadn't actually intended on going this far, but now that I'm almost there, I have no plan for how to stop without it looking like I've chickened out.

My fingers just brush the metal of his zipper when suddenly his hand snatches my wrist. He holds it in place as his dark eyes bore into mine with hunger. It's enough to send a zap right through my body. I'm soaking, and I know it. He knows it.

He glances down at my lap, my legs covered by the tight black denim jeans I'm wearing. My eyes follow suit, falling to his own lap where a very distinct, very large bulge is evident. Both our eyes flick up again. There's a silent conversation going on between us, although I have absolutely no idea if we're understanding each other correctly.

This cannot happen, seems to be the main message. It's the one I'm trying to convey anyway. I want to move away, but his hand is still hot, still wrapped around my wrist, my fingers dangling above his cock. They itch to touch him, but I cannot. Will not. Absolutely should not.

"Well played, Miss Miller."

"Yeah. You too."

He slowly lifts his fingers from my wrist and leans back. I take the opportunity to do the same. My wrist is cold where his heat had once been, and I'm extremely uncomfortable with ignored desire.

Once we're both a safe distance away, he clears his throat. I turn back to my computer; he does the same. We may not be eye-fucking each other anymore, but the air stills crackles with tension. We can both feel it. My eyes drift to him multiple times over the next while, and I notice how stiffly he sits. Rigid and uncomfortable looking. He's been staring at the same thing on his screen, and I've watched him scroll back up to re-read certain passages multiple times.

It seems he is just as affected as I am. This pleases me – on a purely physical level. On another level, though, a level far less loud and annoying, a voice is screaming at me to stop flirting with the man I'm aiding with murder.

Nothing good can come of this.

An hour goes by, and I can't take it anymore. The arousal has not gone away, nor has it abated at all. Roman seems just as frustrated as I am. On more than one occasion, our eyes locked, and we ended up in a silent stare-down that only seemed to make the heat in the room rise.

"I have to go," I say, standing up and grabbing my bag from the floor.

Roman watches me with heat in his eyes, but I see the relief there. He needs to be away from me as much as I need to be away from him right now.

"Where?" he asks. I have no idea why. I'm putting us both out of our horny misery. A thank you would be nice.

"I've got plans...with...home. Just home." My brain is dead.

"So, it's like that," he says.

I have no idea what he means by that, so I choose to ignore him. After wrestling my leather jacket onto my shoulders, unaware that I had even taken it off, I can feel his eyes on me the whole way to the exit.

"Lara," he calls just as I get to the door, eager to make my escape.

"Yeah?"

"You know, even if you fuck *him*, you'll be *thinking* of *me*."

His voice is deeper, lower, and I almost feel it caressing my skin. I frown at him, confused as to who in the world he thinks I would possibly be fucking, and then I realise.

Chase.

He still thinks Chase and I have something going on. Christ.

"I am not fucking *anybody*," I say and mean it. Wholeheartedly. Including him. Especially him.

"Hmm. Then you'll definitely be thinking of me." His gaze drifts down the length of my arm, all the way down to my hand that's still gripping the door knob. I follow his gaze and catch his meaning immediately.

"In your dreams," I say.

His eyes, still latched onto my hand, flare with heat before he says, "Oh, absolutely."

I stomp out the door and down the stairs before I spontaneously combust.

What have I gotten myself into?

CHAPTER 15

My plan to go home and further acquaint myself with my good friend B.O.B. gets derailed when I spot Andi and Soph walking through the door of the office. I stop as I watch them, let my eyes glance longingly towards my apartment, then with a sigh, I force myself to walk towards the office. It's been a while since I've seen my friends.

"What's up, bitches?" I say as I walk in the door, then cringe at myself. I've never used that phrase before in my life, and I am way too old to start now.

"Hello, you filthy whore," Sophie says. Andi and I glance at each other with wide round eyes.

"Jeez. What is this a teen movie? Say hello like normal humans," Andi says, and we all laugh. It feels nice. Normal. With everything going on, it feels nice to just laugh.

"You guys working?" I ask, and they glance at each other.

"Nope," they respond in unison.

Andi adds, "Well, I mean you're kind of my boss, soooo..."

"Great, then we're drinking."

"Who's drinking?" Carey asks as he exits the kitchen,

intrigue in his eyes and a steaming cup of coffee in his hand. "And what are you doing here? I thought you were with Roman."

I feel my face start to flush and look anywhere but at my friends. "Uh... decided to take some time off. Where is everyone?"

"Chase and Luke are out catching a perp. Chase looked like he needed some male bonding time. Thought I'd leave them to it. Feelings make me scratchy."

Ah, reason number thirty-five that I love Carey. He's just like me.

"Eric?" I ask.

"Space," everyone says at once.

"Great. Carey, you're in charge. We're having a girls' night."

"Oh...but...can I—"

"Fuck yeah!" Andi shouts over him, and the three of us exit, leaving Carey looking cute and confused with his coffee.

We walk down the street to one of the only bars in Second that's decent. It's only three-thirty, so the place is empty as we grab a booth and order a round of drinks.

"So..." Sophie starts almost immediately, "what's the reason for this spontaneous girls' night?"

I glance around the room for anything suspicious, an occupational hazard, and shrug. "Can't a girl want to hang out with her friends?"

"A girl definitely can. You, however, don't make quality

time unless there's a reason."

Ouch. That stings a little. It's true, though. I've never been much of a friend. Andi and Soph are practically my first friends, real friends. "I'm sorry," I tell them. "I'll do better."

"Shut up. We love you, prickles and all," Sophie tells me, and I smile genuinely at her.

"But seriously, though...spill. What's got you all jittery and worked up and in need of a female-only alcohol binge?" Andi looks at me with suspicious eyes, and instantly heat crawls up my face. "I...uh..."

Sophie squeals. "Oh my God!"

"You didn't!"

"What?" I ask, feigning innocence. How I thought I'd be able to hide anything from them is beyond me. It's like they've got a sixth sense.

"You fucked Raunchy Roman!" Andi gasps dramatically, and Sophie's eyes go as wide as saucers. Embarrassment floods me as the waitress places our drinks on the table, pretending she didn't overhear scandalous information about my sex life.

I wait until she's gone before I respond. "I did not. And what did you just call him? Also, keep your goddamn voice down!" I have a little look around to see if anyone else might be eavesdropping. God forbid Gideon has someone watching me, and he finds out I'm sleeping with the enemy.

What? No. *I am not sleeping with the enemy.*

"Well, you did something, you little slut. Now spill."

I sigh and take the largest sip of my vodka and cranberry I can manage. It goes down a treat, so I take another, just to avoid talking. When I say nothing, they both glare at me until I finally crack.

"Alright. I didn't sleep with him. I haven't actually done anything with him. But there's been some flirting. And maybe some…little, very small, accidental leg-touching and wrist-grabbing and eye-fucking. Jesus Christ, the eye fucking…I have never been…"

Once I'm started, it's difficult to stop. It all comes pouring out of me in the most horrific case of word vomit I've ever experienced. I talk so much that we have to order a second round of drinks. Andi and Soph listen contentedly, inputting squeals of delight at the naughty parts and sombre head nods when I explain my situation. How confused I am that I could be feeling anything for this guy when my father's life is on the line.

Chase comes up, and the girls look at me like I kicked a puppy when I tell them I've turned him down numerous times. Every time I mention his name Sophie puts a hand to her heart like he's a homeless child who's never been given a gift at Christmas.

"Why would you not want something with Chase?" Andi asks when we're well into our third drink. I'm starting to feel so much better now that I'm getting everything off my chest. "Especially if you were so into him when you were younger?"

I sigh heavily. I've been asking myself that question for weeks, and I feel like I'm nowhere close to being able to answer it. "I don't know. It's like…when I was younger,

I wasn't worried if it would ruin our friendship. I just wanted him. The more he pushed me away because of my age, the more I realised what a great guy he was. Thus, the more I wanted him. But…then I got older, and I realised how much I valued him as my friend…my partner."

Every word I say is true. Chase is my best friend. I couldn't do this without him, don't want to. "If it ended badly, everything would be ruined. I'd lose my boyfriend and my best friend and the best partner I'll ever have. I can't risk it."

"Sweetie…who said it would end badly?" Sophie asks softly, her expression mirroring Andi's look of sympathy.

"Nobody. I just…I said *if*. My mom and dad were best friends before they got together. My dad was ready for the rest of his life with her. When she bailed after she had me…he lost everything. I can't do that to Chase."

I never talk about my mother, and it shows. She isn't worth mentioning; she left my father after I was born, and we haven't seen her since. My dad searched the whole island for her, but she vanished. All she left was a note that said, *"This is not the life I want."* No apology. Nothing. Over the years, I've watched my father try to recover from it. I don't think he really has. I don't know if he ever will.

"You're not your mom, Lara. Not even close." They try to console me, but the alcohol has me, and it's taking no prisoners.

"I know. But I could be. I refuse to let that happen, so no. I can't go there with Chase. Even if I wanted to." The realisation is stark, and it breaks my heart and lifts a weight off my shoulders all at once.

"Alright, this is depressing. So, you won't be with Chase because you're scared you'll break his heart – and yours – by fucking it up. And you can't fuck Roman because you're conspiring to have him killed, and that would be bad karma. Do I have everything?" Sophie asks.

She glances at Andi, who nods before adding, "Don't forget the *raging* mommy issues." I choke on my drink and shoot her a withering glare.

"Yes. The mommy issues," Sophie says and then pauses to think for a minute before an imaginary lightbulb goes off over her head. "I have the perfect way to fix all of your problems."

"You do? Thank God. What?" I ask, hopeful that my friend is about to change my life. Maybe being a good friend has some perks.

A slow, devious smile takes over her face as she looks from me to Andi and then stands abruptly. "Tequila."

"You are brilliant," I say.

ΔΔΔ

Hours later, I am officially drunk. Plastered. Absolutely shit-faced. I lean my back against the oddly sticky wall outside the women's bathroom as I glare at my phone, which doesn't seem to want to cooperate. Every time I try to tap the screen to get into my contacts, the little icon moves all by itself, and I press the wrong thing.

Tricky little bastard.

"Aha!" I say to absolutely no one as I finally pull up Roman's number. My phone might think calling him is a terrible idea, but my tequila-soaked brain thinks it's the best idea I've ever had.

The phone rings twice as I begin to tip to the side before righting myself.

"Lara?" Roman answers, his voice tense and deep.

"Whoa. Almost fell just then," I say, and then I laugh because falling is funny.

"Are you drunk?"

"As a monk. Or…skunk. I don't think monks are allowed to drink. Actually, I'm not even sure monks exist anymore." A small burp escapes, and I slap a hand over my mouth.

"Did you just—"

"No. I'm just calling to inform you that I will be unable to come in your office tomorrow."

"Why? You don't think I could get the job done?" he says, and it takes me a moment to understand.

"Ha. You think you're funny. You are not. I will not make it into the office tomorrow – I foresee myself being ill. Food poisoning, I think." The room spins as I slide down the wall. I grimace as my ass hits the floor. *I hope I don't catch something.*

"Alcohol poisoning would probably be more accurate," Roman says dryly. "Where are you?"

"I am in a bar. In the bathroom. Sophie said she knew

how to fix all my problems, and then she plied me with tequila. You know, I think she might be a genius. I don't recall a single problem right now."

"Try that again tomorrow when your hangover is added to the list. I'll come get you."

"*God no!*" I practically shout. Uncaring if I sound like a bitch. In my state, who knows what I might do to him.

"Alright, then. Fuck me for offering."

I snort. "That was funny."

"You're so wasted. And rude." I don't miss the humour in his voice, even as he feigns annoyance. "I thought you were booty-calling me."

"Ha! As if," I say, although the thought had crossed my mind as I was arguing with my phone for his number.

"You're having dinner with me tomorrow," he says after a long silence.

"I'm sorry. I think you just had a stroke. What?"

He laughs outright this time, and my belly feels all warm at the sound. Or it could be the alcohol.

"Dinner. With me. A *date*."

"Are you malfunctioning right now?" I ask, sure that I must be hallucinating. He's not asking me on a date. We may share a sizzling mutual attraction, but we can't stand each other besides that.

"Just say okay, Lara. Make my life easier. I don't have the time to convince you."

It's my turn to malfunction because before I can stop myself, word vomit rears its ugly head, and I'm whispering a drawn-out *okay* into the phone.

"You're much less stubborn when you're three sheets to the wind," he says, and I frown. His words don't make sense in my head.

"I'm not sure what that means, and I don't have the mental capabilities to figure it out at the moment."

He chuckles again, and I laugh before falling to the side and having to stop myself with my bare hand on the floor. "Ugh, gross," I say, and he laughs again.

"What'd you do?"

"I touched the bathroom floor with my bare hand, and now I'm going to have to get a tetanus shot. Our first date will be in the hospital while my hand is falling off." I push myself up as he bursts into laughter, and then the door is swinging open, and Andi and Sophie stand there.

"Uh oh. I'm in big trouble."

"Who are you talking to?" Sophie asks, and somehow, she seems far less inebriated than I am.

"Roman," I whisper, "my friends just caught me drunk dialling you, and now they're going to ground me." I look sheepishly at my friends as Roman repeats my previous *'uh oh'* into my ear.

"Roman?" Sophie screeches, and then she's stomping towards me and ripping the phone out of my hand.

"Hey!" I shout as she shoves my phone into her back pocket.

"Friends don't let friends drunk-dial sexy murderers," she says and then glares at me until I smile and throw my hands around her neck. "They also don't sneak off to the bathroom while their friends are distracted." She glares at me playfully.

"I love you, you beautiful princess," I mumble into her hair.

"Tell me again tomorrow," she laughs, and then the world goes entirely blank.

CHAPTER 16

The sun burns my retinas the moment I open my eyes. I immediately shut them and am assaulted by the pounding in my head. I groan and roll over, only to see the face of Andi right up in mine. Scrambling backwards as fast as I can, I land on the floor with a thud. The quick movements have my stomach rolling, and I groan as I race to the bathroom and proceed to throw up the entire contents of my stomach.

Who let me drink so much? Why in the world did I think it was a good idea? Flashes of laughing and dancing float around in my head as I puke my guts up. I want to curl up in a ball in the fetal position. Can you die from a hangover?

"Oh God, who hit me with a truck?" Andi groans from my bed. Her voice sounds like sandpaper, if that's at all possible, and I regret the laugh that trickles out of my mouth instantly as it sends actual bullets through my brain.

"Some asshole called Jose," is all I can manage.

"Where the hell is Soph?"

I lift my head off the toilet bowl, struggling to remember even getting home, never mind the whereabouts of the woman who put me in this position.

Tequila to fix all my problems. Worst idea I've ever

heard.

After a few more moments of listening to Andi moan and groan while I remained kneeling on the floor worshipping the porcelain gods, the front door opens, and my nose is greeted by the heavenly scent of grease.

"Ladies!" Sophie screams, and I cringe as the sound batters my head. "I brought nourishment in the form of greasy food and men. Although, the men were not part of my plan. They kind of followed me here like stray dogs."

Two male voices meet my ears as I, *very slowly*, lift myself from the floor. I attack my teeth with my toothbrush and ridiculous amounts of toothpaste and am surprised to realise I feel marginally better.

"You look like shit."

I turn and find Chase standing in the doorway of my bedroom, broad arms folded over his even broader chest. He looks gorgeous, as he always does, and it pisses me off.

"Shouldn't you be in the office?" I ask.

He raises an eyebrow as he looks me up and down. "Shouldn't *you*?"

"*Touché*," I think, but I don't have the energy to say the words out loud, so I settle for a huff as I stomp past him and follow my nose to the bags of food taking over my kitchen table.

"Hello, sunshine." Sophie smiles, looking perfectly put together, bouncing around like she has no hangover and at least eight hours of sleep. I glare at her. How does she look so good? Why does she look so good? How is she so pretty, her skin so flawless?

"Why are you so chipper? Why aren't you dying inside like Andi and me?" The former stumbles out of my room like a zombie.

I can smell the alcohol leaking through her pores, or maybe mine, and almost have to run to the bathroom to throw up again. Andi walks like every step hurts, and I wouldn't be surprised if it did, but she pulls up short when she notices Eric standing in my kitchen, searching my cupboards. She straightens and tries her best to fix her hair.

"There's no fixing that, babe," I say, and she flushes bright red when I send a pointed glance at Eric.

"Why is Sophie floating around your apartment like a butterfly?" she asks me. And then, to Sophie, "Why are you floating around her apartment like a butterfly?"

Soph laughs as she loads mountains of fried food onto plates, causing Andi and me to float towards the table and plop ourselves into seats. "Because, my silly little friends, I am a doctor. I have to work today. I switched to water halfway through the night and ate my weight in food when we got home."

"I hate you," Andi says, but my mouth is too full of bacon to say a word.

I'm just finished eating my breakfast when my life goes to shit.

"You checked your phone yet?" Sophie asks casually. So casually, in fact, that it is not casual at all. Warning lights begin going off in my head as the mother of all flashbacks hits me like a ton of bricks.

"Oh. Oh, no." I run out of the room, hangover completely forgotten, and find my phone plugged in on my nightstand. God bless Sophie. I have three messages, and two missed calls.

All from Roman.

"Kill me now."

The missed calls are both from last night, after the call I had placed to him. The messages came in at three a.m.

At least let me know you got home safe.

I'm looking forward to our date tomorrow. I'll pick you up at seven.

If you don't let me know if you're okay, I'm going to rip this Island apart to find you.

The last message is one Sophie sent from my phone. It's a selfie. Sophie looking wonderfully sober and cheerful while Andi and I are passed out in bed. I'm honestly not sure whether to kiss Sophie for saving my ass and ensuring he didn't show up or kill her for sending him a picture of me with my face smashed into a pillow and my mouth wide open.

There's no way he's actually going to show up, right? He won't actually want to take me out. Maybe he was drunk too. Maybe he was…was…maybe…fuck. There's no way Roman Black says anything he doesn't mean. He certainly wouldn't send a follow-up message. He's going to show up here. He's going to pick me up.

I'm going on a date with Roman Black.

△△△

At six forty-five, I feel like I'm going to puke again. My hangover is gone, thankfully, but my nerves about tonight have increased. This might even be a worse idea than the tequila last night. I check my reflection in the mirror one last time. I didn't overdo it. Unless he plans to take me somewhere in Golden, which I hope he doesn't, there's nowhere in Second that's too fancy. I settle for tight leather trousers and a backless halter, then put my hair up in a high ponytail and make up for it with massive silver hoops. Heels are not my friend, so my feet are comfortable in chunky black boots.

Telling myself I'm only making an effort to get closer to him for the sake of getting information for Gideon, I slip my phone and money into my bag and head into the living room. The knock on the door sends my heart rate into the sky. When I pull it open, he's there.

His eyes take me in in one fell swoop, and my blood heats at the desire in his eyes.

"Still adequate?" I ask, trying to ease the sudden tension.

"Perfectly."

He looks pretty good himself. His light blue shirt is fitted across his chest, the barest hint of more tattoos visible underneath it. The blue looks amazing against his skin, and coupled with the light grey colour of his slacks, I have to swallow the liquid that pools in my mouth.

"I didn't think you'd answer the door," he says, trying to peer over my shoulder and into my apartment as I stand there staring at him.

"I didn't think you'd show up," I say, but that's a lie. I knew he'd show up.

He smirks, takes a step back, and sweeps his arm out, motioning for me to leave my apartment. I do, locking the door behind me while simultaneously begging my heart to stop hammering inside my chest. The walk to the car is silent but not uncomfortable, and when he opens the door for me, taking my hand to help me slip inside, I can't help the smile.

"And they say chivalry is dead," I say before he closes my door.

Roman leans down to look me in the eye. "I'm not a gentleman, Lara. I'm just taking every opportunity to touch you." He closes the door on that note, leaving me gaping like a fish. I'm not entirely sure I'm going to make it out of this night without combusting into flames.

"Where are we going?" I say after we've been driving in silence for ten minutes.

Roman doesn't look at me. His eyes remain on the road, one hand resting on the bottom of the steering wheel, the other on the back of my chair.

"My restaurant. Well, one of them. I think you'll like it." When he flashes me a toothy smile, I consider jumping out of the moving vehicle. This cannot be good for my health.

"I'm sure I'll like it," I say, then proceed to stare out the window in silence, refusing to look at him again for the sake of my sanity.

When the car stops a few minutes later, and I see we've

pulled up outside a somewhat dilapidated building, I can't hide my confusion.

"Um…have you brought me here to kill me?" I ask as he pulls his keys from the car.

The street isn't one of the nicer ones in Second City, but it's not one of the worst, either. The only reason I know which place we're going to is the huge sign that reads BLACK above the door.

The building is painted black. The whole building. Even the windows have been covered in a matte paint that's completely opaque. I've driven past this place on numerous occasions and always just assumed it was a shut-down bar. There's literally nothing to look at. I've never even seen anyone go in or out.

"Maybe. Want to find out?" he asks, flashing me that smile again. Then he gets out of the car and makes his way around to open my door. "Trust me?" he says as he holds out his hand to me.

Oddly enough, I do kind of trust him. Maybe it's stupid, but I can't see him wanting to hurt me. Unless, of course, he finds out I've been deceiving him the past few weeks – then all bets are off. I nod and place my hand in his, the whole time thinking how ironic it is that he asks me to trust him when I'm the one who can't be trusted.

"Wow."

It's all I can say as he leads me through the restaurant. He brought me in through a side door I didn't know existed, and I was immediately transported into another world. Everything in here screams money. The fancy oak-looking floors and beautiful lights hanging from the ceiling, paired with the dark walls and tablecloths, give the place a dark, romantic vibe. From the outside, you would have no idea that this place was completely decked out in the fanciest furniture, that the mouth-watering smell of food would warm your soul.

"This is..."

It's beautiful, that's for sure, but why is it here? Surely a place like this would be welcome in Golden City, but not here in Second, where people can barely afford to pay bills.

"You're wondering why I have a place like this here, aren't you?" he asks, reading my mind as he leads us to a dimly lit booth in the corner of the room.

The rest of the patrons barely glance at us as we pass. The high back of the booth, combined with the placement, gives it an air of privacy. No one can see us.

"Yeah, I guess I am." I can't stop my eyes from wandering all over the room. It really is beautiful.

"I wanted somewhere in Second that didn't feel like it was here. I wanted somewhere close to home that felt... fancy." He seems serious about it, his own eyes looking around.

"But..." I trail off again. I don't want to offend him, not when he's in a good mood. He nods his head, motioning me to go on, so I do. "But who in Second would even be able to eat here? Does anyone even know about it? Because I've never heard of this place. I doubt anyone from Golden would lower themselves to actually eating in Second City."

He gives me a small smile, and I'm glad he hasn't had his

feelings hurt.

"The people here...they're family of the people who work for me. The only people who know about this place are people I've told or invited. Most of them eat for free – or, at least, they eat on a tab. They pay what they can when they can."

He pauses and glances around again before returning his eyes to me. "People in Second deserve to experience fine dining without worrying if they can afford it. It was Amelia's idea. When she died...I made it happen."

My eyes are wide in shock. He opened a restaurant that allows people who can't afford to go to a fancy restaurant in Golden City to eat good food. To enjoy a night out and be normal. To pretend.

"Who are you?" I ask, but he says nothing. He just looks at me with those fiery eyes and a small, haunted smile.

A waiter comes over to hand us some menus, but Roman asks if he can order for me. I allow it, only because it's been so long since I've eaten out in a normal place, never mind somewhere fancy that I'm not sure I could make the choice myself.

He orders, the waiter leaves, and a silence settles over the table. I'm not sure what to say, how to start a conversation. There's so much I want to know, so much I could try to get out of him to give to Gideon, but it feels wrong to do that here. To betray him in a place he built out of his dead sister's dream.

"So...what exactly is happening right now?" I ask when I can't take his gaze anymore.

"Well, we're sitting in a restaurant waiting for our

food." He smirks when I glare at him.

"Don't quit your day job, friend. You're not that funny."

"So that's what we are, then? Friends?" he asks, and I realise he has flipped my own question back around at me. When I just blink at him, he laughs, and I realise he knows exactly what he's done.

"Friends. Co-conspirators. Whatever the hell you want. But that's it. Just because I'm on a date with you doesn't mean I want—"

"I want you. I don't want to be friends. I want to keep you. I want all of you," he says, and I'm shocked into silence.

He doesn't look like he's joking, like this is some sort of game. His face is neutral, his words coming across as if he was just reading from a dictionary. "Does it surprise you that much? You broke into my office, and instead of killing you like I would have anyone else, all I could think was...*fuck,* she's pretty."

"You said you barely noticed I was a woman," I say, remembering how he acted that night, how unimpressed he seemed.

"I lied," Roman says, looking like he notices very much how womanly I am. "That was all I noticed. All I could focus on. All I've been able to focus on ever since."

"This can't happen. It would never work. My career is based around catching men like you." My voice is breathy, shaking with the shock of hearing him admit that he's been just as attracted to me as I have to him.

"There are no other men like me. I could prove it to you if you let me."

I stare. And stare. And when he inclines his head towards me, looking for an answer, I stare some more. It would be so easy to say yes. So easy to let him have me. In this moment, it seems like the simplest thing in the entire world. But it isn't. Nothing about this entire thing is.

"I can't. I...there's too much...we have too much to do. I need to do this for my father. That has to be my focus. If I let you have me...I think you'd consume me."

He eyes me for a moment, and my heart lodges itself in my throat. What if he decides he won't work with me anymore? I don't think he's that kind of man, but I've been wrong before. What if he won't give me the time of day anymore? My father's life depends on this, on Roman trusting me. Shit. What if I just ruined my chance by turning him down?

Roman smiles, scaring the shit out of me a little. "Okay, Lara."

He says nothing else, and before I can respond, the waiter is placing our food before us. Roman slips him some cash, shakes his hand, and tells him that will be all. "Eat. I promise it's not poisoned."

I'm sceptical but also thankful for the change of subject, so I just shovel food into my mouth instead of saying anything. Nothing has ever tasted so good. I moan as I swallow my first bite. My eyes meet Roman's, and I've never seen a man look so pleased to see someone enjoying food.

Conversation over, we eat in a comfortable silence. We share glances and smiles, and he makes jokes, and I pretend I don't find them funny. When conversation starts again, we stay away from anything serious, and before I know it, I'm having a really good time.

A dangerously good time. A woman could get used to nights like this.

The chef approaches our table just as we're finishing up. He's a handsome man, perhaps in his fifties. Roman's face lights up when he sees the man, his eyes sparkling.

"Roman. Haven't seen you here in a while. And never with such a beautiful date," the chef says, reaching out to shake my hand before even looking for Roman's.

"Lara," I say with a smile as his lips graze my knuckles.

"Get your hands off before I fire you, Bo. If she leaves me for you, I'll be heartbroken," Roman seems lighthearted but still reaches out a hand to take mine from Bo's.

Bo smirks at Roman, looking very pleased with himself before raising his hands in surrender but throwing a quick wink my way. Roman doesn't let go of my hand, his thumb burning a path over my knuckles. I shiver.

"It's good to see you around, Boss," Bo tells Roman, a hint of a smile on his face. "Been a long time since you've come around. I lied before…I don't think you've ever actually brought a woman with you."

He winks at me, and I laugh as Roman sighs deeply beside me. Turning my eyes to him, I don't miss the fond smile on his face, the slight redness to his cheeks.

"Keep flirting with my date, and I'll never be able to bring her back. Although, I don't know if I'll be able to keep her away from you now."

Bo throws back his head and laughs, his eyes wrinkling at the corners. "That would be a real shame, you know. I think tonight is the first time I've ever seen you smile."

Roman ignores this, but his eyes lock on mine. I believe him. Bo. I believe that he has never truly seen Roman smile before. Something about me being the person to bring it out in him ignites something inside of me. Our eyes remain locked, and it happens slowly. One corner of his lips tilts up. Then the other. Before I know it, his lips part and his straight, white teeth glow in the faintly lit room, his face glowing with candlelight.

I don't realise I'm smiling back until my cheeks start to hurt, and I don't realise Bo has left at all. In this moment, it's just the two of us smiling at each other despite ourselves. The pounding in my chest intensifies until I think I must be having a heart attack.

Oddly enough, I think I like it.

CHAPTER 17

The phone rings just as Roman and I finish our drinks. Well, I finish mine. He's been nursing water all night. The food is long gone, but we haven't made a move to leave just yet; I don't want to, and he seems to be in no rush, either. It's late, and I have no idea who might be calling. My anxiety spikes for a moment, thinking it might be Gideon, so I discreetly check my screen as Roman downs the rest of his drink. I don't recognise the number, which doesn't ease my worry at all.

"Sorry, I have to take this," I tell Roman as I leave the table and walk towards the restrooms.

"Hello?" I say into the phone but frown when I'm greeted with nothing but silence. I repeat myself, and this time, a sniffle fills my ears, and I realise someone is crying on the other end of the phone.

"Who is this?" I ask again, an urgency in my voice now. The person sniffles again, and when they speak, their voice is quiet and thick with emotion.

"It's Adeline…is…is this Lara?" It takes me a moment to put the name to a face, but the second I catch on, worry turns my blood ice-cold.

"Yes! Yes, this is Lara. Are you okay, sweetie?" I ask, hoping she can hear me over her sniffling.

"I need help." She sounds distraught...terrified. "Can you help me?"

"Yes. Of course. Where are you?"

She rattles off an address, and I commit it to memory. My knowledge of all the places in Purgatory is pretty good, and I recognise the address she gives me as a street not far from where I saw her before.

"Can you tell me what happened?" I ask her, but I don't get a response – not a verbal one anyway. All I can hear is her sobbing into the phone.

"Okay. Alright. I'll be right there."

I rush back to the table where Roman is watching me with curious, worried eyes. "What's wrong?" he asks, and I'm not entirely sure what to tell him.

I gave a random street kid my number and a knife and told her to call me if she needed help, and now she's cashing it in? Yes, that sounds normal.

"I...I have to go somewhere. There's this kid that..." I start but find myself unable to finish. Worry for Adeline has a strange buzz coursing through my body.

"Okay. Let's go," he says, and I want to tell him he doesn't have to come, but he drove here, and honestly, I may end up needing his help.

I stare at him for just a second as he gathers his things. That simple. I tell him there's a problem and, just like that, with no further information, he's ready to help. Roman is surprising me at every turn.

We rush to the car after he throws some money down on the table, and he's already pulling out and racing down the street before I even give him an address. When I finally do, he reaches a hand out to steady my bouncing leg.

"You want to tell me what's going on?" he asks.

"I—Well, a few weeks ago, I was driving through Purgatory, just clearing my head, you know—"

"Alone?" he interrupts, and I turn to scowl at him.

"Yes, alone. I'm fully capable of protecting myself." He gives a grunt of disapproval in response, and I rush to continue.

"I saw this kid. She was alone. Young, you know? Too young. So I pulled over and gave her some cash and my phone number"—I conveniently leave out the blade—"and told her to call me if she ever needed help."

"She called?" he asks, glancing over at my grim face.

"She called."

We don't talk again after that, but I don't fail to notice his foot pressing down harder on the pedal. We had been only about thirty minutes from the address she gave me, and even though we make it there in just over twenty, Roman's hand remains on my knee, halting the bouncing I can't seem to stop.

The car pulls up outside a row of houses, one of the very few of its kind in Purgatory. Most people live in the hotels turned apartment buildings; houses are uncommon. The majority of them are dark, and the one we pull up in front of is no different.

I look around the street and see that it's completely empty, then shove myself out of the car, leaving Roman and his muttered curse to catch up. The outside of the house is in complete disarray, as most of them are. One of the windows is just a wooden board, and the brick outside is chipped and covered in moss and mould. It's not the kind of place anyone walks into of their own free will, and I cringe as I use the side of my fist to pound on the door.

Roman comes up behind me and slips something into my hand. I'd know the feel of a gun anywhere, but I still have to glance down to make sure. I eye him, but he ignores me and pounds his own fist on the door. He looks so out of place here in his expensive suit, and the sight of him pounding on the door is strange.

Nobody answers, and worry is quickly becoming a living thing inside me. Roman motions for me to step behind him then proceeds to not give me a choice in the matter as he shoves in front of me. He tries the handle, but the door is locked. After a quick, and seeming untroublesome shove of his shoulder, wood splinters, and the door swings open, slamming against the wall behind.

Impressive, I guess. If you're into that sort of thing.

Once he's inside the door, I push past him, ignoring his curse. I step slowly and carefully down the hallway, my gun raised in front of me. This isn't the first time I've done this sort of thing, so I'm thankful when Roman keeps his grumbling to a minimum and follows – mostly silently – behind me.

We check the entire downstairs, grimacing at the absolute filth of the place. There are countless beer bottles, random cans, and overflowing ashtrays on almost every surface. We step over piles of clothes and rubbish, sharing looks of disgust as we pass holes in the walls and cracked mirrors. This place is a dumpster fire, and I hate the thought of Addie being here. Of *why* she would be here,

I move cautiously up the stairs that are equally littered with shit, the sound of sobbing getting louder. I make an executive decision to ditch checking the rest of the house and, instead, rush towards where I hear the crying coming from.

I push the door open slowly, calling Adeline's name as I do, and immediately, the smell of blood fills my nostrils. I glance back at Roman who has stopped following me, and is checking out the two other rooms up here. The door stops opening, and after taking a deep breath, I squeeze my way in through the gap.

The first thing that I spot is the large man lying on the floor. His eyes are wide and unseeing, his chest unnaturally still. It doesn't take a genius to realise he's very dead. If I hadn't known that he was dead already, the knife protruding from his side would be a dead giveaway. I tear my gaze away from the body and almost wish I hadn't. Once I'm not focused on the man, it's difficult to understand why it wasn't Adeline my gaze fell on first.

She sits, impossibly small, in the corner of the room, as far away from the body as she could possibly get. Her thin arms are wrapped around her knees, her face buried in her legs, sobs wracking her frail body.

"Oh, honey." The words tumble out of my mouth as my eyes begin to sting.

It's only when I walk towards her that I realise how few clothes she's wearing. Adeline is wearing the same shorts as the first time I saw her, but it's her lack of a shirt that makes my blood boil. The thoughts racing through my brain could not possibly be worse than what has occurred here tonight. Without even knowing the story, I've already determined that man deserves to be dead.

I slip off my jacket as I approach Adeline, and she flinches as I place it around her trembling shoulders while crouching beside her.

"It's just me. It's Lara. It's okay. I've got you."

Her face slowly lifts, her wide, bloodshot eyes meeting mine with a look so full of desperation it almost knocks me over. She throws her arms around my neck, and then I do fall over. One hand wrapping behind her own back, the other reaching to back to stop me hitting the deck. My ass hits the ground with a thump, and once I'm steady, I wrap the other hand around her.

"I've got you. I've got you. Shh. It's okay," I whisper into her ear, stroking the back of her head with one hand.

"I'm sorry. I'm so sorry. He wouldn't…he wouldn't s-s-stop. I said n-n-no. I'm sorry."

I squeeze her tighter, tell her it isn't her fault. I give her a thousand reassurances, and yet it still doesn't seem like enough.

"Jesus Christ."

At the sound of Roman's voice, Adeline scrambles behind me, hands resting on my shoulders while her forehead presses between my shoulder blades. I meet

Roman's horrified eyes, and have no doubt that's exactly how I looked when I first walked into the room. He walks towards the body on the floor, his fingers going to check the man's pulse, even though he's obviously dead.

"I'm sorry," Adeline whispers behind me again, and Roman's eyes flick up towards her.

I've never seen that look on his face before. He looks shocked and…guilty? I can't tell, and before I can even try deciphering it, he looks back down at the body.

"You know who this is?" he asks me. I take another look, but I shake my head. He sighs, and it's a deep, weary sigh.

"Marcus Evans."

I shake my head again; I still don't recognise it. He stares at me, willing me to understand something. Marcus. Evans. The name does ring a bell…I just can't—

Oh.

No. Fucking. Way.

Marcus Evans, victim number three. This is one of the men Roman needed me to find. My eyes widen, and Roman nods.

"Adeline, sweetie, we need to go," I say as gently as I can.

Everything else can wait. Getting her out of this murder scene is the most important thing. I feel her shake her head against my back, so I turn around to look at her. From this position, a quick glance over my shoulder means she sees not only giant, terrifying Roman but the body of the man she just murdered.

Her eyes widen, filling with tears. I turn us both so she

only has to face me and the hideous lime-green wall behind me.

"Hey. Look at me. Just at me. That's Roman. He's my friend, and he is not going to hurt you."

"I don't want to go to prison," she says quietly, and my chest cracks wide open.

"You are *not* going to prison. You're going to come with us. We'll get you out of here, and no one will ever know. I promise."

Her eyes fill with hope, and she nods slightly as she stares at me. Until they move to the man looming in the middle of the room.

"What about you?" she asks.

Roman glances over his shoulder as though she may be talking to somebody else.

"I-what?" he asks, frowning slightly.

"Do you p-promise I won't go to prison?" She looks so terrified yet so hopeful. It's physically painful to witness.

"Christ. *Of course,* you're not going to prison," he says, that strange emotion flickering over his face again.

"Promise me."

"I swear it on my life."

"Okay," I interject, unable to handle the intensity of the moment, "time to go." I stand and hold out my hand to Adeline, who takes it but remains still.

"I'm scared to turn around," she whispers. I open my mouth to respond, but Roman beats me to it.

"Close your eyes," he says.

She does so immediately.

"Okay if I pick you up?"

She nods at his request, and then he's there. Without a sound, he lifts her into her arms. Her small hand releases mine as her arms go around his neck, her head hiding in his neck, legs wrapping around him like a little spider monkey. My heart clenches in my chest at the sight of them.

Wordlessly, the three of us leave the room, then the house.

In my mind, I see myself lighting a match, throwing it inside the toxic wasteland that is that house before stepping back and watching it go up in flames. I wonder quickly if Roman would stop me or if he would be the one to throw the gasoline on top.

I open the door so Roman can ease Adeline into the back seat, reaching over to grab her seatbelt and get it on her. She's so tiny she really should have a booster seat. My jacket dwarfs her, swallowing her whole as she sits in the back of the car.

The minute the door closes and she's safely ensconced in the heat of car, I exhale a sigh of relief. My hand comes up to scrub my eyes and then rest against my cheeks.

"Are you okay?" Roman asks with his hands stuffed into his pockets.

"Yes." I sigh. "No."

"That was a nice thing you did for her."

"I gave her the knife she killed a man with."

"You gave her the knife that saved her life," he says, though it does little to lift my spirits.

That poor girl.

"I know," he says, and at first, I think he read my mind, but then I realise I had just spoken out loud.

Our eyes remain locked for a moment, both of us together in our misery. Mutual guilt connects us in this moment. Guilt over the fact that while we were out having dinner, Adeline was almost raped. While she struggles every single day, we go about our lives like we aren't lucky.

A distant gunshot rings out. The moment passes.

"Get in the car. We have to get out of here."

Roman eyes the surrounding area, brimming with disgust at what he sees. He doesn't like being seen around Purgatory, and he's right to be paranoid. Gideon is coming for his head.

But I can't tell him that, so I just get in the car.

We drop Adeline off at another rundown house in Purgatory. Part of me screams to not let her out of the car, to keep her with me and get her out of this place, but that would be kidnapping.

The house we pull up to looks just like the one we came from – two stories, big windows. The only difference is that it looks like someone is trying to make an effort. The front door has been painted red, though not so recently that the colour is vibrant. Pits of paint are chipped off in places, the colour dull and uninspiring. It looks clean from the outside. The small garden is devoid of trash, at least compared to the rest of the row of houses.

Adeline stares out the window, wide-eyed and pale in the glow from the overhead light of the car. I'm not sure what to say, how to reassure a child after they just had to murder someone to protect themselves, but I need to say something.

"Does your mom know where you were?" I ask, turning in the passenger seat to look at her.

"No. She'd go crazy if she knew. I-I just wanted to make some money. I thought I could do it – what she does. But he was so gross and mean. I couldn't do it." She pauses as tears well up in her eyes. "She's a good mom."

Adeline turns to look at me, eyes imploring me to believe her. "She tries to keep me away when she's working. She feeds me. Looks after my grandparents – they live here too. She…she tries her best. I just wanted to help." A tear slips down her face as her lip trembles.

"You don't have to do that." Roman's strong voice startles me. "She's your mother. She doesn't want you to do what she does." He turns in his own chair, leaning around to see her behind the driver's seat. "Never try that again, kid."

His tone leaves no room for debate, his eyes daring her to disobey him. She doesn't. Adeline simply nods and turns to look back out the window, her soft voice asking what happens now.

I have no idea, so I turn to Roman.

He sighs, looking like the weight of the world rests on

his shoulders. Maybe it does. I really don't know what goes on in the background of his life. Although, after tonight, after our not-date, I feel like I know him better, and that's dangerous territory to be in.

"Nothing. You go in there and get a shower. Throw those clothes away. Tell no one what happened, and never speak about it again to anyone but Lara. You've got her number, and she can give you mine."

My eyebrows raise at his offer. Once again, Roman Black surprises me.

"It never happened. You did nothing wrong. Tomorrow, I'll send someone over here and…we'll get you out. You and your mom. Your grandparents if they want. I've got a place in Second you can stay."

Adeline's eyebrows shoot up her forehead when he tells her about the place in Second, and if she's surprised, then I'm fucking stunned.

"Really?" she asks, unbelieving. So unused to anyone doing anything kind for her. To be fair, I want to know if he's for real too.

"Really. Now go. I think that's your mom." He motions his head outside, and I look to see a woman just a few years older than me run out the door of the house.

Quickly, Adeline surges forward and wraps her arms awkwardly around my neck. Her whispered *thank you* fills my heart with warmth, and I hug her back as best I can from where I sit. Then she's gone, jumping out of the car and into her mother's arms, tears already flowing from both of them.

"Stay here," Roman says.

I bristle, but I do because I don't think I can face her mother after what just happened.

I watch as Roman approaches. Adeline's mother shoves her daughter behind her, distrust written all over her face. I can't hear through the closed doors, and while a part of me wants to know what Roman is saying, another part can't handle any kindness from this man. I don't need another reason to want him.

Adeline's mother starts to cry as he speaks, her eyes wide as her hands cup her mouth in disbelief. She darts forward and hugs him, and I almost laugh at how awkwardly he stands there before patting her softly on the back and allowing her to sob into his chest.

A weird feeling ignites inside of me, and if I was a lesser person, I would call it jealousy. But good people don't get jealous when a very damaged woman hugs a person who has done something nice for her. A good person doesn't get jealous of someone she has no right to get jealous over.

A few more moments pass, and then Roman is back in the car, and we're driving away. I look back to see Adeline being ushered inside.

"You're going to move them into your house?" I ask eventually when I can't resist.

"Not my house. A house. It's just sitting there. Empty," he says, and I wait for more, but it doesn't come.

"That's...that's a really decent thing to do."

"I'm not a monster, Lara. Despite what rumours would have you believe."

Yes. I was starting to figure that out.

The rest of the drive passes in silence, and before I know it, we're pulling up outside of my apartment building. I hadn't even noticed that this was where we'd been driving. Neither of us says a thing as we sit there, the car idling.

Suddenly, quietly, he says, "It was Alisha's. The house. It's empty, and she's not coming back. They need it...she doesn't."

His eyes turn from the window, his body twisting to face me, and I don't know what comes over me. Maybe it's the way his eyes look, almost orange with the glow from the street lights. Maybe it's the look on his face, unguarded and open and almost weak. The sadness seeps from him, and maybe that speaks to me. He just looks so handsome – so strong yet broken at the same time.

It's wrong. It's wrong for so many reasons. I'm lying to him, he's sad, I may be the reason he gets killed. There are so many reasons I shouldn't lean over and kiss him, and yet that's exactly what I do.

Almost impossibly fast, without warning, I'm unfastening my seat belt and leaning over. Both my hands reach for his face, and thank God he seems to understand what's happening, because his own hands reach for my waist, and just as our lips touch, he yanks me out of my chair and onto him.

Roman's lips are softer than I imagined. Firm and wet from his tongue. The moment our lips touch, he groans, a sound so deep it sends thrills through my entire body. I feel that groan everywhere, and it's almost impossible to hold back a moan of my own.

One of his hands squeezes my waist, and the other that's resting on my back pushes me forward so our chests are flush. The feel of my breasts pressed against the impossibly hard planes of his chest makes me moan again, and the moment I do, his hips thrust, and I can feel him, hard as steel under me.

He thrusts again, then his tongue slips inside my mouth, and I die. I die a thousand deaths because this is not supposed to feel so good. I'm not supposed to like this. I'm not supposed to like him, and yet even with this thought in my head, I can't help but roll my hips, my stomach tightening at the friction it causes.

His tongue explores my mouth as his hips continue to grind into me, and I gasp and cry out as his hands wander. One now grips the back of my neck, the other squeezing my ass so tightly I wouldn't be surprised if his handprint remained there forever, branding me as his even though I'm not.

Roman pulls his mouth from mine, and I almost whimper at the loss until he says, "Fuck, baby."

His hot, wet mouth moves to my neck, leaning me back against the steering wheel, his hand at my nape keeping me from losing balance. It feels so good, all of it. Everything. My hands are mindless, unattached, grabbing his hair and his face, scratching at his shoulders and gripping his arms.

The delicious friction between my legs is intensifying, and I can already feel an orgasm building inside of me. Tomorrow, I will be embarrassed about that. Tomorrow, I'll care that all it took was dry humping in his car, and I'm putty in his hands. But now, *now* his fingers are dragging my top down, his lips moving over my chest. *Now*, his hands slip under my top, firm, thick fingers dragging up my side. Pressure builds inside of me.

"Oh, God, I think—" I can't speak.

"It's okay. Give it to me."

Roman's voice is rough, chock full of arousal. His hips pump, and even through his suit trousers, his dick hits just the right spot. His hand is at my breast, pulling the cup of my bra down, and then his thumb brushes over my nipple, and I jerk. The touch travels straight to my pussy, and I call his name as he continues the delicious torture.

"*Roman.*"

"I know."

He squeezes my nipple, his mouth latching back onto mine to swallow my moans, and I erupt. I come, and then I come apart. Pieces of me drift away, floating into space and getting lost in time as my entire body feels the effects of the orgasm. He groans into my mouth as his hips slow their pace, rubbing every last ounce of pleasure from me.

My soul flies away, and I'm boneless in his lap, his hand adjusting my bra and t-shirt back into place, peppering soft kisses everywhere his mouth can reach.

Then his hand leaves my neck, and I lean back against the steering wheel hard enough for the horn to beep. I scream, so shocked by the sudden noise bursting my bubble of languid pleasure that I fly from his lap, scrambling into my seat as quickly as I can. It takes me a moment to realise it had been me to beep the horn and not some stranger who caught us in the act.

With the bubble burst, my mind finally catches up to what just happened.

"Oh my god. I-I'm—" I don't even know where to begin.

Roman smirks at me, a look of pure male smugness on his face.

"Relax. You kissed me. I made you come by barely touching you. Don't freak out. I enjoyed it," he says, and I splutter incomprehensibly a few times.

He sounds so pleased with himself, so smug that I almost can't believe he's the same playful man he was during our dinner tonight.

"It was just the adrenaline. I needed to take the edge off. That was a mistake. One I will not be repeating."

I adjust my clothes and check myself in the mirror to ensure I don't look like I just dry-humped the guy I'm working against to orgasm in his fucking car.

"Yeah, sure. Whatever you want, baby," he says, suddenly stopping, even though it sounds like he had more to say. "Fucking wonderful," he spits, but I don't look at him as I continue to glare at my dumbass self in the mirror. "Fun's over, sweetheart. Your boyfriend is here."

At the word *boyfriend*, I look over at him in confusion but follow his line of sight out the car window. My heart leaps into my throat when I see Chase, frozen at the door of our building, eyes locked on the car.

Fuck. He didn't see, right? There's no way he could see into the car.

"Shit. I have to go," I say.

"We have to talk about what happened."

I turn to him in shock, giving him my best glare. "Actually, we never have to talk about this again," I spit.

"I meant with the kid. Glad to know you can't stop thinking about coming all over my—"

"Shut up. We'll talk. Tomorrow. Goodbye, Mr. Black."

He barks out a laugh as I exit the car, but I don't turn around. I can't. What just happened, and can I please plead temporary insanity? Christ. My eyes lock on Chase, and I sigh. What a fucking mess.

CHAPTER 18

The apartment is silent. I make myself some coffee, even though it's far too late to be drinking it. Chase sits on my sofa, eyes forward, glaring at nothing ahead of him. He'd said nothing to me as I approached, just followed me stoically to my apartment, and has been frozen in that chair for the last ten minutes.

My eyes stray to him for the millionth time, and still nothing. I sigh heavily, pick up my steaming coffee, and take a place on the other end of the sofa. As I sit, I curl my legs up under me and vow that if he doesn't speak in the next few minutes, I'll be the one to break the awkward silence. Thankfully I don't have to.

"How long?" he asks, and though I know exactly what he's asking me, I try my best to delay the inevitable.

"What?"

"How long have you been…making out with him in cars?" Chase swings that wild gaze towards me.

"I haven't been. That was…it just happened. It was a mistake. Not that it's any of your business."

Can you still consider something a mistake if you want it to happen again? *And again. And again.*

"None of my business? Jesus, Lara." I flinch at the use of my real name out of his mouth. "The guy is a fucking psycho. Not to mention the fact that if he was to find out what you're doing, he wouldn't hesitate to kill you." Chase is furious, and I honestly can't tell whether it's jealousy alone or if it's him truly fearing for my safety.

"You don't have to worry about it. It was a mistake, okay? I have no intention of it happening again."

"What about him? Does he know it was just a one-off?" Chase scoffs, standing and putting his hands on his hips, head tilted back to stare at the ceiling. "You should be keeping your distance, not getting closer to him. You know how this ends, and it's not fucking happily ever after."

His tone pisses me off, and I uncurl my legs from beneath me, glaring up at him from my place on the couch.

"I'm not looking for a happily ever after or anything close to it. It was a mistake, Chase. How many times do I need to say it?" I ask, and he looks at me, dead in the eye.

"As many times as it takes you to convince yourself it's true. I saw you, as much as it made me want to gouge my eyes out. I've seen you with him, the way you look at him, the way he looks at you. You're playing a dangerous game. One you better hope you don't lose."

"I've got it under control, Chase," I say, but I know he's right.

I know how I look at him. I know how my thoughts have been changing in regard to Roman, and he's right. It's a dangerous game. I've crossed a line that I'm not entirely sure I know how to get back behind.

"I don't know what's going on with you, but you need to get your head on straight. All of this is for your dad, or have you forgotten him during all dry humping of your enemy on the side of the road?"

His voice is laced with venom, and now I know it's pure jealousy he's feeling. He wants to hurt me, and it sends me off the ledge. I don't care how right he is; he doesn't get to speak to me like that.

"Fuck you, Chase. Don't even try to tell me that this isn't mostly about your jealousy."

His eyebrows rest on his hairline.

"Of course, I'm fucking jealous. Jesus Christ." His annoyance has reached a new level – one I've only seen from Chase a time or two, never directed at me. "You've been avoiding the fact that we almost kissed for weeks now, and I gave you your space. I gave you what I thought you wanted, what I thought you needed, but I'm done with that now. We almost kissed, Lara. We almost kissed, and you would have fucking liked it, so explain that."

"Chase, I—"

"No. You don't get to brush it off. Not anymore. Put me out of my fucking misery. Please. I'm literally begging you."

His honesty is disconcerting. I wasn't prepared to have this conversation. Selfishly, I had been hoping it would go away. I was hoping we would just naturally fall into whichever category fit us, and I wouldn't have to make any tough decisions. I wouldn't have to hurt him or risk ruing the friendship we've built over the last few years.

I understand how selfish it was to leave him hanging, wondering. Especially now. I can't imagine not knowing where you stand with someone, hoping to get more from them, only to see them making out with somebody else. I've been leading him on – not intentionally, but by not telling him what I've been feeling, I've been giving him false hope.

The problem is, I still haven't been able to determine what exactly it is I feel for Chase. Doesn't really matter now. I seem to be out of time.

"Chase, you're my best friend. You know that," I say, pouring all the affection I can into my voice. I need him to know how much I care about him, even if it's not in the way he wants.

"Best friends don't look at friends the way you looked at me. I wasn't imagining that."

"You're right. I know you're right. I'm not saying I've never wanted....I did. It's just...I can't lose you. I can't risk ruining what we have."

I try to convey what I'm feeling through our eyes. Our brains have always been like walkie-talkies, but it seems that right now, the channel is disrupted. He wants to hear the words come out of my mouth. He wants to know exactly what I'm trying to say.

"So, you don't want me. Say it, Lara. I'm not going to hold it against you, but I think you owe me the truth. Look me in the eye and tell me you don't want me."

I look him in the eye. I square my shoulders. The words are on the tip of my tongue. I open my mouth...and nothing comes out. I shut it again, clear my throat, and the same thing happens. His frown increases. He looks genuinely confused, and I feel that way too. How am I supposed to look him in the eye and tell him I'm not attracted to him? I can't. It's not true. I do want him, and I have wanted him, but I can't let myself go there. I don't want to let myself go there.

"I wanted you when I was too young to want you, Chase." This time, the words flow effortlessly. "I wanted you, and you didn't know I existed."

"You were barely an adult. Of course, I didn't want to know you. I couldn't. I couldn't, but you made me," he says, and I know exactly what he's talking about. I made him look.

It took me so long, took every trick younger me had in the book. Months I spent begging him to stop seeing me as a kid, and eventually, he did. Only then I was too scared to go any further.

"You made me notice you. And still, I kept my hands to myself. My thoughts to myself. I didn't look at you, didn't spend time with you. Then you complimented my eyes, and you fucked me up. You got what you wanted – I looked. But then, you avoided me. You've been avoiding me." His words have lost their angry edge. Now they're just filled with hurt and frustration.

"Chase," I whisper because I feel like I know what's coming, and I need to stop this train before it crashes into us both.

"I love you," he says, and the train hits.

Colliding at one hundred miles an hour. I already know it'll result in two casualties, but it's too late now. The words float between us, and I try and push them away before I absorb them. Before I add them to my collection of beautiful moments, of things I cannot have.

"No, you don't," I whisper again.

"I am in love with you," he says, louder this time. Surer. His eyes lock on me, his body vibrating with restraint.

"No. You aren't."

"Don't pretend you didn't know," he shouts. "Don't pretend you haven't been avoiding this thing between us." He laughs, but it's a humourless, self-deprecating laugh. "The great Lara Miller, scared of absolutely nothing except letting me love her. And I would. I would love you, Lara. Forever. With everything that I've got. If you'd just fucking let me."

His chest heaves, his fists clench by his sides while his eye blaze with passion. I've never heard him speak like that. Never heard him lay himself bare. His chest lays open in front of me, and he's giving me permission to reach in and pluck out his heart.

Chase could have anyone, a million choices, and yet here he is, taking up too much space in my living room, bleeding all over my floor in the rarest display of nakedness, allowing himself a moment of weakness.

It would be so easy to reach out and grab it. It would be simple; I could have it all. I take a tiny step towards him, and he mimics me. My heart pounds rapidly against my chest, and I can almost hear myself saying yes. I can almost hear myself saying, "*I love you, too.*"

But a louder voice booms through my head.

"*You'll be thinking of me.*"

Guilt slams into me like a truck, and then I'm taking

two steps backwards. Fear engulfs me at the thought of losing Chase as a friend, but I can't risk loving him. I can't risk loving and losing him. It's not worth it.

He'll forgive me this. He'll forgive me for not being reckless with his heart, but he'd never forgive me for taking it in my palm and dropping it at his feet. There's still time for him to un-love me, and I owe him that.

Chase watches my small backward steps with weary eyes, and then realisation dawns on his face. He closes himself back up, chest stitching back together, heart tucked safely back inside, intact, if not cut up a bit.

"Chase…" My voice cracks, but I don't have to say anything else. Our walkie-talkies are connected again, and even if they weren't, he can read me like a book. It's all over my face.

"I'm sorry," I say, swiping a tear off my cheek. He doesn't need this; he doesn't need my emotions right now. Chase needs my honesty.

"Is it him?" he simply asks, as the last of the love clears from his eyes. Now, it's just hurt and anger back there.

"No. No, it's not him. Or you. It's—"

"If you say, *'It's not you, it's me,'* I will literally never speak to you again."

"I just…I can't. It's not what I want." My guilt rises up my chest at the hurt look in his eyes, and I have to physically hold back the urge I'm getting to vomit.

"Right. Now I know." He turns and looks over my apartment, quickly muttering, "Okay" over and over again, and I'm almost sure it's his way of reassuring himself. "I need some time. I need…just…I have to go."

His feet carry him quickly to the door, and I retake my seat on the sofa, gripping tightly to the arm so I don't run after him.

Chase stops at the threshold, one hand on the handle, the other on the doorframe. He doesn't look back, but I can see the restraint it's taking him. The muscles in his back are bunched tight, his hand white-knuckling the doorframe so tightly I can see it from here.

"When he fucks it – when this all blows up – I'll be here." Another one of those self-deprecating laughs, threatening to cut off my air supply. "I'll always fucking be here."

Then he's gone, the door slamming behind him, and I rest my face in my hands, wondering if, in trying to save our friendship, I ended up fucking it up anyway. I groan into my palms, frustration pouring out of me, ripping my throat to pieces as I swap my hands for a pillow and scream as loudly as I can.

Once I'm finished, I take my cold, forgotten coffee into my bedroom for no reason other than give my hands something to do. I lay face down, barely breathing for a moment, as I try and reassure myself everything will be fine. I'm almost there. My heart rate is back down, the guilt and anxiety in my stomach lessened to a functional point, when my phone beeps.

I slide it out of my back pocket and glance at the screen.

Hope Jace wasn't too pissed off. When you're ready to go again, just let me know.

My phone flies out of my hand and across the room before I'm even aware I've flung it, and then I'm back to square one.

I squish my face into the pillow, take a deep breath, and scream.

△△△

The thought of going to Roman's office on Monday and having to see him after our little…moment…makes me want to vomit. I have never in my entire life been so glad for it to be a weekend. With nothing to do, my plan to spend the day hiding from Chase and everyone else in my life sounded pretty good. I really needed to call Gideon, talk to my dad. I've been too busy to realise just how much I've missed him, but this morning, when I woke up, the silence let all the feelings in.

I've been so busy and so focused on just getting through this shit with Roman, on finding that one piece of information I can give to Gideon to make this all end, that I haven't had time to just…be sad that my dad is stuck in the hands of an evil bastard. I've been so busy stressing about boy problems that I barely recognise myself.

I'm all twisted up and inside out and it's starting to piss me off. I am not this girl. I don't get awkward and shy and weird over a *man*. My inner monologue is driving me up the wall, and it's beginning to sound like a preteen. I know I have more important stuff to be focusing on, but any time there's a moment of silence, my brain strays to Roman and the Earth-shattering orgasm he gave me in the front seat of his car.

It comes as no surprise that when Andi and Soph knock on my door on Saturday, I lose it and blab everything at once.

"So, let me get this straight," Soph says as she stands behind Andi, playing with her hair. "He made you come without even touching your lady bits?"

I sigh and flop back onto the bed. "Technically he did touch me, just through multiple layers of clothes. Why did I even tell you?"

"Because we're your best friends?" says Andi, and Sophie snorts.

"Only friends more like."

"Fuck you," I say with zero venom.

"In your dreams, baby."

I can't see her from where I'm lying, but I could almost hear the wink.

"I should not be having sexy times while my father is being held captive. There are literal lives on the line," I say, putting a voice to my insufferable thoughts.

"Oh, shut up. You're a woman – you can multi-task. Besides, orgasms relieve stress." Andi sighs sadly. "I want a male-induced orgasm."

"I want an orgasm induced by anything other than my vibrator," Sophie says.

"Which one have you got?"

"It's this little…"

I tune them out as they continue their conversation about vibrators. Not because I'm too mature to have a conversation about the powerfulness of sex toys, but because I'm so exhausted, I've actually started to fall asleep. My phone vibrates. I ignore it. It vibrates again. I throw it onto the floor.

Someone knocks on the door.

"Arghh." The noise is unladylike, and I'd be ashamed of it if it hadn't felt so necessary to emit it as I roll from my bed to the floor in order to stand up.

"Jeez," Andi mutters from behind me.

I look through the peephole and almost have a heart attack when Roman's giant head is all I can see. "Shit."

I glance back towards my bedroom, where the girls are still chatting away. There's no avoiding this, really. I say a silent prayer and hope they don't make me want to fling myself out the window.

I steel myself and pull open the door.

"Is my phone broken?" he asks the moment we're face to face.

"Uh, I don't know?"

"Well, it must be because when I call or text, people usually answer. But you're a different story, apparently." He pushes past me into the apartment.

"Oh, do come in," I mutter sarcastically.

Andi and Soph rush from my bedroom. Andi stops abruptly when she sees the large man peering around my living room, and, comically, Sophie slams into her back with a small "Oomph."

"Hello," Roman says, eying the two of them. I've never

seen them so quiet. Their wide eyes take him in from head to toe, and it's difficult not to laugh at their expressions.

"Hello," they reply in unison, and I roll my eyes so hard I'm surprised they don't fall out.

"Why are you here, Roman?" I ask as his gaze roams over my stuff. He looks curious. Surprised even.

"This is nice," he says, ignoring my question.

"Why. Are. You. Here?" I try again, ignoring Andi's whispers behind me, calling me rude.

"You wouldn't pick up. I thought you might be dead."

"Why the fuck would I be dead?"

"There are plenty of reasons you might be dead. Jace might have killed you in a jealous rage." He's dead serious.

"If I was placing bets on who was most likely to murder me, you would be top contender." I walk over, grab his hand and place two of his fingers on my wrist. "Feel my pulse?"

He nods, eyes boring intensely into mine.

"Wonderful. Now that you know I'm alive, you can leave." I glare at him, stepping back and gesturing to the door.

He hmms, and then sits, *sits*, on my sofa. I turn and look at my two friends, both of which give me the same *"what the fuck"* look that I'm giving them.

"Are you busy tomorrow?" he asks.

"Yes." I lie immediately. Quite good at that now.

"No. You're not."

"I am. I have plans."

Roman frowns, glaring up at me as he gets comfortable on my sofa like he's the king or some shit. He looks over at my friends, who I'm pretty sure are shaking their heads to inform him I'm lying.

"Cancel them."

A staring match ensues, and the tension in the room shoots up tenfold.

"*This is so hot. I might come,*" one of the girls whispers, and I can almost hear the other nod in agreement. Roman seems pleased by their confessions. I can't turn to look at them. I will not lose this round.

"We're just gonna go—"

"That would be best," Roman interrupts Sophie as she announces their exit.

"Stay," I bark at them, but they're already scurrying down the hall. *Traitors,* I think as I hear the door slam behind me.

Roman finally sighs and looks away, and childish as it may be, I smirk in triumph. Fuck you, Roman.

"I really do need you for something. I found the next bounty. You're going to help me catch him."

I'm reminded all over again that he really had no use for me. I have no idea why he bothered to ask me to find these men. He could have done it himself. I know he could have.

"Last night. Guy number three. Is Addie gonna have any

problems? If I remember correctly, he was pretty high up with Gideon." I had been worried about her, but calling Roman to ask hadn't been an option. A small smile graces his face, and fondness creeps into his eyes.

"No, I took care of it. Gideon will think it was me. Addie and her family are somewhere safe, hidden just in case. You're welcome."

Something in the way he says you're welcome seems off. He didn't mean it – he didn't save Addie for me. He did it because he…cares. She reminds him of his sister. It's easier now to see through the suit of armour that he wears. To look between the cracks and see the human that he hides beneath the beast. I choose to ignore it. I'm not opening up that discussion right now. I don't want to see him anymore than I have to.

I simply nod and take a seat as far away from him as possible. I try my best not to look at him, but ignoring his presence is almost impossible. I can smell him. Shit, I can still taste him. My stomach flips, and I know I need to get him out of here.

"Alright," I say, hoping to get him out the door faster. "What do you need tomorrow?"

"I thought you had plans?" he asks with a smirk, which I return with my blandest, most unimpressed look. He gives me a real smile then, and spontaneous combustion is imminent.

"I'll come get you. I'll call you when I'm on the way." He stands and makes his way over to my bookshelf. It's full of mainland books, most of which were very hard to come by. Getting things onto the Island yourself is a nightmare, and I'm proud of my collection.

"Hard to get books shipped here. Our government is quite afraid of outside forces contaminating the good people of the Island." He eyes me suspiciously.

"You're not the only one with connections, Black," I reply, and I don't check out his ass as he turns to the bookshelf again.

"Curiouser and curiouser," he says with a little *hmm*, and it takes me a second to recognise the quote from a children's book written long before our island was even built. The fact that he's read it piques my bookworm interest.

"Have you forgotten how to speak good English too?" I ask, remembering the rest of the sentence from the book.

He turns, his eyes gliding over my body in a slow perusal that has my toes curling in my socks.

"You know," he says when his eyes finally make it back up to mine, "I've discovered you often have that effect on me."

Roman leaves, promising to call on his way over tomorrow and warning me to answer the phone. When he's walking away, I feel the most irresistible urge to ask him to stay. In the end, my good sense wins out over my libido, and as I close the door after him, I finally feel like I can breathe.

Things have changed between us. Obviously, I went on a date with him. Now, though, when I argue with him, when I act like I hate his guts, and he bosses me around like I'm nothing but an employee…I *like* it. I want it. I want to push him, argue with him, and piss him off. I want to see all the different masks of Roman Black. I want him.

The problem is that the Roman I saw, the Roman who took me to dinner and saved Adeline and makes my heart race...he would never forgive me if he found out the truth. Myth Roman would hate me, yes, probably kill me. But sweet Roman, human Roman...he'd have his feelings hurt. And that scares me the most.

It's first thing in the morning, and my day is ruined immediately by the sound of Gideon's voice through my phone. I'm barely awake, eyes still half-fused shut, and he's demanding answers I'm not sure I have and don't want to give.

"I told you everything I know. I've got nothing else for you right now."

This isn't the first time I've told him I have nothing. His annoyance is clear even in his silence. It's getting harder and harder for me to find things I'm willing to give him. I've ratted out multiple deliveries. I've told him which restaurants and clubs I found on Roman's books that are worth taking over. I've told him names of his men, dates of certain things. I've given him as much as I can, but he wants more.

I'm running out of time. He's going to move in soon, and I still have no idea what Roman's plan is for Gideon. I've been so preoccupied lately that I haven't asked him. I also haven't wanted to. I don't want to get Roman killed. I might claim to hate him, but I know he's not a monster. Not like Gideon is.

The trouble is, it's him or my dad. That's an easy choice – my dad all the way – but that doesn't mean I feel good about it.

"I need something big. I want something big, little hunter. Am I understood?" Gideon says, and I have to shove my fist into my mouth to keep from barking down the phone at him.

"Yes," I say once I've removed my teeth from my knuckles.

"Wonderful. You'd like to speak to your father?" Gideon asks.

"Yes, of course."

"Ah, well then. You know what to do," he says and hangs up.

"Motherfucker," I mutter to myself, letting my phone fall from my hand to the floor, unbothered to even pick it up.

The only reason I know my father is still alive is because sporadically, Gideon will send me a picture of him with the day's paper, the date clear. It pisses me off to no end because it's just a reminder that it's been almost a month, and all I'm doing is waiting.

The worst thing about this entire situation is that as much as I think I am, I'm not in control. I'm waiting for Gideon, and I'm waiting for Roman, and in the meantime, the best I can do is pit them against each other. I'm useless to my father right now. Everybody is just playing games. Gideon, Roman…hell, even me.

I don't even know who I am anymore.

Distracting myself with paperwork seemed like a good idea when I began, but now, hours later, the letters have begun to blur, and a marching band is going full throttle inside my skull. Tax forms and insurance and countless other important documents are splayed out before me. Most of them make little to no sense to me because our self-governed island got to choose their own rules.

It took years for my father to teach me how to make this company run behind the scenes, and I still struggle. Not because I'm incapable, but because this is the single most boring part of my job. It takes all my concentration to get through it, which in turn, means I don't have to think about the mess my life is in. The only thing I do is ensure my father has a company to return to when I get him back.

Before I know it, the sun has gone down outside, and I have no idea how long I've been sitting here filling out forms, calling people, and trying desperately not to pull my hair out. Surprisingly enough, though, I feel better. Less stressed about my personal life and more stressed about business life. It's good enough for me.

It's already five p.m. and I haven't heard a word from Roman. Which is fine. I'm waiting around for him anyway. Just as I'm shoving a buttload of pages into a filing system, I hear a knock at the door. I almost run towards it but force myself to stop.

When I reach the door, I look through the peephole and am surprised to see Chase standing there. I pull the door open and step aside, inviting him in. He doesn't move, doesn't even look at me for a full five seconds, then saunters past me.

"You walked towards my apartment five and a half times today," he says. "Why didn't you come up?"

"How did you—" I remember the cameras he had installed all over the building after the break-in. "Right. Cameras. You asked for space...I'm trying to respect that."

Chase sighs, leaning his butt against my kitchen counter and crossing his long legs, completely comfortable, while I try to resist the urge to leave. He looks me over, and then he shocks the shit out of me.

"Forget about it. We're good."

What? Yesterday, he hated my guts and today, he's just, *"Meh I'm over it?"*

"Uh, we are?" I ask, moving to lean against the counter opposite him.

"Yep, don't worry about it." His smile is genuine, but his eyes seem sad. When he reaches over and boops my nose, I almost faint.

"Okay then." I say the words slowly, looking over him suspiciously as if he's lying.

He rolls his eyes at me and saunters to the fridge, then pulls out two cans of soda. I take one, and before I know it, he's taking a seat on the couch and telling me all about his day, filling me in on office details I've missed as if yesterday never happened. It's so normal and casual that I find myself making pasta for us like I have a thousand times before. I don't even realise I've forgotten about our fight as I listen to case updates and new case requests.

It's so nice to have this. It's been so long since we've just hung out. Since we've been friends. We talk about Gideon, and I tell him about the phone call. He tells me about Eric and how funny it is watching him fail miserably at flirting with Andi. We laugh as we talk, shovelling pasta into our mouths while consciously avoiding all topics of Roman. When Chase gets up to take the dishes to the kitchen, I take them from him, telling him I have to go to the bathroom anyway. As I leave the room, he picks up the remote control to flick through TV and find something for us to watch. My heart is happy when he settles on the Island's version of reality TV.

As I'm in the bathroom, my phone rings. I pay no attention to it until I hear Chase shout, "I got it," at which point I throw the towel I'm using to dry my hands into the sink and hurry back towards him. When I see him, he looks so ginormous holding the phone to his ear, and it's obvious Roman is on the other side of the line. His back is to me, but I can see the anger in his body.

Chase really fucking hates Roman.

"She can't talk right now," Chase says, and I frown. I should probably take the phone away, but instead, I back up a little, hoping Chase doesn't notice I'm eavesdropping.

"Really? I've been here for hours, and she hasn't mentioned it."

"Maybe she didn't hear her phone. We were, uh, busy."

As I listen to the one-sided conversation, I become very away that a) Chase is a lot sneakier than I've given him credit for, B) he's actively trying to piss Roman off by alluding to the fact that we're doing something bad, and C) Chase is playing Roman's game, and that cannot end well.

I make myself known and once again am baffled by Chase's playful smile. He doesn't look guilty, just mildly amused, and I find myself grinning when he says, "Oh, she's back. Hey, babe. Roland is on the phone."

He winks, and the thought of Roman's pissed-off expression on the other end of the line makes me smile harder. It's not the first time Chase has called me babe, and he absolutely knows that his name is Roman, but the payback is justified, so I just shake my head at him. He hands the phone over after he leans down and plants a very loud kiss on my cheek.

Chase smirks at me as he sits, and I lift the phone to my ear.

"Hello, Roland," I say.

"Call me that one more time, and I'll put your boyfriend in the ground."

"Right. Jeez. What's up?"

"I'm outside. I've been outside. I told you I was coming to get you."

"You never called," I accuse, and I can feel the anger through the phone. He sighs heavily before he speaks.

"I've been busy. Bad day. But I'm calling now. I'm here. We have to go, so hurry up," he says, and then adds, "and leave your fucking puppy at home."

I flinch at the anger in his tone and glance at Chase, who looks pretty smug until I tell Roman I'm coming. Then Chase looks like he just swallowed a wasp. Or a swarm of them.

"I have to go get that last guy with Roman. He found him all by himself," I say, as I slip on my shoes and jacket.

"Great. I'd love to," Chase replies, and I stand up straight to look at him.

"Chase...he told me not to bring you."

"Course he did, Haze. Let's go."

Then he's ushering me out the door, and I find myself wondering how many casualties will occur tonight.

CHAPTER 19

Roman glares as we approach. "Thought I told you to leave the dead weight behind," Roman says as we approach the car. It's a jeep with blacked-out windows, and I take a moment to be thankful that I won't be knocked unconscious as I get into it. I hope.

"Play nice, boys. This doesn't have to be so hostile," I say, but they ignore me, choosing instead to glare each other to death.

"Where she goes, I go. I'm permanent," Chase says.

"Yeah, like herpes."

Chase steps forward, Roman steps forward, and I step between them.

"This is getting boring. Grow up." I shove at both their chests, but neither of them moves an inch. Damn.

I look up at Roman, who finally glances down at me. I notice for the first time that he's not in a suit. He's still wearing slacks and a shirt, but they're more casual, and – sans jacket – he looks almost normal. He watches me check him out and smirks.

"The car's gonna be a little crowded, but I don't mind an audience if you want to go again," Roman says, and my cheeks heat. Chase tries to push forward, but I keep my palm planted on his chest.

"Get in the car," I say, choosing to ignore Roman's jab. It wasn't for my benefit anyway.

Roman pulls the back door open and motions dramatically with the sweep of his arm for Chase and me to climb in. The man in the driver's seat is Trevor, Roman's right-hand man. He turns and nods in my direction. I nod back. Guilt flares in my chest as I realise that I gave Gideon his name. If he winds up dead, it's going to be because of me.

"What's up, man?" he says to Chase, who returns the sentiment. Roman eventually climbs in himself, his head buried in his phone as he types away. There's an awkward tension in the car, and just when I'm really starting to regret getting in, Roman speaks.

"Alright. You ready for some fun?" he asks, turning to look at me. He says *fun*, but the look on his face is worrying. He looks downright evil as he smirks at me from the front seat, and there's mischief glinting in his eyes.

"What kind of fun?" I ask, trepidation in my voice.

"The usual, baby. Some breaking and entering, kidnapping, and if you're lucky, a little grievous bodily harm."

He's in an oddly playful mood considering that on the phone a moment ago, he sounded like an angry bear. It's...charming? Weird? Fuck. Sexy. It's sexy.

"Great," says Chase beside me. "You're going to murder someone in front of her again. Real nice."

"I said grievous bodily harm. You're the only one who mentioned murder. Something on your mind, champ?"

Roman replies, and I can practically see the response on Chase's face, so I jump in.

"Who are we kidnapping, and where did you find him? I haven't even looked at his file yet."

"I'll explain on the way. Let's take a nice little trip to Golden City."

Chase and I glance at each other as the car starts and we get going.

"Explain."

"What do you know about the original founders of the Island?" Roman asks, and Chase and I share another look.

"Not much. A group of rich pricks who were sick of sharing the same air as the poor."

"Bunch of entitled elitist dicks," Trevor chimes in, earning a noise of agreement from all of us.

"Right. Exactly. Well, most of them are dead now – all of them, actually. They kept it quiet, handing the reins on to their children, who now make up our government. That may not be common knowledge. They want people to think it's fair, but it's nepotism through and through," Roman explains.

"What's this little history lesson got to do with anything?" Chase asks.

"Glad you asked, *Jace.* The man in charge of import and export is named Charlie Knox. He has final say over what comes into the island and what goes out. I've got a way around that, but he's still an issue. Wanna know why?" Roman asks.

"Obviously," I say, bored out of my mind.

"Charlie Knox, unbeknownst to the entire Island, except for a select few – including me – is our very own Gideon Bennet's little cousin."

The silence in the car after the revelation is so long that Roman turns in his seat to see if we heard him.

"You're joking, right?" I ask, staring between Roman's odd expression of joy and Chase's look of bewilderment.

"Not even a little. The people running this shit show have no idea that it's not really Charlie running the show – it's Gideon. Gideon, via Charlie, has been working his way into the government, moving up the ranks. It's only a matter of time before Gideon does what he really wants." There's an ominous vibe to his words, and I almost don't want to ask what that is.

Thankfully, I don't have to.

"Which is?" Chase asks.

"Power. Control. Over the whole goddamn island. You wanted to know why I haven't made a move yet? This is why. I've been waiting for the whole story. Now that I've got it, I'm going to set this whole goddamn island on fire. I just need little Charlie to answer some questions."

My mind is reeling. How is it that no one knows this? How has nobody figured it out? It makes sense how Gideon almost has a monopoly on getting contraband onto the island. Why he's so pissed that he doesn't know how Roman is getting his shipments in. It's because he *should* know. He's in charge, and Roman has been flying under his radar without his knowledge. It's why he can't just kill Roman; he needs to know how he's doing it.

Gideon needs me to find the hole in his system before he takes Roman out. Little things begin to take shape, pieces of information and conversation that didn't make sense before do now. His constant pressure to get information on all of Roman's contacts; his frustration at finding shipments that appear unimportant.

Roman has one up on Gideon, and he hates it. He also can't tell anyone, or he loses his power.

A smile takes over my face as I think about how this could work to my advantage. I can keep giving him information, but it doesn't have to be true. He won't know any different, and if I'm clever, I can send him on a wild goose chase that buys me some time. It also means I can assuage my guilt about ratting on Roman. At least until I can sort out my feelings for him. Until then, I can give little pieces of true intel and some false intel and confuse the shit out of Gideon. If it works, it may buy me enough time for Roman to kill him so I can get my father back.

That begs the question – do I trust Roman? Could I tell him the truth? It seems so simple, so easy to just come clean. Tell him everything and work together, for real, to take Gideon down.

It seems simple, but it isn't. Roman could kill me for fucking with him, to begin with. He could punish me by killing Gideon and my father too. Do I trust him? No.

Could I trust him? That remains to be seen.

△△△

The rest of the drive passes with little conversation. At

least involving Chase and me. Roman and Trevor chat in the front, discussing money, shipments, and details about the legit businesses Roman owns. I take mental note of some of the things they say, but now that I've decided to feed Gideon false information, I don't pay too much attention.

Instead, I stare out the window and watch as the scenes go from the normal sights of Second to the dreary, miserable sight of Purgatory. We're heading towards East River Bridge, which means wherever we're heading is on the east of Golden City. Which makes sense seeing as that's where the docks are – it seems appropriate that we would find Charlie close to them.

Chase nudges me as we begin to cross over the nearly empty bridge. He holds out a chocolate bar, my favourite, and I grin at him.

"How'd you know I was hungry?" I ask, smiling as I take the bar from him.

"We've made this drive together enough times for me to notice you always get peckish by the time we make it to the bridge. It's why the glove box in my car is full of snacks."

"For me?" I ask, staring over at him with a small smile. His cheeks redden slightly, and he nods.

"Of course. I always carry random snacks in my pocket. You usually forget to eat. I think I accidentally trained you to be hungry at the sight of the bridge." His eyes dart over my face, bobbing between my two eyes.

"Thank you, I think…" I say, honestly shocked. There are so many little things Chase does and has always done that I think I've started to take for granted.

Him handing me snacks randomly has become so routine that I barely notice anymore. The stash of my favourite snacks in his car – I always just assumed were his. I'm lost in my thoughts, and maybe in Chase's eyes, when Roman interrupts. Only then do I notice the silence in the car.

"How sweet," he says, and his eyes meet mine in the rear-view mirror.

Roman looks angry, and I have no idea why. He glares at me before looking away. My face heats. Chase watches the entire exchange, a sigh falling from his lips before he, too, takes his eyes to the window.

Trevor must feel the sudden tension in the car because not five seconds later, he coughs awkwardly before pointing to the radio. "Music, anyone?"

△△△

By the time the car stops, I'm more than ready to get out. We pull up at a building close to the docks. It's a huge apartment building, and it's only when I see it that I realise I've been here before.

"Holy shit," I say, and then I start to laugh. You cannot make this shit up.

"What?" Chase asks, and I shake my head.

"Charlie Knox is fucking his best friend's seventeen-year-old daughter."

I can't believe I forgot. His wife hired me to find out who he was sleeping with, and I had. How did I not remember the instant I heard his name? I had spent three whole weeks watching his every move just a while ago.

"Oh man, I remember that. That was him?" Chase asks, and I nod enthusiastically. Roman turns to look at me from the front seat.

"Nice. That actually might come in handy as leverage. See, I knew I wanted you for a reason." He winks, and I have to look away. Why did he have to phrase it like that?

"Alright, this is how this is going to go…" Roman begins, and we listen as he goes over the plan in great detail.

"You have got to be kidding me," I deadpan when he's finished.

"It's the best way to get in without making a scene. We've only got a small window of time, so…" Roman thrusts a bag into my hand, and I almost growl when I open it.

"Fuck me." I sigh.

Getting changed in the back of a car while three men wait outside of it is not an easy feat. I pull off my clothes as quickly as I can, grumbling to myself as I do. I pull on the expensive, gorgeous, and minuscule dress. It barely covers my ass, and it's so low cut it's practically daring my boobs to jump out. I have to remove my bra to make extra space for them.

Once the dress is on, I slip into the eight-inch heels Roman has provided. I take a moment to wonder how he knows my size and then dismiss it completely. I don't want to know. I check myself quickly on my phone camera; without makeup, there's not much to be done about my face, but I do have some lipstick and mascara in my purse. With the little amount of makeup I already have on, it will have to do.

I touch up my mascara, add a dramatic red lip, and tousle my hair. Looking myself over, I know I've done the best I could under the circumstances.

Besides, Roman wants me to play a hooker, not a beauty queen. I sigh again as I slip out of the car. When the door shuts, all three men turn. I almost laugh at their reaction. Trevor's eyebrows shoot up to his hairline as he nods approvingly. Chase's mouth falls open slightly as his fists tighten at his sides. His eyes land on my boobs, and he promptly darts his tongue out to lick his lip. Roman smirks, eyes like molten lava as they take in every inch of my body.

He lifts his hand and spins his finger, inviting me to turn around. I grumble but do as I'm told. This is an absolutely ridiculous and sexist plan. I seriously would not be doing this...if I didn't think it would work. Men are notoriously stupid and predictable. If I tell the doorman Gideon sent me as a gift for Charlie, in this dress, he'll know what's up and let me in. He won't be able to refuse my bodyguards, either. Not if he's straight anyway.

I'm turning with a serious scowl on my face, which Roman seems to enjoy. "You're going to have to remove the underwear. We can see it through the dress," he says.

I know he's baiting me, trying to piss me off, and

it's working. So, instead of allowing myself to be humiliated by him, I cock my head to the side and eye him with a challenge.

"Ok," I say sweetly, and right there, in the parking lot, I use one hand to lean on the car and shove the other under the tight dress. I tug one side of my underwear and then the other until they fall and pool around my feet. I tug the dress down as far as it will go and then reach down to step out of my underwear. I take a moment to thank God for the fact I chose to wear a black lace thong.

I pick the underwear up, keeping my eyes locked on Roman's. His eyes are blazing with heat, his jaw is tight as he clenches it, his eyes riveted to between my legs. He can't see a thing, but he knows I'm naked under this dress now. I smirk at him before I turn to Chase, who looks absolutely stunned.

I don't allow myself to feel embarrassed. A breathy "fuck" falls from Chase's lips as I hold my hand with my underwear in it out to him. Chase has seen my underwear so many times. He's always at my place, and I'm not always the cleanest, so handing them to him seems like the safest option.

"Hold these?" I ask, but before he can grab them, Roman's hand closes around my wrist.

"Absolutely fucking not," he says and squeezes my wrist until I'm forced to loosen my fingers and drop my panties into his other hand.

His eyes bore into mine, his hand burning my skin where it holds my wrist. Roman shoves my panties into his pocket, and releases me.

"Let's go," he says, and with a final glare in my direction, he walks off toward the building.

I smirk at his back as he goes, finally feeling like I won a round.

The plan is simple – pretend I'm a hooker that Gideon hired for his little cousin as a surprise. If I had any faith in the intelligence of the human male, it vanishes when the plan goes off without a hitch. The doorman took a giant eyeful of my boobs, heard the word Gideon, and waved me and my two 'security' right on in. Even put in the direct code for the elevator that would take us to Charlie's place.

Trevor is our eyes outside, waiting to inform us of Charlie's impending arrival. The apartment is one of the fanciest things I've ever seen. It's a minimalist design, open, spacious, and airy. The only colours are beige and white, and if I didn't know any better, I would say it was just for show.

Chase lets out a low whistle as he looks at the size of the TV and sound system. Roman walks off, gun in hand, as he sweeps the area to make sure no one is here. I take my time wandering around, seeing if I can find anything that might prove useful. Chase finds a wad of cash tucked into a vase, and his eyes flick up to mine. He shoves the money into his pocket with a wink in my direction.

"I didn't bring you here to loot the place," Roman says, walking back into the room once he's satisfied it's empty.

"No, you brought me here to be an accomplice to murder," Chase replies.

"I didn't bring you here. I brought her. You, I could have done without. Once again, you're the only one bringing up murder."

"Only because I can't stop thinking about the million ways I want murder *you*," Chase spits, and I watch in morbid fascination as they square up to each other. I consider stepping in, but I don't recall signing up to be a referee.

"You know what I can't stop thinking about?" Roman asks, tilting his head to the side in a taunting fashion. "The fact that she was so wet after I made her come that I could feel it through both our clothes."

"You think you're special, Roman? She's been in love with me for years."

"And yet, I'm the one who knows what sounds she makes when she's—"

"You think you've got some kind of claim over her? You've known her for five minutes. We have history you can't even begin to touch on."

"You may have history, but you've got no chance for a future. Not anymore," Roman's cruel smirk and the quick flash of hurt on Chase's face are enough to snap me out of my shocked daze.

"Are you both done?" I snap, and both heads turn to me so quickly that it's obvious they forgot I was in the room.

While they were busy punching each other in the balls and measuring the size of their dicks, they forgot that the woman they were fighting over was right beside them. They both look so guilty, eyes wide in shock as they realise they just said all that right in front of me.

"I'm right here!" I glare at them both. "How fucking dare you talk about me like I'm an inanimate object? I am a person. Neither of you fucking own me, so how about you stop fighting over me like I'm fucking livestock. It's disgusting." I watch with joy as both their mouths open and close over and over.

"Now," I continue, "we've got a fucking job to do. Are you ready to behave like fucking adults and not two adolescent boys?"

Roman's phone beeps just in time; Trevor informs us that Charlie is on his way up. The two men look sheepishly at me before glaring at each other. They each walk away to take their positions, and I take mine.

Let the show begin.

CHAPTER 20

The man who walks through the door is definitely the same guy from my old investigation. Divorce seems to suit him, though, because he sure as hell looks better than the last time I saw him. His eyes are so glued to his phone that he doesn't see me, settled on his couch, one leg crossed over the other, my elbow resting on the back of the chair so my hand can support my head. I cough – very femininely, might I add – to get his attention, and his eyes flicker up in surprise.

"Hello, you," I say in the most seductive voice I can manage. I should probably feel repulsed by this, but it's kind of fun.

"Who are you?" Charlie eyes me suspiciously, his hand clenching around his phone.

"Don't worry, baby. Gideon sent me. He said I'm your gift." And just like that, I've got him.

His body relaxes, both hands falling down by his sides as he looks me over. Idiot. But I do love when men underestimate me.

"Gideon does send the best gifts. I have some things to do…" I level him with a pouty look. "But I guess it can wait." He moves towards me, so I uncross my legs and stand, the heels putting us at about the same height.

"You look stressed," I purr into his ear as I grab his shoulder and shove him onto the sofa. "Let me help you relax."

I drop to my knees before him as he mutters his thanks and tells me how sexy I am. I nod and smile as I undress him. I may appear eager to get him naked, but really I just want to make sure he's unarmed. His fingers run over my neck and shoulders, and I have to resist the urge to grimace at how cold his hands are. I may enjoy the undercover bit, but being fondled by cold hands is not fun.

After what feels like an eternity of dodging his hands – and lips – I finally have him stripped down to just his briefs. He has no weapons on him, which means my part of the plan is finally almost over. Very slowly, I push him back into the chair so he's almost lying down, and then as sexily as I can, I kneel over him, my knees on either side of his thighs. I lean in so that my lips hover right beside his ear, and when I look up, I nod at the two figures hiding in the shadows with a full view of the entire spectacle.

"Are you ready for the main event?" I whisper into Charlie's ear, and he groans in delight, unaware that I'm not part of the show.

His pleasure doesn't last long because, in the next second, Chase is behind me, holding his gun in Charlie's direction, while Roman presses the muzzle right into the back of Charlie's head.

"What the fuck?" he barks and shoves me off him. With the way I'm sitting and the heels I'm wearing, I have no chance of saving myself. I fall backwards, and my ass hits the ground with a thud.

"Ow. Fuck. That hurt, Charlie," I spit as Chase offers his hand to help me up.

"What the fuck is this? Do you know who the fuck I am?" he says, glaring at Chase and me. It's obvious he wants to see who it is that's beside him, but he doesn't risk it.

"I think the better question is, do you know who the fuck *I* am?" Roman grabs the hair on top of Charlie's head and yanks it back until Charlie is staring at him upside down.

He whimpers a little at the pain, but it's when he spots Roman that he really panics. His breath comes more rapid, and little beads of sweat dot his face.

"Ah, so you do know who I am. Brilliant. I hate introductions." Roman walks slowly around the sofa, moving to stand in front of Charlie. "I suppose you know why I'm here then."

"Gideon is going to skin you alive, you piece of shit," Charlie says, and I would give him props for being brave if his hands weren't shaking and he wasn't sitting there in nothing but his underwear. Sometimes bravery is just stupidity in disguise.

"Gideon is going to be dust in the fucking wind by the time I'm finished with him. You give me what I want, and I might let you live. You can keep your cushy little job without him breathing down your neck."

"He'll kill me if you don't."

This is true. If Charlie tells us all his secrets, and we don't kill him, Gideon will find out. Nothing like this can stay secret for long. And while Roman might make his death generally quick and painless, Gideon will boil him alive just for the thrill of it.

"Maybe. It's a risk you have to take. I'm not going to kill you, Charlie, but if you don't tell me what I want to know, I'm going to tell Carl Lightman, your best friend and business partner, that you've been dicking his underage daughter right under his fucking nose. He'll ruin you, and you can kiss your fancy little life goodbye.

"Then, when you come running to Second, or even Purgatory, I'm going to get word to Gideon that you're a rat, and he'll chop your extremities off while you're still alive and feed them to the sharks while you watch. How does that sound?" Roman says it all so calmly, void of any emotion.

Even I feel a sliver of fear running through my veins. Charlie says nothing, his eyes wild and terrified, and I almost feel bad for him. Sometimes it's difficult to remind myself that there are always casualties in war.

"Or," Roman continues casually like he hasn't just promised this man a fate worse than death, "you can tell me what I want to know, and I'll make sure no one finds out about our little meeting. You'll be under my protection, even from Gideon, and I'll make sure he never has a chance to lay a hand on you." Roman can't promise that. I know it, he knows it, poor Charlie knows it. But given the options he's faced with, it's clear that Charlie doesn't have a choice in the matter.

His face pales, and he swallows audibly. For a moment, I think he'll protest, and I'm worried that I'll have to watch Roman torture the information out of him, but then Charlie sighs. He's resigned himself to the fact that he's fucked either way. His time as a double agent is over, and now he's going to sing like a canary.

"What do you want to know?" he asks, and Romans smiles broadly at him before turning his smile on me. I nod and step closer to Chase. Whatever happens, I've given my approval. There's no turning back.

△△△

An hour later, Charlie is all talked out. Roman has pulled every morsel of information regarding Gideon and the docks from him, and Charlie looks exhausted after storytime. Roman now knows the schedule for Gideon's deliveries and how to identify his ships. He knows where on the dock his deliveries are stored until they're picked up and the codes to Gideon's place. He knows everything.

Hope wells up inside of me as Charlie finishes explaining the layout of Gideon's home, the one I think my father may be being kept in. This could be it. This could be exactly what Roman has been waiting for. If Roman makes a move...I could get my father back. If Roman is able to kill Gideon, this could all be over.

I think it might be time to tell Roman everything and hope to God he remains on my side.

"That's everything?" Roman asks, his eyes boring into Charlie's to make sure he's not lying.

"You know everything I do. I swear." His voice is flat, resigned, like he knows what's coming.

"Alright then." Roman stands, and Charlie watches him. Hope flares bright in his eyes as Roman ignores him, and even Chase and I exchange glances, wondering if Charlie will be left alive after all.

"Walk to your bedroom, Charlie," Roman says, and confusion takes over the man's face.

He stands and very slowly turns his back to us to walk towards the hallway that must lead to his bedroom. Roman glances at me, and I see an apology in his eyes, but he doesn't bother to say it out loud. He raises his gun, and I notice the silencer on the end of it. Roman clicks the safety off, and while it barely makes a sound, Charlie stops anyway.

"Make it quick," he whispers.

"Sorry, man. It's better this way," Roman says.

Then he pulls the trigger. The bullet hits Charlie in the back of the head, and it's obvious he dies instantly. His body folds and hits the floor, and in an instant, blood pools around his head.

Roman stares for a moment before sighing and removing the silencer. He shoves it into his pocket and puts the gun into the back of his pants. When he turns and spots Chase and me staring at him, he quickly wipes the tired, guilty expression from his face. His impassive mask returns, and Chase steps closer to me, his arm slightly in front of my body, almost as if he thinks Roman will make a move to kill us now.

He won't. We're a team. And he likes me.

"Better quickly by me than slowly by Gideon. Plus, he would have run straight to him and told him everything," is all Roman says before he's striding towards the door. He pulls it open and waits for us to walk out ahead of him. Surprisingly enough, Trevor and another man I recognise are outside. I don't know how they got in.

"Take care of it," Roman says to them, and they nod, entering the apartment and closing the door behind him.

We walk from the building in complete silence, and when we get into the car, I don't argue when Roman pulls open the passenger seat for me to slide into. Even Chase wisely keeps his mouth shut. I look back at the building and notice something, my stomach souring as an inkling sets in.

"Where's the doorman?" I ask.

Roman glances at the double doors where the man should be standing. A muscle ticks in his jaw, and when his amber eyes look to mine, I get my answer in the form of guilt splashed across every inch of him.

It clicks then, understanding finally rolling around. Roman really is a monster, and he hates himself for it. It's that guilt, that self-loathing, that causes the final wall around my heart to crumble.

△△△

The drive home is completed in heavy silence. Chase glares holes into the back of Roman's head so aggressively that I can feel it from the passenger seat. Roman watches the road in front of him, his eyes dark, full of monsters. And me? I watch Roman.

I find myself unable to pull my gaze away from the side of his face, uncaring of Chase witnessing it from the back seat. I'm drawn to him. I can't help but study the way his eyebrows pull together, forming a V between them. I can't help but stare at the muscle ticking in his jaw.

I want to reach out and touch him. I want to show him gentleness. I want to let him see my hands, hands that are so different from his. Hands that don't take lives just because. I'm not a tender person, but right now, I want to be. For him. I want to kiss him so his latest memory is of my lips and not the blood spilling around Charlie's head. I want him.

He knows I'm watching. His head turns towards me for a moment, long enough for me to realize he knows exactly what I'm thinking. What I want. His hands grip the steering wheel tighter, squeezing and flexing. The tension in the car skyrockets, and I have to force myself to look away.

Squeezing my thighs together does very little to ease the ache that's building between them. It's not the time or the place, and I shove my guilt aside for the fact that Chase remains sitting quietly behind us. I force myself to watch the buildings around me blur as we drive, until finally, we pull up outside of our apartment building. Chase wastes no time unbuckling his seatbelt and slipping from the car. He leans in through his open door, waiting for me to move.

"Are you coming?" he asks.

My eyes flit between the two men. Roman stares

forward impassively. I want him to tell me not to. To ask me to stay. I want him to look at me, to let me see that he's feeling even a fraction of what I am.

He doesn't.

I sigh, turning to grab the door handle. Before I can get the door open, his hand shoots out and grips my forearm. My skin ignites at the contact, and I suck in a sharp breath. His eyes bore into me, and I don't need the words. I remove my fingers from the handle.

"I'll be back later, Chase," I say, barely able to look at him.

"Yeah, thought as much."

The door slams, but Roman still hasn't removed his hand from my arm. Instead, he slides it down until his strong fingers fit between mine. I glance down at our hands, my stomach flipping at the minuscule gesture. We share one last silent look, and then he lets go of my hand and starts to drive.

CHAPTER 21

Walking into the apartment is a strange experience. "I had no idea you lived here," I tell him. I knew there was space above his office, but I didn't expect him to live in it. I notice that the place is bare. It's not much, not as expensive looking as his office. Small but warm somehow, cosy despite it being built inside a warehouse.

"I had it added when I renovated the building because I was sick of going home to a big empty house. I missed Amelia more when I was surrounded by her absence." He pulls a bottle of water from the fridge and takes a large sip. My heart breaks every time he mentions Amelia, and guilt freezes the blood in my veins as I watch him.

"Why did I imagine you sitting in a black leather chair drinking expensive whiskey from a tumbler?" I ask as he sinks onto the light grey couch.

"Why are you imagining me at all?" he asks, his eyes burning with the same fire as they did in the car the other day.

I sit on the opposite end of the couch, facing him. There's less than a foot of space between us. That's too much.

"I don't drink," he finally says, and I frown.

"At all?" I ask.

"My sister was an addict. I usually avoid addictive things." His comment is full of innuendo, and my blood heats at the thought that he might be talking about me.

"Usually?"

"Yes. Usually. Why are you here, Lara?"

I shift in my seat. The tone of his voice is doing things I never thought possible. I am overheating. The look in his eyes is sending me over.

"You brought me here."

"You wanted me to." He leaves his bottle on the small table beside him and leans back, legs spread, arms resting on the back of the chair.

"I did."

"Why?" he asks.

I say nothing, unable to voice it. Unable to tell him what I'm thinking, what I want. I've barely been able to admit it to myself.

"Come here," he says, and while it usually irks me to be commanded to do anything, I find myself rising from my seat almost on autopilot. I stop before him, his broad thighs encasing mine.

"Closer."

Gathering all my courage, I lift one knee and place it on the couch beside him, then do the same with the other. Then I'm straddling him. Feeling everything. *Everything.* My heart races as he looks at me curiously, eyes searching every inch of my face.

"Are you sure you want this?" he asks, but I can barely hear him.

All I can think about is the feel of his hands as he runs them up the outside of my thigh before grabbing a fistful of my ass. I can't help the moan that slips from my mouth as he uses his hands on my ass to grind me down onto him.

"Say yes." He's demanding, but I still can't form words. There are explosions going off in so many different parts of my body. Instead of answering, I do the only thing that makes sense. I kiss him.

He immediately groans into my mouth, his hands gripping me tightly as we continue to move against each other. Roman's tongue slides with mine. It feels good. So good. I can't breathe. My hands take their rightful place in his hair, gripping it tightly enough to pull another groan of pleasure out of him. I'm almost embarrassed at the vigour with which I'm attacking him. I'm desperate. Clingy. Gripping and pulling and scratching at whatever parts of him I can get my hands on.

Roman does the same. His hands slip from my ass to the back of my neck and back to my ass again. His lips and his teeth and his tongue attack my mouth, my neck. He kisses me like a man out of control – and he is. We both are. Nothing has ever felt this good in the history of time.

In the heat of the moment, I had forgotten about my lack of underwear. When his hands slide up my thighs again and under the dress, pushing it up over my ass, he freezes. Completely. Roman's head pulls away from me and his eyes meet mine, alight with lust. I watch as he inhales deeply before his eyes drop to where I sit on his lap. At the first glimpse of me sans underwear, he releases the giant breath he had taken.

"Fuck." It comes out of his mouth as a whisper, a plea. "You have no idea what I want to do to you."

"So show me."

Our eyes connect and stay connected as he manoeuvres us in one swift movement. Before I know it, my back is on the couch, and Roman looms over me, looking every bit the dangerous man that he is.

"Last chance to change your mind," he says, staring intently. "Once I start with you, I don't think I'll be able to stop."

My voice is barely a whisper as I lift my hips, searching for the friction that my body is begging for. "Then don't."

He doesn't hesitate. One minute he's there, and the next, he's gone. Before I can even look for him, I feel him. The stubble on his face tickles the inside of my thighs, and the first touch of his tongue to my centre sends me spiralling. I gasp, fisting his hair and jerking my hips. I am lost, but it feels like I've finally been found. It's been so long since I've had this, so long since I've felt this way, if I ever have. It has only been moments, and already Roman has ruined me for anybody else.

"Give it to me, Lara. Now. Please," he rasps from his position, barely removing his mouth from me and the vibrations send more waves of pleasure through my entire body. I'm moaning, begging, and almost crying at how good it feels. I'm right there already, climbing higher and higher as he licks and sucks and groans against me. "Fucking now, Lara," he growls, and then his fingers are there, and I detonate. I feel it everywhere.

"Roman..."

My entire body vibrates with sheer bliss, and I am boneless. He doesn't stop until he rides out every last wave. Until my moans slow into whispers, and my breath is nothing but pants. I melt into the sofa, unable to move for a moment. Roman rises to his knees, and I almost come all over again when he slips his fingers into his mouth.

"I've been dreaming of how you would taste. Nothing compares," he says, and I smile lazily up at him. "Don't get too comfortable. I'm not finished with you yet."

Roman moves to stand above me, unbuttoning his shirtsleeves and then his collar so slowly it feels like a strip tease. My stare follows the path of his hands as he goes button to button, my mouth salivating at the glimpses of his chest. His abs. The V that disappears into his trousers. My eyes dip south, below his waistband, and they widen. He looks like he's about to burst out of them.

"That looks painful," I say, nodding at his erection as he slips out of his shirt.

"It aches," he says mournfully, unzipping his trousers and pushing them down. "Can you help me with that?"

My pulse races. His eyes are pleading, begging, but only because he knows it's turning me on.

"Make me feel good, baby," he demands, grabbing my

hand and placing it where his boxers cover his dick. He groans when I wrap my fingers around him through the material.

"Please, Lara," he begs, and I don't think he's teasing now.

I sit up and use the band of his boxers to drag him closer. With our eyes locked together, I pull them down then look down to watch as he springs free.

Fuck. It's – *he's* – huge.

Roman's hand reaches out to caress my jaw, softly. His touch is so gentle, his eyes so open, honest, and needy. I lean my face into his hand and turn my head to kiss his palm. Roman looks lost as he watches me, confusion and lust and something else swirling in his brilliant eyes. He closes them briefly before he opens them again, and then they're burning. For me.

"I need you. Now."

Then his hand slips to the back of my head, and he's pulling me towards him. I open my mouth eagerly and take him in. He groans at the contact, and the sound sends a thrill through me. I use my tongue to tease him, but his patience is lost. He uses his hands on the back of my head to control me. So I do what I can. I suck.

"God, yes."

I love how vocal he is. How heavy his breath is coming. I suck him for a few minutes, feeling like a Goddess every time he groans.

"Shit. Fuck. Stop." He grips my hair at the back of my head and then yanks me up. "There's no way I'm coming anywhere but inside of you," he says, and I nod enthusiastically. His hands grips the bottom of my dress and pulls it off, and then we're both completely naked.

"Christ. You're breath-taking."

Then his mouth is on mine, and I'm falling backwards onto the couch. He falls with me but keeps from crushing me with a hand on the back of the sofa. His tongue is in my mouth, and it's almost as difficult to think now as it was when he was between my legs. He kisses a path down to my breasts, and then he lavishes them. I cry out as he bites my nipple, my hips jerking, searching for him.

"Roman, please. I need you."

"You have no idea how long I've wanted to hear you say that."

"How long?" I ask.

"Since you broke into my building."

He reaches between us to position himself. He rubs his dick against my clit over and over until I'm desperate. *Desperate* for him. "Please."

He gives me what I want. The first thrust inside of me has us both crying out. His head falls into my shoulder, and he pauses. I can't stop, though. I move my hips needing to feel him. Needing him.

"Fuck. I'm sorry. I'm gonna fuck you hard and fast. I'll make up for it next time. I have no patience right now."

His words send a thrill through me, as does the sight of him when he kneels up and lifts my ass off the sofa so only my upper back remains down. Roman holds my hips as my calves rest over his forearms.

Then he fucks me. His thrusts are exactly like he said they would be – hard and fast. His eyes take turns staring at the place where we're joined and into my eyes.

The only sounds are the slapping of our skin and both of our mumbled words. Most of them incoherent. He fucks me with skills I don't want to think about, and every thrust gets me closer and closer.

"Tell me you're close," he says, and I nod. Over and over again. Fuck I can't stop nodding.

"Fucking come then," he demands, and I couldn't stop it if I tried. I come. "Say my fucking name," he says, and it spills from my lips like a prayer.

"Roman."

"Fuck. Fuck..." It's a hoarse shout as he slams into me once, twice, three more times. Then he stills. "Fuuuuucking Lara."

He falls down onto me, and our chests are soaked with sweat. I laugh softly as he peppers little kisses into the side of my neck, sending shivers down my spine.

"My God," he mutters, along with a million other things I cannot hear.

I'm liquid. My body is in another dimension, and my soul has left the building. I close my eyes as he whispers gentle praises in my ear, letting my fingers run through his hair.

The last thought I have before I fall asleep nestled under Roman's warm body is that no matter what, I can't let anything happen to him. I don't know what this is between us, but I want to find out.

I have to keep him safe. I have to find a way to keep us all safe.

△△△

I wake up in a bed that isn't mine, surrounded by the smell of him. His heavy arm is draped over my waist, and his breath tickles the back of my neck. I turn slowly to face him, and I'm awed by how peaceful he looks in his sleep. His black eyelashes are so long, fanning his cheeks. I want to reach out and touch him, but I don't want to disturb this moment. I can't imagine he sleeps much, and looking at him now, I realise I wouldn't mind watching him sleep forever. I don't get the chance, though.

"Stop staring at me, creeper." His voice is groggy with sleep, deep and scratchy – and I like it.

"I can't help it. You're so pretty."

He opens one eye and raises an eyebrow, clearly unimpressed with being called pretty. I giggle, then quickly shut my mouth before he calls me out on the absolutely ridiculous sound.

"You know what this means, right?" he asks, and I frown.

"What?"

"You're mine. You don't get to walk out of here and pretend this never happened. You don't get to run back to Jace and play happy family. I told you on our date that

I wanted to keep you, and I meant it. You gave yourself to me, and I intend for you to stay."

"You barely know me," I tell him, "and what if I don't want to be kept?" I ask quietly, but it's lacking all conviction. The words are weak even to my ears. Maybe that's exactly what I want. It's only been a few weeks of knowing him, but... it feels like always.

"You'll just have to grow to like it because I'm keeping you, baby. I'll get to know you." Roman's smile is playful as he pulls me tighter to him, pressing a kiss to the top of my head. His fingers graze my back in slow circles, and I let my eyes close again, enjoying the feeling of it.

"Okay," I whisper into the darkness, giving him permission to keep something I'm not sure he's going to want soon.

"Thank God," is his answering whisper, and then his lips find mine, and I lose myself in him all over again, the rest of the world forgotten as soon as his skin meets mine.

△△△

I wake again the next morning to light streaming in from the window and an empty bed. My palm drifts over the space Roman occupied last night, and I frown when I feel it's cold. As I sit up, my eyes land on his pillow and find a note resting where his head should be. I can't tell if this is the most Roman thing ever or the most *un*-Roman thing ever.

Had to take care of some business. Feel free to hang out here today. If not, here are my car keys. Wherever you decide to go, there's no place I won't find you.

See you soon, baby.

P.S. Jace was looking for you. I told him you were well taken care of.

His keys lay on the pillow where the note had been. Butterflies take flight in my stomach as I read the note again and again. Who is this man, and what has he done with the guy I first met?

I glance down again at the P.S. and barely contain my grin. Jace. Chase. I sigh as I flop back onto the bed. I should have let him know I was okay. Now is not the time to be staying out all night and not letting anyone know. Guilt shoves me from the bed. I search all over for my clothes and am surprised to find them folded on a chair. My heart flutters as I imagine Roman folding them to make my life easier.

I pull open the front door, ready to go home and talk to my team and fix this mess I've gotten myself into. Before I can leave, I stop, jogging back to the bedroom. I reach over and pick up Roman's note, blushing as I smile down at it. *Baby.* God, he's adorable when he wants to be.

With my note safe in the back pocket of my jeans, I walk out of the building and let myself into Roman's car. It dawns on me as I pull out of the parking lot that he just offered me another level of trust that I didn't deserve. Shame clings to my skin for the rest of the ride home.

CHAPTER 22

After I go home to shower and make myself look presentable, I make my way to the office. It's a Monday, so I never can tell who's going to be in the office and who will be out on a case. I'm pleasantly surprised when I walk through the door and find everyone, minus Sophie, inside.

"Oh, good. Everyone's here," I say.

I feel awkward about what I'm getting ready to do. Telling them I'm not working against Roman anymore is going to require an explanation. I'm really not big on telling people things about my personal life, even if these people are my family. People glance up at me from their varying positions, and I smile at the warm greetings. "Emergency meeting, everyone."

Luke and Carey hug me, and I linger in their embraces a moment longer than usual. Andi winks at me from where she sits on the arm of the sofa, her long legs dangling over Eric's lap. I smile at Eric, but the smile he sends back my way isn't his usual. He looks suspicious. Concerned. I look away, automatically searching out Chase, who just hovers outside my office, arms crossed, leaning against the doorframe. He doesn't make a move to come closer, and I don't make him.

"Alright. So…" I had a whole speech planned in my head. What I would tell them, how I would phrase things. But standing in front of them all, I lose the ability to speak, my palms sweating with nerves.

"Any surveillance and taps we have on Roman? End them. Eric, clear my laptop for any and all information I've stored over the last few weeks. From this moment on, Roman is…Roman is on our side."

I don't know what I expected from them, but it was more than confused glances and quiet whispers. I look at Chase, almost afraid of what I'll see, but his face is blank.

"Wait. Are you saying he knows? You told him?" Luke asks, and I let my gaze rest on him.

"No," I say. *But I just might.* "I haven't told him, but the situation has changed. I think instead of working to pit Roman and Gideon against each other, we should focus on helping Roman remove Gideon from the equation. Gideon is the real enemy here. I should have known that from the start."

Chase snorts from his spot by the door, and I frown at him. He knows where we stand. We had an argument, and he knows I'm not going there with him, so why is he still acting like this? He said we were *fine*. I open my mouth to ask him, but Eric speaks before I get a chance.

"Why has the situation changed?" he asks, but from the way he's looking at me, I can tell he somehow already knows. I look at Andi, who gives me a wide-eyed look before shrugging.

"I've just…the time I've spent with Roman? He doesn't deserve to die. I'm not saying he's perfect, but there's a lot that we don't know about him—"

"Exactly. You know almost nothing about him. You're going to trust him now? With your dad's life?" I'm a little shocked at Eric's outburst, and I can tell by looking at him that there's more he's got to say, but thankfully, he remains quiet.

"I have to agree with the kid, Lar," Luke says, looking between the two of us. "Would it not make the most sense to take them both out at once? Like you said before, let them destroy each other. If Gideon was to find out..." he trails off, but I don't need him to finish the sentence.

I know in my own head that it doesn't make sense. That it seems like I'm taking a very big risk; basically, taking my father's life out of my hands and putting it into Roman's. Eric is right; I barely know him. But I can't deny that what I do know about him is enough to believe he doesn't deserve to die. Unless he's harbouring some truly evil secrets, but I doubt it. There's something about him. Something about the way he is, the way he makes me feel that tells me I can trust him. He's important to me, now more than ever, whether I want him to be or not.

"Look. I know it sounds crazy. I know it seems like I'm just playing chicken with my father's life, but I'm not. Roman is not a bad guy. He isn't. He saved a little girl's life in Purgatory. Covered up the fact that she killed the man who tried to rape her by implicating himself. He's...he's...I won't say he's a good person. He's done some terrible things, but never at the expense of innocent people." I pause, looking around at everyone, including Chase, who's listening but staring at the ceiling above my head. "I wouldn't do this if I didn't know in my gut it was the right thing. Roman can kill Gideon. We can get my father back, and who knows... maybe Roman can make some changes in Purgatory without Gideon in the way."

Luke studies me, his eyes stuck on my face, thoughts so loud in his head I can practically hear them. Carey's looking at Luke, waiting to see what his partner decides so he knows whether to crack a joke or get annoyed. Eric is looking at me like there's something he needs to say but won't. Andi is winking at me dramatically; her female intuition and her bearing witness to my confession on Thursday means she knows exactly what has changed my mind.

To my surprise, it's Chase who speaks. His voice is sombre, serious. He still doesn't look at me, only at the others in the room. "She hasn't let us down yet, has she? It's her dad. She would never risk his life for something unless she thought it would work. If she says this is the way it's going to be, then this is the way it's going to be."

He finally lets his eyes reach mine, and so much passes between us, none of which I get to focus on because he turns and lets himself into my office. The sound of something smashing follows the slam of the door, and Eric's narrowed eyes meet mine, giving me a look that says, *"Look what you've done."*

"Alright then," Luke finally says, standing. "I trust you. I'll focus on Gideon. I hope you know what you're doing, sweetheart."

He continues to stare at me for a moment, opening his mouth like he has something to say, but he only shakes his head, walking out of the room and into the kitchen.

I don't know if that was disappointment or something else on his face. Luke had always supported me one hundred percent, but he's also my dad's longest friend. This has been hard for him too.

"Thank God!" Carey says, his whole body deflating. "I really thought he was gonna say he didn't want to do it your way for a minute there. The tension in here was," he fans himself dramatically, "whew." He lifts his coffee cup to his mouth and takes a long sip as he and I both wait for Eric to speak.

"Your dad dated my mom a long time ago," he finally says, "but he was the only man who ever made me feel like I had a dad. You made it feel like I had a sister."

My heart slams painfully against my chest. I don't dare speak yet; he looks like he's not near finished. "I thought you were both dead the day Gideon took you. I've never wanted to murder someone more in my life. If you say Roman can get your dad back and kill Gideon, fine. But I'd feel a lot better about it if this little talk didn't come right after you slept with him."

My mouth falls open, and my face flames while he continues. "I don't think you'd ever let personal feelings get in the way of saving your dad. I just…I hope you're right about Roman. We hunt men like him. You taught me to hunt men like him." He sighs heavily before letting a hand scrub down his face.

"Eric, I—" I start, but I don't know what to say. Eventually, he stops waiting and walks off towards his closet. Andi is close on his heels, but she stops at my shoulder before following him.

"Don't worry. I'll talk to him. I'm pretty sure he was just

rooting for you and Chase. I think…I don't know. I'll talk to him. Later, though, I want every. Single. Detail." She runs off after Eric, and I can't stop the sigh that falls from my mouth as I let myself flop into the first seat I find.

I had almost forgotten Carey was sitting beside me until he turns with his eyebrows raised and says, "You're *fucking* Roman Black?"

△△△

"Hi."

After enduring an entirely too-long conversation with Carey, who wanted every single detail about my situation with Roman, followed by a discussion about our next move, I finally escape to my office once Chase heads home. Roman calling was a surprise, an oddity even. He wants to keep me…what does that even mean? He wants to keep me. The real issue is will *I* be able to keep *him*?

"Hi, yourself. You left." Roman's voice is calm and playful. Light in a way I don't think I've heard before.

"I did. I wasn't a prisoner, was I?"

"No. Although, the idea of tying you to my bed had occurred to me. Leaving you this morning was a lesson in restraint. No pun intended."

I can't help the laugh that bubbles up my throat. When Roman jokes with me, it seems so unnatural. Like seeing a dog wearing shoes.

"Not a chance. If anyone's getting tied up, it's you."

"Hmm..." He goes silent for a moment as if he's pondering the thought. "Okay."

"You'd let me?" I ask quietly. Shocked that he'd let me put him in such a vulnerable position.

"Sweetheart, I'd let you do anything you want to me."

I'm momentarily stunned by his confession and more than a little turned on too. I remain quiet, unsure what to say next.

"Where are you?" he asks, finally breaking the silence.

"I thought you could find me anywhere, Mr. Black. Are your abilities that lacking?"

He huffs out a laugh, and I hear the tell-tale creak of his office chair. The image of him sitting there, spinning from side to side, brings a smile to my face. "You're in your office. You've been there since this morning. You went back to your apartment first, showered, and then went straight over. Wet hair and all."

My fingers reach up to touch the still damp strands of hair that trail over my shoulder. That's not creepy at all. Automatically, my head scans the office, looking for any signs of cameras or listening devices. Roman chuckles at my silence, aware that he's made me uncomfortable.

As I glance around the room, I can't help but wonder if my slight distrust of Roman is simply because I know I'm deceiving him. In the grand scheme of things, Roman has never actually given me a reason not to trust him. He's not overtly forthcoming with information, but I've never caught him in a lie. Maybe I'm just projecting.

"That was creepy. Who's following me?" Trevor probably.

Roman pauses, the silence heavy over the phone. "We haven't talked much about Gideon. What we're doing – it's dangerous." Another pause.

"Part of me wants to lock you up and hide you away until it's all over," I scoff, making sure he knows that would never be an option. "I know you'd never let me. But that part of me is new, this…thing between us, it's new, but it's strong. I feel it. I've been feeling it. I just want you to know that all the wheels are in motion. All the players are in place. It's going to get messy, but I'm going to keep you safe."

"I don't need you to keep me safe," I say, but I can barely hear myself.

"I know. But let me do it anyway."

△△△

Roman didn't come over last night. Shortly after our conversation, he said he had work to do. I wanted to ask what it was, wanted to know where he was going, but I didn't. Couldn't. I didn't want to know anything anymore. I wanted no information that Gideon might want. The less I knew, the less I could give to Gideon if he tortured me for it.

My phone rings when I get home that evening. I know who's calling before I even look. That sick feeling in my stomach is a tell-tale sign.

"Hello," I say, my voice flat, void of any emotion.

"Hello, little hunter. You sound...sad." Gideon almost sounds concerned. Like our relationship going beyond kidnapper and daughter of the kidnapped. Or adult-napped. Abducted. Whatever.

"Not sad. Nauseated. Your phone calls do that to me." I know I shouldn't poke the bear. Not now. Not when I'm crossing him. I should do everything in my power to keep on his good side, but I really don't have it in me. The longer this goes on, the harder it is to keep my cool around him.

"Watch yourself, girl. I've killed people for saying less." A chill runs down my spine. I don't doubt it for a second.

I mumble an apology that tastes like shit in my mouth. Then I wait.

"Well?" he says after I let the silence go on. "Have you nothing to report?"

"No. Honestly, he's been pulling back. He's gone a lot lately." I can tell he isn't pleased through the phone, so I rack my brain for something, anything.

"There's some discord with his men, though. There's been a lot of arguing, shouting. They all seem stressed like something big is coming up that they aren't prepared for. I don't know what yet, but I will soon. It's big, though, whatever it is."

This is all true. I've heard them all arguing, yelling at each other when I'm in the office. Something about a huge shipment and ensuring they do everything right. It's the thing that has Roman constantly working, doing "things" that I don't want to ask about.

"Hmm. You know, I think I might already know what you're talking about. I'm very glad that you've confirmed it, though. I can take precautions now. You know...I think I might have done enough damage to his business. Maybe I should just go ahead and kill hi—"

"No!" I realise my mistake the minute I make it and am left flailing around to find a reason for my outburst. "I-he-he's not hurt that badly. Just the other day, he was telling Trevor, you know, his second in command or whatever, that he's thinking about opening two more bars in Golden and giving Trevor more power."

A lie, obviously, but I need something. "He said he's got some new contact, something about someone new controlling the docks. I didn't want to say anything until I knew for sure but...yeah. If you strike now while things are still good, his whole organisation will live on. You can cut the head off the beast, but another will take its place."

My heart is racing. That was a whole load of shit, and I wouldn't be surprised at all if Gideon saw right through it. The silence on the other end seems to stretch forever, causing my anxiety to spike to new levels.

"You seem eager to ruin him before I kill him. It's interesting." He pauses, and I feel sick to my stomach. "Tell me why. If you lie to me, I'll start removing your father's fingers one by one and force you to listen to his screams."

Shit. Fuck. "I-It's just...I don't trust you." I throw it out there. It's the truth. I can't risk him being able to tell that I'm lying. So I go for honesty, hoping it'll buy me some time. "I don't trust that you'll give me back my dad if everything doesn't go smoothly. I want…I want Roman ruined and d-dead just like you want, but it needs to be executed properly because I don't trust that you won't keep my dad and force me to keep working for you for longer." Please believe me. Please.

After what feels like years, Gideon laughs. A huge booming laugh that honestly frightens the shit out of me. "That does sound like something I'd do, doesn't it? Ha! Yes, indeed. Alright, I'll take my time to ensure there are no hiccups."

"Good," I say, my heart finally returning to its usual beat. "Then, when it's done, I never want to hear from you again.

"Fine," Gideon says, and I know I've pissed him off, but I have no idea how.

"Can I talk to my dad?" I ask, though I already know the answer. He *hmms* for a moment pretending to think. His 'no' is final, and I don't bother trying to change his mind. Roman has a plan. The wheels are in motion; it will all be over soon.

"Lara?"

"Yes?"

"You find out what this big thing is. You've got two days. Then I want to know everything you do. If I find out you've been holding back on me, you won't like the consequences."

It takes me hours to fall asleep, and when I do, I watch my father die over and over again, his screams the new soundtrack for my nightmares.

CHAPTER 23

The knock on my door the next morning surprises me. It's eight a.m. and Roman already texted to say he'd stop by later. I trudge to my door, cranky after a horrible sleep. Surprised is all I feel when I see Chase standing opposite me. He hasn't spoken a word to me since…well…since I chose Roman.

"Is he here?" he asks, peering over my shoulder as if Roman might jump out any second.

"No. You coming in?" I ask, stepping aside for him, but he hesitates. "Chase?" I ask, and he sighs before following me into the kitchen.

I make us coffee and almost cry in relief when I take my first sip. One look at Chase's body language, though, and I know I'm about to cry for an entirely different reason.

"I can't do this anymore. I can't…I…fuck." His whole body looks tight like he's about ready to explode. My own arms come to wrap around my torso, maybe to protect myself from this explosion or to hold myself together while Chase rips me apart.

"Chase, I'm sorry, I—"

"No. Don't. Just let me say this, and then I'm gonna go. You have nothing to apologise for. You told me how you felt. That's it. As much as I wish I could make you love me, I can't—"

"Chase, I—"

"Lara. Please. Don't say you love me. Don't say it, because if you say it, I'm going to want to kiss you. You don't want me to kiss you, but if you say those words, I'm going to try, and I don't think there's any coming back from that. Just let me – God, fuck…this is harder than I thought it would be." He finally looks at me, and I know what's coming.

"When we get your dad back, and when everything is settled down, I'm leaving. I can't work for you, with you, anymore. It's too hard. I can't watch you with him, and I know that's unfair because you owe me nothing, but I can't do it, and I won't. So I'm done. Once everything is settled, I'm out."

My heart cracks right down the middle. I want to beg him to stay. I want to say, *"Please don't leave me, Chase. You're my best friend. I need you. Please."*

But I don't. Instead, I force the tears that are trying to escape to evaporate, and I look at him.

"If that's…if that's what you need. I just want you to be happy."

He smiles at me then, not a real one, not even a big one, but a smile nonetheless. I've never worked a day without him…can't remember a day without him in it.

"I know you do."

Fuck. I lose my fight against the tears.

"Please don't. Don't leave. You're my best friend, Chase. I need you. I don't know how to do this without you beside me. I lo—" I cut myself off. I don't want to hurt him. Tell him something that might make him feel like there's a chance. "I want you here."

He looks torn, but I know Chase. Once his mind is made up, there's no changing it back. He's going to leave. He's going to work somewhere else; he'll probably move out. Then he'll be gone, and I won't have him by my side for the first time in years.

"I'm sorry," he says, and then he stands.

I know he's not leaving yet, but this goodbye somehow feels permanent. I want to hug him; I want to wrap myself around him and make him stay. Go back to when everything was normal and ok. But I just stand there as he brings his cup to the sink and washes it. I stare at his back as he moves the cup to the cupboard. It seems so silly, so starnge, but... but he always leaves it in the sink. It feels oddly... final.

"Chase..." he freezes at the sound of my voice. Turns. Walks towards me slowly.

I take a tiny step forward, then force a tiny step back, bumping lightly into the wall behind me.

Please don't kiss me.

As if he hears my thoughts, he shakes his head, clearing it like that was exactly what he was going to do. Instead, his palms meet my face, his pretty hazel eyes looking down at me.

"I'll always be your best friend. I just need some time to accept that that is all I'll ever be." He leans down, pressing his lips to the top of my head, and I inhale as much of him as I can, only feeling less creepy because I know he's breathing me in too. It's weird, seeing as we'll see each other in the office soon, but we need this. He needs it.

Finally, he lets go, clears his throat, and walks out the door. He leaves, and I'm left wondering how the hell I tried to protect us and ended up losing him anyway. My dad is going to be so mad at me.

When get to the office I tell everyone that we're closing for a while. Things have been so stressful lately, and with them all taking on my cases as well as their own and whatever new stuff has come up, I know they could use the break. Besides, I've got two days before Gideon wants answers, and it's time for me to figure out what to tell Roman. Time for me to woman up.

"A whole week off?" Carey asks. "Paid?"

I roll my eyes. "Yes, paid. Everyone go home and rest. I have a feeling things are about to heat up, and I need you all on your A-game. Hopefully, we'll be getting my dad back."

There are mumbles of agreement as they all pack up their stuff.

"What about digging dirt on Gideon? Finding a way into his fortress?" Eric asks.

"I still want to keep an eye on my dad, so yeah, keep on checking up. But get some rest too and…" I pause. "Take Andi on a date."

Andi's face lights up as she looks at Eric, her excitement visible while Eric's entire face is red as a tomato. He grumbles something I don't hear but has Andi looking at him like he hung the moon. Carey and Luke make plans together. I watch them, and a pang goes through my heart. This is my family. I glance up and watch

Chase as he sits behind the desk in my office, pouring over something. My family.

I watch them all walk out the door a few minutes later, even Chase, who is telling Eric about the house he's thinking of buying, and then I am utterly alone.

I turn off everything I can. Make sure the place is clean so there's no mess to return to. I switch off the lights as I go, then lock the doors. As I make my way towards my car in the parking lot, I can't help but feel like I might never return to the office. Or that if I do, nothing will be the same again.

△△△

Roman's car is nowhere in sight when I pull up outside his building. Trevor and a few other henchmen stand outside.

"Hey," I say as I approach, unsure whether or not I'm supposed to speak to them.

It's strange. I've been here a lot over the past month, and yet, I never really see his people around. At least not as often as I thought, and never without him present.

"There she is," Trevor says with a smile on his face. "Man, Lara. When you took your panties off under that dress, I thought for sure Roman was going to explode." He laughs as he reminds me of the awkward experience.

"Yeah, well, he deserved it. He did make me pretend to be a prostitute." I laugh, glancing awkwardly at the other guys who seem as uncomfortable as I do.

"I bet he had a serious case of blue balls after that." He

laughs again, but I don't really know what to say now, so I stand in the awkward silence for a moment.

"Anyway, uh, is he here? Or will he be?" I ask, praying that he's upstairs and just didn't leave his car here.

"Uh, he's out…solving some problems. Go on up, though. He said to make yourself at home." Trevor moves out of the way so I can get past. I smile and say goodbye to them, then walk to Roman's as quickly as I can without running.

The door is unlocked, which strikes me as odd. Actually, the fact that I'm here at all, alone, is odd. I glance around the room. I could snoop. Everyone snoops, right? Except not everyone was actually spying on the snoopee, so it feels like a betrayal. I don't even want to open a drawer. Not even the fridge.

Instead, I sit down on the sofa and am bombarded with memories of our night here. Heat curls low in my stomach, and I shiver. I'm just taking out my phone to call him when the door opens.

"Oh," he says, looking confused at me sitting on his sofa. Shit, was I not supposed to come here? "I thought for sure you'd be elbows deep in my underwear drawer by now."

I laugh softly, but all I really want to do is kiss his face off.

"Hello," he whispers when we're toe to toe, and kisses me. And kisses me. And kisses me. My knees are weak by the time he pulls back, my heart racing.

"Wow. What was that for?" I ask, settling down onto the chair beside him.

"I missed you." He looks uncomfortable at the thought, eyebrows pulling together comically.

"You saw me, like, yesterday."

He frowns at me then, and I reach to smooth the line between his brows. "Yes, I did. You're becoming a problem."

"Oh dear." I widen my eyes innocently. "I can go if you want." I move to stand, and he grabs me around the waist.

"Stay." His lashes lower, eyes pleading. "Please."

Oh, God. Can humans melt?

Roman's kiss is soft, gentle. His lips just barely touching mine, his tongue sweeping out to taste me, and taste me he does. The kiss changes as he delves deeper into me, and I have no other choice but to hold onto him for dear life.

I could kiss him forever. The thought startles me, and I pull away to gather myself. That was…intense.

"Are you hungry? 'Cause I'm starving," I say, and he gives me a quizzical look, one of those dark eyebrows rising.

He looks like he wants to ask what just happened but stops himself. Instead, he tells me he knows just the place and goes to order us some food.

At least twenty times during the evening, I open my mouth, prepared to come clean. I have to tell him. I can't keep it in anymore, not when things are progressing this way. This fast. I try, I really do, but every time I try to say the words, I freeze.

How do I do it? How am I supposed to tell him this whole thing was a lie from the beginning and expect him to believe that it's real now? I've already broken his trust, and Roman does not seem like the type to make the same mistake twice.

I'm still deep in my thoughts after we eat. All night, Roman has refrained from asking me what's wrong, though I can tell it's bothering him. He looks at me now, and I know it's coming.

"What's going on? Are you regretting this?"

Shame washes over me when I see the almost worried look on his face. It's not an expression I ever thought I'd see on him, and it cuts me up.

"I-Roman...No, I'm not regretting this. I want to be here. I just...It's..." I have to tell him. Sooner or later, I have to find a way to get Gideon to let my dad go before we make our move, but how am I supposed to explain that to Roman? Telling him after everything is over is the worst possible thing that I can do.

"Look, it's about my dad...he...well—"

"He would hate me?" Roman says, and I rear back in shock. "That's what you're thinking, isn't it? I mean, if he was alive, he'd hate me. He spent his life putting men like me behind bars, and now..." His face is passive like he's putting on a mask. His eyes search mine as he waits for my input.

"No,"—*I mean yes, he would, but*—"it's not...Roman, you are a good man. You... you're good. My dad would see that. He would have seen that." I stand up and go to him, settling myself onto his lap.

I know Roman hates himself. I can see it in his eyes when he thinks too hard. When he killed Charlie, I watched that look cross his face. Like he'd resigned himself to the fact that that was all he was. A murderer. But I see him, and maybe that makes me foolish. Maybe that makes me one of those girls who thinks they can fix a broken man, but…I don't think Roman needs to be fixed. I think he just needs to be *loved.*

I look him in the eye as my hands clasp the sides of his face, gently running my thumbs over his cheeks. He seems surprised by the gesture for a moment, but then he leans into it. His eyes close as he sighs, and I literally feel all the tension leave his body.

"I see you, Roman. You do bad things, but you're not a bad man. You saved Adeline and avenged your sister. You opened up somewhere nice for people to eat and pretend for a while. I wouldn't be here if I didn't think you deserved it."

His eyes open and search my face, maybe looking for any sign of a lie. I look back, knowing that all he's going to find on my face is evidence of the truth.

"I'm *not* a good man, Lara. I've never claimed to be. I have more blood on my hands than I'll ever be able to wash off. I've done things even I have nightmares about, and I will always do what I have to do to survive."

It's his turn to hold his huge hands against my face. "But if I choose you, and I *have* chosen you, the blood on my hands will never be yours. I will destroy anyone who hurts the people I love. The people I care about. Someone bothers you, Lara, say the word, and I will burn the fucking world down to make it right."

"I believe you," I whisper because it's all I can say. My heart races violently in my chest.

He stares intently for a moment, and then his lips are on mine, brutal in their ministrations. He kisses me like I'm the only thing he has left in the world. Like it's the first time. Like it's the last.

Then he stands, and my legs automatically wrap around him, clinging to him like he is all I have left too. We kiss each other as he walks us to his bed, and at some point, I realise I can't really breathe, but that's okay. He's breathing for me. He steals my breath, then fills me up with him. Kisses me until he consumes me, until I know nothing but the taste and the feel of him.

Before I know it, before I can even process it, I'm naked, and he's between my legs. I fly, I soar. He is everywhere, and he is perfect. Everything in me shifts. Maybe the stars realign. Maybe the whole fucking world explodes. I don't know. All I know is that the way this feels could not be replicated. All I know is the sounds he makes, the sounds I make. The way he touches me. Holds me.

"You are…" I can barely hear him, but *I agree.*

"You have no idea…" *Whatever you say, Roman.*

"God, I can't even…" *Yes, me too.*

"Don't want to stop…" *So don't, ever.*

"Lara. Lara. Lara. Lara. Lara…" *Roman. Roman. Roman. Roman.*

"You own me…" *You fucking own me too.*

I don't know if I say the words out loud or if I just think them, but either way, I know he understands. I know he knows. He rarely stops kissing me, touching me. Right before we both explode, our eyes meet. Lock. His beautiful amber eyes tell me everything. Then we are falling, falling, falling.

When it's over, Roman lays beside me, his front pressed to my back. He kisses my shoulder, the back of my neck. His arm is a welcome weight across my waist as he pulls me in tight to him.

Tomorrow, I will tell him everything. Tomorrow, we can wipe the slate clean and begin again. For now…I close my eyes. Squeeze his hand where it rests under my breasts.

For now, I'll sleep beside him. I'll memorise the way his body feels against mine, just in case it's the last time.

△△△

"Good morning."

I groan as Roman speaks into my ear. I pull the covers up over my face but smile when I hear him chuckle. He pulls them back down enough for me to poke one eye out.

"Hi," I say, but it's muffled by the duvet covering my mouth.

"Hi." He kisses my forehead. "Look. I have to go. Today is…I've got some shit happening today. I'm not kicking you out, but…I'd rather you not be here."

I pull the blankets away from my face and sit up when I realise how serious he is. "Is everything ok?"

A look crosses his face that I can't determine, and an unwelcome bout of anxiety blossoms in my stomach.

"Yes. Fine. You just can't be here. It's not safe. Come on. I'll take you home." He stands and grabs a pile of clothes resting on the chair, then hands them to me with barely a glance. I'm spinning with this sudden mood change. What the fuck is going on? Last night, last night was…

"Roman…What's going on? We have to talk. I need to—"

He cuts me off, his impatience getting the better of him, and I rear away from him as he suddenly spins to face me.

"Lara, I'm serious. You cannot be here. We need to go."

Uh? Okay. Fuck this guy.

"Why are you being such a dick? What the fuck is wrong with you?" I stand, shoving my legs into my trousers without even putting on underwear.

"I'm sorry. Sorry. Something big is happening. I can't have you around."

"Can't or won't?" I ask, pulling on my t-shirt, sans bra, and grabbing my shoes.

"Both. I'll pick you up later." He starts to turn but instead leans forward and kisses me. Gently. So at odds with this weird mood that he's in.

Talk about a head spin.

"Forget about it if you're still in a mood," I say, and he smacks my ass lightly as I walk past. Where did playful Roman come from? "You're going to give me whiplash with these little mood shifts."

"I'm a grown man. I'm not in a mood. I'm protecting what's mine," he says – growls, really.

We walk silently out to the car. Him, in stoic, annoyed silence. Me, in utter confusion and, oddly enough, arousal. He's kind of hot when he's protecting what's his.

"What exactly do I need protection from?" I ask as we drive, and he shoots me a sidelong glance, his hands twisting on the steering wheel.

"Nothing you need to worry about."

"You just woke me up and hustled me out of your place like a cheap one-night stand to 'protect' me, and now you're saying I shouldn't worry?"

"Precisely."

I glare at him, throwing all the faux annoyance I can muster into the look. Doesn't matter, though. He barely pulls his eyes off the road.

When we make it to my building, he finally looks at me. His mask is on. Hardly any emotion in his handsome eyes, a blank slate across his face. I wonder if it will always be like this. Me wondering which Roman I'm going to get that day.

"I don't need you to protect me," I tell him, remembering myself saying the same thing the other night.

He smiles slightly and reaches over, his hand wrapping around the back of my head as he pulls me in for a short but sexy kiss. When he pulls back, his eyes are finally familiar. That warmth, that Roman warmth, is back inside of them. Just the corner of his mouth tips up slightly.

"Let me anyway."

I sigh as I watch him pull away. The ball of anxiety in my stomach isn't letting up. Not one bit.

My apartment feels different when I step into it. I was here yesterday, and yet it feels like a lifetime ago – like everything has changed since then. I step into the shower and try to wash away the feeling in my stomach, but it doesn't go anywhere.

It lingers as I eat breakfast, as I down my coffee. It persists when I try distracting myself with cleaning. After checking my phone for the tenth time in ten minutes, I finally give in. Except, instead of calling Roman like I want to, I text my friends in the hopes they can tell me everything is going to be fine. Talking with friends is a great way to get rid of this ball of anxiety in my stomach, right?

I send a message into our group chat, asking them to meet me in the same bar as the last time. Although, I very strongly inform them that it's not for alcohol. They just so happen to do a really good lunch, and I feel like eating my feelings. Their replies are almost instantaneous.

YES, BITCH, ON MY WAY.

I'LL BE THERE. NO TEQUILA, THOUGH?

I smile to myself as I get dressed, hoping that talking this out with my friends will ease the worry I feel. Maybe they'll even have some advice about how to tell

Roman the truth tonight.

Either way, I have to come up with something because tomorrow, Gideon is going to call. Tomorrow, I have to have a plan.

Hopefully, Roman will be involved in this one.

CHAPTER 24

The moment I step out of my building, I realise someone is watching me. Awareness prickles down my spine as I lock the door behind me. Acting normally, I calmly reach for the phone in my pocket. My first instinct is to call Roman, but if this has something to do with Gideon, then that isn't a possibility.

With my phone in my grasp, I turn away from the door and glance around as nonchalantly as I can. It's always best to let people think you're unaware of what's going on around you. If they don't expect you to put up a fight, you get a slight upper hand. I see nothing out of the ordinary in my glance, so I continue on my way, stepping down off the footpath to cross the road over to the bar.

The streets are empty, and the lack of cars and pedestrians makes me extremely nervous. I type out my message to Chase as I walk, hoping he's in his own apartment and will be able to get to my aid quickly if I need him. I hear the irritating swoosh of the message being sent and, almost simultaneously, the growl of an engine quickly followed by a screech as a black jeep swings out of an alleyway and begins gunning towards me.

I turn, quickly breaking into a run as I curse myself for not having a weapon on me for the first time in I don't know how long. The jeep speeds up behind me, and with nowhere to run on the straight road, it eats up the distance between us before it overtakes me, swerving to pull in right in front of me. I stop to avoid face-planting the shiny black metal and jump backwards when the door swings open. Benny jumps out.

"Now, love," he says, holding both hands up in front of him as if in surrender, one empty, the other wrapped around a gun. "Just get in the car and make this easy for all of us. I don't want to have to chase you, but I will."

I survey my options. I could run – Benny is huge and old, and I have little doubt that I could outrun him. The issue is that I can't outrun a bullet no matter how highly I think of myself. My other choice is remaining calm and getting into the car, and when I think about it like that, there was never really any other choice.

I sigh as I roll my shoulders, glaring at Benny as ferociously as I can manage. I stomp over to the car, urging myself not to wipe the smile off the bastard's face as I go. That is not a fight I would win. I mutter a curse and aim a not-so-nice word toward him before I reach the handle. I've got the door open and one foot in when Benny's beefy hand wraps around my mouth, and the pungent smell of chloroform invades my senses.

"Sorry, love. Precautionary measures," he shrugs casually, "you understand."

I struggle against him but ultimately breathe under the material covering my mouth and nose. He holds it harder against me, and eventually, even my own stubbornness isn't enough to resist the drowsy pull the chloroform has on me. I kick my foot back once more for good measure, connecting with his shin before I lose consciousness and embrace the blackness.

△△△

I wake up handcuffed to a chair. Again. I'm in a different room this time, though. It appears to be a garage – two fancy cars are parked in front of me, and all signs point to a domestic car garage. I don't pretend to be asleep this time, instead choosing to focus on erasing the grogginess from my mind.

Once again, I've been abducted in broad daylight, even though I was more than willing to hop in the car myself. I inhale in order to try to stamp down my irritation, tugging at the handcuffs on the off chance that I'll be able to get myself out. I stop trying when a door to my left opens, and in walks Gideon. The fucking bane of my existence.

"Really, little bounty hunter, we must stop meeting like this," he says and then enjoys a little laugh at his own attempt at humour.

"I wish your henchmen would stop rendering me unconscious any time he takes me for a ride. I never get to enjoy the scenery," I spit, and he laughs.

Gideon closes the door behind him and leans against it in the way only villains can. I can't find it in me to be scared of him anymore; only mildly worried for the safety of my father. I rack my brain to try to think of any reason Gideon might have hauled my ass here without warning, and for a moment, I think he knows about Roman and me, but that's ridiculous. It's not as if we've been traipsing all over the Island like a devoted couple. I tire of trying to figure it out and decide to skip to it.

"Why am I here, Gideon? You said I had two days. You only gave me one," I say, annoyance clear in my tone. He folds his arms across his chest and narrows his eyes at me.

"Hmm. Changed my mind, it seems. Why do you think you're here?" he counters, and I roll my eyes.

"I don't know. That's why I asked."

He stares at me for a long time – so long that I start to panic. He knows. What the fuck am I supposed to do now?

"You ever heard the name Charlie Knox?"

My stomach plummets. Is that what this is about? I only have a second to weigh my options, and I can only hope I'm making the right decision.

"Yes, actually. Roman was talking about him the other day. He's government, right?" Gideon's eyes narrow, and I pray that my acting holds up.

"He's dead is what he is."

"Yeah," I begin, sweat dripping down my back. "I heard Roman say someone killed him, that he wished he'd thought of it himself." Gideon continues to stare at me, so I keep going.

"I would have told you, but I just...it didn't seem relevant. Politics isn't what you asked me to listen out for. Also, I assumed you would have heard on the news like everyone else. I...is that why I'm here? Was it important?" I feel like I've said too much, gone too far.

The way Gideon is watching me tells me nothing about what he's thinking. He cocks his head to the side like a curious dog, weighing up my answer. Gideon pulls himself away from the wall before walking over and leaning on the bonnet of one of his cars.

"Alright, then." And that's it. He switches back into the other persona, his mood different, Charlie Knox forgotten. "The information you've given me over the last while has all been...useless," he continues, and I begin to calm down. If he thought I knew about Roman killing his little cousin, surely he'd be ripping off my fingernails right now.

"It's been nothing worth my time, and yet that is exactly what it has taken. My time. Care to explain?"

"Roman's a hard nut to crack, alright. He doesn't give me anything. Rarely leaves me alone in his office. He switches phones so often I've never even gotten a chance to bug him."

All true, except he does have one phone that he constantly uses that very few people know about, but I'm not about to spill that secret.

"I can't give you what I don't have. And besides, haven't you done enough? You've intercepted almost every single delivery he's had since I started this. I know I said to be thorough, but I didn't think you'd really listen..." My stomach sours as I force the next words out of my mouth. "Why haven't you just killed him yet?"

Gideon eyes me suspiciously. His eyes roaming, calculating. It makes me nervous, how quiet he is. How he seems to look right through me, into my soul. He begins nodding his head slowly, and my anxiety kicks up a notch.

"Yes," he finally speaks, "*almost* every single delivery. Oddly, the ones I've intercepted haven't had anything that pertains to me. Nothing. Seems weird that the deliveries you clue me in on rarely hold any drugs. No guns. Nothing."

"What are you implying?" I ask, heart in my mouth. If he knows.... If he's hurt my father in any way, I'll never be able to forgive myself.

"Nothing, nothing. Just seems convenient, especially now that you're fucking him."

My heart stops and then speeds up as shock makes its way through my body. He sees the confirmation on my face before I have time to school my features. I need to play this right. I need to ensure he doesn't suspect that I'm playing for the other team now.

"You said do whatever it takes. I'm not above using myself and my body to get what I want."

Gideon laughs out loud, clapping his hands as he does so.

"So you're saying you're sleeping with him for information? Not because you've grown fond of the little...pest."

Hearing someone refer to Roman as little almost makes me laugh, and I have to resist the urge to defend him, the urge strange in and of itself.

"I was trying to expedite the process, get you something good. Men are simple-minded like that. Get them naked, and it's easier to grab them by the balls."

I sincerely hope he can't tell that I'm lying, that the last few weeks of lying have made me an above-average fraud. I can't tell with the way he watches me. Nothing about Gideon is easy to read. He's too unhinged, too... psychotic. He never reacts how I expect him to and definitely doesn't show emotion in the way I'm used to.

"Well then, I applaud you. And rest assured, I have plans to end him soon."

I fight to keep my face impassive, even as my pulse skyrockets and fear shoots its way through my veins. I need to find out every single thing I can. It's time to lie through my teeth and put on the performance of my life.

"Brilliant. Then I get my father back, and we can never see each other again." I don't have to pretend to be thrilled by that prospect. The thought of Gideon disappearing from my life, let alone the planet, fills me with nothing but joy.

"Yes, yes, of course. But there's one more thing I need you to do for me."

Unease blossoms in my stomach at the thought of all that he could ask me to do, and I find myself praying that it's something I'm willing to go through with.

"I really do hate to inform you of how truly monstrous the man you're sleeping with is, but it's best you know. I'm shocked you haven't figured it out already."

"What?" I ask, and my dread is all real.

"Ah...so you truly don't know?"

I shake my head at him, giving the most withering glare I'm capable of. It's difficult to look threatening when you're cuffed to a chair. I don't know what he's about to come out with, but knowing him like I do, chances are it will be bullshit. More lies or threats to ensure I won't back out of doing his bidding. Well, as soon as I get out of this fucking chair, I'm going straight to Roman and coming clean.

"Tragic. Truly. Well..." he takes a deep breath and pretends he doesn't want to deliver whatever bad news he's about to. I'd believe him if it wasn't for that slight smile, the gleam of enjoyment in his eyes. "Your little lover boy has been smuggling women and their children onto the island. Roman has started bringing in his own...*talent.* He's luring them in with the promise of a better life on the Island, only to force them into prostitution the moment they arrive. It's absolutely diabolical. Brilliant, yes, but diabolical all the same."

Well, I was not expecting that. I almost laugh at the absurdity of it. At the absolute untrueness of Gideon's little fable. Does he really think I'm going to believe him? Clearly, he expects me to if the look on his face is anything to go by.

"Uh...I really don't think that's true," I reply, at a complete and utter loss for words.

"Ah. Love is blind, little hunter. Of course, you don't think the man who's fucking you is capable of being a glorified pimp. Alas...it's true. Brilliant plan, really. I wish I had thought of it myself. Anyway, I can't have that. Not on my island. My girls barely get enough attention as it is. I will not have them losing clients because of some new fucking pussy."

I flinch at the harshness in his voice when he talks about

the women. He is such a pig, and I'm suddenly thankful that this man hasn't had the chance to procreate.

The problem, though, is that his lie is almost too absurd to be a lie. Right? It seems too...convenient. If it wasn't true, why wouldn't he be using the idea himself? If it isn't true, why does he seem genuinely angry about the prospect of losing money? My brain spins as I try to think it through, so I remain quiet as Gideon paces, his face a mask of fury.

Roman is absolutely not capable of something like this. I'd know. I'd have heard something. Even if I hadn't heard something from Roman himself, surely if he was bringing boatloads of women and children onto the Island and selling them as fucking sex slaves or whatever, I'd have heard something. Someone would have heard something.

I try to rack my brain for anything I might have heard, tuning out Gideon who has gone on the expected villain rant. I think back to every phone call I overheard, every piece of paperwork I've scoured. Something tickles my memory, somewhere in the back of my head, and as I reach for it, I almost fall out of my chair. Surely, it's a coincidence. My brain locks in on the memory of the shipping form, the one that simply claimed it was shipping 'The Assets.' Could that be? It couldn't.

Roman may not be one of the good guys, but I know where his morals lie. He wouldn't...and suddenly, my mind whirls to the moment we arrived to save Addie. The strange look on his face when he saw the situation she was in. That was...guilt wasn't it? I had assumed that it was because he had so much and she had so little. I assumed his guilt was for the same reason as mine, but what if it wasn't. What if the guilt had more to do with the fact that he…

No. I shut my brain down. There's not an actual chance in hell that I'm going to believe a word out of Gideon's mouth. The man is a liar, a thief, and a cheat, and I would be just as bad as him if I just believed the words that he was saying. I know Roman. I've spent time with him. He wouldn't…there's no way he would do something so utterly disgusting.

I'm so lost in my thoughts that I don't even realise Gideon has ceased his incessant chatter and is holding out a manila folder in my direction.

"Proof. Just in case you need it."

I stare at him incredulously for a few seconds before he barks out a laugh. "Ah, yes. Excuse me. I forgot."

He uncuffs my wrists, and I twist and turn them before taking the folder in my numb, tingling fingers. My blood runs cold when I pull out the images. I have to admit that it's difficult to make excuses when I'm staring at grainy, black and white images of Roman, standing at the back of a truck, a phone pressed to his ear. Beside him, the two back doors of the truck are flung wide open, and inside sit at least seven women and some children.

My face falls, and I can *feel* the triumphant smile spread across Gideon's face as he watches my reaction to the images. This proves nothing. Not really. I shake my head and then stand and step away when his hand comes to rest on my shoulder. I can do nothing but glare at him as I shove the images back at him, but he shakes his head.

"Keep them. In case you forget that you were sleeping with the enemy." He winks at me, and I mentally vomit in my mouth.

"Find out when his next shipment comes in. I want to know the very minute you do. Don't worry, little hunter, I'm going to shut it down, and this will all be over soon."

His voice is condescending, irritating. I hate him. If I had a weapon on me right now, I know I wouldn't hesitate to fucking put a bullet through him, or stab him, or bludgeon him to death. It's infuriating that, once again, he's ensured that nothing in my life would be able to remain the same.

Gideon calls for Benny, and when I threaten to castrate him the next time I see him if he even attempts to knock me out again, Gideon tells him to let me remain awake. He smiles at me as he says it. Like allowing me to stay conscious is some great, selfless act. Like he's doing me a favour. I asked to see my father, begged, but Gideon must have used up all of his generosity. He leaves me there with Benny, who leers at me. I glare at him, vowing in my head that one day I will kill him. I will make them both pay for everything that they have done.

Benny turns his huge frame and walks, summoning me after him and I have no choice but to follow. I slip silently into the car he leads me to and welcome the quiet. I welcome this moment to think. Something's coming. Something big. As I sit in the back of this car I can feel something in the air change. There's a chaotic charge pulsating all around me. I wonder if I'm the only one who feels it. Anxiety settles in my chest, my heart pounding.

I need... I don't know what I need anymore. In the beginning I thought I could handle this. I thought that because of my job, because of how my father raised me that I would survive this.

Not anymore. I realise now that I am just a girl. I'm just a girl who has no real idea what she's doing.

CHAPTER 25

Benny throws my phone to me as I sit in the back seat, and I fumble to catch it, lost in my own muddled thoughts. I turn it on and type in my code, and it immediately buzzes and beeps with missed calls and messages – most of them from Chase and the rest of the team. I'm about to reply to one of his messages when my phone begins to ring.

It's Chase, and the minute I answer, he immediately begins shouting down the phone. I've never heard so many curse words fly from his mouth in such rapid succession.

"Chase-Chase, it's me. Stop-No, stop shouting. Jesus, it's me." I interrupt his tirade, and he immediately sighs in relief.

"Where are you? What the fuck happened?" he shouts, and I hold the phone away from my ear in order to avoid a shattered eardrum.

I don't want to tell him about what Gideon told me. Not until I can get to Roman. Not until I can ask him to his face what the truth is.

"Benny picked me up. Gideon wanted to see me, but it's fine, and I'm fine. You can relax."

"Relax. Ha. Relax." He sighs again. "Jesus, you just took years off my life. Where are you now? I've been driving around aimlessly for the last two hours!"

"I'm...uh...I'm in the car with Benny. Gideon wasn't happy with the information I've been giving. I have to see Roman," I say.

"No, you have to come home so I can lay eyes on you and convince my heart that you're still alive."

"I'm alive. I'm fine – seriously. Look, Chase, I have to see Roman. It's important, and I...I just...wait around, okay? I'll call you. I'm fine. Just wait at home, please?"

"What's going on, Hazel?"

"Nothing," I reply, but I want to spill my heart out. I want to tell him everything and have him reassure me that nothing is ever what it seems.

The chances of Chase defending Roman instead of instantly believing the worst in him are slim to none, so I don't do that. "I promise I'm okay. There's just something I need to do. I'll call you."

I hang up so I don't have to listen to him beg, then use the next few minutes to respond to messages from everyone else. I do everything possible to avoid thinking about confronting Roman, but eventually, I run out of texts to respond to. I look out the window, surprised to see that I'm a close enough distance to Roman's warehouse that I could walk from here. It's not great without my car, but if I go home, I'll see Chase, and if I see Chase, he'll know something's wrong.

"Pull over," I say, and Benny does so without question.

I ignore him as I exit the car, not responding to his taunts, choosing instead to give him the finger over my shoulder as I walk away, making my way towards

Roman's building. I don't even know if he's there. I only had one text from him telling me he was busy but wanted to see me later. My stomach flips as I respond to it, asking where he is.

We had plans tonight. I was probably going to sleep with him again, wrap myself around him, touch him. I feel sick at the thought that that might never happen again. If this turns out to be true, if I discover in the next few moments that Roman isn't who I thought he was, then… I can't even let myself imagine it. Not yet.

How does one get over having sex with a man who forces women to sell their bodies just so he can make money?

After a few moments, the building comes into view, and I still haven't received a reply from Roman. I see his car in the lot, but that means nothing. He often goes out in one of the SUVs that his men drive.

I steel myself as I walk slowly towards the building, taking longer than I probably should in order to delay the conversation. The thing is, if I confront Roman and he proves it isn't true, then I still have to come clean. No matter what happens, the truth will come out, and I have no idea how the hell anything is going to go after today.

I walk through the door almost robotically and am surprised by the number of people in the building. I smile at the few I've gotten to know over the last while, and each of them gives me a surprised but genuine smile back. I'm so nervous my palms are sweating, so I discreetly wipe them on the side of my jeans. I eat away the distance between where I was and Roman's office, and I can't tell if I'm relieved or terrified when I hear his voice flit through the cracked-open doorway.

"What the fuck do you mean?" he asks, and I pause my movements to hover and listen. There's no response, so I assume he's on the phone.

"No. No. Listen, they need to be in the van and on that fucking ship. I'll be there at seven tonight. Am I understood?"

My heart begins to race. What is he talking about?

"How many?"

"Well, we've got enough food and water and clothes and shit for twelve, but no more. Once they're on the ship, they're in that container, and they don't get out until it docks again. Make it work. I have something to deal with, then I'll meet you back here and we'll go."

No. *No.* I almost can't believe my ears. I can't understand the words I hear coming out of his mouth. Any other day, and I probably wouldn't have batted an eye. Any other day, and none of this would make sense. It's almost too much of a coincidence for me to even be hearing this conversation right now. I try to deny it. I try, but all I can hear is the voice in my head telling me it's true.

It's true. It's all fucking true. There's no possible way he could be talking about anything else. Nothing else makes any sense. Even as I think it, my brain is trying to provide other scenarios, other situations in which people would be in a container on a ship. In which they would need food and water. I come up empty. Empty and devastated. Furious. Terrified.

Roman continues to speak, but I don't want to hear another word. I don't want to know anything else. There's too much proof. Too much irrefutable evidence, and all of it points to the fact that Roman has been trafficking people. I fight back the vomit that's threatening to rise the moment I hear silence.

I steel myself. My spine. I stand up straight and try to wipe any emotion from my face. I can't leave; I can't just avoid this. I have to say my piece, and whatever happens, happens.

I pull the door open and walk inside the office, my eyes immediately finding him hunched over behind his desk, texting on one phone while the other sits in the opposite hand.

"What?" he barks, without even looking at me.

I take the moment to watch him, to study him. I can still feel his hands on me, still taste his lips. I almost run, but instead, I stay rooted to the spot, even though my brain screams at me to abort mission. I can't. Not now.

"I said— oh. What are you doing here?" he asks and uses his cold business voice. The one I was used to, the only one I knew before the moment we kissed.

It crosses my mind that I might never hear that soft, teasing tone he was giving me just last night ever again. He looks slightly panicked at my presence, and it's another stab to the heart. Is he wondering what I might have overheard?

"I just...I need to—"

He cuts me off before I get a chance to speak.

"Lara," he says, getting up from his desk, "I'm up to my

neck right now. I can't do this with you."

"No, this is important. I really need—"

Once again, his rough voice cuts me off. Annoyance and anger build inside me like a tidal wave. How dare he act like I'm an inconvenience when he's off doing God-awful things without me knowing?

"Jesus! Lara, I told you I'd see you later. I have a...delivery that's going to fucking shit that's more important than you know. I've got a restaurant with a chef who just quit and a nightclub without a fucking DJ. I cannot do this right now. Whatever it is, it's going to have to wait. I'm late."

He brushes passed me, turning around only to plant a soft, swift kiss on my lips. I stand there, unable to move, whiplash from his fucking outburst threatening to bowl me over. As much as I want to demand that he stay and tell me that what I think I know isn't true, I also feel like I've seen and heard enough.

"I'm sorry. I'm an asshole. But later, alright?" He peers at me from the doorway, eyes boring into mine, and instead of demanding his attention, I nod, barely conscious, and give him a tight, fake smile.

Roman nods back, and then he's gone, footsteps pounding down the steps. I'm surprised I can hear them over the sound of blood in my ears and my heart slamming against my aching chest.

Once he's gone, I make my way towards the desk. It's unusually messy – a sure sign that he's stressed. Roman is always neat, always organised; minimalistic and clutter-free. I eye the paperwork on his desk, truly afraid to riffle through it, unsure if I can handle anything else.

Rifling is unnecessary because before I even have to lift a finger, my eyes fall over a sticky note stuck to the top of his closed laptop.

My eyes shut of their own accord, and a sigh rushes from my nose. I almost don't feel myself pull my cell phone from my pocket. I glance down, fingers itching to touch the tiny yellow piece of paper, to scrunch it up and throw it in the bin so I can pretend it doesn't exist. But it does.

I grip my phone in my hand, and as my eyes roam over the sticky note, the small scrap of paper that he somehow managed to fit the names of eleven women on, I make the call.

"I want you to let my father go." I skip a formal greeting. I don't have it in me. "Now. I got what you wanted, so now you need to let my dad go."

"Well, you certainly work quick, little hunter. Tell me what you know, and I'll tell you if it warrants your father's freedom."

Another time, I probably would have done it better. Another time, I would have done it in person, exchanged information for my dad like a late-night ransom. But I'm dazed and disappointed and a little bit heartbroken. I just want it all to be over. I tell him everything. Everything I've heard, everything I know.

"Tonight, at the dock. You'll get everything you want."

Gideon laughs on the other side of the phone. The sound is like nails on a chalkboard, and I can't stand it. "I knew you'd do it, little hunter. I'm proud of you."

Tears well inside my eyes at his words, and for once, I let them fall. They burn my cheeks as they go, and before long, I can taste the salt on my tongue.

Gideon rattles off an address in my ear. "What's that?" I ask, doing my damnedest to keep the sadness from my voice.

"You can pick your father up there in exactly two hours. Nice working with you, Lara."

Gideon prattles of a address that I have to scramble to take down and promptly hangs up before I get a chance to say anything. He's letting him go. In two hours...in two hours, I'll have my dad back. Relief like I have never felt before settles into my bones as a weight falls from my shoulders. Some of the cracks in my heart start to stitch together again, like maybe things might be okay.

I have to call Chase.

"Lara, where the fuck are you?" He asks, answering on the first ring.

"Two hours. You have to go get my dad in exactly two hours." I give him the address.

"Wait, what? What is going on, how is this- what's fucking happening?"

"Chase just- please. I'll explain everything. I promise. I'm sorry. I need you to get my dad, and call me the minute you have him. I just- can you do that for me? Please."

The silence lingers, I can almost hear his stress on the phone. I know him. He wants to know everything, he wants to ask a million questions but I cant do it. Not right now.

"I'll get your dad. Of course I will."

I know he wants to say more, but he refrains. He trusts me, and the thought that usually makes me feel better, only makes me feel worse. We hang up, but he's worried.

Thoughts spinning and heart aching, I spend the next two hours waiting for Roman to return, wondering how the fuck everything got so messed up so quickly.

CHAPTER 26

Roman walks back into his office almost two hours later, immaculately in place as usual. My stomach flips at the thought of what might happen now. What might he do once he knows that I know? It's hard to imagine him hurting me.

A few weeks ago, I wouldn't have doubted for a second that he might hurt me, but now, knowing him like I do, I struggle to find any fear inside myself. I take him in as he watches me curiously. His eyes roam over me, clearly trying to read through my silence and figure out why I'm here. If I'd ever thought this would be easy, I was dead wrong. Knowing the truth now only makes this more difficult. I let him in, I let him touch me, and now I wanted him to tell me to my face what I already know.

"What are you still doing here?" he asks.

"I'm here for the truth," I say, unmoving from my position, leaning against the window as if this wasn't one of the hardest conversations I was ever going to have.

"Truth?" he asks, clearly confused. "I can't stay long, Lara. I have to be somewhere. Why don't you wait for me upstairs?" His voice is calm, and I know he doesn't know.

He thinks I'm here for him. For sex. To continue on as we have been the past few days. How comfortable he must be behind that mask he wears. How easy it must be for him to slip from man to monster. I betrayed him, yes, but his is worse. His cuts deeper. Because what I've been doing this whole time was for someone I care about, while Roman has been using his dead sister as an excuse to do terrible things. Unforgivable things.

"Were you ever going to tell me, Roman?" I ask, looking directly into those eyes, those eyes that just last night roamed over my naked body. "You must have had a great laugh with your friends, right? Little Lara the Bounty Hunter fell for the bad guy."

"What the fuck are you talking about?" He looks concerned, his eyebrows dipping low as he makes his way towards me, stopping abruptly when I take my own small step backwards, bumping into the window behind me. "Baby, what's going on?"

Roman's voice is full of worry now, and I feel my heart crack all over again. God, what a beautiful little liar. There's no possible way he could care about me and still do what he has been doing. There's no way he's given himself to me while refusing to admit his sins.

"You're going to make me drag it out of you, aren't you? God, I feel so stupid. I thought you were good. I thought you were different. Jesus, it's been happening right in front of my eyes. You've been telling me almost daily since we met that you're no good, and I just fucking ignored you." I laugh, but it's empty, hollow, much like all the words he has whispered to me this last week.

"I don't—"

"Don't fucking lie to me, Roman. The girls. The women. Tell me about the women." I don't expect my voice to come out so loud. The shout seems to startle him as his eyes widen and his eyebrows inch their way back up his forehead. He shifts on his feet, just slightly, stepping closer to me.

"The women?" he questions, but I can see it on his face now. I can see that he knows. The flash of guilt in his eyes is all the admission I need, and I feel sick to my stomach.

"Don't. I heard you on the phone today. I already know, but the least you can do is say it to my fucking face. Tell me the truth."

Roman thinks for a moment, emotions flitting over his face, and I know it's only because he's allowing me to see them. If he wanted to, he could have this entire argument with a bland look on his face, regardless of what he feels. Finally, he seems to come to some sort of realisation, and his glare becomes cold enough to freeze lava.

"What do you think you know?" he asks, and his voice matches that glare. It's a tone he hasn't used with me since the first time we met, and just like then, it sends a shiver down my spine.

"I'm not stupid, Roman. Although, considering the situation I'm currently in, perhaps that's not entirely true." His jaw ticks at my words, and he walks to his desk to perch on it, arms folded across his chest.

"Okay, Lara, I'll play. I'll play whatever game this is. The problem is that I think I know exactly what you're talking about. I think I know what you think you know, but I need you to say it. I need you to say what you believe I'm doing."

He's looking at me like I'm a mystery again; the difference now is that he's looking at me like a mystery he doesn't want to solve. My anger is boiling over as he studies me so calmly. The only sign he's bothered by this conversation is the continuous clenching of his jaw, the muscle popping.

"You're..." I start and then find I can't say the words. They choke me, struggling to work their way out of my throat.

My stomach is rolling inside of me, and I can feel my hands shaking. I can't explain why, but there are hundreds of alarm bells going off in my head, and my body is telling me to run, telling me I've walked into a trap. I shake my head, clearing my thoughts, and try again.

"You're smuggling them. Women...and children. You're smuggling them like they're fucking guns. Like they're nothing."

He looks me dead in the eye and nods. "I am."

My world shatters. I feel like I'm going to throw up. I knew it, and yet hearing him admit to it, hearing the confirmation come from his mouth is like a dagger to the heart. "Oh, God," I moan, bending over and clutching my stomach, desperately trying not to throw up.

I can't look at him, can't see the calm on his face after he openly admitted to smuggling women and children onto the Island for...I can't even think it. How could I have trusted him? How could I have thought he was any different? He told me he was the bad guy, and I didn't believe him.

"Ask me where I'm smuggling them to. Ask me why. Ask me what's really going on." Roman's voice is granite – he doesn't even have to raise it like I do. Confusion rolls through me, and I flinch when I see it's him who's looking at me with disgust.

"What?" I say, standing up straight again, watching as he loosens his tie and gives a cold, humourless laugh.

He turns his back to me and rests both palms on his desk as he bows his head forward.

"Fucking ask me!" he roars, slamming a hand down on the wood before he turns back to me.

It would be impossible to miss the shock he seems to feel when he sees me taking a step away from him. His eyes widen slightly before confusion transforms his face.

"What, are you scared of me now? What the fuck, Lara? What kind of monster do you think I am?" Roman's voice is softer now, and I realise he's wounded. I've cut him, and I don't know how. How is he the one who seems hurt by this? How dare he!

"The kind of monster who smuggles women onto an island so they can become sex slaves to the highest bidder," I spit, and his face drops, morphing as shock and anger battle for precedence. He lifts a hand to rub his jaw and laughs angrily. His head nods, over and over, eyes burning into mine. This isnt right. This isn't right. He looks so... dissapointed.

"*Off* the Island, Lara. I smuggle them *off the Island*." Everything goes silent. "When they ask me to." The world stops. "Not so they have to sell themselves." I can hear my own heartbeat. "So that they can have a better life." I think I might throw up. "I take the women under Gideon's fat thumb, and I give them the option of getting on a boat and sailing away and having a place to go when they get there."

This is not happening. I can't have gotten it this wrong.

"Lara…I set them up on the mainland. I have a place they can go. I don't…Jesus, I don't take them and force them to come *here*. Jesus Christ."

"No," I whisper, voice barely audible, "that's not true."

"Yes. It is. You know me. You fucking know me. How could you ever think for a second that I would do something so disgusting?"

I can hear the truth in his voice, see it on his face. I can hear the disgust at just the assumption of him doing such a thing. Then it dawns on me. The reality of what's happened.

Gideon played me. He really fucked me. He told me something about himself that he knew would repulse me, except he put Roman in his place. He knew, all along, he knew my resolve to bring Roman down was faltering, so he gave me something he knew would make me turn my back on him.

Oh, God. What have I done?

"But the phone call…I heard…"

"Yeah, you heard me wanting to get the women off the island because word has it something is going down with Gideon. Something big. I needed to get the women and children out of the way before something happened and they got hurt," Roman says, a lot calmer now, and

I can tell he knows I believe him because his face is softening, eyes lightening as they watch me realize the truth.

"I thought..."

"I get why you thought that," he says, coming towards me, using his fingertip to lift my chin, forcing my eyes to meet his. "I would have explained when you asked, but everything was falling apart, and I had to go take care of it. Jesus, if I had known that's the thought you would jump to, I would have stuck around to explain."

His hand slides over my cheek, then around to the back of my neck as he pulls my head into his chest. The tears immediately fall and soak through his shirt. "Don't cry, baby. I'm furious you thought I would do such a thing, but don't cry."

I take a moment to enjoy his embrace. To feel his warmth, to hear the steady beat of his heart, and to inhale the unique and manly smell of him. I take a deep breath, wanting to hold as much of his air inside my lungs as I can. My heart slams against my chest as I whisper apologies. Over and over again, I say it. "I'm sorry. I'm so sorry."

He pulls my face from his chest and leans in to kiss me, thumbs wiping the tears from my cheek. I want his kiss more than I want to take my next breath, but I pull back, turning my face to the side so he can't kiss me.

"Roman... I... I'm so sorry, I—"

"It's fine. It's fine." He leans in to kiss me again, but this time, I have to push at his chest. I need space. I need *distance*.

"No. No, Roman. It's not," I take a deep breath, readying myself for the disaster that is about to occur. "Roman. I'm sorry. Oh, God. I don't…I don't even I didn't know. He said…he said that you were bringing the women here, that you were making them…"

Finally, Roman looks as concerned as he should. He leans away from me, those eyes studying me as I physically cave in on myself. My body seems to want to make itself as small as possible, but I'm thankful for it as I feel my arms wrap around myself.

"Who?" Roman asks.

"I tried to end it. I did. I didn't believe him, and I was coming here to tell you everything. I wanted to tell you the truth, but then I heard the phone call, and you were talking about the women…and I thought…I thought…" I can't say the words. I try, but all that comes out is more rambling nonsense.

Roman's eyes are suspicious, his entire body seems wary of me, untrusting.

"Lara. Look at me. Look. At. Me."

I have no choice. I look.

"What did you do?" His voice. That voice.

"I told him. I told him everything. He knows where the truck is, the women. He knows what time the ship leaves. Fuck. I'm sorry. I'm so sorry. I had no choice. I have no choice. He's got…he's got my dad."

I feel physically sick. If Gideon knows where the women are, he's going to take them back…or worse. Gideon might just kill them for betraying him.

Roman's face wears an expression I've never seen before, but his voice stays calm. Like this is not the worst possible thing that could happen. Like I haven't just betrayed him in the worst way.

"Who?" he asks. The simple word buries a knife into me. I'm bleeding all over the goddamn floor.

Our eyes meet, and I know he knows. He can see it. I watch him as he reads my face, and I know he can see the devastation there. He's smart. Too smart not to have already figured this out.

"Gideon."

The name floats between us. It's a heavy, physical thing. It seeps into the air we're breathing, and it coats the walls in its vile connotation. It's a curse, a secret I've kept for too long. I wish I could appreciate the weight that's been lifted off my shoulders, the relief of not holding that in anymore. But the weight is replaced and tripled by the consequences of my actions. There is no relief to be had, not when Roman is looking at me the way that he is.

Not when his eyes are the darkest I've ever seen them, and his face is unrecognizable in his fury. I don't know what else to say. I don't know what else I'm supposed to do. Everything has blown up in my face so quickly, and I'm at a loss on how to proceed.

I open my mouth to speak, but Roman raises a hand, stopping me, then drops all his fingers except the index one, indicating for me to give him a minute. I slam my mouth shut, the taste of salty tears penetrating my dulled senses. Nothing feels real right now…like I'm floating, living a fever dream in real time.

"Your father isn't dead?" he asks.

I drop my head in shame and embarrassment and everything else.

"No." My voice is barely a whisper.

"Gideon's got him?"

"Yes."

"This whole time...this whole fucking time you've been working for him. Spying for him?"

I nod.

"Everything that's gone wrong...that's all been you?"

Another nod.

"You've been lying. This whole time. This whole thing has been a lie?"

"Yes."

His face crumples, distorted in the pain I've inflicted, and I rush to correct myself.

"No. No! Not us. Not how I feel about you. Just...I can explain, Roman. I can...Everything I feel about you is real. Everything I told you, apart from my father being dead, is real. I wanted to come clean. I was going to... I... Roman?"

He has his back turned to me, and I can see the heavy rise and fall, the controlled breaths he only takes when he is right about to lose it.

"What did he want?" he asks.

"What?"

"Gideon. He took your father. Why? What does he

want?"

I take a breath before answering. Before delivering the killing blow.

"You. He wanted you dead. He wanted me to find an in, to get everything I could on you, so he could take everything. Then he was going to take you out."

I try to stop the tears, but they have a life of their own. They mix with the blood from the hole in my chest on the floor, and it's only when I look up to find Roman has turned back to me that I see he's haemorrhaging too.

"You were playing me. The whole time. You were just giving him my fucking secrets, smiling and flirting your way into my business, into my bed, into my fucking life, just until he put a bullet in my skull?"

"No. It wasn't like that," He glares at me, hatred evident in every inch of him. "Okay, maybe at the beginning. You were a means to an end. I needed my dad back. I didn't know you, I thought…"

Even I can hear how little my words change things. How weak my argument is. Defending myself is futile. There is no defence to the crime I have committed.

"It's not like that *now*. Things changed. We changed. I know that I lied, I know it looks bad, but—"

His loud, slow clapping cuts me off, and I flinch at the coldness of it, the harshness on his face.

"Wow. Jesus." He laughs coldly. "Fuck, Lara. Well done. Well-fucking-played. You got me. Hook line and fucking sinker."

"Roman, I didn't…I didn't mean to—"

"Hurt me? Play me? Well fuck Lara, you did it. Congratulations. They say I'm a monster. They've talked about my cold, empty heart for years. Said it couldn't be thawed…but you fucking did it. You put on the show of your life, and what a show it was."

He resumes his slow clapping, and every clash of his hands hits me like a blow to the face. I remain silent as his applause rains on; I take the blows as my penance.

"Are you going to put the bullet in me yourself, or are we expecting company sometime soon?" he asks coldly.

"He knows you're here. I told him you would be." Shame. I am a ball of shame, guilt, and regret.

"Well then. What are we going to do about that?" he asks, and I see him pulling the gun from the desk drawer. He checks it and flicks the safety off.

"You need to leave. You need to go before they get here. We have to go to them, we…we have to stop him."

"We?" he asks, incredulous. "And what makes you think I won't kill you right here? What makes you think I won't end your lying ass right now?"

Fear engulfs me, but I ignore it. I made my bed, and now it's time for me to claw my way out of it.

"I can help. Let me help. I did this, Roman, so please let me see it out to the end. After…after, you can do whatever you want. I won't fight you. But please let me try and fix what I—"

My words are cut off by the sound of the door flinging open, and without thinking, I dive, shoving my body in front of Roman's as a shot rings out. I feel the bullet fly by my face, narrowly missing me and Roman's chest before it lodges into the drywall behind us. I feel Roman lift his gun as I turn, pulling my gun from my waistband and taking aim at the two armed men standing in the doorway.

Roman aims his gun as bullets fly towards us, one grazing my arm. A bullet hits the man closest to us in the head, and he hits the ground, blood pooling around him. My bullet lands in the chest of the second guy, who manages to stay up and take another shot, but he's way off due to his injury, and Roman ends him with another shot to the head. His body hits the ground with a thud.

Roman and I remain frozen, ears ringing from the gunshots, hearts racing, and blood pumping full of adrenaline. It lasted five seconds, tops. They hadn't expected him to be ready, to be armed, and with the layout I had given Gideon, they knew where they were shooting. I let out a long breath as I eye the two dead men before turning to Roman.

"Are you okay? Are you hit?" My eyes roam over every single inch of him, scouring him for any signs of bleeding. My relief is immediate when I can't spot any. "Thank God," I whisper, but he ignores me.

His eyes linger on the graze on my arm, and I look and see that it's bleeding freely. I can't feel it, the adrenaline numbing the pain in my arm as well as in my chest. Roman's eyes look over me, checking me for more injuries before darting to where I had been standing before, to where I'm standing now, right in front of him, his own personal human shield. If I had been expecting thanks, which I wasn't, I would have been disappointed when he glares at me with all the hatred in the world.

He walks forward, grabbing his jacket off the rack where he left it and slipping his arms through. He pulls out his phone.

"Don't meet me here. Then turn the fuck around and get there. Now." He says to whoever is on the other line.

I watch in silence as Roman walks back, grabs his car keys from where they rest on his desk, and then stomps towards the door. I grab my jacket and follow, invited or not. I try not to look at the bodies as I step over them. We walk down the stairs in silence, steps hurried. I don't need to ask where he's going. I already know.

Roman stops at the threshold of the building so suddenly I slam into his back and almost land on my ass when he spins abruptly. "You help me end this mess you made. You help me, and then…" he trails off before spinning on his heel and marching towards the car.

He barely waits for me to open the door and get in before he takes off, tires spinning on the gravel, sending a cloud of smoke and dust into the sky.

I can't take my eyes off him as he drives us towards the dock's warehouse, the one where the women are waiting to be taken to a better life. I send a silent prayer up to whatever God is listening that it isn't too late. That I'm not too late.

Roman remains quiet, his harsh amber eyes glaring at the road in front of him, and he remains quiet even as I beg him to speak.

CHAPTER 27

Queitness. It echos in the care. So quiet I can hear my heart thudding in my ears.

"Yell at me, Roman. Scream at me. Please. Do something."

The words are a prayer from my lips as I stare at his profile. His face is a mask of fury, his lips tight and his eyebrows pulled close together on his forehead. The muscle ticking in his jaw is once again the only indication that my words have any effect on him.

His hands grip the steering wheel so tight that his knuckles bleach, and as we speed down the road towards whatever war is waiting for us, I know that he won't forgive me for this. Can't forgive me.

"Please, Roman. Anything is better than your silence. I'll take anything. Anything but nothing." I whisper the words softly, letting every ounce of guilt and misery seep into them. I destroyed everything. Ruined everything, and I have no one to blame but myself.

He finally looks at me, a glance, a meeting of our eyes that feels almost physical – so much so that I lean towards the passenger side window, trying to escape the anger emanating from him.

"I can't, Lara. Fuck." He slams one hand against the steering wheel once, then twice, and the blaring of the horn makes me flinch.

"I can't look at you because I'm trying so hard not to fucking explode. I can't shout at you because I'll say things I can't take back. Things I wouldn't want to take back. You have no idea what you've done. Right now, all I need from you is cooperation. We're going to pray we aren't too late, and we're going to kill whatever motherfuckers try to come for us. After that..." he shakes his head, trailing off and leaving the end of his sentence unfinished. But I hear the words anyway.

After that...he'll probably kill me. He needs my help now, but once I stop being useful, I'm dead. We take a sharp corner, and the street blurs past as we race to the docks in Golden City. I glance at my watch and see that it's 6:15. It's been two hours. My phone buzzes right at that moment, and I pull it out to see Chase's name. My heart races as I glance at Roman before answering it.

"I've got him," Chase's voice comes through immediately, and relief sinks into my bones. "He's unconscious but he's... fine. Can you tell me what's happening now?" I go to answer but Roman snatches the phone from my hand and flings it out of his open window.

"Well, your dad's safe. You happy now?" Roman won't even look at me, and his voice is laced in fury.

"No." I whisper, and I settle into my seat and watch out the window as I consider the mess I've made. I ruined everything – worse than I thought possible.

The noise of gunshots and screams and the smell of smoke permeates the car as we approach the dock, and I look up to see the carnage. Some of the fighting has spilled outside of the warehouse, and I watch as Trevor takes a shot at someone before throwing his empty gun to the floor and rushing to grab another man by the throat, throwing a punch so hard the man immediately drops.

I've never been in a situation like this before, and knowing I've caused it, knowing I'll be the one to blame for all the death here today, makes me sick to my stomach. It's messy and violent. It's a bloody brawl with some of the deadliest men on either side. I glance at the bridge in the distance, but no one is coming. The army stationed there is probably hoping we kill ourselves so they can have their island back.

In the water, I see the ship, the one I'm guessing was for the girls. There's chaos on the deck, fires and fights and gunshots. The setting sun casts an orange glow across the dock as the boats bob in the water, and what should be an idyllic scene has become a nightmare. I have turned the pinks and purples of the evening sky into blood and bruises. The sound of birds and crashing waves into gunshots and sounds of pain.

I glance quickly at Roman. Enemy, turned lover, turned enemy.

The car screeches to a stop, and I have to brace a hand on the dash to catch myself while Roman pulls a gun from his waist and jumps out of the car, leaving it running in his haste. I follow suit, racing to catch up with him. No one has spotted us yet, and Roman grabs my wrist to stop me as I move to walk forward.

"I don't know whose fucking side you're on anymore. If I see you kill or harm any of my men, I will end you myself, do you hear me? You've fooled me once, and that's on me for not seeing through you, but you're needed right now. Don't fool me again."

His words are icy, cutting through me violently, and the look in his eyes is like he's speaking to a complete stranger. I suppose he is. Almost everything he knows about me is a lie. My betrayal and deceit have turned me into someone he doesn't know.

"I'm on your side," I whisper, hoping he can hear the sincerity in my voice.

"We'll see."

He tugs me after him, and then we're crouched behind a small wall in front of the warehouse. A loud pop fills my ears, and I realize Roman has already begun shooting. My hands are shaking, but I copy him, leaning up over the wall and aiming for anyone I don't recognize. It's easy now to tell the two groups apart. I've spent so much time with these guys over the last few weeks, and even thinking that I had signed some of their death warrants dims more lights in me than I can count.

Men begin falling to the ground as bullets fly from our guns and others. Finally, the attention is on us. Trevor spots us first, followed by some of the other guys.

"Let's move!" Roman barks, and then we're up and over the wall, running towards the door to the warehouse where more bullets are flying, and the sounds of flesh hitting flesh is louder.

The dull smacks of fists into faces settled in my ears, finding a place in my brain to hide so they can return later and ruin any sleep I ever hope to get. It's carnage.

Bodies are strewn all over the bloodied cement floor, and few men remain standing. I see the truck, the huge container that is set to take the women and children to the docks and off the Island. The door is open, and I almost throw up when I notice the bodies inside.

Some are small enough to be children. The acidic taste of vomit burns my throat as tears fill my eyes. Oh God, what have I done? How could I have been so stupid? How could I have believed for one second that Roman was the one trafficking girls onto the Island? It doesn't take long for me to think of Adeline. Is her body in there? Have I killed her?

When I glance over, I see Roman find the same thing I have, and when his eyes meet mine, the rage in them is unlike anything I've ever seen before. I drop my gaze from his, shame seeping into my bones, curling its way around my soul.

We are still partly hidden by huge containers filled with God knows what, and without another thought, spurred only by guilt and a desperate need to right my wrongs however I can, I step out with my gun raised and begin firing.

I don't duck or cower. I can't. If I die today, so be it – chances are, I won't live to see tomorrow regardless. Adrenaline keeps me moving forward, not an ounce of fear in my body. I hear Roman call my name from behind me, but I can't stand to look at him for another second. To see the hatred in his eyes. So, I do the only thing I can. I walk into the fray and fire off round after round, aiming for anyone who isn't a part of Roman's crew.

Most guns have been abandoned, probably empty before we even arrived. It's almost easy to aim and fire at the men who are fighting hand to hand or hiding behind whatever they can. I try not to think of the lives I'm taking, the pain I'm causing.

I spot some of Gideon's men dragging wounded behind containers, and I take the opportunity to kill them too. I'm surprised to find I don't feel bad about it. Not like I should. There's only so much a single person can feel guilt for, and right now, my mind is occupied by the dead women and children whose blood is on my hands, by the fact that I betrayed Roman. That I had gotten some of his men, his brothers, killed. My capacity for guilt is completely full.

When I find my gun empty, I toss it to the floor, reaching behind me to pull out the other and continue walking forward. Sweat drips down my forehead, and my back is either damp or bleeding, but I barely feel it. A man I vaguely know as Miles is on the ground, a huge bald guy bent over him, smashing his fist into Miles's face over and over. I walk up behind him, my steps silent in the chaos, and hold my gun to the back of his head.

He freezes instantly, and Miles's head lolls to the side. I'm unsure if he's dead or alive. His lifeless face makes my next move easier as I pull the trigger, blood splattering over my hand, arm, and face. I can taste it on my tongue and see it out of the corner of my eye. My body is vibrating with adrenaline, and a strange kind of bloodlust casts a hazy red mist over my vision.

A stab of pain enters my left thigh, but I ignore it, pushing on. I take two steps before someone comes for me, but he has no gun. It isn't fair, not really, but I don't think about that as I narrowly avoid his fist. I raise my hand again and barely register that I've shot him until I feel his blood stinging my eyes.

I pause and use the back of my hand to wipe the blood away, and someone takes this opportunity to grab me from behind. I swing my elbow out, ignoring the pain as it meets the nose of whoever my attacker is. He immediately releases me to hold a hand to his broken nose, but the back of his other hands is free to catch me right in the eye. I barely feel the pain, even as my vision swims. I kick out, catching him in the stomach and sending him to the floor.

His hands leave his face, and he uses them and his feet to scoot backwards away from me. I watch him and barely flinch at the fear in his young, handsome face. His brown eyes are wide in terror, and I find I like it a lot better than betrayal. So, I shoot him. He stops moving instantly, his hands going out from behind him and the back of his head hitting the ground with an inaudible smack. The terror fades from his face until his eyes show nothing but emptiness.

I glance around and notice there aren't many men left – no one needing my help anyway. I'm just getting ready to jump into another scuffle when my eyes roam over the truck, and a flash of blonde hair and a familiar face has me running in that direction.

My suspicion is confirmed as I get closer. Fucking Benny. Gideon's brother and right-hand man. Rage like I've never known before fuels me, and I am in front of him before I even realize I've moved. This has been a long time coming. His name has been on my list since the day he drove past me at the office, since he came into my apartment while I slept. Since he put a bag over my head and stuffed me into the trunk of his car.

He kickstarted all of this. This may have been my fault, but he and his brother were the architects of the whole situation. Benny is hiding, leaning against the huge wheel of the truck, his hands pressed against what I assume is a nasty bullet wound in his thigh.

I crouch down in front of him, and his eyes widen as he realizes who has suddenly invaded his space. The roaring of men is quietening, the brawl dying down, and I can only hope it's Roman's men with the upper hand.

"Hello, Benny," I say coolly through the strange, quiet calm that seems to have taken over my body. I've heard that it's quietest in the eye of the storm. That while all around the chaos, the eye of the storm is deathly silent. That's how I feel inside. "You're not looking so good."

"What the fuck are you doing here?" he asks through gritted teeth. His face is pale from blood loss, and he almost looks like a fragile old man, even though he's barely a day over forty-five. "Call Gideon. Get him to get someone for me. This was a good catch, girl, but they were fucking prepared."

His voice is weak, and I get a fraction of perverse pleasure from that. They don't know yet. They don't know that I went to Roman, that I blew the whistle on the whole fucking thing. This is the first bit of good news I've heard.

"I'm not getting anybody. You bastards lied to me. You fucking...God, you really fucking played me. And I mean, well done. Really, you had me fooled."

Hysterical laughter bubbles up my throat as I lean my hand on top of his wound, covering his own cold hands as he tries to staunch the blood. I press down, and he hisses in pain.

"What the fuck are you doing? You work for us!" He spits at me, and that laugh erupts from my throat again. I barely recognize the sound of my own voice when I speak again.

"You let my father go, Ben. He's safe now. I don't work for you anymore. And since you made me betray Roman, I don't work for him anymore, either. In fact, Roman's probably going to put a bullet in my head for what went down here tonight."

Benny's eyes widen as he realizes the situation he's in.

"That's right, Benny. I've got nothing left to lose."

There's nothing more dangerous than a girl with nothing left. I shove his hands from his leg and press the tip of my gun down into the bullet hole, smiling maliciously at the sound of his screams.

"You'll fucking regret this, you stupid little bitch. He's going to fucking kill you, you double-crossing whore."

His words float right over my head. I'm not afraid. My fate is already decided either way. If I'm going to die today, I at least want to rid the world of one final scumbag on my way out.

"Doesn't matter, does it? I'm dead either way, old man. Save me a seat in hell."

Benny's mouth opens to say something, but before he can utter a sound, I rip my gun from the wound in his leg and force it into his mouth. With his horrified eyes locked on mine, I pull the trigger. I close my eyes against the spray of blood on my face. I'm sure I look like a mad woman, but I don't care.

My ears ring from the noise of the shot, and I take a second to enjoy this moment. This last good thing. It was the right thing to do. I could have made it last longer, could have drawn it out and given a speech like they do in the movies. I could have, but why waste more breath on him? He isn't going to be a problem for Roman now.

Hours pass – or maybe just minutes – as I kneel on the floor. The only thing holding me to reality is the sharp pain in my knees from the harsh concrete floor. That's how Roman finds me. On my knees with my eyes closed, my gun still inside the mouth of a dead man, the blood of his enemy dripping off my face. It's only when I open my eyes that I realize it's quiet. There's only the sound of men barking orders, and the fact that Roman is here, before me, alerts me to the fact that it's his men still standing.

Roman's eyes meet mine, and I can't help the tears that fall. The salty, metallic taste coats my tongue as I let the gun drop to the floor with a thud.

"Everybody get the fuck out. Now!" he roars, and from my place on the ground beside the truck, I can't see them, but I hear their scuffled footsteps and murmurs as they leave, the noise of the door slamming behind them, startling me.

"You did this." His voice is gravelly as he takes in the dead man beside me without an ounce of sympathy. "You may have helped us end it, but you caused it. Your betrayal cost me a lot of good men. It cost…it cost those women their lives."

Roman's words send an ache through my chest that almost knocks me over. There's nothing I can say, so I remain silent as he drags his gaze away from Benny and back to me. Then he raises his gun.

As our eyes lock, I become entranced by the look on his face. Locked in this moment, a moment that would define everything forever. For a second, his guard is down, and for that second, I can see straight through him. Into the darkest recesses of his soul. There's no light left inside of him now, no resemblance of the man I have come to know, the man I have come to maybe love. If he weren't standing above me, holding a gun aimed at my head, I'd think I was staring into the eyes of a corpse. There is nothing inside of him I can see that hints at forgiveness.

I did this. I turned him into this. He's become the monster we all portrayed him as, and it was time for him to live up to his reputation. I had told him that he could trust me. I made him think a relationship wasn't a foolish thing, that if he could just try, he would see. And then I broke his trust, and even though he hasn't said it, maybe even his heart. It's time for me to pay the price for my mistakes.

He takes a step forward, and now the gun is digging into my forehead, still hot from the shots he fired before he found me here, bloody and on my knees. Our eyes remain locked together, and I want so badly to see something in his face. I want to find even a hint of doubt. To think for just a second that he won't blow my fucking brains all over this God-forsaken room. But there is only darkness. Only anger and hatred and… revenge.

Roman's eyebrows pull together, and I want more than anything to reach out. To smooth that little line between them and run my fingers through his hair like I have before. But the time for that is gone. Dead and buried. He'll put a bullet in my brain for what I have done. For the betrayal I had no choice but to commit. Any moment now.

I let my guard down, let him see it all. The grief, the pain, the sorrow. I let him see how sorry I am. I shuffle forward as far as I can, his gun digging further into my skin, and he swallows visibly at the movement.

"It's okay. It's okay." The words slip out of my mouth as a whisper, giving him my consent to kill me. I never expected to try to comfort my murderer before they ended me, but I can't help it. I don't want him to see him like this anymore. This is what I deserve.

In a sudden movement, he shoves the gun forward, almost tipping me over from my knees. I turn my eyes up towards the gun, but all I see is the tremor in his hand. His hand is shaking violently. I look at his face again, his own eyes staring at his hand like it's betraying him. My eyes roam down over his body, and I realize that it isn't just his hand; his whole body is shaking.

Before I can say anything, he pulls the trigger. I squeeze my eyes shut as I hear the faint click of the chamber, but nothing happens. I wait for the pain, but it never comes. My eyes stay shut until I hear his quick sigh of relief. I open them, letting my confusion show as I look at him, at the relief all over his handsome face.

Finally, after what has seemed like hours of silence, he speaks.

"I can't even fucking kill you, Lara." He laughs, but it's humourless. "Fuck you. FUCK YOU!" he screams and throws the gun across the room, where it smashes into a wall, before pulling another out of the back of his waistband. He levels the gun at my head again, and I'm more confused than I've ever been in my life.

"Get the fuck up."

I do as I'm told instantly. My legs are shaky as I try to get to my feet, the adrenaline fading, leaving me weak and unsteady.

"Leave. Get the hell out of my fucking city. No, better yet, off of my fucking island. I don't want to see your goddamn face again. I don't want to hear your fucking name. You no longer exist. You are a fucking ghost. You have nothing, and you are nothing. I may not have the strength to end your miserable existence right now, but I will spend every moment away from you ensuring that if I ever see you again, I won't hesitate to put you in an unmarked fucking grave."

I'm already nodding my head, my heart racing so fast it feels like it might explode. He's letting me live. He's not going to kill me.

"I—" he cuts me off before I can say anything. Before I can thank him.

"Don't fucking speak. Just go. Fucking go."

Tears slip down my cheeks as I nod, moving around him and walking back towards the closest door in the decrepit warehouse, moving slowly to not trip over any bodies on my way. He may have let me live, but I don't trust that he'll be able to resist putting a bullet in my back as I walk away. Just another few steps, and I can run. I can run so fast and so far that he'll never have to see me again. I can give him that. I may have ruined what we had, maybe even all that he has built, but I can give him this.

Just before I reach the door, he lowers his gun, and then he's marching towards me. Fuck. He's changed his fucking mind. I speed up, still stepping backwards, but he makes it to me in a few large strides and raises the gun again. I squeeze my eyes shut, convinced for the second time in as many minutes that I'm about to die. Instead, his hands come to the sides of my face, the one with the gun making me wince as the metal digs into my head. Then his lips are on mine.

He kisses me like it's the last time he ever will, and I know that it is. For that reason alone, I kiss him back with as much emotion as I possibly can. I pour everything into that kiss, our tongues sliding together in each other's mouths, all teeth, lips, and quiet, breathless kisses. I savour the taste of him, the feel of him, knowing without any doubt that nothing will ever compare to this.

I get ten seconds of this glorious kiss before his hands leave my face and land on my shoulders, shoving me away from him before he wipes his mouth with the back of his hand, disgust shining in his beautiful, cold eyes.

"I regret every single moment between us. Every. Single. Moment. Including that one," he says, and my heart shatters into a thousand tiny pieces, all of them stabbing my lungs and causing physical, throbbing pain in my chest. "Now leave. From this moment on, you mean absolutely nothing to me."

His words have a cold finality to them, and despite my better judgment, I turn my back to the man with the gun – the man I just might love – and I run as fast as I can. My broken heart and shattered soul protest against the agony of leaving like this. Leaving him to clean up the monumental mess I've made.

I let my tears fall as I go, stumbling over my own feet, until finally, I'm out the door, sprinting in the harsh sunlight away from the man who made me feel alive.

The man who now wants me dead.

CHAPTER 28

I'm so out of it that I barely notice Chase's car sitting on the side of the road. My eyes only seem willing to acknowledge the slew of bodies. My body can only feel the burning gaze of Roman's surviving men as they glare daggers through my skull.

Chase stands beside the car, shoulders square and gun held out before him. He looks like he's been in a brawl himself, but that wouldn't surprise me. If he heard about the trouble and showed up to help, I'd say that sounded about right.

His eyes finally lift off the group of men trying to kill us with sight alone and land on me. He doesn't smile, doesn't do anything but stare until I stop before him. Our eyes lock.

"We have a problem," I tell him.

"We have more than one problem," he gestures towards the car. I follow, walking closer so I can see inside the back window. Only, the moment I do, I wish I hadn't.

"He wouldn't leave without you," Chase tells me, already yanking the driver's side door open and jumping inside quickly.

I follow suit, jumping in the back as fast as I can, and almost crying the instant I do.

"Oh, Eric. What did you do?"

"S'okay. I'm fine. Just a little blood." His words end in a cough that sends blood spluttering out of his mouth.

I laugh softly through my tears, but only because he's trying to smile. His red-coated teeth taunt me.

"Just a little blood," I repeat.

He tries to smile again, but his eyes flicker and then close. I squeeze his hand tightly as I can. Like if I don't let go of him, he can't go anywhere.

"Stay with us, Eric," I give him a little shake, and his eyes flutter open for a brief moment. "We've got you. I'm sorry. I'm sorry."

I don't know what to do. What to say. I meet Chase's eyes in the rear-view mirror. His eyes are haunted, tired.

"What did I do, Chase?" I ask, but he doesn't answer.

What have I done?

I hold Eric's clammy hand as we race home, nudging him sporadically to ensure he's still alive. Chase hasn't said a word, and I don't blame him. Everything seems to be happening at a snail's pace, but my mind is going a hundred miles an hour. Guilt. Fear. Worry. Excitement. I get to see my father again. I get to see him alive and in the flesh. It's probably the only thing that keeps me going.

We pull up outside the office with a screech of the brakes, and then Chase is there pulling Eric from the car, cradling him in his arms as if he were a small child. I have to force myself to follow him, beg my legs to hold me up, but I'm crippled with fear.

"What the hell happened?" It's my father's voice, and

my head snaps up towards the sound.

Seeing him, seeing proof that he's alive and well is what tips me over the edge. My legs crumple beneath me, and I land on the pavement, my knees smacking off the hard cement with enough force to break the skin. My dad's confused gaze flicks between Chase and me as he carries Eric inside. I hear Andi gasp, Eric's name falling from her lips with a cry. It's enough. It's too much.

"Dad," I croak, and that's it. Decision made, he runs towards me.

I can barely contain my sobs, and yet I'm not even sure which particular thing I'm crying about. I feel like a child. My whole world is spinning on its axis, and all I want is my dad. The minute his arms wrap around me, I lose it. I try to explain what happened, what I've done, but the words are nonsensical. Unintelligible. He says nothing, just helps me to my feet and walks me to the door.

"Lara, you need to focus now. You can have all the time you want afterwards to feel whatever it is you're feeling, but look..." Just inside the door, he gestures to Eric, passed out on that stupid sofa, skin pale and blood on almost every inch of him. "He needs you now – we need you. Get it together. Just a little while longer."

My mind latches onto his every word, and with each breath, I feel myself settle. I feel my despair slither away, deep inside me. My fear abates little by little until there's nothing left but a steely resolve. My dad's hands come up to each side of my face, his eyes boring into mine, and a thousand words are passed between us.

I nod. He nods.

"What the hell happened?" My father repeats his earlier question, his head snapping over to our injured friend.

"We showed up to get Lara," Chase says as he and Sophie work on tearing Eric's shirt from his body to see his injuries. I hadn't even noticed that everyone else was here. "But everything was already over. Nobody was outside. Just a bunch of dead bodies. We were getting ready to barge in when all of Roman's goons came pouring out the door." Chase looks over at me briefly, and I feel a stab of guilt.

They came outside because Roman kicked them out. Kicked them out so that he could tell me to leave.

"They said Roman was inside…. They said he was going to kill Lara, and the kid just lost it. It happened so quickly. Before I even had a chance to reel him in, it was done. He tried to barge in, and they shot him. Twice. Fucking trigger-happy motherfuckers. I tried to get him in the car once he was down, but he kept fighting me. Even with two holes in him, he fought me. He wouldn't leave. He wouldn't leave without you."

He directs that at me, and I know he doesn't mean it, but it feels like an accusation. It feels like blame.

"I'm sorry." It's barely a whisper, and my dad's hand squeezes my shoulder, but nobody else says a word.

"Roman knows," I admit, though I'm sure they've figured it out. "He knows I was spying on him. I… Gideon, he…"

I try to find the right words to explain what happened. I try, but as I look around at the worried faces – at Sophie, who's poking and prodding at Eric, at Andi, who's clasping his hand so tightly in hers I'm almost sure she'll break it – I'm not sure there are words good enough to describe how monumentally I fucked up.

"Gideon told me Roman was smuggling women and children onto the Island. That he was forcing them into prostitution. I didn't believe it...but then the evidence stacked up. I tried to confront him, but he wouldn't listen. He just wouldn't listen. And when it was all too much, when there were too many signs pointing to it being true...I gave Gideon what he wanted."

"Lara...Gideon was the one trafficking women." Dad's voice is confused, gentle, like he wants to get the truth out of me but doesn't want to break me in the process.

"Yes, I found that out after. Roman was transporting women...but he's getting them *off* the Island. He was saving them, and Gideon killed them all. I made the wrong choice. I did the wrong thing. I ruined everything."

"Where's Roman now? Why are you alive?" my dad asks.

"Because Roman and I...because we..." I can't even look at him as I say the words. Shame barrels into me.

Nobody responds. The only sounds are Sophie as she works on Eric.

"Why didn't you tell anyone?" Luke's voice startles me, and I look towards him slowly. His hand rests on Carey's shoulder. Carey, who stares at me with so much sympathy I can barely stand it. "We could have helped you. We could have figured it out together."

"I wanted to keep you all out of it. I wanted to—"

"We're supposed to be a fucking team, Lara!" Chase's

shout startles all of us. "We're supposed to be in this together. We could have figured this out. You could have been killed, and Eric might fucking die. Jesus. Fuck. You called me and told me nothing. Do you know how worried I was? How worried we all were?"

"I'm sorry."

"You're sorry? Fuck. Fuck, you could have been killed, and I—and we—"

"Stop." Andi's voice is gentle but serious. "Just stop. We all make mistakes. We all fuck up. Just stop. Please."

Her voice breaks, and so does my heart for the millionth time. The silence is deafening. Nobody moves but Sophie. Nobody speaks. I'm not even sure if I breathe; it stays that way as she works. I can feel Chase's anger, my dad's confusion, Luke and Carey's worry, my guilt. So much guilt.

Eventually, Sophie slows and then stops. She blows out a breath, pushes stray curls from her face, then turns to look at us.

"I've done all I can, but I need to get him to the hospital. I stopped the bleeding. One bullet went straight through, and the other is out. I did some stitches, but he lost a lot of blood. I can't fix that here."

Eric's eyes flutter as he lays there, then they open. He finds me, or at least it feels like he does, so I walk over and let my hand grip his. He looks at me, barely, and I choke back tears. I watch as his mouth moves, trying to form words. I dont... I can't... I lean in closer.

"Chicago,"

"What?"

"I gotta see Chicago, remember?" His words, muffled, barely decipherable, hit me right in the chest. Immediately I'm transported back to that day outside the office. God, that feels like a life time ago.

Luke interupts, offering to drive them to the hospital. Eric's skin is pale and clammy, but the relief I feel at hearing him speak, watching his chest rise and fall, is insurmountable.

"Come home soon," I whisper as I squeeze his hand, and I'm flooded with emotion when Andi's hand closes over mine, a small, sad smile on her face, reassurance if I ever needed it. Eric's eyes flutter open slightly, eyes unfocused.

There's a small commotion as Luke lifts him into his arms, and Andi grabs Sophie's hand to get to the car. My dad holds open the door, and we all watch from there as Carey helps Luke put him in the car. Then they're gone.

There's an atmosphere unlike any other when we come back into the office. Our silence is tense and uncomfortable. My hands are still shaking, my chest barely capable of breathing without collapsing. So much has happened. Too much.

"What the fuck do we do now?" Carey asks, and I'm not sure if he means right now while we wait or if he means in general. After everything that just went down. We all look towards my father, who looks slimmer. Older. He's aged in the few weeks he's been gone, and it's another splinter in my heart. When my father says nothing, Carey's inquisitive gaze locks on me.

What do we do now?

Roman knows I played him. Gideon knows I betrayed him and I've killed his brother. Eric is bleeding out in the back of a car. Chase hates me.

What the *fuck do we do now?*

"I have no idea."

ACKNOWLEDGEMENTS

I don't think I quite know to explain what a journey this has been. I began writing Second City during lockdown. It was mostly just me and my son at home at the time, he was one then. He's four now. I didn't really know where I was heading with this book, but I'm so glad to have ended up here.

There are so many people who made this possible. Jaxon, my son, who got ino such a good sleep routine I actually had a second to myself. You are an angel baby. Ed, who encouraged me to keep writing when I really did not think I could. There would be no Second City without you. I love you. My family, who had so many different versions of this book shoved down their throats as the writing process went on. Editors, ARC readers, anonymous members of a discord. So many people helped me not only finish and edit this book, but gave me the confidence to actually go through with publishing it. Thank you. From the bottom of my heart.

I have always wanted to be writer. I love books. If you're here then you probably do too, so you get it. I wanted to write stories that would make people feel the ways I have felt after a good book. I hope (really, really hope) you enjoyed this book. This is my first. My baby. There are so many more, hundreds, just floating around up there in my brain along side lyrics to songs I haven't listened to in years and the entire script for Mean Girls. I hope soon all of these stories in my head will be in your hands, and I hope they make you feel like life is a little bit easier, a little bit lighter and a little bit more magical.

Find me on my socials and my website to subscribe for bonus content and chapters and all information on my new releases.

Thank you, reader, for getting this far. I hope you stick around.

Chelsea

Printed in France by Amazon
Brétigny-sur-Orge, FR